A Latter-day Novel

Spirit of Fire

JOHN M. PONTIUS

MILLENNIAL QUEST

SERIES

ISBN: 1-55517-385-3

Published by and distributed by:
925 North Main, Springville, UT 84663 • 801/489-4084

CFI Publishing and Distribution Since 1986
Cedar Fort, Incorporated
CFI Distribution • CFI Books • Council Press • Bonneville Books

Cover design by Lyle Mortimer
Page layout by Corinne A. Bischoff
Printed in the United States of America

Table of Contents

Acknowledgment

Many people have contributed freely to this work through friendship, encouragement, proof reading, praise and well-deserved criticism. It would be folly to try to name them all. However, a few deserve special mention for their selfless contributions.

Many thanks to my Parents who have edited, encouraged, prayed, buoyed up, and done everything exactly right. When I grow up, I want to be just like you. Kathy, I love you. Shayne, you are my anchor. Evan, you are the most Christian and unselfish man with whom I have ever done business. Warm fuzzy thanks to Bonnie and Lisa, my gorgeous daughters, for actually being faltered I used their names in the book. Big proud thanks to Matt and Ben, my missionary sons. Special thanks to Lyle Mortimer of CFI for believing in me twice in a row — certainly a new record for me.

Most of all, my eternal gratitude to Heavenly Father, and to my dear Savior. It turns out, all things really are possible to those who believe.

Introduction

Angels in Coveralls began as a suggestion made by a friend and former fellow missionary. After reading *Following the Light of Christ into His Presence*, he called me up and made many astute observations. His only criticism was that the message of the book needed to reach a broader audience than the style of the book would appeal to. In a way, I was preaching to the choir.

In essence, he said: "Why not deliver the same message as a series of stories, or a novel? Make it heart warming and entertaining. Teach them this great message through the lives of people who have actually lived them. Entertain them, and they won't mind being taught these truths which will prove precious to their souls."

As I thought upon his suggestion, a whole series of prior feelings and impressions fell into place. I had frequently pondered the idea of writing just such a book, but had not yet considered using it as a vehicle to teach these precious truths. His words caused a long series of strivings within my soul to suddenly take on solid form.

All the stories in this book are fictional. The primary value of these stories is to illustrate the process of spiritual greatness. Even though many of these stories are based on real events, none of them are intended to represent real people. I have carefully changed names, places, and surrounding events where necessary. These stories are not intended to establish doctrine, nor to propose that all people must, or even might walk a similar path.

All of the characters in this book are fictional. I'm sorry to say, this is not a biography of my life. In many ways, I wish I had the courage, and spiritual greatness I ascribe to some of my characters. All of them are a part of these stories to illustrate the very real process we all go through in our spiritual journey.

It is my profound belief that this life has a single grand purpose. That purpose often has very little to do with what we spend the majority of our time actually doing. To learn what that purpose is, is to pierce the confusion of this world, and find the path of righteousness. However, understanding the purpose of life may not necessarily give us a concrete means of achieving it.

One of the rather recent additions to my testimony of Jesus Christ and his glorious Gospel, is the witness that, in addition to being true, the Gospel works. In other words, the promises are profoundly true. We can, I can, achieve every promised blessing. There is nothing withheld, nothing missing, nothing omitted we must have to, walk the path to great righteousness, and the promised rewards thereof. Having found this to be true, it has fallen very sweetly upon my understanding that the principle outcome of these things is the happiness and meaning to life we all seek.

It is these very ideas that I have attempted to put into novel form in *Spirit of Fire*, namely, that it is possible, even probable, indeed specifically ordained, that we can achieve every promised gift and blessing in this life. Secondly, this novel was written with the firm belief that the process of achieving those very gifts, though fraught with trials, is delightful and filled with joy.

If you feel nothing else from reading *Spirit of Fire*, I hope you feel, at the very core of your being, the witness that it *is* possible for you, regardless of your limitations, or self doubt, to luxuriate in that joy which surpasses the understanding of man.

one

Jimmy

Jim Mahoy stuffed the tractor keys into his pants and bent to ruffle Jimmy's hair. His son's temper was still aflame.

"Thtop it Daddy!" he pouted, his lower lip protruding.

"You hurt the kitty, Jimmy. That's why she scratched you."

"No. Kitty hurt me!" Jimmy countered with perfect two-year-old logic.

"She was afraid. You need to hold Kitty easy, like a baby. Be nice to Kitty."

"You be nice!"

"Don't talk to Daddy that way…"

"Kitty hates me. You hate me. I don't like you!" he shouted, his arms rigid at his sides.

"Jimmy, that's not true. I love…" Just then Mom called everyone to breakfast. Jimmy spun around and was gone before he could say another word. It was a typical exchange with Jimmy. Not typical in its anger, but typical in its abruptness and in Jimmy's surprising certainty that he was right.

Just as Jimmy disappeared around the corner Jim heard the Spirit whisper, "This is the one." He felt stunned. In his heart he felt himself say, "Oh, no. Not Jimmy." As he joined the family for breakfast the feeling did not subside.

Jimmy was a vividly happy child, always busy, always challenging, always experimenting with his new world. He was unusually willful, seldom willing to take second seat, even to his parents, yet he was unselfish and loving. He had started talking quite young, apparently out of the sheer necessity of having a way to take control of his little world. He spoke with a vocabulary worthy of a child several years his senior. His hair was bright red, almost orange, and he possessed a sudden Irish temper. He was the youngest of seven and the joy of every member of his large family, which consisted of his two brothers and four sisters.

Jimmy's dad, Jim Mahoy, was a man of medium height, almost as broad across the shoulders as he was tall. He came from a long line of burly Mahoys who, for four generations, had coaxed crops from the fertile Utah valley. He was a quiet man, wise in his own way, and deeply spiritual. While his education stopped one year short of a high school diploma, he could add a column of numbers of almost any length simply by glancing at it. He could multiply, divide, do square roots, and convert from metric to English measures all in his head.

As breakfast ended, and each family member piled their dishes into the sink, Jimmy's mom turned on impulse just as Jimmy ran from the kitchen after his big brother Sam. A strange feeling of concern touched her, but she had things to do. She smiled, and busied herself with assigning cleanup and chores to the older children.

Jimmy's mom, Laura Mahoy, was forty-two, a blond beauty from California, soft spoken and infinitely patient. Still it was she from whom Jimmy had inherited his quick temper. It made her chuckle to watch him stomp his feet and put his fists on his hips. Sometimes his face would turn red simply because his two year-old vocabulary did not have enough words in it. She saw herself in her youngest's fiery ways.

Sam almost fell over as Jimmy wrapped himself around his right leg. He sat down the milking equipment and knelt down. As he did so, Jimmy flung his arms around his big brother's neck, so that their noses were almost touching.

"Pleath Tham, pleath let me go to the cowth with you," he begged, his lisp becoming somewhat exaggerated due to his excitement. At times the lisp was completely absent, and only surfaced when he was upset, or especially excited. Sam smiled. He loved it when Jimmy called him Tham. Sam and Jimmy had a special relationship, one which neither understood, yet one in which they both rejoiced.

Because their family was so large, the last three children had been tended and raised, as much by the older children, as by Laura. Consequently, each of the babies had bonded with one of the older children, creating an almost paternal relationship between them. Jimmy was Sam's baby. They were bonded by the purest love siblings can have. It wasn't uncommon for Jimmy to run past his parents to Sam to seek sympathy, or to show a hurt. It was certainly to Sam he came to seek justice, or more commonly, revenge, from an older child. He was almost never disappointed.

"You have your pajamas on. Big boys don't milk cows in pajamas, and I have to go now," Sam told him. Besides, Sam knew what a bother Jimmy was in the milking parlor. It took as much work to keep Jimmy out from under the cows as it did to milk them.

"I will dreth me," he said, pulling at his pajama tops with chubby little hands. "I can milk cowth, and feed the baby cowth. You will take me to cowth? Pleath?"

Sam was the second oldest after sixteen-year-old Emily. He was fourteen, and stocky like his dad, but not at all eager to farm for a living. He hated milking cows with a heated passion. At fourteen, he was nearly the strongest boy in his school, and the slowest afoot. He could lift the back end of a VW beetle, but finished last in every race he ever entered. He was quiet, made friends slowly, and was often the brunt of teasing, but when he found a friend, they remained his friend for life. He had inherited his father's hands, but his mother's fingers. His hands were broad and powerful, his fingers long and agile. Even at fourteen, few adult men could outgrip him. He had a heart so big and tender that it oft times felt on the verge of breaking.

These were his blessings. His curse was that without glasses he was virtually blind. Behind the heavy lenses he could see just well enough to get along. The thick glasses made his eyes look smaller, giving him a piggish, unintelligent appearance. He had never caught a ball in his life, except perhaps on accident. He could not see well enough, so if someone actually did throw to him, the ball almost always hit him, making other kids laugh at him.

In a desperate gamble to give her young boy a chance to succeed, his mom had started him playing the flute at age six. Why the flute? Because, for some odd reason, they had one. He took to it with a delight, and by age fourteen was a surprisingly accomplished artist. He read music well, but his most beautiful songs came from deep within him, music which was at times bright and prancing, sometimes soft and wistful, occasionally thundering, often brilliant. But, even this talent made him seem odd. In his big hands the small silver flute looked misplaced, and his peers misunderstood his gift. From a body that big, one expected a grunt or belch, not a haunting melody. Consequently, he never, ever played for anyone not directly related to him, and no coaxing in the world could have made him do so. Even Miles, his best friend in the whole world, didn't know he played like an angel's dream.

Sam lifted Jimmy and swung him around until he laughed. "I don't think so, Jimmy. Tham is in a hurry today," he said using Jimmy's pronunciation of his name. "Maybe tomorrow, OK?"

"OK Tham. I love you Tham. You are my biggetht betht brother. You milk cowth today, and me milk cowth tomorrow, and feed baby cowth," he said shaking a small finger in Sam's face. As far as Jimmy was concerned, they had a contract. Sam put on his most serious face, and nodded solemnly. It was all he could do to not laugh at his baby brother.

Jimmy unlaced his arms from his big brothers neck. Just as they broke contact, he suddenly felt like taking him along. He started to say something, but Jimmy was already off onto something else, and out of sight. He heard the kitten complain as he picked it up in the other room. The love Jimmy felt for his kitten was not mutual.

Sam walked through the garage and loaded the equipment into the old GMC truck. He stopped for a moment to examine his bicycle. He and Jimmy loved to ride together. They rode long distances with Jimmy astraddle the center bar, but when Jimmy had graduated from diapers, the bar hurt him. For a while they taped a bath towel around the bar, but that had a tendency to roll sideways. Dad had helped Sam weld another bicycle seat to the bar just behind the handlebars. He smiled to himself. Jimmy would love it. This way he would have his own seat, and could hold onto the handlebars. They had even welded on some foot rests for him to keep his feet safely away from the front wheel. He promised himself that after chores they would go on a big ride together.

Sam wasn't old enough to legally drive, but in a farming community, boys were expected to be able to operate all the equipment. Because of his size, Sam had begun early, and driving the old truck was old-hat now. As he turned onto the lane to the barn he had that uneasy feeling again, and almost went back to bundle up Jimmy to go with him. But, he had work to do, and he pressed the accelerator hard. He would hurry back.

Chores usually took several hours, but this morning one of the cows, Rosie, had been reluctant to enter the stanchion, and it had taken longer. He fed the calves, mixed chopped grain and water for the pigs, fed fifty rabbits, broke open twelve bales of hay for the cows, loaded nearly forty gallons of milk in ten-gallon cans onto the truck, washed the milking equipment in large sinks of scalding hot water, pressure cleaned the parlor floor, and started back toward the house.

All along the half-mile lane back to the house, that uneasy feeling persisted, making it seem much longer today. He wanted to speed up, but if he did, the milk cans would slide off the truck. He came to the bridge over the big irrigation ditch behind their house. He glanced at his watch to see if there would be time to take Jimmy on that bike ride before his nap. It was two minutes to eleven. As he came off the other side of the bridge, he saw Jimmy's kitten standing on the bank. It was obviously soaking wet. He had a sudden urge to look up and down the ditch, but, the feeling was indistinct, and swallowed up by the need to concentrate on steering the truck off the bridge. Once across, he felt like he should go back to the ditch, but the milk needed to get into the cooler. He sped up, and as he approached the house, his mother was standing on the back porch with her hand shielding her eyes, looking back and forth.

"Mom, where's Jimmy?" he asked from the truck, struggling to keep calm in his voice.

"I was just looking for him. I heard him asking to go with you to milk the cows. I thought you had taken him."

A lump rose in his throat. "No, I didn't."

Laura swallowed, but calmly said. "Well, he's around somewhere. You check the chicken coop. You know how he sneaks out there sometimes."

"Mom, I'm going to look in the ditch."

His mother flashed him a frightened look. "Why? He never goes near it."

"Mom, I saw his kitten by the bridge. It was soaking wet. I'm afraid he threw it into the ditch. Maybe he fell in too. I don't know. I just have a bad feeling."

Without saying another word she started for the bridge. The kitten was still there, licking itself off. The ditch was full, and moving slowly. They walked to the first bend and then the next, but found nothing.

"Go get your dad," she commanded, and strode off downstream. Sam complied and began trotting toward the house.

Sixteen-year-old Emily bolted from the back door, alarm showing on her face. "What's wrong? Why is Mom walking the ditch?"

"Em, we can't find Jimmy. Go get Dad, will you?" She nodded, dropped the dish towel to the ground, and ran toward the south fields. She stopped, ran back, hopped on her bike, and raced away.

Sam began calling Jimmy's name. Seconds later their only close neighbors came out onto their porch. They lived directly across the street, and had heard him calling. Without asking what was going on, they ran across the street and to the ditch behind their house. There was no hesitation, they just did what had to be done. The Carters were both inactive in the church, but had been good neighbors for many years. Mr. Carter jumped into the water above his waist, and began pulling boards from the dam. The water changed course, and began dumping into the drain ditch. He hung onto the metal frame of the dam to keep from being washed away.

"I'll stand in the water here. If he's in the ditch he won't go past me. Besides, it will stop the water from going further downstream."

Sam nodded. The ditch went underground shortly after it left their farm. Sam turned to rejoin his mother.

She had walked almost a quarter mile, and was in the middle of the hay field. Sam was about halfway to her when she suddenly jumped into the ditch. He heard her frantic calls for help from the ditch. He turned and shouted to the Carters, and broke into a run. Mrs. Carter shouted something about an ambulance. He got there just as his mom crawled from the ditch with Jimmy in her arms. He was blue, and not moving. Sam tried to take Jimmy, but Laura ignored him. Instead, he helped her climb out. Quickly, she laid Jimmy on the grass and felt for a pulse. Sam began to rub Jimmy's arms. They were ice cold. Jimmy's eyes were closed, his lids almost black, his lips a dark blue.

Laura bent Jimmy's head back and leaned over, blowing air into his mouth. A gush of water came from his mouth. With an icy calm, she cleared his mouth and blew again, and again. She then began pushing on Jimmy's chest. Sam didn't know what she was doing, or why, but he trusted his mother. She knew things he didn't, and was dead calm in emergencies. For Sam, time seemed to stand still. His dad arrived, and following Laura's directions, began pushing on Jimmy's chest. After a long time Laura straightened. Her face, a mask of exhaustion and grief, was streaked with tears, her eyes puffy. Her lips were purple and swollen. Oddly, except for being discolored, Jimmy's mouth looked perfectly normal.

Jim gently pushed her aside and they changed places. She, rhythmically massaging his chest, while he blew air into his son's mouth time after time. After what seemed like a long time, and in reality, was over an hour, he straightened up and felt for a pulse at Jimmy's neck. Tears began to course down his face.

"Honey. Laura. I don't think we should continue." Laura didn't seem to hear him. "Honey, there's no use. It's not right. He's gone," he said softly.

"No!" she screamed. "He's not dead. We have to try longer. Do it!" The intensity and volume of her response shocked everyone. He nodded and resumed his work. By this time a sizable crowd had gathered. Some had walked, a few had driven tractors, and quite a few cars had driven out onto the hayfield. The wail of a siren punctuated the distance. Laura looked around across their dismayed, sympathetic faces. They looked helplessly back. A few looked away.

She looked at Jim, and knew he could not stop working on her son to give Jimmy a blessing. Her eyes were frantic as she scanned the group of onlookers.

"Don't we have any priesthood holders here? Someone give my baby a blessing!" she shouted. The whole crowd took a step back, a dozen active priesthood holders among them. She flared at them. "You! Brother Carter. You're an Elder. I know you hold the priesthood. You give my baby a blessing!"

Brother Carter was the only inactive Priesthood holder in the crowd, and the only one who had not taken a step back. He hung his head.

"Sister Mahoy, I can't. I ain't worthy. I've been inactive more'n twenty years. I don't even remember how." It was the first time he had ever called her "Sister Mahoy." For years it had just been "Laura."

"My baby is dying! God will bless my baby, you only need to say the words. Please!" she pleaded, barely glancing in his direction.

He looked helplessly to the left and right. Every face he saw looked away from him. A look of grim determination mixed with tremendous anxiety settled on his face, and he slowly came around and knelt by Jimmy's head. Tears were coursing down his leathery face. He placed his large calloused hands on Jimmy's tiny head, and after a long pause, in a voice almost too small to be heard, said:

"Heavenly Father, I know I'm a sinful man, please forgive me, and please don't hold my sins against this little baby. Jimmy, in the name of Jesus Christ I command you to live. Amen."

The blessing was so simple, so direct and honest, that Jim Mahoy momentarily stopped, and looked up at Brother Carter. For just a second neither he nor Laura continued to work on Jimmy. Unexpectedly, Jimmy coughed, and a spatter of muddy water sprayed from his mouth onto Laura's dress. She gasped. Jim pressed his fingers to Jimmy's neck.

"I feel a pulse!" he cried. People applauded. A hundred "thank God's" were mumbled simultaneously. "Roll him onto his side. Here, raise his hips. Come on Jimmy, cough it all out." People were laughing and crying, hugging each other. Sam found himself hugging Emily. Other brothers and sisters joined them. Brother Carter knelt in stunned silence, as if he had been turned to stone.

By that time an ambulance had arrived, and Jimmy and his parents were loaded into the back, still working with him, urging him to cough, speaking words of love and encouragement. The ambulance was one of the old kind that looked like a pregnant station wagon. The drivers fumbled with the oxygen bottle, and decided they didn't know how to turn it on. A piece was missing. Jim grabbed it from them and got it going. By cupping his hands around Jimmy's face, he improvised to replace the missing piece. He ordered them to drive. They slammed the back doors and shortly they were gone in a cloud of dust, sirens, and flashing lights. In those days, ambulance drivers were trained to do little more than transport sick people. The idea of trained paramedics treating someone at the scene was an idea still years away.

———

Sam couldn't remember walking back to the house, nor putting the milk into the cooler, nor finishing the rest of the chores which could not be postponed, even for something as terrible as this. The worst part was the grief-stricken quiet. For a house full of seven kids ranging from sixteen to five, silence was an ominous thing. It was probably the first time the house had ever been dead-silent in the middle of the day. Emily urged the kids to complete their chores to take their minds off Jimmy. They plodded ahead slowly, each struggling with fear, hope, and disbelief.

What little talk there was centered on the idea that he had begun to breathe, and the hope that they would all come home from the hospital together, and their lives would be whole again. Emily spoke words of hope and assurance, drawing deeply from the fragile resources of her own hope, pushing aside logic and reason in favor of comforting the little ones.

Sam walked back to the bridge. The kitten was still there, looking at the water as if waiting for Jimmy to return from it. Mr. Carter had replaced the dam, and the ditch was once again full. Sam found a piece of wood and tossed it into the ditch. It floated away slowly. He timed it until it arrived at the place where they had found Jimmy. It took thirty-six minutes to arrive at the spot. Somewhere he had heard that three minutes was the most a person could go without oxygen. He knelt on the bank and alternately cried and prayed.

———

When the phone finally rang it was like a cannon going off in dead silence. For the briefest moment no one moved. Finally, Sam answered it. It was their dad. The news was not good, but not without hope.

Jimmy was breathing on his own, and his pulse was strong and steady. His body temperature had returned to normal. The only problem was that he had not regained consciousness. The doctors were amazed that he was alive. To further confuse the issue, his lungs were completely free of water. It was a miracle by any measure. The doctors speculated that he had been without oxygen for over an hour. They all agreed that if Jimmy regained consciousness, at best, he would surely suffer some sort of brain damage. At worse, he would not awaken, not ever.

Neither parent came home that evening. Someone brought food, and Mrs. Carter stayed long enough to see that everyone was tucked in bed. Her demeanor was kind and grandmotherly, and everyone appreciated her care. Sam cried himself to sleep, as did many of the others.

Jimmy neither improved, nor deteriorated, but simply remained as if asleep, breathing easily. Each of the kids was allowed to go to the hospital to visit Jimmy. Each came away with the feeling that everything would be OK. The mood in the home brightened after several days. Laura refused to leave the hospital, so Dad came home each evening, ate, held family prayers, slept a few hours, and returned to the hospital. Sam tended the farm. Emily watched the family. They would make do. After fourteen days, Jim finally prevailed upon Laura to go home and sleep. She had eaten little, and had not bathed for over a week. She had changed from her muddy dress only after insisting that the nurse let her change by Jimmy's bedside.

Jim and Laura stood by Jimmy's bedside, their arms wrapped around each other. Laura had a hand on Jimmy's forehead, and Jim held his small hand. His flesh was warm and alive. In a few minutes Laura would leave. Unexpectedly, Jimmy's eyes fluttered open and focused upon his mother.

"Hi, baby," she whispered lovingly.

"Mommy, I love you," he said, smiled softly, and closed his eyes again. His breathing continued undisturbed. They hugged for a long time, confident for the first time that everything would be OK. They knew that he could not speak or remember who they were if he were brain damaged. Laura hummed to herself as she made the long drive home.

After family prayers, she tucked her loved ones in bed. Even Sam, and those too old for such things, got tucked in, and kissed goodnight. After a long, hot bath Laura fell to her knees beside her bed. She shed many tears of gratitude for this blessed sparkle of hope. For the first time in many days she climbed into bed with a peaceful heart.

She slept what seemed like the whole night until she had a dream. She dreamed that she sat down to do genealogy. Their family group sheet grew large in her vision until she focused upon the last entry on the page. She read Jimmy's full name, birth date, place of birth, age at death 2 years, 2 months. Death date, 24 July 1965, that very day. She awoke suddenly, and sat up in bed. Oddly, there was no panic, no grief, no wrenching anguish, just peace. It was to be. It was only a little after midnight. Seconds later the phone rang. It was Jim. Jimmy had passed away peacefully just moments before.

———

In a small community the death of a child is a tragedy felt by all, and Jimmy's funeral was overflowing with people. A small, baby blue casket covered with countless flowers, stood just in front of the pulpit. All of Jimmy's family sat in the first row with dozens of aunts, uncles, and cousins in rows behind. Behind them, a sea of mourners flowed into the cultural hall and out onto the grass. The funeral seemed to go on a long time, but in reality, was only as long as necessary.

Finally, the bishop stood and said: "I was just passed a note that one of the family wanted a few minutes." He returned to his seat. Almost a full minute elapsed in silence before anyone stirred. When Sam finally did stand, every eye in that large assembly turned toward him, but he did not feel them. Sam walked to the small, blue casket, and without turning to face the people, brought his flute to his lips. He heard his mother begin to weep, then heard his father draw a ragged breath. Finally, he blew a quivering note, and softly, ever so softly, he played "I Am a Child of God." It was Jimmy's favorite song, and one which he had played for Jimmy many times. The music was sweet, pure and haunting, like an angel's hymn at evening. Then, quite unexpectedly the music danced away, laughing, playing, bubbling with little songs Jimmy had loved and sung; Primary songs his Mother had taught him, nursery tunes, the theme from Sesame Street, Mister Rogers, and others. Next, a thundering passage from Bach, and a magical, aching tune from deep within Sam. Then at last came the lullaby. The music was so pure, the tone so clarion and sweet, that the words seemed to float in the air. "Lullaby, and good night, may angels attend you. Lullaby, and good night, my little one, good night." It was as if there was no one else in the chapel but Sam and Jimmy, and their love touched hearts until every eye was flowing.

The music ceased. Sam stood there for a long time, as if reluctant to finally say goodbye. At long last, he gently laid the precious flute beside his baby brother, and slowly returned to his seat without looking up. This was the last time he would play it, until Jimmy again asked him to play "I Am a Child of God," in his joyful, innocent way.

––––

It seemed like an invasion, all the people who came to their home. For hours they came, bringing food, leaving food, eating food, clearing away food. And all the while, they remembered, laughed, and cried. Some brought a photo or two they had taken of Jimmy, others offered help, saying, "Call if you need anything, anything at all."

Brother Carter didn't come to the house along with everyone else. Instead, he got on his tractor and baled the hay that Sam hadn't been able to get to. It was his way of being there for them in their hour of need. Of all the flowers, food, and warm wishes they received those days, Brother Carter's gift was the one which most touched their hearts.

Finally, they all left, and miraculously, so did all the clutter they had brought. Jim and Laura collapsed onto the big sofa, and after a few minutes the whole family gathered around them. It would have been a typical evening at the Mahoys, except that every heart was burdened beyond tears, and each had sought their parents in the hope of receiving comfort. It was Mother who spoke first.

"Kids, you have all been very brave these last few days. I'm proud of you. But now that all this is behind us, it's time to cry." The kids exchanged confused glances.

"What I mean is, it's important to let your feelings of hurt come out. One of the worst things one of us could do to ourselves is to let Jimmy's death ruin something inside us, or make us angry at God. The time will come when you feel like crying for days and days. When that happens, I want you to know that it's OK, and that you should go ahead and cry until there are no more tears. We will all understand."

"Mama, I already feel like crying for days and days," Beth exclaimed, her bright blue eyes wide and shining with tears. Beth and Angela were twins, blond haired, blue eyed, ruffles, ribbons and mischief. They were twelve years old, going on twenty one. "Me too, Mama," Angela replied in her twinnish way. They arose simultaneously and snuggled on either side of Laura, who tucked them against her.

"Mama, me too," little Rachel sobbed, not sure what it all meant. At five, and suddenly the youngest again, she had yet to fully understand why Jimmy was getting all this attention, and why he was "spending the night" somewhere else. She took a place on Laura's lap. The twins both reached up to take one of her hands.

"I don't need to cry," Benjamin interjected in a gruff voice, made lower for emphasis. At 7 years, he was going through the tough stage. It was Jim who responded.

"I used to think that big boys don't cry, and I suppose when it comes to a cut finger, or a black eye, maybe they don't. But when the hurt is coming from your heart, then it's OK to cry. Actually, I think that if you don't cry, it will all eventually build up inside until you just explode with sorrow. If that happens, you will hurt yourself, maybe other people you love too."

For a moment there was silence, and a few sniffles from the twins. Finally, Dad knelt down. It was their silent cue for family prayers. They all shifted to the floor, but before he called on someone to pray, he said: "In a few days, after we have cried all our tears, we'll talk again. It's been my experience that people sometimes feel angry after they feel sad, and after that, they might blame themselves for what happened. I want to talk about those feelings, 'cause no one is to blame. Jimmy's death was…"

"My fault!" Sam bellowed, as if the burden of his guilt would burst his soul. Everyone was stunned by Sam's fury. He had jumped to his feet. "I should have listened! He didn't have to die! It's my fault! It's the same as if I had killed him!" His fists were clenched, his body rigid, veins standing out on his neck and face. He turned as if to leave the room, but stopped abruptly when his mother calmly asked.

"Was this when Jimmy asked if he could go to chores with you?"

"How did you know? How…" he stammered, his face contorted with grief and confusion.

"Because, just after breakfast, I had a feeling like I should keep him near me. That's why I thought maybe you had a similar impression."

"The point is," Sam interjected, his voice icy with self indictment, "I *didn't* listen. If I *had* listened he…"

"If I had listened," his mother interrupted, "he would still be here too. If anyone is guilty, I am! I'm his mother, for crying out loud!" She choked back an angry sob. "It was my job to keep him safe. I…"

"While I was washing dishes," Emily interrupted, her voice choked with emotion, "I had a feeling several times to go find Jimmy. I could see the bridge from the kitchen window. If I had even been responsive enough to just look up, I would have seen…"

"While I was feeding the chickens," Benjamin interrupted in a whisper, "I felt worried about Jimmy, and thought about the ditch. I just ignored it 'cause I thought it was stupid. The ditch goes right behind the chicken coop…"

There was a painful silence. After a moment Sam sat down on the floor as everyone else returned to their seats.

"I also have a confession to make," Jim admitted. Every one turned their eyes toward him, even Laura. She had no idea what he was going to say. "Three days ago as I was fueling up the tractor I looked into the back yard where you were all going about your chores. For some odd reason you were all there. You were so happy and beautiful. I thought to myself how lucky I was, and how I loved each one of you. I distinctly heard a voice say: "One of these will shortly be called home. Their work is done." There was a feeling of peace that came with it, and I knew that one of you would be leaving our home." He stopped for a long while as his body was racked by a silent sob.

"I knew it was from God, because of the peace I felt. I have long known that one of the things Satan can't imitate, is peace. I knew better than to try to beg the Lord to not let it happen. What I was hearing wasn't a prophecy, so much as a loving word to prepare me for these last few days.

"That morning, as I was helping Jimmy because his kitten scratched him, I heard the spirit whisper that it was Jimmy who would be called home. I don't know why, but I knew then, and I know now, that it was Jimmy's time to leave us."

"Then, if it was inevitable," Emily asked aloud, giving voice to the question they all wanted to ask, "why prompt so many of us to feel something that would have saved him? And why did we all ignore it? Why? It seems so futile, and so…so unfair!"

Jim waited a few moments before replying. "Well, I'm not sure I know the answer to that. I still have many questions myself, but I think it has to do with free agency."

"In what way, Jim?" This time it was Laura whose heart was begging for understanding. She had a master's degree in marriage and family counseling, yet nothing in her extensive training had prepared her for the violence done to her heart these last few days.

It was obvious to all, especially to Jim, that he was struggling for understanding, even as he was trying to explain it to his loved ones. "Perhaps it works like this. Heavenly Father knew that Jimmy had to come home, that his work was done. He wouldn't just strike Jimmy down. We have great faith that He wouldn't do such a thing, and we pray constantly for His protection. Perhaps Jimmy decided to throw the kitten into the ditch to punish it for scratching him that morning. Jimmy was a little like that, you know. Somehow, it happened that Jimmy also fell into the water. Perhaps Kitty scratched him, or hung onto him, and he got too close. I don't know, but he fell into the water because of poor choices on his part, not because God pushed him in, or sent angels to do it, or something. He fell in because of poor use of his free agency. However, it was God's plan to call him home, so he allowed this error on Jimmy's part to accomplish that. He warned us because we love Jimmy, and because the Holy Spirit always warns and protects. He warned us because it's our right to receive such things. We didn't listen because we were busy. Just like Jimmy, we used our agency unwisely, and Heavenly Father used this also to complete His plan. I think any one of us could have stopped Jimmy from drowning, but since we didn't, Heavenly Father used our actions to bring Jimmy home. Heavenly Father allowed our weaknesses, including Jimmy's, to accomplish His divine will."

"Then what is the point in warning us?" Laura asked, as much for her benefit as for the kids.

"Because, I suppose, we have the right to the promptings of the Holy Spirit, and because He wanted to teach us a lesson we would never forget. I don't think He took Jimmy home to teach us. I think

He just used his passing as an opportunity to teach. I believe Heavenly Father loves us enough to use even a tragic event like this, to teach us a lesson we must learn before we can reach the Celestial Kingdom."

"What lesson were we supposed to learn from this?" Angela asked dubiously. Beth nodded in twin-like agreement.

"What do you think we were supposed to learn?" Jim asked in response.

Angela thought a while, but it was Beth who replied. "I think we are to learn that Heavenly Father loves us. I think it was loving and kind of Him to warn us, and to give us the opportunity to save Jimmy, even though He knew we wouldn't do it. Imagine how we would all feel if He hadn't told Daddy that Jimmy's work was done, and that He would be coming home. We would all feel like we had killed Jimmy ourselves by not watching him closer, or not listening, or something."

"I think," Sam added quietly, "that we are to learn to listen, and to obey promptings which we receive. At least, that's what I'm going to do. I'll never ignore another one if I know it's from God." A chorus of "me either"s followed.

"I think," Emily said slowly, her voice nearly a whisper, "that He warned us because he loves us, not to make us feel guilty. I just don't think He'd do that. I know he wouldn't."

"It breaks my heart that Jimmy is no longer with us." Laura's voice was soft, yet certain. "Yet, he is sealed to us in the Temple, and I know that he will always be a part of our family. His life had meaning. He brought us love, happiness, joy, wonder, and laughter. He brought us all these things and more. His being a part of our family had a purpose, and that purpose was complete, so he went home to Heavenly Father. I promise each of you, and I promise Heavenly Father, that I will never forget Jimmy, and I will never forget the lessons he taught me in his short life. Nor, the lessons Heavenly Father taught us in his passing. This I promise."

"This, I promise," Sam said to himself, and he meant it more than any promise he had ever made.

two

Cheryl

By the time December rolled around, every tear which needed to be shed, had rolled from reddened eyes to the floor. With the final drop, a semblance of normality came upon them, and the joy of the Christmas season slowly warmed them.

The Mahoys loved Christmas time more than any other time of year. With so many kids in the house, a sense of breathless wonder hung in the air, like crystalline fog on a winter's eve that sparkles like diamonds in the moonlight. Christmas was Laura's season of joy. She loved no time of year better, and her happiness overlaid the family's collective spirit like a warm comforter. For her, Christmas meant secret plans and special gifts, surprises, decorations, and fun. It meant remembering old friends, Christmas cards from far away, and new friends unexpectedly made. It meant walking through crunching snow with frozen toes to sing carols at friends' doors. It meant shopping for hours for that special gift, wrapping it just so, and thrilling inwardly for days at the joy the receiver might feel when it was finally opened.

Jim Mahoy's favorite part of the season was watching Laura. He never loved her more than when she was alight with the spirit of Christmas. At times it felt as if his heart would just burst from sheer love. It seemed as if she were super-human, inexhaustible, and angelic all packaged in a small, soft bundle. For Jim, Christmas was the Christ child born in a manger, and it was Laura. He cared but little for gifts, bright paper and ribbons, Christmas trees and ornaments, the thousand feet of outdoor lights he hung each year for Laura. He didn't really care about caroling and the like, but he would have wrapped the entire world in strings of Christmas lights just to see his precious wife laugh and clap with joy like a four-year-old when he plugged them in each year. It was as if she had never seen them before, and her happiness was so pure it was spiritual.

Emily's favorite part of Christmas was cooking. She loved to bake, and Christmas was a blank check to cook anything she could conceive, and cook she did; cookies, cakes, pies, candies, pastries, gingerbread houses, and much more, some of it too beautiful to eat. For weeks the air was filled with a carefully orchestrated symphony of sweet spices. The aromas wove a tapestry of Christmas more beautiful than any masterpiece on canvas, and she loved every moment she spent weaving it. There was one other part of Christmas that Emily cherished. She had never told a soul and probably never would, but she loved watching her Papa watch her Mama. Deep inside her soul she understood his passion, and everything feminine within her thrilled that a man could love a woman so. Every Christmas she renewed her vow that her heart would also have just such a love.

For Sam the best of Christmas was the tree. Each year he would hunt and hunt for the perfect tree, and when he found it he would bring it home. It would first spend a few days in the barn, then in the garage, then in the back room to gradually warm it up. It took him more than a week to get the tree into the house. But, with Sam in charge, it had to be done just so. Finally, the tree would stand unadorned before the big living room window, carefully watered, until its branches relaxed enough to suit him. In the mean time, he carefully planned how to decorate it. One year he flocked it white with small red lights, big red bows, and candy canes. Another year it was blue lights, white origami birds, and silver garland. This year, he had decided, it was going to be multicolored lights, large calico bows, strings of red popcorn garland, and a large angel in calico coveralls on top. He didn't even try to explain the angel, and no one asked. One does not question the master, and when it came to the tree, he was in charge.

For Angela and Beth, the twins, Christmas time was snow. Snow to play in, build forts in, and sled on. Soft snow, hard snow, powdery or wet, it didn't matter. The only way to ruin Christmas for them was for it to not snow. If there was snow outside, they were outside. It seemed as if the only time they came in was to get warm enough to go back out.

For the first time ever, five-year-old Rachel was melancholy this Christmas. No one understood why, least of all Rachel. But it seemed as if all she could do was gaze out a window or into the tree, hour after hour. It was so unlike her that Laura worried about her, and tried to draw her into the joy in her own soul. But Rachel resisted gently, and wisdom seemed to dictate letting her find her own solace.

It was a perfect Christmas eve. Fresh snow was falling heavily, so Angela and Beth were breathless with anticipation. All the presents were carefully wrapped and hidden, cookies and cakes covered every flat surface in the house, and a quiet calm had fallen over the house. In the background the Mormon Tabernacle Choir quietly sang "Away in a Manger." The whole family had gathered near the tree, now perfectly resplendent in its calico bows and red popcorn stringers, to hear their father read the account of Christ's birth from the Gospel of St. Luke. They had scarcely begun when the phone rang. It was nearly ten o'clock at night and unexpected. Laura hurried to answer it, expecting a late holiday greeting from family far away. After a moment, she handed the phone to Emily, a look of concern on her face.

Emily took it in Jim's small office, and after a few long moments came back to where the family sat waiting to resume their Christmas Eve.

"Mama, Papa, that was Cheryl. You know, Cheryl Cantello, the inactive girl? Well, she needs a place to stay, just for tonight. I guess her Dad threw her out of the house. She says she'll call her married sister in the morning, and work out something after that."

Jim and Laura exchanged glances, nodded once, and in a way which mystified the younger kids and thrilled Emily, they made a decision without a single word being spoken. "Of course she can spend the night, Honey," Laura told her. "You and I will go get her. It's too stormy for you to drive alone tonight. Call her back and tell her we will be there in about half an hour."

"Mama, Cheryl is at the gas station pay phone. The station is closed. She walked there without a coat, and she was crying. She was really cold, and afraid. Can't we go sooner?"

Laura quickly dialed the phone and got elderly Sister France who lived next to the gas station. Sister France was on her way out the door almost before hanging up the phone. "Come on, Emily. We will pick her up at Sister France's home. It will still take us about twenty minutes to get there. We will have to drive slowly in the snow, but she will be safe until then."

After they had departed, Jim gathered the family around him. "You all heard what is happening. This means that Cheryl doesn't have any Christmas. The stores are closed by now. Let's come up with some ideas for a Christmas for Cheryl."

"How old is she Dad?" Sam asked. He couldn't remember her too well.

"She's Emily's age. And about the same size I'd say. Any ideas?"

"Daddy, you got each of us a couple of things, right?" Beth asked contemplatively. Jim nodded. "Well, you, and Santa," she added with a quick glance at Rachel, "know what they are. Would any of them be good for Cheryl? I mean, she can have one of mine."

"Yeah, mine too," Angela agreed. Beth nodded enthusiastically, and added, "And we can hang another stocking, and share our candy."

"I wanted a teddy bear. If you, I mean Santa, was going to give me one, I want Cheryl to have it," five-year-old Rachel volunteered happily, with an 'I already know about Santa,' look at Beth. It was the first time she had risen above her melancholy for days.

"I don't know what to give her," seven-year-old Benjamin said. I doubt if any of my gifts would work for her. I'm just a kid, and she's a grown up." That brought a chuckle from the older ones. But, he was so busy thinking, he didn't notice. Finally, his face brightened. He ran from the room, and returned in a few minutes holding Jimmy's kitten in his arms. It laid there listlessly. "You know how Kitty hasn't been playful since…well you know, since Jimmy left. We thought she was sick, but she isn't. I think she needs to be loved again by someone special. Well, I think Cheryl needs to be loved again too maybe they need each other. Maybe this is their Christmas to find a new family for both of them."

Jim was touched by his son's compassion. "I think that's a wonderful idea. Why don't you make her a gift box with holes in it, and a soft bed inside. You all have come up with wonderful ideas."

Only Sam had not come up with a gift. It was hard for him to imagine what Cheryl needed, or wanted, especially among the things he possessed. Finally, his face brightened, and he knew what to do. "I have an idea," he said, and walked away to work on it.

Cheryl was the last one to walk through the front door. She was taller than Emily by almost an inch, and as pretty a girl as Sam had ever seen. He wondered why he hadn't seen her at school. Her hair was almost the color Jimmy's had been, dark red, almost chestnut. She was clutching a paper shopping bag to her chest. It contained all she possessed in this world. Her eyes were red and frightened, and she looked at the floor as if wishing she could sink into it and disappear. Emily and Mom hustled her upstairs and drew her a hot bath. They found her a night gown, and without another word, tucked her into the spare bed in Emily's room.

Christmas morning was the most magical morning of the year. Both Jim and Sam left the house at four A.M. to milk the cows. When they arrived home, the festivities would begin. They returned around six, and the whole family gathered around the tree. Jim and Laura studied their family with wondering eyes, wanting to hold onto this moment in their memories. Jim snapped a few pictures, then handed the camera to Laura. She was a better photographer anyway, and family tradition demanded that Papa hand out the presents.

"Where's Cheryl?" Jim asked. Emily gave him a sideways look.

"Still in bed."

"Well, go get her. It's Christmas morning."

"I already told her, but she said she doesn't want to interfere with our Christmas."

"Our Christmas? It's hers too! You go tell her we aren't starting without her."

"Yeah, and tell her to hurry, too!" Rachel added enthusiastically.

After a few long minutes Cheryl came down the stairs wrapped in Emily's thick, blue bathrobe. She smiled weakly, and took a seat on the couch, as far away from the tree as she could get and still be in the same room. She folded her arms across her chest, and lowered her head until her long, red hair hid her face.

"Let's see, the first one here is for Rachel." Rachel laughed happily and hopped up to grab her gift. Without returning to her seat, she ripped the wrapping apart. It was a doll with long blond hair, just like her own. Everyone was appropriately impressed as she hugged the doll to her chest and rocked back and forth. Mama flashed a picture of her.

The next one was for Benjamin, who received a baseball glove. They continued from youngest to eldest until each had a gift. Angela received slippers with bunny rabbit faces on the toes, and Beth got a pair of fluffy mittens. Sam got a harmonica which he immediately began to play as if he had owned it for years. Emily received the new blouse she had been hoping for.

"Well, look. This one says 'To Cheryl, from Santa.'" Cheryl looked up for the first time, a look of disbelief on her face, tears beginning to form in her eyes. She honestly believed they were mocking her, and wanted to run away. But, no one was laughing, and Jim really was holding a Christmas gift out to her. Slowly, with wonder in her eyes, she stood and walked to where she could take it.

"There must be some mistake. I didn't…"

"Open it Honey," Laura urged. She slowly undid the ribbon, and removed the paper with great care. A small, blue, teddy bear was inside. She took it and pressed it to her cheek. From where Sam sat he could see tears running down her face.

Suddenly, all the rest of the presents were forgotten. Someone pressed another box into Cheryl's hands. It contained a pair of bunny slippers exactly like Angela's. Another box held mittens, exactly like Beth's. Another bigger box contained a winter coat with a faux fur collar, exactly her, (and Emily's) size. Sam shoved his gift into her hands. She looked at him with a shocked expression, then down at the box, and then back at his face. She carefully unwrapped the box, and removed the Christmas tree angel wearing calico coveralls.

She began to cry, then to laugh. "It's true," she said. "Angels do sometimes wear coveralls. I just never realized it before." She gave

Sam a meaningful smile, and he blushed deeply.

Benjamin handed her the box he had wrapped. "This one is moving!" she exclaimed gleefully. She carefully opened it and lifted out the yellow and white kitten. As soon as she touched it, it began to purr in a loud, contented way.

"See, Daddy. See, it loves her!" Benjamin exclaimed happily. Cheryl didn't know, but they all did, that the kitten hadn't purred since Jimmy had died five months ago.

She just stood there holding her gifts, pressing the kitten to her cheek, her eyes aglow with wonder and happiness. "You guys. How did you...?"

"Santa did it!" Rachel declared.

"Baby Jesus did it," Benjamin corrected, and everyone laughed.

"Hey, here's a gift for Mommy," Jim said, handing his wife a shiny box. Cheryl knelt down amongst her gifts and new friends, and laughed happily as they finished their Christmas giving. But every so often, her voice would unexplainably go quiet, and she would have to wipe away a few tears before she could laugh again.

When it was all over, the room looked like the aftermath of a cheerful tornado. Everyone carried their treasures to their rooms, but Cheryl continued to sit amidst the bright Christmas clutter, stroking her kitten, rocking gently from side to side, and humming softly to herself. It was a time of sweetness for her, and everyone sensed it was also a time of healing.

———

Later that evening they knelt for family prayers. Cheryl knelt next to Emily. Her eyes were bright and happy, and she held her kitten in her arms, its purr motor running loudly.

"Before we pray, can I say something?" Cheryl asked timidly. Jim just nodded and smiled.

"This has been the happiest day of my life. Since my mother died when I was seven, we haven't had Christmas. I have hated Christmas all these years. I think I hated it so I wouldn't have to be sad at not having it. I didn't realize that until this morning.

My dad kicked me out last night because I didn't have dinner fixed when he came home. He was drunk, and didn't realize it was almost ten o'clock. We had eaten without him hours earlier. He grabbed me by the hair and threw me out into the snow. He said I was a worthless bitch, even more worthless than my mother had been. I laid down in the snow and cried, and waited to die. I wanted him to find my frozen body when he left the house the next day. I wanted him to know how he has made my life miserable all these years, and how much I hated him. He opened the door and threw a paper bag of my clothes at me. He didn't even care that I was lying in the snow without a coat.

As I was lying there shivering, a feeling of warmth came over me, and I thought about my mother, and I knew she wouldn't want me to die this way. I got up and stumbled a couple of blocks to the gas station. It was closed. I had forgotten it was Christmas Eve. I just stood there shivering, thinking about dying, until this warm feeling came over me again, and I thought about Emily, and I knew she was warm and safe and loved. I thought if I could just spend one night being loved like Emily..." She stopped, her voice wouldn't go on. She wiped tears away with the back of her hand, and smiled sadly. "I thought, if I could spend just one day being like Emily, then I would be happy to die. But I wasn't going to let my father cheat me out of that one day. So I called Emily. I called because somehow I hoped I could just experience love, even for one day." There was a long pause. "I know you don't love me like one of your own, like you do Emily, but I have seen the love you have for each other, and you have shared more love with me than I thought existed in the whole world. I got my wish; I got my day of love.

"I will be going to my sister's house tomorrow, or the next day, but I wanted you all to know how special you have made me feel. It's the only time I can remember being this close to being loved. I just wanted to thank you. That's all, I guess."

When Jim finally spoke, his voice was husky with emotion. "You were only wrong about one thing, Cheryl. We do love you like one of our own." A chorus of agreement filled the room. The twins rushed over to hug her, then everyone joined in, and for a few minutes she was surrounded by love more powerful than she thought possible anywhere in the universe. It was more than her fragile soul could stand, and she wept openly for joy. These were not just words; this was love, pure and unfeigned. It warmed her through and through, and the icy pain deep within her began to melt away.

Several days later, they all gathered for Family Home Evening. It was Angela's turn to give the lesson, and naturally, Beth did exactly half of it. Cheryl was still there. She had not been able to get her sister on the phone, and had written a letter instead. It would be a few more days before she left. No one was in a hurry for her to leave, especially she.

"Tonight's lesson is on what is good," Angela said in her best sunday school teacher voice. "Who can tell me what is good?"

"Love is good," Cheryl said, then blushed deeply. It was one of those slips that opens a window into another's heart.

"I think Christmas is good," Rachel said in her enthusiastic way. "I especially liked the part about giving Cheryl presents she didn't expect." Everyone agreed with this. Again, Cheryl blushed.

Angela cleared her throat importantly. The room fell silent again. "How can you tell if something is good?"

"It makes you feel good inside," Laura answered, a thing she had discovered herself.

"It makes me want to thank Heavenly Father," Jim added. He always felt like praying when something good came his way, even something as ordinary as a beautiful sunrise, or a bird's song after a summer rain.

"Daddy, would you please read Moroni 7 verses 12 and 13?" Jim waited while others found the scripture, then closed his eyes and quoted from memory:

> *Wherefore, all things which are good cometh of God; and that which is evil cometh of the devil; for the devil is an enemy unto God, and fighteth against him continually, and inviteth and enticeth to sin, and to do that which is evil continually. But behold, that which is of God inviteth and enticeth to do good continually; wherefore, every thing which inviteth and enticeth to do good, and to love God, and to serve him, is inspired of God. (Moroni 7:12-13)*

"So," Angela continued, "If something makes us feel like doing good, then that thing came from God. Does that also mean if something ends up being good, then the things that made it happen were good too? Is that right Daddy?"

"I think that is generally true, especially if it felt good inside."

"But what if you didn't feel good inside, like you were sad at the time, but later it turned out good?" Beth wanted to know.

"Then, I suppose you could say that Heavenly Father made good come of it," Jim replied.

After a silent, twin-like signal, Beth took over the lesson. "OK," she drew a deep breath as if preparing herself, "here is what the lesson is about. We think this is the best Christmas we have ever had. And we think it's because Cheryl came to spend it with us. Daddy, do you think this was good, I mean, like Heavenly Father wanted Cheryl to spend Christmas with us?"

"Very much so."

"OK then, do you remember when she said she got this warm feeling at the gas station that made her want to call Emily, do you think that was Heavenly Father too?"

Instead of answering himself, Jim asked: "What do you think, Cheryl?"

Cheryl started, looked around the room as if in panic, then cleared her throat. A look of calm came over her, and she smiled. "I was thinking about that this morning. It's funny that Beth has brought it up. I do think that warm feeling, and the thoughts about Emily, came from the Spirit. The other thoughts I was having were that I wanted to die."

"See? That's what we mean," Angela took over as if it was all in the script. Beth looked at her sister with an expression of perfect harmony. "On the one hand, she had this bad feeling telling her to lie in the snow and die. But then she also had this warm feeling telling her to look for love, and where to find it. I think that is what Moroni was trying to tell us in the scripture. Things which tell us to do bad come from the devil, and everything which tells us to do good, comes from God."

"That is really neat," Cheryl volunteered with wonder in her voice. "I hadn't realized that. I was actually in a battle for my life, and was receiving real revelation from Heavenly Father on how to win. I didn't realize..." She fell silent for a moment. "I didn't realize how much Heavenly Father loves me. I had no idea. I thought I was nobody, a total write-off. I thought God only loved the prophets — and Emily." This brought a collective smile from the Mahoys, but Cheryl was serious. "Boy," she continued, her voice almost too quiet to hear, "this really is turning out to be an amazing Christmas. It seems as if I am suddenly surrounded by love."

"There's one more part to our lesson," Beth added without missing a beat. "We think that since Heavenly Father sent Cheryl to us, she should not be in such a hurry to leave. If Heavenly Father wanted her here, maybe she should find out if Heavenly Father wants her to stay here, I mean like for a long time. I mean if it's all right with Mommy and Daddy."

"Oh yes, Cheryl." Laura interjected enthusiastically. "I was thinking just this morning how sad it will be when you leave. I think Beth and Angela..."

"Angela and Beth," Angela corrected.

"She was born first, Mama. You know the A B C's, Angela then Beth," Beth added teasingly.

"...that Angela and Beth have given us an inspired Family Home

Evening. I hope you'll consider their words."

All eyes except Cheryl's turned on Jim as he searched for the right words. This was unexpected, yet it had the feeling of truth to him. "Cheryl," he said as her big brown eyes turned from Laura to himself. "You are family now, whether you leave tomorrow, or stay for the rest of your life. You just remember that you have a home here, and that you'll always be loved." A tear rolled down Cheryl's cheek.

After a moment, Jim slid to his knees, and everyone followed. As he looked around the room, waiting for the Spirit to whisper who should pray, his eyes fell upon Cheryl. Her face was bright with the light he knew to be from the Spirit of God. "Cheryl, would you pray tonight?"

Her head snapped up, startled, and for a moment she looked as if she might say no. Instead, she bowed her head, and they waited a long time for her to begin.

"Dear Heavenly Father, I think you are the most wonderful Heavenly Father in the whole, wide world. You treated me so nice to let me have Christmas with…with my new family. I didn't know you loved me…it kind of surprised me to learn that you did…that you do. God forgive me for not knowing sooner…God bless Mama Laura. God bless Papa Jim. God bless Emily, and Sam, Angela and Beth, Benjamin and Rachel,…and please tell Jimmy we love him. God bless Kitty, and the angel in coveralls. God bless Jesus, Amen."

No one moved for a full minute. "I don't think I did so good," Cheryl said timidly. "I've never prayed out loud before, actually, to myself either."

"It was the most beautiful prayer I've ever heard," Sam said quietly, mostly to himself. A chorus of happy hugs assured her that everyone present agreed.

My Angel in Coveralls

Cheryl never did move to her sister's, but stayed with her new family. Cheryl turned seventeen the same month Sam turned fifteen. He was a junior in high school, and she a senior. It was the fall of 1966. Fall had gripped the air, and Halloween decorations hung all through the school. When you're a senior girl, the most important consideration is who will take you to the Senior Prom, which was only three days away. Cheryl held no hopes that she would be asked. She was not popular at school, because she did not join in the things that would have made her so. She was too shy to join in without being almost forced to participate. Still, her heart ached to go to the dance.

Sam was sweet on Jenny, a dark-haired junior from the Seventh Ward. Jenny was pretty, and a cheerleader. She was popular, bubbly and enthusiastic, and Sam was hopelessly smitten with her. He thought Jenny was perfection wearing lipstick. Sam was on the football team, and showed considerable talent at it. By his junior year he was the varsity center, and consequently, more popular with the other kids. The best thing about that position was that he didn't ever have to catch the ball, a skill he was still not good at.

He had grown nearly an inch and gotten contacts, and suddenly his broad features and dark hair were attractive. It was as if the old Sam had moved away, and his handsome cousin had taken his place. He was still shy, but too caught up in the momentum of life to be overly affected by it.

He and Jenny had planned for weeks to go to the prom, and he made arrangements for a tux, corsage, dinner, and the works. Cheryl watched all this from a distance, happy for Sam's happiness, yet saddened that she had not achieved the same.

The night before the prom, Sam called Jenny. After a long conversation, a thousand promises, and a few tears from Jenny, he made arrangements for her to go with her cousin, Tim, Sam's good friend, also a junior. He told her he had a family obligation he could not shirk, and he would see her at the dance. They would still dance a few. She understood, and admired him for his decision, but still, she was not pleased.

The evening was waning to darkness when Sam walked up to

Cheryl who was sitting at the kitchen table, supposedly studying for an Algebra final.

"Cheryl? Uh, I have a problem. I have spent all this money, see, and made reservations and all, and Jenny says she has to go with her cousin to the prom because her parents insisted. I was wondering, would you like to go with me? I know we're family and all, but if you weren't, I mean, given other circumstances, I would have liked to go with you. You're real pretty, and fun to be with and all. I mean, what do you think, Go with me?"

"As a favor to you? To save you money?" she asked dubiously.

"Well, yes."

"I don't believe a word of it. I talked to Jenny yesterday, and she was so excited about the prom she couldn't think straight. It was all she could talk about. Her parents were happy about it too. Tell me the truth, or forget it."

"Well, it's sort of the truth, except that I asked her to go with her cousin. I didn't want you to miss the only Senior Prom you'll ever get to go to. You are more important to me than a date with Jenny, and we will have our own Senior Prom next year. But you can bet that if you say no, Jenny will still go with her cousin just to spite me. So you are doing me a favor."

"Yeah, she would do that, and so would I probably. You will have to do some fancy footwork to get back into Jenny's good graces." Sam shrugged. He knew what she said was true. "Well, as long as it's only as a favor to you, not because you feel obligated to take me."

"As a very big favor to me," he echoed, and she smiled a big smile.

"I don't have a dress. I don't know how to do my hair. I don't have high heels or anything. This is awful! Actually, it's very sweet." She kissed him on the cheek, and hurried off to find Emily and Mama Laura. He had already discussed it with them, and they had been working on it for days. They had lengthened one of Emily's dresses, and borrowed a pair of shoes. Preparations were much further along than Cheryl could have ever guessed.

That next evening, when Cheryl came down the stairs, Sam had to struggle to keep his mouth closed. Since Christmas Eve a year ago, he had looked at Cheryl as his sister, not as a dateable female. What he saw coming down the stairs could have walked across any beauty pageant stage and won hands down. Her dark, red hair was done up with large ringlets falling softly by her cheeks. Her dress was black, and did stunning things to her figure.

"Wow, you look fantastic!" he gushed. "Who are you? Where's

Cheryl?"

She hit him playfully with her handbag. Sam pinned a corsage on her, and she pinned a boutonniere on him. She took his arm and they left in the family car. Jim and Laura stood on the porch, huddling against the chill, and inwardly glowing with contentment.

The dance was the highlight of the school year, and everybody who was anybody was there. A few nobodies showed up as well. There were kids there in tuxes and tails, and also leather jackets and faded jeans.

Surprisingly, Cheryl was graceful on the dance floor. Sam had secretly taken lessons from his mother for several weeks, and he knew the basics. Before long, they were oblivious to anyone else, and danced in a cloud of discovery and happiness.

It surprised him when he felt a tap on his shoulder. It was a boy he didn't recognize, but he was dressed in a suit and looked harmless. Cheryl shrugged and smiled, so he stepped aside. That he was a much better dancer than Sam was obvious from the second step, and Cheryl glided away like magic.

Suddenly alone, he thought of Jenny, and after a few minutes found her dancing with her cousin. Following the stranger's example, he tapped in, and was soon gliding around the floor with Jenny. She was pleased to finally dance with him, and didn't show any sign of being angry.

"I understand why you wanted to come with Cheryl," she said finally. "It would be a shame for her to miss this." He was grateful she understood. "Look how much fun she's having." Just then, the crowd shifted and he caught sight of her dancing away. Her partner had drawn her close to him, and they were spinning around the floor. All he needed to see was the smile on her face to know he needn't hurry back.

He and Jenny talked and danced for most of an hour before he again caught sight of Cheryl. The music had slowed, and they were dancing very close, except that Cheryl was arching her back, trying to keep his head off her shoulder. He was leaning into her with his hands low on her back. Too low.

"I think I better go rescue Cheryl," he said, and nodded toward them. Jenny gasped, and released him. He immediately walked away.

"Excuse me. May I cut in?" he said as he tapped him on the shoulder. The look of relief on Cheryl's face was enough to tell him he had come just in the nick of time.

"No!" he said, at the same moment Cheryl had said, "Sure."

He danced away, and Sam followed. "I'm cutting in," he said. Cheryl turned to join Sam, but her partner jerked her back.

"Please. It's been nice, but I'm tired now. Thanks." But still he wouldn't stop. Finally Cheryl just stopped dancing, and the stranger had to stop also. Sam held out his hand and she reached for it, but the stranger gave him a menacing look. He returned the glare without lowering his hand.

The stranger gave Sam a dangerous look. "She's dancing with me, and if you know what's good for you, you'll leave. You can have her back when I'm finished with her. Now beat it!"

Sam took her hand without blinking an eye, and pulled her away. The stranger shrugged. "Well, I guess I lose." He started to turn away, but added, "On second thought, you lose." Without warning, he spun on one foot and swung at Sam. Sam wasn't expecting an attack, and the blow caught him on the side of the head. Sam stumbled one step, his head ringing, and his ear turning puffy. The fellow swung another time, but Sam stepped into the blow, and it hit him on the shoulder.

The same defect that made him poor at catching a ball also made him a poor fighter. Sam knew he had one chance to end this fight successfully. He waited until the fellow swung again. He ducked beneath the blow and with all his strength hammered the stranger under the chin. The fellow's head snapped back. He fell backwards with a loud thud onto the polished floor. Sam took four quick steps and grabbed him by the suit lapels. In a single motion he lifted him until only his toes were touching the floor. The stranger was still gasping for breath as Sam shook him, his head snapping back and forth.

Two people in leather jackets and jeans pulled their friend from Sam's grasp, and were about to finish it for him when several teachers appeared. They separated them, and kicked the stranger and his friends out of the dance. Sam didn't realize the music had stopped until it began again, and people started to turn away in disinterest.

Cheryl was instantly by his side, inspecting his ear. It was sore, but not bleeding. "A cow can kick harder than that fool can hit," he said quite honestly. He should know, he had taken blows from many cows. Cheryl chuckled, put her arms around his neck, and kissed him on the forehead.

"You really are my angel in coveralls, aren't you?" He blushed, as he took her hand and they danced until the band put away their instruments.

There weren't very many cars left in the parking lot when Sam and Cheryl came out. Sam helped Cheryl into the driver's side of the car, but as he was doing so, he spotted four cars parked on the far side of the lot. Only the glow of cigarettes in the dark told him that someone was there. He had a sinking feeling and knew they were in trouble. Instead of going to the other side, he slid behind the wheel, pushing her to the other side. He didn't have a driver's license, but he knew how to drive as well as anyone who did.

"What's wrong?" she asked in a worried voice.

"I think those punks waited for us. I wanted to drive. Just in case. It's a long drive home, and they may be planning something."

"Let's go back inside and call Mom and Dad," she insisted. Sam thought that was a good idea, but they could see the janitor locking the doors to the school.

"Cheryl, you pray, and I'll drive. We'll be all right. What can they do to us as long as we drive straight home? They surely won't run us off the road."

"I suppose you're right." He started the car and pulled away. After watching for a while, it didn't appear they were being followed. They began to relax and talk about the dance. They came to an intersection where they had to turn left to go home. If they turned right it took them to a long, winding road in the hills which eventually dead-ended at a lake. When they came to the intersection, there were three cars completely blocking the left road. Sam panicked and started to back up, but several cars were directly behind him, honking their horns. They had no choice but to turn right. He knew the road was a dead end, and hoped they could find a way to turn around before they caught up. He gunned the car and sped off. After a mile, the road turned to dirt.

He didn't dare go too fast, mostly because he didn't want to reach the dead end any time soon. But he did want to find a place to turn around before they caught up. All of a sudden, a car loaded with teenagers roared past them like they were standing still. Before he could react, another car zoomed past, its exhaust roaring loudly. Cheryl screamed in fright, and turned terrified eyes on Sam.

"Whatever happens," Sam told her, his fists clenched white on the wheel. "I won't let them hurt you. It's me they want to get. So when they start onto me, you just run away into the woods. Take off your heels, and run barefooted. I've seen you run on the farm, and you can really move. You have on a black dress, and they won't be able to find you."

"I couldn't leave you. I couldn't!" she protested.

"You have to!"

"But, I won't!"

"Promise me you will if it comes to that!" he nearly shouted.

"OK. I promise, if I have to, I'll run. But I won't like it."

"Listen, they can't hurt me too much. I'm tough from football and working on the farm. I'll fight them a little, then roll up and pretend to be whipped. They'll get tired and leave. But I'm afraid what they might do to a beautiful girl in the middle of the night. So you have to remember your promise. I'm going to get it either way. It will only make it worse on you to stick around."

"OK, OK!" she said, her voice angry. "Let's figure out a better solution before it comes to that." At that moment the two cars in front of them pulled side by side and began braking. They had no choice but to also slow down. Four cars pulled up behind them, swaying back and forth, honking and flashing their lights. They were obviously spoiling for whatever they had planned. It only took them a few minutes to force Sam to a complete stop.

Sam knew better than to get out of the car as the boys from the front car started walking back toward him. One of them was the stranger in the suit. He had a baseball bat in his hands which he was swinging back and forth. He walked straight up to Sam's car, and without saying a word, shattered their windshield. A million pieces of glass sprayed into their faces and laps. Cheryl screamed in terror.

He leaned through the broken windshield on Sam's side, his face plastered with an evil smirk. Cheryl cowered back into her seat. Suddenly the rear window exploded inward as someone smashed it to atoms.

"First," he glowered, "I'm going to beat the living crap out of your boyfriend here, and make it so he never thinks about another girl as long as he lives. Then you and me are going to finish what we had going at the dance. And you're going to like it, whether you do or not!"

As he was saying this, Sam was praying silently. He knew only a miracle could save them. At the exact moment the threats ended, he had a wild idea. It was impossible, dangerous, foolish, and a hundred other things, but with the idea came a feeling of peace. His father's words rang in his ears. "Satan can't imitate peace."

He lunged forward and grabbed the kid's tie and a part of his jacket. Luckily, it was not a snap-on tie. He wound a beefy hand into the fabric such, that nothing short of a crow bar could have opened it. With his other hand he shifted into reverse, grabbed the steering wheel, and simultaneously jammed his foot onto the gas.

The family car was a fairly new Rambler Ambassador station wagon. It outweighed the punks cars by almost a thousand pounds. His action was so sudden, so unexpected, that the kid in his grasp dropped the bat, and screamed in wide-eyed terror. The big, V8 engine roared as the car slammed into the car behind them. A side window exploded from an invisible blow. Shouts, screams, and curses were rending the night air.

"Get down!" he shouted at Cheryl, who complied the best she could. He jammed the car into first gear, and gunned the motor. He didn't dare hit the front cars as hard. He had watched a few demolition derbies, and knew that to puncture the radiator was to lose. He picked the smallest of the two cars in front of him and hit it as hard as he dared. It jolted forward six feet. He was hardly aware of the screaming face still suspended in his front window as he jammed the car into reverse and plowed into the cars behind. The car he hit jumped ten feet. He jammed it into forward, and hit the other car. People were running everywhere, trying to get out of his way. There were four cars behind him, and they were having a hard time getting them out of his way. He hit them again and again. Finally, there was an opening between the two cars in front of them, and he sped through the opening, letting go of the punk on their hood just as they cleared the two cars. He saw him flip end over end onto the side of the road. He hoped he hadn't hurt him too much, and simultaneously hoped he was stone dead.

He steered the car down the winding road in total darkness. He had smashed out the headlights in his escape. Cheryl was sitting up, blinking in the rush of wind through the open windshield.

"That was the most amazing thing I have ever seen!" she exclaimed without taking her eyes off the winding road. I think your Dad is going to kill us when he sees what we have done to his new car!"

Sam thought about this for only a second before replying. "Maybe, but I'll bet he'll consider it a small price for bringing you home safe." She looked at him with a strange expression on her face.

"You really would let them beat you if it would let me escape, wouldn't you?"

He just shrugged. "It isn't over yet. This is a dead end road. I doubt they will give up after I messed up their cars like that. We have to figure out something else." After what seemed like too short a time, they arrived at the small campground on the lake. It was deserted. When they pulled into the parking lot, they were almost immediately surrounded by six other cars. They couldn't tell they had been followed because their headlights were also smashed. This time they pulled in bumper to bumper. Sam gunned the big engine, but the wheels just flipped gravel and billowed smoke. It was no use.

"OK. This is back to plan 'A'." He reached up to the dome light and ripped it off the ceiling with one almost effortless movement. "When I jump out, you wait five seconds, then head off the other way. If you do it right, they won't see you. Remember, you promised. No matter what you hear. Keep running." She nodded, wide eyed, tears streaking her face.

He pushed his door open the few inches he could, and climbed out onto the hood of the car that was blocking him. A head appeared and he kicked it. Whoever it was fell backwards and didn't return. He jumped up onto the roof of the car blocking him, jumped over a baseball bat which someone swung at his legs, and ran down the trunk. He didn't even look back to see if Cheryl had followed his instructions. He had his work cut out for him at the moment.

He knew where he was headed. He had spotted an old fire pit not far away, and it had branches hanging out of it he could use as a club. He almost made it, but was not fast enough. Someone tackled him from behind. He fell, skidding forward, someone clinging to his legs. He easily pulled a leg loose and kicked the offender in the face. Just then, a terrible blow landed on the side of his head, and he was dazed momentarily. He could feel other blows coming down on him. He could feel his body contorting, trying to roll into the fetal position. He had never felt such pain. It made his mind seem to grind to a stop. He forced himself to think. His vision cleared just as a fist came at his nose. Reflexively his hand shot out and caught the fist. He closed with all his strength and twisted. He felt the other's bones breaking, accompanied by a scream of pain. It was a sickening feeling, but he was fighting for survival. He rolled to his knees, and was immediately bowled back over by a kick in the ribs. The only thing that was saving him was that there were too many of them on him to swing a weapon at him without hitting someone else. It was small consolation.

Blackness was just about to overcome him when he saw a body fly over his head. He dimly heard someone curse, and the beating seemed to slow, then suddenly stopped. Dimly, he identified the sound of another fight going on nearby. He had a sinking thought that Cheryl had returned, but the blows were too solid. His vision cleared a bit, and he saw a black coated punk spin away and drop to his knees. He sat up, and saw his attackers converge on a single person standing in the headlights of an old truck, his legs spread. Whoever it was moved like a ballet dancer, swinging what appeared to be a shovel. The improvised weapon moved faster than it was possible to follow in the dim light. It blurred this way and then that. A foot lashed out to the crunch of breaking bones, then the flat of the shovel bashed another senseless. In mere minutes it was all over. Those who could move were crawling away. Engines gunned, and cars sped away into the darkness.

It wasn't until his unidentified benefactor leaned over Sam that he realized it was his dad. He still had the shovel in one hand, his eyes wary and darting. Jim examined his son, and satisfied that his injuries were not life-threatening, helped him stand. Sam felt like passing out and throwing up at the same time. He hurt in every part of his body. He took a step and realized he had been kicked in the crotch.

Sam heard a heavy whack off in the darkness to their right, followed by a grunt and a heavy thud. A moment later, Cheryl trotted into the circle of light carrying a red necktie and a baseball bat.

After she had satisfied herself Sam was not mortally wounded, she chuckled and held up the necktie. "I collected a trophy for you."

Sam fell asleep on Cheryl's shoulder as they bounced home in the old truck. His dad said nothing, his face a grim mask of anger and pride. Cheryl told Jim the whole story as they ground their way home, taking extra care to not hit any bumps which made Sam groan in his sleep.

They put Sam to bed after dressing his wounds, and he slept for three days. When he finally looked in the mirror he was surprised to see a black and blue stranger looking back at him. In the final tally he had four broken ribs, three broken fingers, two black eyes, a concussion, and a zillion cuts and bruises, but he was alive, and Cheryl was unharmed. He tried to smile at the thought, but it hurt too much. The station wagon was a total loss. The insurance company took one glance at it and wrote it off. Most of the punks were caught and punished. Several received prison sentences. They weren't hard to identify. They drove battered cars and most had broken bones and bruises the shape of a shovel.

Sam later found out that the story had been in the newspapers and on the TV. He was a kind of hero, which only made him uncomfortable.

Cheryl was in charge of Family Home Evening the following Monday. He hobbled downstairs, and was greeted by a room full of balloons and crepe paper. A large cake Emily had baked was on the coffee table. On its surface, Emily had very carefully crafted a frosting angel wearing coveralls.

Cheryl's lesson was a retelling of their experience. None of them had heard it from start to finish, and they all listened with rapt attention. She was gushing in her praise of Sam, and of Papa Jim. When the telling was all done, and they were about to kneel down to family prayers, Sam asked the question that had been tickling the back of his mind for days.

"Dad, where did you learn to fight like that? You weren't in the army or nothing. How did you do it? And how did you find us? We were miles off the way home, and it seems like a miracle you ever found us."

Jim straightened in his chair, and considered his answer. "We called family prayers about eleven o'clock that night, and while your Mother was praying, I had a feeling something was very wrong. It was just a feeling, but quite clear. I knew you two were in danger. I didn't wait for the prayer to end, but jumped into the old truck and drove toward the school. As I went I prayed. You know how the Lord and me are. I do everything He says, and He makes it rain on my crops. Well, I needed some rain, and told Him so. I about drove past the turn off to the lake when I had the strong feeling that I should turn up there. It was a long shot, and I knew it, but I had asked for help and it seemed absurd to ignore it when it came. I turned onto the road. I knew I was on the right track when I saw hubcaps, fenders, and glass all over the road about halfway there. I drove as fast as I could until I came upon the station wagon surrounded by cars. From its condition I knew you had tried to get away by bashing into them. It was also obvious it hadn't been entirely successful. I saw a pile of guys off to the side, and knew you were under them. As I was getting out of the truck, I had the thought to grab the irrigation shovel. I did, and when they came at me, I just did everything I felt impressed to do. I swung, ducked, kicked, punched, and fought by the Spirit. It was the most incredible experience I've ever had. It was as if I was another person. During it all, I had this incredible sense of calm come over me. I would sense the need to swing before I became aware of someone being there, and smack, someone would go down. When it was all over, the feeling left me, and I was just standing there holding a bloody shovel. Son, the answer to your question is that I did it by the grace of God. I think this is what Moroni meant when he said God strengthened their arms so they could defend their families from the armies of the Lamanites, even though the were vastly out numbered. I'm quite certain that had we not discussed what we did following Jimmy's accident, about listening to the Spirit, and following directions even when it's hard to understand, and had I not taken it to heart, that both you and Cheryl would have died up there."

"You know what I don't understand, though, Dad. It's the difference in the promptings. You described the feelings you had as being quite strong. I can see how that could be the Holy Ghost directing you to come save us. But at other times, the promptings are so small, so difficult to hear, so…"

"Still, and small?" Jim interjected.

"Exactly. Sometimes I can't tell the difference between the whisperings of the Spirit and my own thoughts. I can get the big promptings, but the little ones I miss a lot."

Laura cleared her throat, and everyone turned toward her. "The same thing has bothered me since Jimmy's passing. There were both kinds of promptings for me that day. I had many little promptings, and I ignored them because I didn't recognize them as promptings. By the time the big one came there really was a problem, and I had waited too long…" Her voice trailed off. "I have often wondered why Heavenly Father didn't warn me louder, so I couldn't miss it. Why even use the still small voice, if we humans are so prone to not hear it?"

"We keep talking about two voices, the still small voice, and the louder one. Are there actually two voices? Or is it just that we have our ears turned low some times, and it sounds still and quiet?" Benjamin asked, a note of confusion in his voice.

Jim turned to Cheryl. "Is it all right with you, Cheryl, if I take a minute and explain what I think is going on? I know it's your Family Home Evening."

"Please do. I'm as confused as I can possibly be. I have heard both of these voices too. I always assumed it was because I just don't listen well enough, or if I were more righteous, the voice would be louder. I turn the time over to you."

"Thanks, Cheryl. There is only one Holy Ghost." Everyone smiled at such an obvious statement. "But He speaks in two different ways."

"Why Daddy?" Beth asked in exact stereo with Angela.

"Well, you know how Bishop Connell serves as our Bishop, but he is also our home teacher? When he comes home teaching, does he act and speak differently than when he's being the Bishop at church?"

"He smiles more when he's our home teacher, and laughs." Rachel observed enthusiastically. "When he's the Bishop, he acts all serious."

"Well, it's kind of the same thing with the Holy Ghost. One of the great blessings that Jesus Christ has given us is that he is the 'Light of Truth'. Has anyone heard that term before?"

"Is that the same thing as our conscience?" Sam asked.

"The same. It's something that every person has, and it has the job of teaching every person right from wrong. This is the still small voice we keep talking about. We have it as a result of the Atonement. It's one of the very precious gifts from Jesus Christ. The scriptures indicate that one of the reasons Jesus had to suffer so much was so that he would know how to guide us when we have problems."

"Wow. I didn't know that." Cheryl put both hands on her cheeks with her elbows on both knees. "So does the still small voice only tell us not to steal candy bars, and that kind of thing? Or, does it have another purpose too?"

"It has several purposes in addition to telling us not to do wrong things. One of the greatest of these, and the hardest to learn to hear, is the prompting to do good things. It seems easier to hear the ones not to do something bad, but there are a lot of promptings to do good things too."

"You mean, like say your prayers, be kind to someone, that kind of thing?" Benjamin asked. "I've heard those a lot. Sometimes I ignore them because they always seem to want me to do something I don't want to at the moment. I thought they were just my own thoughts, and not very important."

"I'd like to share a scripture," Jim said, and drawing on his unique memory and love of the scriptures, he closed his eyes, and recited:

> *And the Spirit giveth light to every man that cometh into the world; and the Spirit enlighteneth every man through the world, that hearkeneth to the voice of the Spirit. And every one that hearkeneth to the voice of the Spirit cometh unto God, even the Father. (D&C 84:46-47)*

"I think the important part here is the last sentence. 'And every one that hearkeneth to the voice of the Spirit cometh unto God, even the Father.' That's the whole purpose of life, to return to Heavenly Father. It says that we must learn to hearken, or obey, the still small voice in order to return to Him. Unless you realize that these promptings are actually revelation from God, then you may feel free to just ignore the ones that are inconvenient."

"Boy. I do that a lot." Emily commented. "But you know what? I always feel kind of empty inside when I do."

"Me too," several said at once.

"But I'm still confused." Cheryl leaned forward in her chair. "How do I tell the promptings apart from my own thoughts? I always thought they were just my own thinking."

"Well," Jim began, "here's how I do it. I still miss some, but this helps me. It's like the scripture in Moroni we read in Family Home Evening a while ago. Everything that is good, and teaches us to love and serve God, to pray and be kind, comes from God. Everything which teaches us to do bad, to be mean, or to not pray, these things come from the devil."

"I can see that," Laura interjected. "But I also hear a lot of confusing things. I hear a lot of discussions, questions, even arguments in my head. I hear the good and the bad, but I also hear these other things."

"It's my opinion that this is our own mind working. I think what happens is the Holy Spirit prompts us to do good. After that, the devil tries to get us to not do that good thing, and then our minds try to decide what to do. What we are hearing is that argument going on in our minds."

"Hey!" Emily said enthusiastically. "I think I understand. It's called the still small voice because it sounds like our own thoughts. But it's not, at least not all of it. The Holy Spirit says to do some good thing. It just says 'Say your prayers,' or something like that. After that you hear reasons why you shouldn't from Satan, like you're too tired, or too mad to say prayers. After that you hear this long discussion trying to decide what to do. I get it. This is how revelation works. We get prompted by both sides, and we must decide what we will do."

"Let me read another scripture." Again he closed his eyes and recited.

> And they are free to choose liberty and eternal life, through the great Mediator of all men, or to choose captivity and death, according to the captivity and power of the devil; for he seeketh that all men might be miserable like unto himself. And now, my sons, I would that ye should…choose eternal life, according to the will of his Holy Spirit; And not choose eternal death, according to the will of the flesh and the evil which is therein, which giveth the spirit of the devil power to captivate, to bring you down to hell, that he may reign over you in his own kingdom. (2 Nephi 2:27-29)

"I think this is a great key. I believe almost all revelation works this way, that it comes quietly, and we receive our greatest blessings by being obedient to what is sort of a divine hint, or suggestion. Promptings aren't the same as commandments, but they are revelation, and anyone who learns to obey them will eventually enter the Celestial Kingdom."

"So," Laura added, "we choose eternal life by choosing to obey the Holy Spirit, and we choose captivity and eternal death by choosing to obey the will of the flesh, which is what Satan uses to tempt us. It all seems so clear and precise when you look at it that way. This will make it easier for me to decipher the complex conversations I hear in my head sometimes. Jim, why haven't you explained this to us before?"

"I think it has only crystallized in my own mind in the last little while. It's been a principle I've apparently been having trouble learning myself."

"But then, what is the louder voice?" This question came from Benjamin.

"I believe that the louder voice is the Holy Ghost speaking in His other role as a revelator. It seems to me that these louder messages are reserved until after we have become fully obedient to the still small voice."

"Dad? Why do you suppose you heard the louder voice to warn you to come help Cheryl and me? Why not use the still small voice like when Jimmy was in trouble?"

There was a conspicuous silence before Laura said: "I think I can answer that. Since Jimmy's death, I have seen a tremendous change in your father. I can honestly say that I have never seen anyone try harder to hear and obey every prompting than your dad. I think because of his obedience and his faithful heart, that it wouldn't have mattered. I think Jim would have heard, and come to save you, even if he had only heard the tiniest whisper from the still small voice. I personally feel that because of his perfectly obedient heart, when a time of danger arrived, the Holy Ghost spoke in an unmistakable voice. Perhaps if we have used our free agency wisely, and been obedient in all things, then it doesn't make any difference, and Heavenly Father will speak to us in a louder voice when it really matters."

"All I know," Jim said, "is that I am grateful beyond words to Heavenly Father for allowing me to come to your aid. It has given me greater faith in Jesus Christ and in the promptings of the Holy Spirit, and caused me to be even more diligent in obedience. I can honestly say, that my cup of joy is full, and runneth over. I'm sure that this experience was partly to teach us this lesson."

"And," Cheryl added with great soberness. "I'm just as sure that all this was meant to teach me a lesson. I haven't got it figured out yet, though. I wasn't going to go to the prom. Sam was motivated by kindness to take me there, and he was inspired in the way he handled incredible odds, but it was overwhelming. He was my angel in coveralls. Papa Jim was inspired to find and save us by a long line of impossible events, and he was my angel in coveralls too.

"Before, when I wanted to die, He wouldn't let me. Now that I want to live, I seem to keep getting into life threatening situations, and God keeps bailing me out. This has never happened to me before. It's more than my poor brain can grasp. Someone help me understand all this."

Benjamin observed: "I don't think the war you won at the gas station is over. I think Satan is mad 'cause you got away from him the first time."

Six year old Rachel raised her hand, and Papa motioned to her. "Cheryl, I think it's just Heavenly Father's way of saying He loves you, and that you matter a whole lot."

"You matter enough that he is willing to send angels to save you," Laura added quietly.

"Angels in coveralls," Cheryl whispered reverently.

———

The following Sunday was Fast Sunday. In those days, Sunday meetings were held in two blocks. In the morning, Priesthood began at 9:00 a.m. At 10:00, the sisters and children came, and Sunday school lasted until 11:30. After that, people went home, fixed and ate their Sunday meal, did necessary chores, and rested. At 7:00 everyone returned for Sacrament meeting which lasted until 8:30. Fast Sunday usually meant fasting until Testimony meeting was over in the evening.

It was the first time in Cheryl's life that she had fasted, and her tummy rumbled fiercely. Yet even with the discomfort of hunger, she felt the warm glow she had only recently learned to recognize as the presence of the Holy Spirit. She fidgeted with her hands, fighting the urge to stand and bear her testimony. She desperately wanted to, yet could not quite bring herself to overcome the pull of fear upon her.

There was a long silence during which no one stood. Cheryl was just about to stand when a brother walked past their row. Startled, and simultaneously relieved and disappointed, she quickly relaxed. She didn't recognize the man who slowly walked to the stand.

He stood before the pulpit for a long moment before taking a step closer. Then with trembling hands, he pulled the microphone toward him. It groaned loudly in protest.

"I hope you'll forgive me for coming to the pulpit today," he began, his voice subdued. "I knew that I didn't have the courage to stand and bear my testimony, but figured I could make my feet walk up here. I just figured once I got up here, I'd think of somethin' to say." A soft chuckle flowed across the congregation.

"For those of you who don't know who I am, my name's Rulen Carter. I live 'cross the street from the Mahoys. I've been a member of this church all my life, and haven't seen fit to darken the doorway for longer than most of you are alive." This he said with some emphasis, as if he felt some justification for staying away.

"I ain't proud of that. I knew every Sunday that I should a gone to church. I done raised my whole family without the Gospel, and...until a short while ago, I didn't care one whit.

"Before I lose my starch, I gotta tell you why I'm here today. I hope Brother and Sister Mahoy will forgive me, 'cause I sure don't mean to play upon their loss, but I gotta do this if they'll forgive me." Brother Carter looked meaningfully at Jim Mahoy, who nodded once. Brother Carter smiled, as if relieved.

"Not long ago, little Jimmy Mahoy fell into the irrigation ditch and drowned. Ya'll know about that. What ya probably don't know is that I was there. I helped hunt for Jimmy, and was standing there while Brother and Sister Mahoy tried desperately to get him to breathe.

"I knew Jimmy was dead, and it made my heart ache as fiercely as if it had been my own baby layin' there on the ground. I was about to turn and go back to my own house when Sister Mahoy looks directly at me and says, 'Somebody give my baby a blessing.' Well, her words drove through me like a sword. I was stunned, 'cause I knew she was talking to me. I looked around, I knew a dozen other priesthood holders was there, and when I looked, they was all turned away.

"Laura looked directly at me, and said, 'Brother Carter, you're an elder, you give my baby a blessing.' I ain't proud of what I said. I says that I wasn't worthy, and didn't know how on account a bein' inactive all these years. I don't know why she said what she said next, but it was words which have echoed in my mind ever since. She says to me, 'God will bless my baby, all you have to do is say the words.' Well, I kneeled down, and asked God to forgive me, and not count my sins contrary to little Jimmy, cause God knows, and you all know I'm a sinful man. Was then, and still am now. But my mind fastened on those words, and I knew they was true. I did my best to say the right words, and to let God give that baby a blessing. Well, I wanted to say beautiful, powerful things, and instead was saying all the wrong words, but the feelings was right, and inside me I knew that God was going to bless Jimmy. Almost immediately after I said the words, why Jimmy takes a breath, you see." He paused to swallow back emotion. When he continued his voice was small. It was the most fantastic thing I have ever heared. He coughed, and started making noises. And, he was alive, and I knew that it was the power of God what had brought him back to life. Well, they took Jimmy away, and he stayed alive for a couple weeks until God made it right with Laura and Jim, and then he took Jimmy home. But that don't make no never mind to the fact that he came back to life. Now, here's the thing what has got me inside this here church after all these years of sinnin'. Its that God has kind of sucker-punched me. I know that sounds bad, but its kind of what He did. You see, I was living my sinful life feeling pretty content, and by bein' in the wrong place, at the right time, I was called upon to use my priesthood what I had plumb forgot I even had. So here I was, kneeling there with a stone-dead baby, and surrounded by Jimmy's angels, and I put my hands on this baby's head, and by God, he looked past me, and plumb poured out the power of heaven through my soiled hands into that baby. Brothers and Sisters, I felt it. I was there. I was an instrument in God's hands, when He could of picked a hundred better men, he picked me. I'll live all the rest of my life without knowin' why. But by God, by all that's holy, and all that's true, I'll live it with my heart and hands clean before God. Maybe it was plumb orneryness, or stupidity, or just bein' too busy, but what ever my reasons was for not serving God before, have been flat washed away, so's I can't even remember what they all was. Well I'm here before you to ask God's pardon, and you all's pardon, and the Bishop's and who all else I gotta beg forgiveness to, that's what I'll do. I'm here to serve God, and here to try to make myself worthy of the miracle what God wrought through my soiled hands."

He stood there in the stunned silence which followed his words. His eyes misted over, and he gripped both sides of the pulpit. His head fell, and his voice quivered as he said:

"I most humbly bear you my witness that God lives, and that he loves us. I also bear you my witness that Jimmy's death has bought me my salvation. Brother and Sister Mahoy, if Jimmy's death means nothing else, to me, it is the key which unlocked my stony heart. God forgive me for being so wretched that only a baby's death could touch me. It's a terrible price to pay. God forgive me…"

four

Chris

It isn't often identical twins have different birth dates, but Angela and Beth did. Angela was born May 1, 1956, at 11:49 p.m. Beth was born May 2, 1956, at 12:02 a.m. It made perfect sense therefore, at least to Angela and Beth, to celebrate their fourteenth birthdays at midnight. Mama and Emily had made a cake with two identical halves, each half with fourteen candles. As the grandfather clock was striking twelve, they each blew out their half of the cake. Such a clatter of clapping, clocks, and cheering followed that they didn't hear the doorbell the first time it rang. Jim hurried to the door the second ring.

It was Grandma Pearl, Papa's mother. She excused herself for calling so late, and stepped into the entryway. Behind her came a small boy holding a little battered suitcase without a handle. His hair was almost black, cut very short. He was barely four feet tall, with bony arms and wrists. His black eyes were sunken, giving his face a feral quality. His face was emotionless, even while he exuded fear.

"Jim, this is Chris. He's my niece, Lois's boy. He's six years old, and he needs a place to stay for a few days. His real name is Buddy Brown, but he was born on Christmas day, and goes by Chris. Lois and her husband are having marriage difficulties, and, well, he needs a home for a few days."

"Hi, Chris." Laura bent over and smiled at him. "It just so happens that we have an extra bed in Benjamin's room." It was Jimmy's bed. She hadn't been able to bring herself to let someone sleep in it for several years. But Chris's plight was more important than a sentimental silliness. "We were just having cake and icecream. You want some?" Chris nodded enthusiastically.

"Wait!" Grandma Pearl commanded, and Chris halted amid-stride. "Let's look at the list." She produced a three page document from her purse and studied it for a minute. "Nope. No wheat. No sugar. Sorry, Chris honey. But it lists icecream as being OK. But you will have to have a shot before you go to bed. OK?" Chris smiled and nodded.

By this time the rest of the family had gathered around. Angela and Beth took him by both hands and led him into the kitchen. Emily, Sam, and Cheryl stayed with the adults who moved into the family room.

Grandma Pearl unbuttoned her sweater and took a seat in the

recliner. She was so short that her feet dangled six inches from the floor.

"I went to visit my sister, Maryanne, Lois's mother, yesterday. They live side by side in a development outside Salt Lake. As I was driving up to Maryanne's house I saw Chris sitting on the front doorstep of Lois's apartment. It was late in the afternoon, and he was sitting there in his pajamas. I walked up to him, and he smelled like urine. His pajamas were horrible. I could see that he had been crying. As I walked up to him he looked at me with those big brown eyes, and said: "Will you be my Mommy?"

"I tell you, it melted my heart. I scooped that boy up and banged on the door. It took a long time for her to answer. When she came, she was still in bed clothes. I told that young woman that I wanted Chris's clothes. She bundled them up, and handed them to me without asking where I was taking him. I'm not even sure she remembered who I was. "The only thing she said was that Chris was being punished for wetting his bed last night. The poor thing hadn't had breakfast or lunch. I didn't know what to do with him, so I brought him here. I'll work things out with my sister tomorrow. I appreciate your taking the boy in. He's a handful. He's a full-blown diabetic. Hyperactive. Can't eat a blessed thing. Allergic to everything under the sun. Every one of his teeth are rotten. I'm so mad I could skin someone alive!" Grandma Pearl scooted forward and slid off the big chair. She buttoned up her sweater, said her goodbyes, and vanished.

Chris was finishing his second bowl of icecream when they entered the kitchen. He ate like a wolf, food flying off his spoon, running down his chin, splattered all around his bowl. He was reaching for another helping when Laura intervened, and sent all the kids to bed.

Chris still smelled like urine, even in his street clothes, so Laura hustled him off to the bathroom. She started a tub of water running, and pulled his shirt off over his head. Her heart sank, and tears came to her eyes. She opened the door and called to Jim who was beside her in an instant. After closing the door she turned Chris's back toward him. His back was a mass of scars and bruises. Old cigarette burns were everywhere, and long red welts ran across his bottom. They questioned him about how they got there, but he would only say, "fell down playing." It was the only answer he dared give.

All her other kids could bathe themselves by the time they were six, but Chris seemed to not have a clue what to do. Laura scrubbed him from stem to stern, and rubbed him dry. He stared at her the whole time expressionlessly. She found a pair of Benjamin's pajamas that would fit him, and showed him his bed.

"Need shot," he said emotionlessly. Laura had forgotten about it. He retrieved his insulin kit from his small suitcase. She had seen these before, and quickly filled the syringe. He pulled down his pajamas, and she administered the shot in his hip. He didn't flinch.

"Are you a big boy and won't wet the bed, or do you need to wear diapers to bed?"

"Big boy!" he said with a wounded voice.

"That's a good boy. I'm glad you can spend the night. My room is right down the hall. The door is open all night. If you need something, you come knock on the door, OK?" He nodded. She kissed him on the forehead, kissed Benjamin who was already asleep, and turned out the light. Chris rolled onto his side and yawned. It had been a big day for him too.

Laura had earned a Master's degree in marriage and family counseling, which she had set aside to raise her family. She often felt grateful for her education, especially when their family grew to accommodate foster children, some of whom, like Chris, needed special attention. It was her gentle ways and her love of counseling which made it possible for her to draw these foster children out of their frightening worlds, and into her love. She loved being a mom, and in spite of occasionally feeling as if she wanted to scream, she wouldn't have traded it for anything.

Neither Laura nor Jim could sleep. The memory of Chris's back was haunting. It troubled them both deeply that anyone could harm a child, and they needed to talk. It was almost two A.M. when they finally turned out the lights.

"I didn't put away the cake," Laura mumbled as she rolled over. "It will have to take care of itself until morning." Sleep had already taken her away when she suddenly sat up. She glanced at the clock which said three A.M. She had little difficulty arousing Jim, who was a very light sleeper. "Jim, I just realized I ignored a whispering of the Spirit. I said I didn't put away the cake, but what I was really thinking about was the candles and matches."

"I'll get them, Honey. You've had more than your share of troubles today." He swung his legs out of bed and pulled his pants on, looping one suspender over his shoulder. When he pulled open their bedroom door, a strong odor of smoke swirled into the room. Laura was at his side instantly.

"You get the kids up. I'm going to stop the fire. Get everyone out, then come back and help." He ran down the stairs. Bright images of flames danced on the floor at the bottom of the stairs. He turned left toward the family room and skidded to a stop, momentarily immobilized by what he saw. Chris was standing in front of him, a single flickering match in his hand. The couch was on fire, the wrappings from the birthday presents burning hotly. As he watched, the fire jumped to the curtains behind the couch. Chris was transfixed, as if hypnotized. He grabbed Chris by the pajamas and yanked him away from the flames.

"Fire." He said, almost reverently.

Jim flung upon the front door and tossed Chris onto the grass. The garden hose lay sprawled across the lawn. He spun the faucet and ran to the sprinkler. He twirled it off as he ran back. By the time he got the hose to the fire it was too hot to approach. Behind him, terrified kids were streaming through the front door. He aimed the hose at the fire, and knew almost immediately it was hopeless. The glass in the window behind the couch burst at the first sprinkle of water, and the fire roared bigger with the fresh oxygen. The paneling on the walls was beginning to buckle and burn. The carpet was burning, making a choking, blue smoke.

At the very moment he decided it was hopeless, he heard the glass break on the opposite side of the room, and a thick column of water roared past him. The fire retreated against the blast of muddy water, and in minutes it was defeated. Jim used his garden hose to put out the remaining hot spots.

Sam ran into the house from the back door, naked except for underpants. He had started the sprinkler pump, and turned one of the big flexible hoses from the garden into the house. His quick thinking had saved their home, but the aftermath was unbelievable. What was not burned was soaked with muddy water. The smell was a nauseating combination of acrid smoke and pond water.

Cheryl tapped him on the shoulder. He turned his stare from the devastation in their family room to her. "You better put on your coveralls, or I'll have to start calling you my angel in underpants," she said in dead seriousness. He looked down, and as if for the first time, realized he had nothing on. He disappeared into the back hall, and returned wearing a pair of muddy coveralls.

"Mama, look!" It was Angela's voice. She was pointing out onto the front lawn. Chris was standing in the blackness of the morning, his face visible only by the flickering light of the single match he held in his hands. His eyes were glazed and hypnotic, his pajama bottoms dripping with urine.

It took months to repair the damage, both physical and psychological. Insurance paid for all the repairs, but the worse damage could not be repaired with money. No one trusted Chris. Everything he ate made him hyper. Sugar put him into a zombie state, and he started lighting matches again. Already he had burned down the chicken coop and a neighbor's pasture before they figured out the sugar connection. Everyone except Laura wanted to strangle the little runt.

The most frustrating thing about Chris was that punishment had no effect on him. After he burned down the chicken coop Jim had spanked him, a rare occurrence in their home, but not unheard of. Chris had taken the spanking without emotion or crying, and had walked away apparently unfazed. Moments later he purposely broke one of Benjamin's toys by smashing it against the wall of the house. Jim spanked him again, this time more soundly. Again without any tears from Chris. Mere moments later Chris went out to the chicken run, caught a chicken, and kicked it until it stopped moving. When Jim and Laura found him, he was standing there with the dead chicken dangling from his hand.

They both had an urge to ring his neck, but some greater force prevailed. Laura knelt down before Chris, so they were almost eye to eye.

"Chris, I know you are angry, and that you are breaking things because you think we are punishing you out of meanness. Maybe some big people did that to you in the past, but not in our home. In our home, we only punish when you do something wrong. What you have done here is wrong. Do you understand that it's wrong to kill things out of anger?" Chris nodded, and let the chicken drop to the ground.

"Do you understand that when we do wrong things, that painful things happen back to us? Sometimes its a punishment, sometimes another thing?" Again Chris nodded sullenly.

"Do you remember when I spanked Benjamin the other day? What did he do?"

"He cried." Chris shoved his hands into his pockets and wet his pants. Laura ignored the latter.

"That's right Chris. Little boys cry when they are hurt or when they are spanked. Why don't you cry Chris? You don't even cry when you hurt yourself."

"My papa says if I cry, I get more. Only babies cry, and babies get more whippings. If I'm bad and cry, then Mister Cigarette will punish me. I'm too big for Mister Cigarette any more," he said with an air of fear and defiance.

"Your Papa was wrong, Chris. Mister Cigarette is bad, and little boys should never ever be punished by Mister Cigarette. Mister Cigarette can't come here to our house, and we won't let him punish you ever again. Do you believe that?" Chris nodded uncertainly.

"Chris, I want to ask you a question. Will you try to tell me what you are feeling no matter what, even if it scares you a little?" Again, Chris nodded, his face a mask of uncertainty.

"First, will you smile for me?" It was such an unexpected request that Chris's eyes grew wide. Laura smiled broadly, and after a moment of silence, Chris smiled back.

"That's much better. I want you to smile because what I'm going to ask you is a happy question, and not something to be afraid of. So, you can answer without feeling afraid, OK?"

"OK," he mumbled.

"What makes you feel the worst inside? Was it Mister Cigarette hurting you or was it that your Papa helped Mister Cigarette hurt you."

"My Papa," Chris said quietly. When he glanced up into Laura's eyes they flashed with anger and betrayal.

"Chris, will you smile again for me?" Laura asked.

"Why?" Chris asked.

Because it is against the law of our house for Mister Cigarette to come here. You never, ever, have to be afraid again. Does that make you feel like smiling?"

"Yes," he replied, and a little smile appeared on his face.

"Good. There's one more law at our house that is also happy, but might seem a little hard to understand. Will you help me with this other happy law, Chris?" she asked tenderly, gazing into his eyes, both hands on his shoulders.

"Yes," he responded carefully. Still, he answered without asking what the law was. Trust was slowly forming in his heart.

"Thank you Chris. I really need your help with this one. This law is that when little boys feel sad inside, they cry until they don't feel like crying any more."

"Really?"

"Look into my eyes Chris," Laura instructed gently. "See these tears in my eyes?" she asked. Chris nodded slowly. "I feel sad inside my heart because of what Mister Cigarette did to you. So, I'm going to cry for a few minutes because of your sad experience. Will you cry with me?"

Jim felt his own eyes flood with tears as he saw twin tears streak his wife's face. He resisted the urge to swallow back his tears, or to wipe them away hurriedly as he had all his life. Chris looked up at him just as tears fell from his chin.

Suddenly, as if a great dam broke somewhere inside Chris, he began to sob. At first it sounded like a bleating goat, "Blaaaa! Blaaaa!" It was as if he had never cried before, and didn't really know what sound to make. Then it changed. "Bluuuur, Bluuuur, Bluuuuur," he cried. Laura held him close to her, and whispered love to him.

"That's right, baby. Cry now. Cry hard. Cry those nasty feelings out. Cry until it doesn't hurt anymore. Mama will hold you until you no longer hurt inside. Cry away all those bad feelings." And he did. For a long time, and during it all Laura held him, rocking him back and fourth, kneeling there in the chicken coop. When Chris finally exhausted his pent-up emotions, he was a little boy again, and they were both covered with chicken manure, urine, snot and smiles.

Afterwards, it was as if the sweet spirit that was Chris finally had been liberated from the terrible prison Mister Cigarette had put him in. Before, he was a tough little boy who wouldn't have cried if he broke his arm. Now he cried over everything, and Mommy Laura, as he called her, would hold him until he no longer needed to cry.

In time, with good fresh farm food and an abundance of love, he outgrew his insulin dependence, and was able to eat anything. He discovered a world filled with love, family, and strawberries. He would do anything for a fresh strawberry, a bribe that worked until he discovered the precious little gems grew on plants in the garden. They considered putting an electric fence around the patch, but in the end, it became Chris's strawberry patch. At least they always knew where to find him.

Months later, Jim and Laura were lying in one another's arms, as was their happy custom, just before going to sleep.

"Do you remember when you cried with Chris until he cried?" He felt her head nod against his chest. "At the time it was very uncomfortable for me. I was standing there with anger in my heart while you were administering love. I'm ashamed to say I thought you were wasting your time. I just wanted to say I'm sorry for doubting you."

Laura twisted so she could see his face, then gave him a kiss on the cheek. "You know, it was a unique and wonderful experience for me. All my training, everything I knew about mothering, seemed to be useless at that moment. But inside, I knew what had to be done. It took a lot of faith to do what I knew to be rightAs I was doing it, I knew with every fiber of my being that it was right. I just knew it."

"Just watching Chris since that day has vindicated your

unorthodox therapy. He is a happy little boy, and if we can just get him to quit wetting the bed, he will be quite well, adjusted."

"He's almost there," Laura said a little wistfully.

"I can't quit thinking about that day. I was ready to hog tie him and send him to a mental institution. But you, in a single act of inspired love, changed him.

She shook her head slowly. "It is rare for a life to be changed so suddenly. Most problem children like Chris take years and years to reach. What occurred that day in the chicken coop was an act of God, a miracle, and had little to do with me."

"You are far too modest, I think. Laura, as I watched you that day, I was awed. Overwhelmed. I am convinced that you saved his life, possibly his soul.

If you had failed to act as Heavenly Father wanted you to, who knows what would have become of him. Perhaps he would have ended up in prison having killing some innocent person out of anger." He fell silent.

"I think you're making more of it than it really was. I just did what had to be done. I'm no heroine. I'm just a mom. Besides, I almost burned the house down by ignoring a prompting."

"You are a heroine to me. You heard the prompting, and your spirit was sensitive enough to truth that it later woke you back up. You saved our home, my love, not almost burned it down. And with Chris, you had the courage to do what was right in a very difficult situation. In my book that makes you a heroine. More specifically, it makes you MY heroine."

"In my book," she said happily as she snuggled closer, "that makes you the person I love most in the whole world. Want another kiss?"

five

The Farm

No one, except Mom and Dad, was sure why they all loaded into the station wagon early one morning and drove for a very long time. There was excitement, and secrets in the air. After the car warmed up, and the scenery began to roll by in monotonous reiterations of sameness, they quieted down and began to play "I spy," games.

Finally, the car followed a series of dirt roads and pulled into an abandoned farm. It was an impressive place; big, brick home, two new barns, six grain silos and row after row of big tractors and equipment. The newest barn had two huge combines and various new equipment. The home was large, with five bedrooms, a living room and family room, two bathrooms, and a large kitchen. Someone had spent lots of time and money decorating with long beautiful draperies and deep carpets. Everything about the farm spoke of prosperity and security. They explored for hours before they finally all returned to the car. It was a warm, spring day, with patches of snow still on the north side of the buildings. Laura spread out their picnic lunch on the tailgate of the wagon.

"Well, what do you think?" Dad asked, a strangely neutral expression on his face. Various expressions of; "Big. New. Pretty. Amazing," were his replies.

"How big is it, Dad?" Sam asked.

"It's 840 acres, all sprinkler irrigated. It produces an average of eighty bushels to the acre of wheat and barley. It has eighty acres in alfalfa, and…"

"Dad," Sam interrupted, anxious to get to the point, "why are you showing us this place?"

"Well, we're thinking of buying it. What do you think?" The excitement in his voice was too much to suppress, and he sounded like he was on the verge of fulfilling every dream he ever had.

In reality, the family had often heard their papa talk about his dream farm. To Sam, this farm seemed to fit that description in every way. It did seem like a wonderful place, and he began to feel excitement building inside him.

They loaded into the car and drove around huge fields thick with grain stubble. The farm was "L" shaped, long and narrow, and stretched for two miles in one direction, and one in the other. The fields were a quarter mile wide in most cases. There were three other homes on the farm, one of which was still inhabitable, and had its own small collection of barns and a milking parlor. The other two had long been abandoned, and had at one time or another housed cattle. One of the small homes had twelve, small, triple-bunk beds built along the walls of two small bedrooms. They learned later that a family named Christiansen had raised a wonderful family of twelve kids in that small home.

The community was small, but large enough for two thriving wards. Their church was an old converted grade school, complete with flagpole. Comically, the bishop's door still had Principal lettered on the glass. The other farms in the area were well kept and prosperous looking. Everyone they stopped and talked to was enthusiastic about the farm they were proposing to buy, and welcomed them as potential neighbors. It was a wonderful, positive day, and they all returned home exhausted but happy.

Two weeks later the papers were signed, and Sam moved onto the new farm immediately to begin spring plowing. The family began packing for the unbelievable task of moving twenty years of accumulated possessions to their new home.

It was with a sense of adventure and exhilaration that Sam went out that first morning to hook up the plow. He selected the largest of four tractors. It started like a dream. No grinding and grinding, spraying starting fluid, and hunting for booster cables that he was used to. He selected a six bottom plow and hooked it up. He chose the field closest to the house and lowered the plows. They slid into the rich brown soil and started effortlessly rolling over the earth. Sam had spent hundreds of hours plowing, albeit, never on a rig this big. Yet his senses told him something was wrong. There was a jerkiness to the flow of the tractor which concerned him. He stopped and walked back to the plow. To his amazement, he was picking up large stones. He was plowing too deep.

Back in the big cab, he turned the dials which adjusted the plow depth. Again he picked up stones, and had to raise the plows to where they were almost not able to roll over the dirt. After a whole day of fighting the shallow soil he moved to another field and found it just the same.

With a heavy heart he called his Dad on the phone, and told him of the shallow soil. They consulted for a long while before deciding it was not a tragedy. It would just take a different tool to till the ground.

Still, they wondered why the plow was even on the property if it was not usable.

The new disk was sixteen feet wide with twenty-four-inch diameter disks. It could be adjusted from inside the cab to cut exactly six inches deep. It rolled the soil as neatly as any plow with half the effort, and it didn't pick up rocks. The big tractor pulled it like it wasn't even there. Sam hooked the big set of harrows behind the disk and began preparing the soil with a single pass. The big equipment worked like a dream. In the air conditioned cab you could turn on stereo music and drive for hours without so much as a moment's discomfort. With their old, open air tractors, plowing was a freezing, runny-nosed, dusty, bouncy, exhausting job. With their new tractors, it hardly seemed like work. The hardest part was the amount of time it took. A quick calculation told them they would have to plow almost twenty-four hours a day to be done in time. It became obvious why the big equipment was there. Not for comfort, but for speed. They settled into six hour shifts. Sam plowed for six, then Jim, then Sam again, over and over. It took almost two weeks to prepare the fields. Spreading fertilizer took another week.

They hooked two smaller tractors to the seeders, and Emily and Cheryl each took one. At seventeen, they were adept drivers, careful to not miss a patch, and mindful to keep the hoppers full. The girls worked at it about ten hours each day, and then Sam and Jim took over. Finally, after six weeks of round the clock labor, it was done, and the whole family slept for two straight days.

The spring was glorious, with flowers blossoming and green appearing everywhere. When the grain finally began to peek through the soil it was a wonder to look across eight hundred acres of rolling fields carpeted with the slightest haze of green. It was the miracle of spring as far as the eye could see, and it was the hope of a future filled with promise slowly peeking through the soil.

Shortly thereafter, it was time to begin irrigating the fields. The big pumps were carefully oiled and adjusted. There was no way to test the sprinkler equipment other than to pressurize it with water, so after as many tests as could be done dry, the big pump was switched on. The water exploded into the big mainline with a roar like a jet engine. The first mile of mainline was buried until it reached the two irrigation circles.

An irrigation circle is a large irrigation machine. One end is anchored in the center of a large 160 acre field and pivots around it. The machine itself looks like a quarter mile long suspension bridge on wheels. The wheels slowly turn as it slowly moves around the field like the large hand of a clock. As it goes, it sprinkles water on the thirsty ground. The further from the center, the larger the sprinklers become.

In mere seconds water began to stream from the first sprinklers. As the water moved down the quarter mile length of the big circle, the rainbirds began to click their life-giving rhythm, each one slightly larger than the one before it, until the mighty nozzle on the end burst to life spraying it's one-inch-thick jet of water over fifty feet as it came to the corners of the field.

Their new ward was wonderful and welcomed them with enthusiasm. They were loved and accepted from the first day at church. It was like finding family, like coming home, and the whole family basked in the warmth of their fellowship. Their chapel had been a small gymnasium in the old school, and the organ was pedal powered and sounded asthmatic. To make matters more frustrating, not a soul in the ward could play more than one hand. Sam could play one hand and a finger, so he was almost instantly the new ward organist. He took the calling seriously, and spent hours practicing until he could squeeze as much music from the old gasping organ as was physically possible.

Not long after they moved there, the ward announced plans to modify the old church house and add on. In those days, the ward members were either expected to raise half the money, or do half the labor. Since money is not a surplus item in a farming community, and work is second nature to them, they opted to do the labor. Each priesthood holder was asked to invest two hours a day, or ten hours a week, to building the church. Sam and Jim accepted the challenge. So, in addition to the physical demands of activating and maintaining a new farm, they happily worked on the new addition to the church.

Six months after moving into the ward Jim was called to be the bishop. It was a surprise to Jim, who considered himself a plow horse suitable for the fields, not a race horse to prance in front of people. He accepted with as much humility as a human soul can possess and still be able to breathe. His sweet spirit touched the hearts of the ward members and things began to happen. He plainly confessed to everyone his lack of knowledge and understanding on how to run a ward, especially to Heavenly Father. As a result, he relied entirely on the Lord, and inspired decisions were made again and again.

Bishop Jim, as the ward members affectionately called him, found there were quite a few inactive members in his ward. He began visiting them wherever he could find them. New faces began showing up at church, and the marvelous little ward loved them so openly, they came back again and again. It was a time of great spiritual growth for Jim as the mantle of his office settled upon his shoulders. It was a time of rejuvenation for his ward.

For Sam, the change that came over his father was startling, and also a powerful education. His father's quiet humility seemed to deepen, but the power behind that quietness was most amazing. All this came a quiet dignity which made him seem majestic in an unassuming away.

Sam watched all this with a quiet wonder. His Dad was still quite human, prone to err, and occasionally moved to anger. It would have seemed hypocritical, except that he knew his father well enough to know that his heart was rock solid in his faith. He knew his Dad wanted to be perfect, both personally and as the bishop. Yet he knew his Dad well enough to respect the fact that he did not pretend perfection. With Jim Mahoy, his exterior was a perfect reflection of his soul. He spoke and acted the same on the fields as at the pulpit.

On one occasion toward the middle of summer, Sam and his Dad were loading sacks of chicken feed at the feed store when another truck backed up beside theirs, and a man with a full, black beard climbed out. The man was unfamiliar to them, and in the way of country folk, they immediately shook hands and introduced themselves. The man's name was Jake Please. It was a name Sam had heard many times. Whenever the subject of enemies to the church came up, this man's name seemed to top everyone's list.

Jim smiled at this new man, and before he could withdraw his hand said: "Jake, I'm your new bishop."

Jake's eyes narrowed, and he forcibly withdrew his hand. "Ya ain't my bishop. I don't belong to your church. And if you know what's good for you, you'll drop the subject." He glared for a second, then walked away.

Sam breathed a sigh of relief. Jake Please was a large and powerful man, and his face had an edge of steely sharpness which made Sam want to follow his advice and let the man leave.

Jim, however, said: "I need you to be my ward clerk," loud enough that everyone on the loading platform stopped and looked up. They were nearly all members, and knew Jake Please's reputation and antagonism toward the church very well. But it was noisy, and they could hear nothing more of the conversation which followed.

"I told you. Let it drop. I don't want to have to rough up a good man, just because his mouth got to runnin' away with him." Again he turned away.

"It isn't going to be easy." Jim said just as loud as before.

"What isn't going to be easy?" Jake demanded, thinking Jim was saying it wouldn't be easy to rough him up, but there was a slight edge of curiosity softening his hostility.

"Getting you ready to serve the Lord as my ward clerk," he replied matter-of-factly.

There was almost an explosion of anger, but his curiosity won. "What are you talking about," he demanded.

"I'm going to have to excommunicate you first," Jim replied with a thumb and finger on his chin, as if considering the situation carefully.

"You can't excommunicate me! I ain't done nothin' that bad!"

"Then why don't you come to church?"

"Because I don't like it. That's all! I ain't been to church since I was ten years old. Didn't like it then. Don't like it now."

"I always found that when someone doesn't like church, it's because they've done something that they need to be excommunicated for. So that's what I'm gonna do."

"But I ain't done nothin' that bad!"

"What have ya done then? You better fess up so you can be my ward clerk like the Lord wants, and I don't have to "x" ya. It's up to you."

"Well, everything. Me and the wife, well we 'bout broke every commandment I suppose, except the really bad stuff. But nothing to get x'd for!"

"Hmm. Well, maybe we can get this cleared up after all. But you and the wife had better come see me tonight at the church. Come prepared to get your lives in order, and we can maybe avoid the excommunication. Seven o'clock OK?"

"You're damn right it is. We'll be there! And don't you go x'n us before we get there, you hear?"

"I'll wait for you. Don't be late. Nice to finally meet you Jake."

"Yeah, maybe. See you at seven." They shook hands, and Jake stomped off.

Jim stepped over to Sam and pushed his mouth back closed. Sam didn't even realize he was standing there agape. They loaded the feed in silence and started home.

"Dad?"

"What is it, Sam?"

"How did you know Jake wouldn't hit you for saying what you did to him?"

"I didn't."

"What you said though. You can't excommunicate someone like that can you? I mean, just because they don't like coming to church?"

"No. Of course not."

"Then why did you say you would?"

"To be honest with you, I don't know. I felt the Spirit come over me as soon as we shook hands. I have learned over the years that when the Holy Spirit touches me, I just let go, and say or do whatever I'm supposed to. I have had some amazing experiences, and this one was one of the strangest. It was probably the only thing I could have said to get them into the bishop's office. Perhaps, ultimately, they would have been excommunicated if they hadn't agreed to come tonight. Whatever the eternal truth of this matter is, it was what the Lord wanted me to say. I said it, and Jake responded. That's what really matters. When they come tonight I'm going to explain the whole process of church discipline so they understand. I'll set it all straight so they aren't acting under a misunderstanding. However, they are coming, and that's a wonderful start."

"Is he really going to be the ward clerk?"

"As soon as I touched his hand, I knew I was supposed to call him to that position. If he carries through with his part of it, I will call him to that position, just as the Lord wants."

Brother and Sister Please kept the meeting with the bishop that night, and were both disfellowshipped. Part of the conditions of their repentance was that they could not miss a single sacrament meeting for six months. Accordingly, the very next Sunday, they came to sacrament meeting. Brother Please wore his work clothes, but had buttoned up his collar and tied a dark, string tie around his neck. He looked extremely uncomfortable, but plowed through the small crowd of faithfuls. He shook everyone's hand with a painful grip, laughed with a loud voice, and acted like he had never missed a Sunday in his life. With his full, black beard he looked like a charging bear. Even so, not a single member backed away or acted surprised to see him.

Sister Please wore a red miniskirt, red high heels, red beads, bright red lipstick, and a full do of red hair. She looked like a lady of the night, and was the exact opposite of Jake. She spoke to almost no one and clung to her husband's hand like a frightened child. It took three sisters to lovingly pry her loose to get her to attend relief society. They had three children, all girls, all dressed in worn pants. They ranged form fourteen to nine, and obviously wanted desperately to be somewhere else.

Before church had even begun, they had accepted a dinner invitation to a neighbor's home, and the magic of the Holy Spirit and love had begun to work.

As the weeks progressed, the Please family continued to come. Each week, Brother Please's beard grew shorter, and Sister Please's dresses grew longer. The third week, all three girls showed up in cute dresses, and each carried a new copy of the Book of Mormon. The transformation which gradually occurred was a miracle as surely as the dividing of the Red Sea. In exactly six months, Brother Please accepted the position of ward clerk, and Sister Please, a position in the Primary presidency. Their girls looked as if they had never missed a day of church in their lives.

But the most amazing transformation of all occurred in Brother Please's soul. Where once there was bitterness and a hardened heart, now there was a gentleness which only the influence of the Holy Ghost can bring. On the day he was called to his new position, the Bishop asked him to bear his testimony. He walked slowly up to the pulpit, and steadied himself with both hands.

"I want you to know that Bishop Jim tricked me into repenting!" This brought a ripple of laughter, but, Brother Please was serious. "The first time we met, he threatened to excommunicate me if I didn't become the ward clerk. At that time, I was an angry, violent, unforgiving person. Everything inside of me told me to beat him senseless. I once spent a week in jail for hitting someone who shoved religion in my face. But something was different about Bishop Jim. I could feel his love for me. Or probably what I was feeling, was Heavenly Father's love for me. But it felt good, and I desperately wanted to know why it was coming from Bishop Jim at the very moment he should have been afraid of me. I wanted it bad enough to go to the bishop's office to find out how to get it.

"Over the years I had convinced myself that God didn't love me, and so I didn't love him back. I believed I was too nasty for anyone to love, including God. I thought my wife stayed because I fed and housed her. I didn't think anyone, including her, could love me. But it was that morning that I felt God's love for the first time. Since that time, I have come to the amazing realization that not only does God love me, but so does my wife and my girls. I freely admit that I didn't deserve their love. But finally realizing they do has literally melted my soul. I feel inclined to forgive Bishop Jim for tricking me, because I know he was acting as the Lord's servant. Besides, he told us straight out that first meeting that he owed me a better explanation, so he didn't really trick me. As I think about it, he probably said the only thing in the world that could have induced me to set foot inside this church.

"You have all witnessed the change that has come over me and my family. Look how beautiful my daughters are in their new dresses. They had never worn a dress before in their lives. I can hardly believe how beautiful they are. Look how my wife glows with the Holy Spirit. I've seen her in every kind of clothing imaginable, but I have never seen her look as beautiful as she does this very minute, radiating love and goodness." He paused here to smile at his family on the third row. They squirmed uncomfortably, but for a full half minute he waited.

"Thanks to you all, I have come to the startling, breathtaking conclusion that not only is the church true, but that the Gospel is true. By that I mean that not only is this His true church, but it works. It blesses lives. It changes people. It purifies and uplifts. It takes mean, nasty, sinful people like me, and helps them repent and leaves them feeling clean inside. For that, I will be eternally grateful. In the name of Jesus Christ, amen."

He remained at the pulpit for a few more seconds before adding in dead seriousness, "I offer as a witness the fact that I just said that whole bit without cursing a single time. That in itself, my brothers and sisters, was a miracle." Those who knew him, nodded vigorously in agreement.

During this time, the farm continued to look more dismal. It was exhausting, unrelenting, and hopeless work. There was not enough water. As the summer progressed, even the big well began losing pressure and began sucking air. They had to throttle it back, and the water going onto the fields was insufficient. The grain suffered and matured slowly. Over two-hundred acres had been lost to faulty or missing equipment.

Harvest was both frightening and exciting that year. They prepared the big combines, swept out the big grain silos, put the grain bed on the big truck, and made everything ready. Jim lowered the cutter bar and started into the grain on the field beside the house. Sam was riding on the combine, making adjustments and helping. After a few minutes a trickle of grain began to flow into the hopper, then a stream, then a steady pour. After many stops to adjust the settings on the big machine, they were ready, and the grain began to pour into the hopper. Each of the fields was forty acres, and before they had gone all the way around the first field, the combine was full. They pulled the big truck beside the combine and transferred the burden of golden wheat. It made a surprisingly small pile in the bottom of the truck. It was a process they would repeat a thousand times for nearly two weeks.

Once harvest began, it would continue nearly twenty-four hours a day, until it was done. If it was during the day, they drove the truck to the local mill where the truck was weighed and the grain dumped off. If it was night, the grain was pumped into their own big grain silos where it would wait until after harvest. When the fields were bare, they would begin taking it a truck load at a time to the mill.

The precious wheat was most vulnerable during harvest. As the days progressed, the stalks and heads grew more fragile, and even a brisk wind could knock grain onto the ground. Once on the ground, there was no way to recover it. No effort was spared to get the grain in as soon as possible. If a frost came, the heads would swell, and the combine could not efficiently harvest it. If it snowed or rained, the brittle straw stalks would become soft, and lay down where the combines could not pick it up.

Nearly every hour the combine had to be readjusted to accommodate the changing conditions. As the day warmed the grain heads grew dryer, the grain lighter, and the combine fans and screens had to be adjusted to accommodate. As the evening came, the chaff became damp, and the fans had to be set higher to blow it away without blowing the grain out the back end of the combine.

Jim and Sam ran the big combines. Cheryl and Emily, both graduated from high school now, drove the big truck. Angela and Beth baled straw, and Benjamin, now age eleven, drove the fuel truck out to the combines to refuel them.

Running a combine is the nastiest job man has invented for himself to do. The combine engine runs at full throttle; the belts, chains, fans and machinery scream and shake as if they are going to fly apart, and the roar is deafening. The big cutter head hovers just above the ground, requiring constant adjustment. To pick up a rock or dirt is to damage the machine and cause hours, or days of repair. The back end of the combine dumps out the straw and chaff. By far the worst, the chaff hovers in the air in a choking cloud not unlike some ancient pestilence decreed by the voice of an angry God. It fills the cab until the windows are coated, the driver's skin itches, noses run, and eyes are red and puffy. Before long, Jim and Sam had scarves wrapped around their faces, but that was not sufficient and they coughed and sneezed constantly. They tried gauze masks, but they got plugged in minutes. Finally, they bought big dust masks designed especially for mines, and those kept the chaff out of their lungs but not their eyes. They had to run the windshield wipers to knock the dust off the window every few minutes and wipe the inside of the glass with a rag every few minutes. During the day it was hot and dusty. During the night it was cold and dusty.

They were amazed at how much grain they harvested. On the fields that had had adequate water, they harvested about thirty-five bushels to the acre. Some fields did even more. Even on the fields that had suffered most, they harvested enough grain to break even. Before long it became apparent that they would have a good harvest. They began to rejoice as truck after truck of grain went to the mill.

By the end of the harvest they had delivered over 21,000 bushels of grain to the mill. The current price of grain was $4.35 per bushel. Simple math told them they could make all their payments and still have plenty to live on until next year. It wasn't as good as they had hoped, but it was enough.

Every aspect of farming is a gamble, but that which comes closest to true, Las Vegas type gambling is deciding when to sell your wheat. The price of wheat is always lowest during harvest, because there is an abundance of grain and because many farmers must sell immediately, so there is more supply than demand.

However, most grain mills offered to store the wheat for a few pennies a bushel until the farmer was ready to sell. If you could hold off, the price usually rose by the first of the next year. It was considered prudent to wait as long as possible to sell your harvest. Accordingly, Jim decided to wait. Even a few pennies per bushel raise yielded thousands of dollars in additional income.

It was September 21st, 1972, when the news came. The United States announced a total grain embargo against the Russians. Frantically, farmers rushed to sell before the prices plummeted. All grain sales were immediately suspended by the mill. All across the nation, farmers watched helplessly as the price of wheat slid and finally stuck at $2.85 per bushel. Without hope that the price would rise any time soon, Jim sold the wheat for a huge loss. Their actual cost of growing the grain was $3.95 per bushel.

Jim and Sam went to the local bank from whom they had borrowed the money to grow their crop, expecting the worst. To their surprise, the bank was willing to wait, and to loan them money again next year too. They had seen the good job they had done on the farm, and they knew the price of wheat was beyond their control. It was the best they could expect, and they mentally prepared themselves to do much better next year.

During the winter they worked steadily rebuilding several engines, repairing equipment, and welding sprinkler pipe. They worked every daylight hour, and many dark ones. It was a peaceful, happy time, and one of almost total poverty.

Christmas time found them without funds, except for the barest necessities. They gathered the family around and explained the situation. Rather than feeling dejected, the kids welcomed the challenge, and enthusiastically set themselves to making gifts. They plotted, planned, schemed, and worked their magic in secret little huddles. Instead of Christmas lasting a week, it lasted a month because their preparations were so lengthy.

The girls sewed, painted, knitted, wrote poetry, made photo albums, cooked special treats, and invented a hundred small, but loving gifts. The boys built, sawed, welded, and otherwise crafted thoughtful and fun gifts for everyone. Jim built Laura an apple cider press from old machinery parts and wood, something she had often spoken about. Sam made her a butter mold from a small but perfect piece of maple he found. It was a time of joyful anticipation, and very little money was spent.

Christmas morning was magical beyond magic. Cheryl put her angel, still wearing coveralls, atop the tree, and everything was perfect. There were fewer gifts to give, but each was highly special, both in thought and in the amount of effort and time it had taken to create it. The gifts were unwrapped slowly with everyone else watching. Many tears were shed, both by the receiver and the giver.

They spent the day appreciating their gifts, laughing about their efforts and joys, and making fresh apple cider. The press worked perfectly, and they sipped the sweet cider as if it were the nectar of life. Far sweeter than the juice was the love which flowed in glorious abundance. For many years thereafter, everyone would say it was the best Christmas ever.

After days of fasting and prayer, they decided to hang on and farm again next year. They were, afterall, farmers, and the decision was as much genetic as it was logical.

Even more important, was their attachment to the ward. Their father, Bishop Jim as the ward members called him, was making dramatic headway in reactivating lost members. The ward had grown in size by almost half again, all of whom were previously inactive members. There was a time when nearly ten percent of the adult members of the ward were disfellowshipped. One family simply showed up to church and never wavered thereafter. Their reason? To keep from having Bishop Jim come to their home and disfellowship them too, they laughingly insisted. It wasn't really their reason, but it had played a part in their thinking.

Early next spring they dug new wells, deepened and improved old ones, and bought enough sprinkler equipment to cover the entire farm. When the freeze left the ground they worked around the clock. No effort was spared. They labored like dragons, and after four weeks had all eight-hundred acres seeded. The new sprinkler equipment functioned perfectly, and the farm turned a lush green. They waited with breathless suspense for something to go wrong, but nothing did. The crops came up, the water burst from the ground as if by a miracle, and hope returned.

During all this time they labored on the church as before, fasted weekly, studied the scriptures, held numerous church jobs, sang in the choir, and taught classes. It was a time of sweet joy, and a joyful season in the sun. They developed one unique farming practice which all their neighbors allowed would cost them their farm. After much discussion, it was decided that moving the sprinklers on Sunday was breaking the Sabbath, and they decided to cease to do so. It was Jim who said: "The Lord called me to be Bishop to labor in his kingdom, and He expects me to keep the Sabbath day holy. The Lord needs a bishop, and I need a miracle so the crops won't die without water on Sundays. We'll both do our jobs." So they both did. People drove a hundred miles to see the crops that didn't need water on Sundays, shook their heads and drove away thinking it was a trick.

Chris turned ten that year and started first grade. A little old, but ready. His little body was stunted by years of malnutrition, and was about the size of a six year-old. He hadn't touched a match in three years, and was a happy, loving, and loved child. His thick black hair still had two wild tufts where the hair grew around large scars left by 'Mister Cigarette.' Laura's heart ached every time she combed his hair before school, but Chris seemed to have no memory of those days, not so long ago.

Laura had taught him the alphabet, and he could read exactly fifty words from flash cards. He could recognize all the numbers and knew all the do's and don'ts about school. Do say please and thank you. Don't pick your nose, or forget to zip your pants after the bathroom. School boys don't wet their pants, hit other kids — especially girls, or throw things. They do mind the teacher and pay attention whenever she is talking; practical things like that. The fact that he understood such things was nearly a miracle. He came to them with almost no social skills, and lacked even those most instinctual thought — like don't take your clothes off in public. Mommy Laura, as Chris lovingly called her, had drilled him endlessly until he knew them all and probably a few extra just in case.

For unsophisticated farming folk, getting a certified letter was a rare, frightening experience. Before Angela was back in the house from the mailbox, the whole family knew about it from her excited shouting. It was addressed to Jim Mahoy, and Laura dispatched

Rachel to get him from the equipment shed. The return address was from the State of Utah, Dept. of Family and Youth Services.

Jim sat down and carefully opened the letter with his pocket knife. He read it for a few minutes before handing it to Laura. She read for a few minutes before having to sit down herself, her eyes filling with tears.

"What's wrong?!" Beth demanded, in exact unison with Angela. Cheryl reached for the letter, which Laura let her take. She read for a few minutes, then looked around the room as if searching for someone. All of the boys were outside.

"Chris's father wants him back," she said quietly, still looking at the letter. She looked up to see if she had spoken out of turn, but both Jim and Laura were looking at her as if grateful she had spoken the hated words. She read on. "There is to be a hearing before a judge to determine custody. Papa Jim is supposed to appear with Chris a week from Monday."

By that next Monday morning everyone but Chris knew what was going on. They packed his small suitcase, as well as a larger one. He was excited and laughed as he lugged his suitcases to the car. Each of the kids gave him a hug, told him they loved him, and walked him to the car. Jim and Laura got into the front seat of the station wagon with Chris between them. They drove away and were gone, but not before Cheryl was in tears. This was too close to her own experience, and she had a bad feeling about it.

The drive seemed to go by, both too fast and too slow. Before they were ready, they were sitting in a small room, oppressively dark with wood paneling, and worn, red carpeting. Chris squirmed between them, and seemed both excited and afraid. They had told him this was a meeting to see if he wanted to live with his real father again. Chris seemed both happy and fearful. When he saw his father he hesitated, then ran to him and gave him a big hug. They both seemed happy to see each other. He was with another woman, obviously not Chris's mother, who also gave him a hug and seemed pleased to meet him. Jim and Laura waited patiently. Tony, Chris's father, walked up to Jim and shook his hand.

"I want to thank you for taking care of Chris these last few years. I'm sorry I haven't contacted you sooner. This has been a terribly difficult divorce. I knew Chris was safe, and that he was being spared much of the pain in our lives. As you can see, I have remarried and made a lot of personal improvements. I'm sorry for any pain taking Chris back might cause you. I can see you love him. What you can't see, is that I do too. Very much. I'm ready and anxious to be his daddy again."

Tony had a lawyer who presented their case and read from state statutes. The judge listened attentively and nodded frequently. When it was their turn, Jim stood and began telling about how Chris had come to live with them and his deplorable physical condition, but the Judge interrupted him and said it was irrelevant. Jim tried to explain that Chris had been burned with cigarettes and beaten. The judge asked curtly if they had evidence, or if Chris had ever said that his father had done it. They had to say no. The judge wouldn't listen to more. He simply said that the law stated that natural parents had a right to their children unless there was obvious evidence of their being unfit, unable to provide, or abusive. He banged the gavel, and Chris no longer lived with Papa Jim and Mommy Laura. His new family swept him away, and before they could even say goodbye he was gone.

Laura cried all the way back home, and Jim drove with a grim determination. She could hear his teeth grinding. When they returned home without Chris, Cheryl ran to her room and stayed there the rest of the day.

That evening, just before family prayers, everyone was quiet an air of sadness hung over them like a rain cloud.

Laura cleared her throat, obviously fighting back strong emotions. "Kids, I know it's hard to see Chris leave after living with us for four years. We all loved him. Sometimes, patients in a hospital fall in love with their doctors and the doctors love them back. But the time always comes when they have to leave, because they can't live at the hospital. It's better that they get well and return to their real lives. We were Chris's hospital, and because we loved him when he most needed it, he got well. While he was getting well with us, his father was getting well at his own hospital. Now they are together, and we mustn't mourn the fact that he has his family back. Let's be happy for him and remember him with happy hearts."

Jim felt like giving her a standing ovation. His heart swelled with pride for her courage and perfect heart. As he slid to his knees, in his soul and in his prayer that evening, he wished everyone could be blessed with such a mother to love them so perfectly and to heal their young lives. When he finished, he looked up to see Laura staring at him, a radiant look of wonder and tender love on her face. Her words had healed the family's hearts, his prayer had healed hers.

The year 1973 was slow a birthing, and by the time the ground was thawed enough to begin planting, it was late into the spring. In order to have a reasonable expectation of a good harvest, the planting had to be done by the first week in May. They started working the soil the first day in May, leaving them less than a week to complete a four week project. Their only choice was to purchase another tractor. It arrived in a few days, and they worked around the clock until the crops were in. They did it in exactly ten days. It was a feat which left them semi-conscious from exhaustion, but it was done, and done well.

Both Emily and Cheryl had graduated from high school that previous fall, and come spring left to attend Ricks College. It was an exciting time for them, and they left with many tears and much laughter. They arranged to share a dorm room at college and took comfort in the fact that they were together. They were a good couple. Emily was a whiz at school and could give Cheryl much needed help in her classes. Cheryl had shed her defensive shell, and was a natural with boys and almost any social setting, and helped shy Emily find a comfortable nitch in college society. Together they eased their mutual transition into college life.

Jim and Sam had learned much over the winter. They had read many books, consulted with neighbors, hired an agricultural specialist to calculate optimum fertilizer rates, and set schedules for spraying. They carried out their plan like clockwork, and the crops began to grow. Again, they refused to water the crops on Sunday, and oddly enough, the crops didn't seem to mind. Instead they grew thick and lush. The fields were solid green as far as you could look in any direction. No crop of grain had ever been as lush as these. Neighbors stopped their cars beside the fields and walked out into them just to experience the rich feeling of such a lush stand of grain. They returned to their own fields with renewed determination and faith in the valley and its thin, but fertile soil.

Sam turned nineteen that fall, and received his mission call to South Africa. They had to get out the big atlas to see where he was to go. They rejoiced, Mother cried, and plans were made to take Sam to the mission home right after harvest.

The fall chill was already in the air, and the sprinklers had been turned off weeks earlier. The fields were a golden sea, heavy with grain. Old timers could not remember a time when such a crop of grain had been grown in the valley. A ten foot square piece of ground was cut, thrashed by hand, and measured. It represented over one hundred bushels to the acre. That Sunday the family held a special day of fasting to thank Heavenly Father and to rejoice in His blessings and kind favor. The new church had been dedicated the week before, and their long labors on it suddenly came to an end. It truly was a time of joy.

Sam pushed open the big, double doors of the red barn and backed the huge combine out into the yard. Even though as big as a small house, they were complex, finicky machines, prone to break downs and failures. They required constant maintenance and careful operation to keep them from breaking down. Both he and his dad worked till noon on the big machines before they were comfortable that they were ready to go. Sam was working in the John Deere combine when he felt a chill blow through the cabin. He glanced up to see a black cloud rolling across the valley. It looked like a thunder cloud, but much lower to the ground. Within several minutes the cloud reached the far edge of their farm and immediately the cloud unleashed a barrage of hail more devastating than a bombing. The cloud swept across their farm from end to end, and when it came to the furthest field, the hail quit, the cloud lifted and blew off into nonexistence.

Sam ran into the fields with his father. In minutes the whole family was there staring at the ground in wordless shock. The ground was a perfect sheet of golden grain and glistening hail stones. Little, if any, grain remained on the stocks. There was no point in even driving the combines out into the fields. There is no efficient way to recover grain on the ground, and the loss was tragic and complete.

Several weeks later the banks foreclosed on the farm. Dealers came and repossessed sprinkler equipment and tractors. Everything was mortgaged to pay for the massive loans on the farm, and within weeks an auction was held, wherein everything they possessed of any value was sold to pay the debt. Everything was sold; furniture, clothing, tools, jewelry, vehicles, even a stack of fence posts. In the final analysis, they had lost everything. In actual fact they were penniless, homeless, and destitute. The farm was repossessed, and proceeds from the auction barely canceled the mortgage debt. But they still owed over a hundred thousand dollars to the small bank who had loaned them money to operate the farm.

The night before they were to leave their beautiful farm, Sam did not eat. Even though they had spent the day loading their old GMC truck with their last few possessions, he had fasted. His heart was heavy and his faith shaken. They had spent three years joyfully serving the Lord, doing everything they could conceive, obeying every commandment, observing every law, fasting, serving, and worshipping. They had risked all to keep the Sabbath Day holy. Their father had worked to exhaustion to serve as the Lord's bishop, his powerful service a great blessing to the ward.

Their farming had been a success, and yet, in an act that was apparently divinely engineered, they had lost their all. In fact, theirs was the only farm affected by the hail, and the destruction on their lives had been thorough and complete.

That night he spent a long time on his knees, asking, wondering, begging, and even complaining a bit. It did not seem fair. It seemed so useless, so unkind, so unjust. He was young, and in time he would recover, but his parents had lost a lifetime of work and savings. They had nowhere to go and no hope for a future. He climbed into bed with a heavy heart and slept. In the night he had a dream, one which he would never forget. So impressed was he by the experience that he hunted up a few pieces of paper the next morning and recorded it as follows:

Last night I had a dream. It was so vivid that I was unsure if it was a dream or reality until I woke up the next morning.

I dreamed that I was standing in a field of ripe grain. As I looked out over this field of grain I instantly knew many things about it, as if I had lived there all my life. The field was lush and deep, as rich a crop as ever was grown on earth. Along the borders of the fields were flowering shrub bushes which grew spontaneously. The roads leading to the fields were lined with flowering trees and bushes more beautiful than any formal garden I could conceive, yet they had not been planted but had grown there spontaneously or by decree. I knew that the rains had come to water the fields every night, and there were no weeds or noxious plants anywhere.

In one corner of the field a huge machine was harvesting the grain. The machine made little noise or dust and never broke down. It moved across the fields cutting the grain which poured into the hopper in a heavy stream of gold. The man driving the machine barely gave thought to what he was doing, but sang as he ran his hands through the flowing grain and danced on the machine as much as drove it.

Immediately in front of this huge machine were women and men dressed in beautiful robes of bright colors, with flowers in long streamers running through their hair and across their shoulders. They were singing and dancing, walking ahead of the machine as its big cutter bars bit into the thick grain. I instantly knew that they were not afraid of the machine because it was against the laws of nature for them to be harmed by it in any way. Neither they, nor the person operating it, had any fear that they could be injured. They simply were in the joy of harvest, and it seemed to consume their whole soul.

Somehow I knew that the laws of nature had been altered, that the law of opposition in all things had been done away. Anything they tried to do yielded to their efforts. If they tried to move a rock a hundred times larger than themselves, it was obligated by divine decree to move. If they wanted to farm, they would be successful by divine decree. If they wanted to run a business they would succeed by divine decree. I also understood that it was impossible for them to injure one another physically or any other way. The laws of God would not allow it. Nothing could be lost, damaged, stolen, misplaced, ruined, abused, or otherwise become unusable, unbeautiful, or undesirable.

Their society was perfect, with no crime, no taxes, no corruption, no sin. Their government was by divine decree and perfectly just. There were no courts, criminals, or jails. There was no such thing as hospitals, doctors, illness, disease, or death.

I watched all this with a thrill in my heart, experiencing their joy, yearning to join them, and yet aware that I was still bound to this other world where things were much less perfect. I thought this must be the Celestial Kingdom, and I yearned with all my heart to be there.

As I watched, a kindly voice from behind me asked: "Sam, is this what you want?"

"Oh yes," I replied with all my heart. "This is the life I long for." There was a moment of silence before the voice replied. "What you see is the Telestial Kingdom, the least of all the rewards I give unto men. If you seek a life without opposition and refuse to learn the lessons of this life, this will be your reward. If you desire a greater reward, then endure with patience and great shall be your blessings, even greater than the mind of man can comprehend."

It was then that I understood that these people had lost their free agency. They could choose any righteous act, but it was physically impossible for them to choose to disobey or to sin. It has always been that we have been free to choose righteousness. What I did not understand until then was that free agency is largely the right to choose to do evil. They had lost this right.

I knew that they were not organized into families. Their relationships were according to their chosen vocation and common interests. They loved one another, but did not marry or have children. They were without authority, except over their own possessions, and never progressed beyond what they were at that time. They had no priesthood, and without it, they could never return to the presence of God.

No sooner had I perceived these thoughts than the vision closed, and I found myself sitting up in bed, marveling at all that I had seen. I knew many things about their world as if I had lived there all my life, but have recorded only a few of greatest interest to me at this time in my life.

———

That next morning Sam called the family together and related the dream he had had and the many impressions he had received while in the vision. The greatest of these was that everything would be all right. Everyone took comfort from the dream, even in the idea that Heavenly Father had seen fit to bless them with this word of comfort at the very time when they felt abandoned by Him.

As they loaded their last things onto the old truck, Jim took Sam aside. "Son, I'm so proud of you. I didn't have a vision last night, but I did have a peaceful feeling. I too know everything is going to work out. The family really took comfort from your dream."

"Dad, I will write a letter to the church and ask them to postpone my mission for a year. I know we can no longer afford to pay my way. The ward can't afford it either. Besides, we're leaving town. I hate to do it, but I don't see an alternative."

"Sam, this spring, as we were planting the fields, the Spirit whispered to me to take the money for your mission and put it in a savings account under your name. I took five-thousand dollars and put it in your name, in a bank in Utah. You have your mission money. The Lord has seen fit to preserve that part of our dreams."

"But Dad, you and the family are penniless. How can I take all that money and leave you? You need me to help you start over. I'm sure the Lord will understand. This is just a delay, not an abandonment of my plans. Don't you see..."

"Now you listen to me, my young son. The Lord instructed me to set that money aside for your mission. I obeyed, and He sanctified that money to your use. Those funds are sacred, don't you see? We would have lost them along with everything else, but we didn't. It would be sacrilege to misuse them even to buy gas to leave the farm. We have enough money to see us safely to Salt Lake. From there you will go on your mission, and from there we will find a place to go to start a new life. As you said, it will all work out."

Sam could not keep the tears from his eyes and merely nodded. He climbed into the station wagon with the family, and his dad got into the old truck. His moist eyes were only two of many as they pulled out onto the dirt road. A heavy snow began to fall as if the heavens were mourning with them.

They had one stop to make before leaving town. They still owed the bank a lot of money, and Jim wanted to stop and thank them for investing in his dream and to assure them that he would repay the debt as soon as he was able. In a small town, even the failure of one farm can burden a small bank. He felt bad that he had placed them under hardship.

The bank was small even by small standards. It consisted of one teller window and an attached room wherein sat the bank president, Paul Richards. Brother Richards was a member of the other ward in town, and was fully aware of their plight. Brother Richards had loaned them money to run the farm. Even though he had not held the mortgage on their farm, his investment exceeded a hundred thousand dollars. Had he been able, he would have loaned them enough money to farm another year, but it was beyond the resources of their small bank to do so. It was with much regret and many apologies that he had had to deny their request, and consequently, they lost the farm.

Jim and Brother Richards shook hands solemnly. Jim was the first to speak. "Brother Richards, we have said all we need to, except that I want to thank you for your kindness and to assure you that I will repay every cent of what I owe you."

Paul got a strange look on his face, and responded. "But you don't owe me anything."

"You know better. I owe you many thousands of dollars."

"But you don't. I received payment just two days ago. Payment was made by bank draft transfer, and I assumed it came from assets you still held in Utah."

"I no longer own anything in Utah. There must be an error. Someone misdeposited those funds. You'd best look it up and correct the mistake."

"Brother Mahoy, I checked and double checked. The money came from Utah and had your name on the draft. That's all I know. That's all I need to know. Your account is paid in full."

"Do you mean to tell me that I owe you nothing?"

"Actually, I owe you money. The bank draft was $10,000 more than the amount you owe. I have a cashier's check for you here." He pulled an envelope from his drawer and handed it to a stunned Jim.

"Are you sure...there's got to be some mistake. I..."

"Jim, I have lived in this area all my life. In forty years I have never seen a family move into our area and do greater good, set a greater example, or live a richer, more Christ-like life. You and your family practically built our new church. You have had a greater influence for good upon this area than you could possibly know. If you insist that this money didn't come from you, then it came directly from God, or from someone acting as his agent. Don't argue with God or with me. Take the check, and God bless you on your journey. I can assure you, for years to come, whenever people refer to 'the Bishop,' they will be talking about 'Bishop Jim.'"

Jim swallowed hard, and wiped his eyes with the back of his hand. "I'll always remember this place as my first spiritual home. I'll miss you all powerfully. But I have to ask. Paul, is this money from you?"

"No. In all candor, I know exactly what I told you. It came from Utah with your name on it. Accept the fact that you have a miracle here and rejoice over it."

They embraced, and Jim left walking slowly, the check held out before him as if it were the most amazing possession of his life.

"Who could have done such a thing? Who could have paid all that money?" Laura exclaimed after she had heard the story.

It was Cheryl who said with great conviction, "an angel in coveralls."

In reality, they would never know, and the origin of that vast sum of money remained a mystery.

In the final analysis, Cheryl had been right. As long as Cheryl lived with them, whenever she was asked to pray, she always said, "and God bless the angel in coveralls." They all knew she meant their unnamed benefactor.

six

North and South

The family arrived in Salt Lake City, December 4th, 1973, late in the afternoon. For reasons they did not quite understand, they drove directly to Temple Square. They parked and slowly walked across the Temple grounds, brightly lit with a million, tiny, white lights. It was like walking through a frozen Celestial Kingdom, so bright, peaceful, and beautiful. There was a sweet spirit there, and it warmed their souls after their long, mournful journey from the farm. Because of slick roads and car trouble, it had taken them several days, during which time they had slept two nights in the car and eaten all their meals in their laps. They knew no one in the city and had no concrete idea of where to go. They just assumed they would find a motel or some other meager accommodations. Even though they had the big check, they had not been able to cash it. It was drawn on an Idaho bank and since they had no accounts in Utah, banks had refused to cash it for them. Consequently, they had been reduced to living on the few dollars they had scraped together before leaving the farm.

The Visitor's Center was still open, so they walked reverently into its vast foyer, savoring the warmth, the peace, and the richness of spirit they found. They clustered together, almost as if afraid to be any distance apart. They moved as a group to the large paintings on the far wall. They were life sized paintings of scenes from the life of Christ and were breathtaking.

"Good evening." They turned in unison toward the white haired man behind them. Jim took several steps and shook his hand. "My name's Elder Carlson. I'm the director of the Visitor's Center, and want to welcome you to Temple Square."

Jim thanked him and was about to turn back to the paintings, but the man persisted.

"Have you had a long trip?" he asked, an edge of hidden meaning in his voice. Laura joined Jim and shook his hand as Jim introduced her. The kids continued to look at the beautiful paintings. Soon, they were out of sight.

"We just drove several days from Idaho," she told him. "We haven't gotten a hotel room yet, but several of the younger kids have never seen Temple Square at Christmas time, and we wanted to visit it before it closed." She wanted to apologize for their crumpled appearance, but instinctively knew the older gentleman hadn't noticed, or at least didn't care.

"How did you know we've been on a long trip?" Jim wondered aloud. Brother Carlson smiled. "Well, I didn't really. But when you all came through the door you just stood there, as if you had just stepped foot on foreign soil and weren't quite sure what to do. That usually means you are more than visiting Temple Square, but that you are pilgrims, so to speak."

"What do you mean, pilgrims?" Laura shoved her hands into her coat pockets as if subconsciously seeking protection from the answer she knew was coming, and didn't want to believe herself.

Brother Carlson smiled and shrugged. It was so gentle and disarming that they all smiled. "A pilgrim is usually from some place, going to some place which they have yet to determine. They are just — going — traveling, to some unspecified destination."

"Is it that obvious?" Jim asked quietly, looking around as if to see who else might have noticed. There was almost no one else in the building.

"Only to those who choose to notice. What brings you to Salt Lake?" he asked as he motioned to a grouping of chairs. He pulled around his chair to face them and waited. Before long, they had told him the whole story. He listened carefully, nodding, frowning, occasionally laughing. They really didn't know how long they talked, but by the time they were finished the custodians had locked the doors to the Visitor's Center. Jim looked at his watch and realized with a start that it was 9:00 p.m. They had stayed over an hour past closing. Elder Carlson stood as a white haired woman approached. He put his arm around her waist and introduced her as "Sister Carlson, my bride." She shook Jim's hand, and unexpectedly, gave Laura a hug.

"Elder Carlson," she scolded, "you have been keeping these good folks talking so long they have about missed supper." She took Laura's hand and walked toward the elevator. Brother Carlson chuckled, and ignoring Jim's protests about needing to get along and find a hotel room, herded him into the elevator which descended one floor. They walked along a carpeted passageway until they arrived at a cafeteria. Only one table was occupied, and that with the Mahoy's children. Before them was a mountain of food which was rapidly growing smaller.

"Come. You've almost missed it. We already said the blessing," Sister Carlson insisted as she pulled out a chair for Laura. Brother and Sister Carlson began eating, and Jim and Laura joined. It was hot and very good. They had all forgotten how hungry they were. Sister

Carlson disappeared into the kitchen and returned shortly with plates of pie and ice cream. Before long it was all gone.

When they were finished, Jim reached for his wallet, but Elder Carlson caught his arm. "We have this wonderful arrangement. We are on a mission, you see, and run the Visitor's Center for the church. One of our little blessings is that every evening we come down here and eat our dinner. This is the staff cafeteria and is under the temple annex. The cafeteria cooks always leave out something nice. We have specific instructions to share it with anyone we like. So you needn't feel obligated to pay anything. You are our guests."

Jim began to express thanks, and to insist they needed to leave, but Elder Carlson again placed a hand on his arm. "Brother Mahoy. This is Christmas time, and every hotel and motel in this city is packed to capacity. I know you are capable people, and don't need any assistance caring for yourselves. However, we are old people and have no family to share the Christmas season with. We have a large apartment just a short distance from here, also provided by the Visitor's Center. We have two extra bedrooms and no one to help decorate our Christmas tree. We were even considering not putting one up this year. But look at these children, they need a Christmas tree."

Sister Carlson took Laura's hand. "Laura, I have been trying to finish a quilt for my daughter who is having a baby, and my slow old fingers aren't getting it done very fast. Besides, I miss having children in the house, and it is Christmas. Won't you please spend the holidays with us? At least until you get settled? It would be such a nice thing to do for two lonely people."

Laura sputtered, and Jim sat there wide-eyed. They had turned the whole situation around into making it a favor to the Carlsons to stay. He knew it would be nearly impossible to find a room, and was actually planning on spending another night in the car. But this kindly couple was giving them exactly what they needed, and were making them feel as if they were doing a favor, not receiving one. They exchanged one of those meaningful glances, and Laura nodded. The relief and happiness in Sister Carlson's face was genuine, and almost enough to convince them the Clarlsons did consider it a big favor.

They walked less than a block on freshly fallen snow to their apartment. It was on the fourth floor of a large building. Their apartment was indeed large, and the Mahoy's had two bedrooms and a bath all to themselves.

Upon awakening, they happily discovered the Carlsons had already fixed a huge breakfast. They spent the morning putting up the tree, quilting, and baking Christmas goodies. The Carlsons were genuinely pleased to have company, and it was as comfortable as staying with family. The Carlsons left at noon to do their job at the Visitor's Center. They gave Jim a key to the apartment, and told them to join them in the cafeteria below the Visitor's Center at 7:00 p.m.

As they were eating dinner, Sam mentioned that he was entering the mission home January 2nd to go on a mission to South Africa. Brother and Sister Carlson both dropped their forks. There was a stunned silence during which the Carlsons stared wide-eyed at one another.

Finally, Elder Carlson explained: "Sister Carlson and I have been called to preside over the Johannesburg, South Africa mission. We will be entering the mission home on the very same day!" The news was electric and almost beyond comprehension. Suddenly everyone was laughing, shaking hands, and talking all at once. A glowing sense of grand design, of divine providence settled over them, and they let the joy wash over them, and salve their wounds.

Time seemed to go into slow motion, as if this glorious Christmas season would last forever. Every day was filled with wonders, Christmas shopping the big, new malls, visiting Church historical sites, and, best of all, listening to the Tabernacle Choir sing Handel's Messiah. It was powerful, magnificent, and deeply spiritual. Christmas morning was delightful, with laughter, hugs, and gifts for everyone.

After what seemed like months, January 2nd finally came. The Carlsons made arrangements for the family to stay on at the apartment for another week. They drove the Carlsons to their destination in Provo, and tearfully bid them goodby. Shortly thereafter, they took Sam to the mission home in Provo, and after many hugs, kissed him goodbye.

"Dad?" Sam asked as he picked up his bag. "Where will you and the family go?" Do you have plans?"

Jim and Laura exchanged one of those magical glances before Jim replied. "Sam, we have decided to go to Alaska. The economy is booming there. Uncle Ben lives there, as you know, and he tells me that I can find a job almost without trying. Your mother and I figure that we will have an adventure too."

Sam thought about this for a few moments before a feeling of peace swept over him. He knew he wouldn't have to worry about his family, that he could concentrate on his mission and trust God to everything else. "Then north to your future, and south to mine it is." He embraced his father, then his mother one more time, and turned and strode through the big, double doors.

seven

South Africa

There was a new world on the other side of those doors, a vast sea of white shirts, suitcases, and organized pandemonium. Sam was directed to a table by a white haired lady with a gentle smile. Here he handed in his papers. He was shown where to deposit his bags, and before many minutes, was sitting in a large hall with nearly a thousand other prospective missionaries. The mood was apprehensive yet calmly determined. He felt the Holy Spirit warming his soul, and he felt at peace. Music began to play, and before many minutes they were singing "Ye Elders of Israel." The voices of those missionaries drowned out the organ in a rendition so enthusiastic it sent chills of joy up his spine. A white haired man took the pulpit and introduced himself as Elder Whitehall, Mission President of the Mission Home. He heartily welcomed them, and gave them needed instruction. He turned the time over to Elder Bruce R. McConkie, who delivered a stern, yet inspiring message about personal worthiness, dedication, service, and personal integrity. He bore his testimony, and the words reverberated in Sam's soul.

The new missionaries were bused to the BYU campus, assigned a room in the ancient Knight Halls dorms, and after meeting their new companions, eating dinner, and studying the scriptures for two hours, they fell exhausted into bed.

The next day began at 6:00 a.m. with a shower, scripture study, companion prayers, and breakfast. Each new missionary's companion had been there for at least 3 week, and knew the routine. They enthusiastically instructed their "greenie" companions in their duties. By 9:00 they gathered in a room no larger than twelve feet square that smelled of furniture polish. All four walls of the room, floor and ceiling were wood, and except for the bright overhead lighting, would have been oppressive. There were twelve elders there; six senior companions and their respective "greenies."

A skinny, serious-faced young man stood before them, and introduced himself as their zone leader. Elder Toleman was a returned missionary from South Africa, and would spend the next eight weeks teaching them Afrikaans, the language of their mission. He also informed them that they would be learning the discussions in both English and Afrikaans, in that the mission field was bilingual, and both languages would be used for teaching. This brought a groan from the new missionaries and a sympathetic chuckle from the "seniors."

Elder Toleman had them all stand. He said "Good morning," in Afrikaans, then had everyone repeat it at the top of their voice. He then told them what it meant. They repeated the sentence again and again. Then he taught them "How are you," which they repeated endlessly in loud voices. This went on for three hours. When they broke for lunch they could conduct a rudimentary door approach in Afrikaans. It was amazing, and the new elders enthusiastically practiced their new language skills at lunch.

After lunch they repeated the process but took lines from the first discussion. By break time at 4:00 they could say the first two exchanges in the discussion, including "Brother Brown's" unrealistically golden responses.

From 4:00 to 5:30 PM was vigorous exercise and a shower. Dinner was at 6:00 PM, with more language training from 7:00 to 9:00 PM. Scripture study and journal writing were from 9:00 to 10:00 PM, with lights out at 10:00 PM. Every other day they had a "devotional," with some member of the General Authorities. Sundays were a spiritual feast, with more language training. Monday was preparation day, and they had four hours in the morning to roam BYU campus, write letters home, and otherwise unwind. The rest of the day was language training.

By the end of the eight weeks, Sam was supercharged spiritually, his prayers had found a dimension of communication he had never thought possible, and his bosom burned with the presence of the Holy Spirit almost constantly. His desire was to do the Lord's work, and nothing else mattered.

Emily and Cheryl came to see him off at the airport. They had enrolled at BYU, and hugged him, or held both his hands the whole two hours they had together. His family had departed weeks earlier for the long drive to Alaska. His parents had each written him a long letter, with instructions that he was to open them on the plane, and not before. When it came time to leave, Emily gave him a big hug, and kiss. Cheryl held him tightly and kissed him hard. It surprised him and took his breath away. She pressed a letter into his hand, and spun away as tears streamed down her face. Emily stayed to cheerfully wave as he walked down the ramp, tears rolling down her cheeks.

Their flight was scheduled to take them from Salt Lake City through Chicago, New York, and London. After almost a full day in London they boarded another plane which made several mysterious refueling stops in the middle east at places the pilot claimed he was not at liberty to name. From there it was a long flight to Jan Smuts airport in Johannesburg, South Africa.

When they wearily stepped from the plane three days later, they could not believe they had finally arrived. For three days they had not slept anywhere but sitting up on planes. The saying popped into Sam's head, "No matter where you go, there you are." He knew it was silly, but South Africa seemed much more real than he had expected. In his mind his mission started the moment he set foot in Africa, and now that he had arrived, there seemed to be a conspicuous absence of heralding angels, or pillar of fire over the airport. It was just another hot, muggy place, and he was the same, though much more tired, hungry and dirty. His suit smelled, and his shirt seemed permanently glued to his back.

Four missionaries met them at the airport, shook their hands unceremoniously, and herded them to several vans. They crowded inside and drove a considerable distance through the bustling city of Johannesburg. Finally, they crossed into a quiet neighborhood filled with huge homes.

The Elder driving their van was explaining. "When Israel became a nation again after Yom Kippur war, many Jewish people sold their homes in South Africa dirt cheap and moved to Jerusalem. There was a period of time when homes were sold for a tenth of their value. During that time the church had bought a jewish mansion for almost nothing, which has been used as the mission home ever since."

Sam later learned that there are few economies in the world like South Africa's. Based on the two pillars of fantastically rich natural resources and almost unlimited cheap labor, there were more millionaires per capita in South Africa by almost double, than in the United States. The screaming difference was that South Africa had almost no middle class. One was either mind-bogglingly rich or groveling poor. What middle class there was fell to those who chose some profession, such as lawyers, doctors, and the like. Thus, the middle class, such as it was, would have be classed as wealthy or well-to-do in America. Anyone or any race who made their living by the sweat of their brow, eeked out an existance living in tiny houses on minimal income. With labor so incredibly available and cheap, there was no pressing need to pay anyone more than survival wages.

About this time, Sam's van turned from a well-manicured lane onto the long drive of the mission home. The drive took them toward a sprawling, red-brick mansion, with expansive glass windows, flowing architecture, and a five-car garage. They rounded a fountain and stopped before massive, double wooden doors. Sam was delighted to see Elder and Sister Carlson standing on the front steps. They hadn't gone to the language training mission, but had come directly to South Africa. Elder Carlson shook his hand exactly like every other Elder, and Sister Carlson gave him a wink as she shook his hand. He didn't expect special treatment, and could see that they were very pleased to see him there finally.

The double doors opened into a broad foyer. A massive circular stair dominated the room, with a six foot wide crystal chandelier hanging from the high, domed ceiling. The stair treads were nearly three feet deep, and rose a mere four inches with each step, which gave one an almost fluid appearance when traversing them.

They were ushered into a huge living room with a massive, white, velvet couch, and a ten, foot Steinway grand piano sitting in a bay window. Over the couch hung a painting of exquisite beauty. It was of a peaceful, pastoral scene nearly ten feet in length. It depicted small stucco homes with thick thatched roofs on a picturesque dirt lane bordered by a stream on one side, and a meadow on the other. He later learned that they had bought the home furnished, and that the art and furnishings were virtually priceless. The painting which hung over the couch was worth more than they had paid for the whole mansion.

Sister Carlson brought them sandwiches and milk while President Carlson interviewed each of them in turn. In what seemed like a very brief time, Elder Mahoy was loaded into a VW beetle and driven several hours to his new area.

Elder Tilley met him in front of the boarding house where they would be staying. He was tall and blond, with a perpetual smile. Sam decided he liked his new companion almost immediately. Elder Tilley helped him unload his two bags and carry them through the house. The house was oppressively dark, with small windows and high ceilings. As they went through he was introduced to a huge woman in a dirty apron. The introduction was done in Afrikaans, and he understood none of it. He shook her plump hand, and assumed she was the landlady. He could see into the big kitchen, and was amazed to see that they were cooking on a big wood burning stove. Several black servant girls were scurrying around the kitchen.

Their apartment was an attachment to the back of the house with an outside entrance. The room was about ten feet square, with painted concrete floor, and a high sculpted tin ceiling. The room was unheated, and had no plumbing. They had to go into the house to take showers. He remembered having been told this, but it finally sank home that they would not be cooking for themselves. They lived in boarding houses, which meant the landlady cooked for them. He flopped on his bed and let his eyes roll up into his head. He was exhausted to the point of death, having had no true sleep in three days. He was no sooner horizontal than his companion prodded him in the side. Sam opened his bloodshot eyes to look at Elder Tilley's who had a broad grin on his face. He wasn't sure, but he suspected Elder Tilley enjoyed what he said next.

"Elder. Dinner is in ten minutes. Then we have several appointments and some tracting. Don't go to sleep. We don't go to bed until 10:00 P.M."

Sam rolled to a sitting position, a little chafed, but glad to hear that missionary work was waiting to be done. Dinner consisted of two small, fried, beef sausages his companion called 'boer worst,' farmer sausage, two fried tomato slices with a couple of fried onion loops, a small pile of white rice, and a cup of tea. He couldn't believe his eyes, or his stomach. The sausages were floating in oil, he had never eaten a fried tomato slice in his life, he detested rice, and was relatively certain tea was still against the Word of Wisdom. He looked at his companion who was slicing his sausage. He stabbed a piece still holding the fork upside down in his left hand, scraped a pile of rice onto the sausage with his knife, wiped the knife on the side of the fork, and stuffed it into his mouth all with the fork in his left hand.

Elder Tilley said something in Afrikaans, which Sam correctly interpreted as a compliment on the food. Sam blinked in surprised, and sliced a piece of sausage. He nearly gagged. The sausage had no spices other than salt and a lot of pepper, and tasted like lard. He forced himself to swallow. He then tried the rice which he found dry and tasteless. Surprisingly, the tomatoes and onions were wonderful. Problem was, they had almost no bulk. Sam forced himself to eat. When he was done, he felt no less hungry than before. Elder Tilley picked up his tea, and stirred in milk and sugar.

Elder Tilley leaned toward him and said. "It's herb tea, and we have permission from the first presidency to drink it. Its almost a national drink. It is completely healthy and tastes good. Try it."

Sam watched his companion sip the tea with considerable doubt. He almost felt as if he was watching him commit some grievous sin, yet a feeling of peace came over him unexpectedly, and he prepared his tea similar to Elder Tilley's. He carefully sipped, and was surprised to find a sweet, fully, bodied, earthy taste on his tongue. It seemed very pleasant, and he enjoyed the whole cup. Had he been at home, or more confident of himself, he would have had about three more cups of the tea, and several more plates of something besides lard sausage and tasteless rice. As it was, they thanked the landlady and departed.

Pretoria was the capital city of South Africa, and an important point of commerce. The wide streets were packed with buses, trucks, cars, bicycles and pedestrians. To make it more confusing, they were all driving on the wrong side of the street. Sam was amazed to observe that there were ten black faces to every white one, and everyone seemed to be shouting in a foreign language. He felt dizzy, tired, hungry, nauseous, and terrified all at the same time.

He and Elder Tilley walked what seemed like a very long distance before coming to a high rise apartment building. There was one elevator for the odd numbered floors, and another for the even numbered floors. There was no 13th floor, since it was presumably unlucky. But there was a floor numbered 12 1/2, witch was apparently an odd number, since the odd elevator stopped there. He found out later that some buildings skipped the 13th floor completely due to the fact that some of the more astute tenants figured out that 12 1/2 was just a ruse to cover up the fact that this was, in fact the 13th floor, no matter how you numbered it, and still unlucky. In order to preserve the even/odd rhythm there was also no 14th floor. On some buildings the 13th floor was actually there, but was used for storage or something other than for apartments. The whole preoccupation with 13 struck Sam as comical every time he saw a new attempt to avoid it.

Their appointment was on the 11th floor, but the odd elevator was broken, so they rode the even elevator to the 12th floor and walked down one flight.

Elder Tilley introduced Sam to Mister Van der Merva. He said "pleasure to meet you," in Afrikaans, pleased to have followed the conversation thus far. From that point on, he didn't comprehend a single word, not even one. They talked a hundred times faster than the teachers in the Language Training Mission, and they pronounced the words differently. Sam felt his heart sinking further into his empty stomach moment by moment. After about 15 minutes, Elder Tilley turned to him, and asked him in Afrikaans to continue the discussion. He barely understood what Elder Tilley said, but realized with a start that he was supposed to give the next concept. His brain flashed, a vague memory surfaced, he remembered the words, but suddenly without confidence he turned to Elder Tilley and thanked him, but asked him to continue. There was perspiration on his companion's forehead. He frowned, nodded, and continued. After a while, the discussion became heated. In spite of not being able to understand the words, it was clear that an argument had erupted. Mister Van der Merva fetched his bible, and began quoting scripture. A few minutes later Elder Tilley stood without warning, politely excused himself, shook hands, and walked to the door. Sam followed, not real sure what had just happened.

Once back in the elevator, Elder Tilley switched back to English. "I guess he just wanted to argue. When the spirit of contention comes, I just leave. Some elders like to argue. We call it bashing. But I refuse to do it. I'm here to teach the Gospel, not to argue about it."

"Sorry about not doing my concept in there. I was lost and actually, I didn't understand a thing you two were saying," Sam admitted.

"Don't worry. It took me weeks to begin to understand what was going on. The LTM gives you a false sense of the language. It will click for you. Our other appointment is several blocks away and we need to hurry. She is an English speaking sister. She's had three discussions. Do you know the fourth in English?"

"I thought I knew them all. In both languages," Sam added despondently.

Elder Tilley chuckled. "Ah, to be green again." To call a missionary green was about the same as calling a teenager a baby. It was not a compliment. But he sensed that Elder Tilley didn't mean to insult him, just to comment on his own memories of being a 'greenie.'

The walk was short, and the apartment complex newer looking. They took the odd elevator to the 7th floor and walked to #722. A note was stuck to the door in a fashion Sam had never seen before. The envelope had been licked, and the flap stuck to the door. When Elder Tilley pulled it off it left a white inverted "V" on the door.

Dear Mormon Elders,

I am no longer interested in continuing our discussions. Thank you for calling,

Eva

"Someone got to her," Elder Tilley lamented as he stuffed the note into his pocket. "It happens a lot. Well, our tracting area is not far from here. We still have several hours of daylight."

"Why didn't she call? It seems rude to just stick a note to your door," Sam commented as they walked briskly to their tracting area.

"We don't have a phone, as you may have noticed. Things are different here. Most people don't have telephones, and you have to pay by the call so they are expensive to use. Most people only call for very important things or for emergencies. We never use the phone, it scares people. They think only bad news comes when the phone rings so we don't call. Besides, we can't afford it. You wouldn't believe the cost to get a phone installed. In addition to all that, there's a five year waiting list to get a phone installed I'm told."

They had turned several corners and entered a residential area of small homes. Sam guessed the homes were no bigger than one or two bedrooms at most. Each home had a tiny front yard surrounded by a short, ornate, concrete fence. The yards were immaculately kept, with breathtaking displays of flowers and shrubs. Africa was, after all, a arid-tropic climate, and flowers seemed to spring from the cracks in the sidewalks.

Elder Tilley walked up to the first gate. A pit bull ran from the porch to the gate and began barking. He pushed open the gate and marched toward the house. Sam hesitated, then followed. The dog nipped at his heels as he hurried to keep up.

The doorbell was a buzzer that reminded him of the timer built into his mother's stove. A woman in her 40's slowly opened the door just a few inches. When she saw who they were, or who she thought they were, she slammed it back shut.

"Foot sack!" she called from the other side of the door. He knew it was a curse, usually reserved for dogs and rapists. It literally meant, 'Go away, I say!' but carried an array of colorful threats and insults, several of which were threats of physical violence and suggestions about non-human ancestry. When someone said foot sack, they really meant it. In reality the word she had said was Afrikaans, but sounded exactly like foot sack in English.

Elder Tilley slid a blue pamphlet under the door. As they walked away, they could hear it being ripped into shreds.

"Happens a lot," was all he said. Somehow, it seemed to make it less disappointing, almost normal. But it still bothered Sam. He found himself wondering why the lady was so angry, and if they shouldn't go back and reason with her. Elder Tilley seemed to have no such misgivings as he marched away.

The next house had a bull mastiff. It was so big that it could almost look them in the eye over the concrete fence. Elder Tilley marched right up, spoke something soothing to the dog, and opened the gate. He marched up the short lane. Sam followed, trembling with fear the dog. Instead of biting him, it followed him, sniffing at his behind. Just as the owner opened the door, the big dog put its nose on his heel, and slid his big slobbery nose all the way up into his crotch. He couldn't help himself from uttering a startled cry. The owner saw what had happened, laughed at them, and slammed the door.

Elder Tilley glanced at Sam as he wiped slobber out of his crotch. "Happens a lot," he said.

After three more doors Elder Tilley turned to Sam. "Elder, this one is yours. I do five, you do five."

"But!"

"If you get stuck, I'll help you. But don't expect me to bail you out until you are really stuck. I'm there, just relax and you'll do fine." He pushed open the gate and motioned for Sam to lead the way.

"But I don't know what to say."

"Say whatever the Spirit directs or whatever you have memorized, whichever comes to mind first." He chuckled.

"I'm not sure I can handle it if its not in English."

"OK, tell you what. If its in Afrikaans, I'll take it. If its in English, you take it. Now do it."

Sam took a breath and strode in. He didn't even notice the barking dog as he walked past it. He knocked, and waited. Someone stirred inside and pulled open the door. A young woman stood there holding a little girl. The baby was about two years old, and as pretty a little girl as Sam had ever seen.

His eyes were pulled toward the child, and for a moment he entirely forgot why he was there. The woman turned the child toward Sam. He reached out to her. The little girl cocked her head, then reached out a small hand with a big smile. Her hand was tiny compared to his, and sticky with something. Sam smiled, and still holding her hand, suddenly remembered why he was there. With a start he turned back to the baby's mother. To his surprise, she was studying his face with interest. He forced the smile from his face and introduced himself in Afrikaans. He could do that much.

"I prefer English," she said in Afrikaans, then added in English, "and I think you might too."

"Yes, Ma'am," Sam said with a little too much relief. Today's my first day in South Africa, and I can't understand a word anyone says. Even the English people are hard for me to understand."

This made her laugh, which sounded musical to his ears. "You have an American accent," she observed.

"Yes, I suppose I do. I'm from Idaho, in the western United States. We're missionaries for the Church of Jesus Christ of Latter-day Saints."

"Mormons?" she asked.

"We're sometimes called Mormons. We ..."

"I don't mean to be rude, but I'm not interested in your church. My husband and I are happy in our church. I hope you'll forgive me."

Elder Tilley turned to leave, and the woman started to close the door.

"Believe me, you are not being rude," Sam muttered as he turned. The door stopped closing. She had a quizzical look on her face.

Sam hurried to explain. "What I mean is, the previous five doors got slammed in our faces, and I've almost been bitten by two dogs, and was molested by another one. Not being interested I understand. Slamming the door, or putting your dog on someone is rude. You certainly haven't been rude. I thank you for allowing me to speak to someone who understands what being a Christian means."

She frowned at this, then said. "If I truly understood what being a Christian means, I probably wouldn't turn you away would I? But really, I'm not interested."

Sam had to think about this before answering. "I can't imagine you doing anything unchristian. Forgive me for intruding on your evening. It was worth it just to see your daughter. She's so cute. Is she about two?"

"She'll be two in three weeks."

"Reminds me of my baby sister when she was that age." Sam turned to leave, and the woman slowly closed the door.

When they were back on the sidewalk, Sam suddenly had an idea.

"Just a minute," he said, and hurried back up the walk. He rang the bell. When she opened the door, he handed her a Joseph Smith tract. She seemed reluctant to accept it, so he handed it to the child who snatched it from him.

"Ma'am, I came over 6000 miles to be a missionary. So far, you're the nicest person I've met in this country, and the most wonderful thing I possess is in that pamphlet. I know you aren't interested and won't read it. Just the same, I wouldn't feel right about not giving you something in return for your kindness." He smiled and trotted back down the steps. When he closed the gate, she was still standing in the door. She had a confused expression on her face. He waved and in response, she took her daughter's arm, and waved it back at them.

As they were walking away, Elder Tilley put an X next to 355, their house number.

"Why'd you do that?"

"They sacked us. The 'X' warns the next Elders not to knock on that door again," he explained matter-of-factly.

"I know what the 'X' means, what I mean is, why did you 'X' her, she didn't sack us."

"Did too."

"Did not."

"Are we in her house teaching her the first discussion?"

"Well no."

"Do we have an appointment to come back?"

"No."

"She sacked us."

"But I have this feeling. I think maybe we planted a seed."

"Maybe you wasted a Joseph Smith tract. Do you realize we have to buy those things ourselves? Give away ten of them, and it's worth one soft drink. Don't waste them. We can give out the little blue ones for free. If they sack us, give em a blue one, OK?"

"She didn't sack us," Sam insisted.

His companion moaned, and muttered something in Afrikaans about greenies as he turned into the next gate. Ten door slams later, they headed for home. It took them almost an hour to walk home, and each step brought on more exhaustion until Sam was not sure he could make it home. The town was hilly, like San Francisco, and seemed an endless series of climbs and equally wearying descents. By the time they stopped at their boarding house Sam was exhausted and completely lost. He didn't recognize the building and thought they were going to tract one more house before going home. He was startled when Tilley opened the door and just walked in.

When Sam got to his bed, he fell onto it and almost immediately began to snore. Elder Tilley rousted him, and said something about scripture study and companion prayers. Sam felt like he was talking to someone in a dream.

"Elder Tilley, did you ever notice how much bigger I am than you?"

"Yes, but…"

"This body is going to sleep, whether you or I tell it not to. If you want to knock yourself out trying to get it up, help yourself, but I'm not going to fight it, or you. Good night."

"I'll pray for your soul, you sinful Elder," Tilley said in mock seriousness.

"Light a candle for me," Sam muttered, and promptly fell asleep.

Elder Tilley let Sam sleep until about eight AM the following morning, two hours past normal. He was still tired when he awoke. Elder Tilley was sitting on his bed, reading the scriptures. They just made it to breakfast on time. Breakfast was a shallow bowl of white corn mush. With a pat of butter, salt, sugar and milk it was tasty, and only a quarter of what his stomach was hoping for.

After breakfast, Elder Tilley announced they were going thumb tracting. Sam had no idea of what this meant, but followed gamely. They walked out onto a busy street, and Tilley stuck out his thumb. Sam did the same. In less than two minutes a big, old Buick screeched to a stop in front of them. The brakes were metal to metal. In America this car would have been a classic. In Africa, it was a taxi stuffed with about ten black people. Sam couldn't believe that many people could fit into that car. The springs were collapsed from the weight, with the bumper almost touching the ground. As soon as it stopped, the driver leaned toward them, and talked with a big smile on his face.

"Good morning my bossies, do you need a ride into town my bossies? I have much plenty room, if you like, I drive you to town."

Sam had several black friends back home, yet this man's face were truly black. His skin was so dark that Sam could not easily distinguish his features. All he could clearly see was two eyes suspended above a set of huge teeth which appeared and disappeared in rhythm with his speech.

His accent was lilting, with a sing-song beat. Sam could not imagine what room he was talking about. But, as he was speaking, four people got out to make room for them. Tilley thanked them, and told them they would never make someone else walk so they could ride. After much persuasion, they went on.

"The blacks offer us rides about ten to one over whites. They know we are missionaries, and they have taboos and strong beliefs about missionaries. It's considered good luck to give a missionary a ride, and to give foreign missionaries a ride is a big honor. They were probably real disappointed we didn't take them up on it."

"Why did they call us bossie? I had a cow we called bossie," Sam said.

"Well, they call anyone they respect their boss. If they are speaking to someone younger, they often call them "bossie." In our language it's a compliment, like a small boss, bossie. See? But in Zulu, "bossie"means something like 'little smart ass,' or something like that. It's not a compliment."

"I thought you said they would be honored to have us ride in their car. Why insult us then?"

"They would have been. In that situation, they had the power, and offering us a ride put them in a position of power over us. They weren't offering us a ride to honor us, they were offering a ride to honor themselves, to be able to have power over us."

"That sounds pretty cynical. Are you sure about that? It sounds petty and cheap," Sam said with a note of disgust in his voice.

"I have heard many people comment on that aspect of black culture."

"Have you ever heard a black person say that?"

"I don't speak Zulu."

"I won't believe all that until I hear a black person say it. Why don't we just take one of them up on their offer. Why not ride with the black people?"

"Well, there's two reasons," Elder Tilley explained. "The first is that I don't like the idea of putting four people afoot so we can ride." Sam agreed with that.

"The second is, that it is actually illegal."

"What?" Sam exclaimed. He could not believe his ears.

"It is," Elder Tilley insisted. "The church has a binding agreement with the South African government that no LDS missionaries will meet with a group of blacks larger than four persons. It also absolutely prohibits us teaching them the gospel."

"You're joking," Sam said.

Elder Tilley turned to face Sam, his face stern. Sam could tell he was not joking. "Elder Mahoy, this is not America. The laws here are very different. When we return to boarding I will show it to you in writing in our missionary handbook. To avoid the appearance of holding meetings with black citizens we do not accept rides from car loads of blacks."

"I think that's terrible," Sam said adamantly.

"Actually, I do too Elder. I do too. But I can't change the way things are."

Elder Tilley was muttering something about greenies when another car load of blacks pulled up. They turned it down and one more before a white man pulled up in a car all by himself. They got in, and while driving to town, almost taught him the first discussion. He was very nice, but not interested, and the subject changed to the weather. He let them out near the center of town.

Pretoria was a bustling city of high rise apartments. The street level floor was shops, stores, and businesses. The apartments above the shopping district were new looking and appeared recently built. The signs along the street were about half Afrikaans and half English. Sam could see Coca Cola, Kodak, General Electric, Sony, and a hundred other names familiar to him. They walked a short distance to a camera shop and went in. Elder Tilley's camera was being repaired. They picked it up and after paying, looked around the store. Everything seemed expensive. Everything he could have bought in a camera store in America was on the shelves, but things were much more expensive. It turned out that Elder Tilley loved photography and came here occasionally to look at the latest equipment. His camera was new and expensive.

They decided to walk to the park and meet people there before lunch. Their attempt at proselytizing in the park was a disaster. Every conversation they tried to start ended up in a curt refusal. It seemed that everyone was in too big a hurry to listen to their message. By lunch time, they were both a bit discouraged. They couldn't get home in time for lunch at the boarding, and Sam didn't have enough money to buy anything. Elder Tilley bought them fish and chips at a small shop. The little café was no bigger than a walk-in closet and had a line of people waiting. It was worth the wait. Sam finally tasted something he liked, but could have eaten twice as much.

They decided to take the bus home and found the correct bus stop, which was not a simple task. They had to study the bus schedule for twenty minutes, tracing routes and studying maps to see which bus or combination of buses would take them nearest home. In the end, the fast way home was a direct ride that left them within a half mile of their boarding. The combination of buses that would have let them off within a block of home would have gotten them home several hours later. Sam was surprised to learn it only cost five cents to ride the bus.

As they were waiting, Sam noticed that they were just a few doors from a music store. He loved music and had left his harmonica with his parents. They had several hours to wait. Sam finally persuaded Elder Tilley to go in and browse around. Most of the instruments were used, showing obvious signs of wear. Yet the shop looked prosperous. Sam gazed at the instruments, wondering what stories each instrument could tell, who had owned them, and why they had sold them.

He was so deep in thought that he was startled when the store owner spoke to them. "Looking for something particular gentlemen?"

"Huh? Oh, no. Mostly waiting for the bus. But I love music. Hope you don't mind."

"Certainly not. Do you play?" The store owner was a young man in his thirties, dressed like an American hippie. He had long hair held back by a scarf tied around his head, a flowered shirt, faded bell-bottom Levis, and sandals over white socks. It was almost comical, but he seemed very comfortable in his costume.

"I used to play the flute and the harmonica. I tinker on the organ and piano. Nothing spectacular. I gave up the flute years ago."

"You're American!" The shop owner nearly shouted.

"Yes. We..." He wanted to tell them they were missionaries, but the man grabbed his hand and started pumping it up and down.

"I am too! Except that I've never been there, I mean. I love everything American. In my office I have an American flag, and I collect American stamps, and American anything I can touch. I love American clothes, American music, John Wayne, Walt Disney, American everything." He was so enthusiastic that Sam felt embarrassed. Even he didn't love American everything.

"My name's Thomas Snodgrass. Pleased to meet you."

"Elder Sam Mahoy, and Elder John Tilley." Sam introduced themselves. Tom finally stopped shaking his hand and worked over Elder Tilley's. Elder Tilley was smiling like he was watching a comedy act.

"Do you play Dixie Land Jazz? That's my favorite."

"I don't know that I've ever tried," Sam admitted.

"What! You said you are American. You really a Russian spy? Just kidding. I thought all Americans loved Dixie Land Jazz."

"Well some do I'm sure. But ..."

"No buts. Which instrument do you prefer? Pick one, and I'll get my trumpet."

Sam looked at Elder Tilley, who shrugged his indifference. Sam wandered over to a piano and sat down. Oddly enough, or perhaps not oddly at all, it was an American made, Baldwin, baby grand. It was obviously a used piano, but was in perfect tune. Sam played a primary song and felt a feeling of peace come over him. The piano was in great condition and he felt musical inside.

Tom returned with a long silver trumpet and blew an exuberant note. Without warning he launched into "When The Saints Come Marching In." When Sam didn't play along, he stopped.

"What's the matter? You're a Mormon missionary, a Latter-day Saint. This is your American song. Don't you know it?" he asked in mock amazement.

"I've heard it but..."

"OK. I'll play the opening line, and whatever I do, you do the same thing. OK? Good. Key of C"

"What is the key of C?"

"Oh, one of those. No black notes," he answered with surprising patience.

"Got it." Sam said, understanding perfectly.

Tom puffed out his cheeks and belted out "Oh when the Saints."

Sam hammered out the same thing.

Tom played "Come marching in."

Sam copied him, but added a few flourishes.

They played back and fourth until they had worn the song to a frazzle. Tom would stop and periodically give him some instruction.

"OK. Now go up a key, play a forth, then the fifth, then add the seventh. See how that leads to a natural key change? Now, just play everything with two sharps, F and C." When explained that way, it made perfect sense to Sam. He played by feeling, by hearing, and every previous attempt to explain music theory to him had gone over his head. But Tom had a way of saying it that just made sense. Sam played until his fingers ached, and they had missed their bus.

By the time they stopped playing the store was jammed with people who had come in to listen. Tom stood his horn on the piano and turned to the people. In a few minutes, he had sold one lady trumpet lessons for her son, and another man said he would bring his wife back to see the piano Sam had been playing.

"Hey, you Mormons are good for business," Tom proclaimed loudly. Many people in the store laughed. Tom disappeared and returned with a flute. He handed it to Sam, who took it reluctantly. "Elder, play us some flute." The people clapped and urged him on. Elder Tilley urged him to do it. Sam laid the flute onto the piano and stood.

"I'm sorry. I don't play the flute anymore," Sam explained quietly. "That was a long time ago."

As they left, so did the crowd. One man wanted to know who they were, and several others asked if this was part of their mission. A woman wanted Sam to teach her daughter piano lessons. He said that he was here to teach the gospel not the piano. The woman considered this, and then invited them to come to her home to teach the gospel, if he would play too. They made an appointment with her. While the Elders stood at the bus stop, they talked with several people about the gospel and made another appointment. By the time they arrived home, they had made three appointments, taught two discussions, and were feeling full of the spirit. It was a wonderful day.

After companion prayers that evening, Elder Tilley complimented him on his playing and the result it had had on people. He suggested they return every Tuesday and do the same thing. Sam was delighted.

As the weeks progressed, their Tuesday "music tracting," as they came to call it, turned into Tuesday and Thursday, then Tuesday, Thursday, and Saturday. Tom loved it. People actually planned ahead to be at his store, and a few made reservations. He had to have his wife, Linda, come to the store to man the store so he could make music. Tom started handing Sam different instruments just to see what he could do. With a few dismal exceptions, Sam picked up on them quickly.

The third week, Tom handed him a violin.

"Gosh. I've never touched one of these. Don't have a clue what to do." Tom handed him the bow and showed him how to hold the violin. He showed him how to press down the strings to make different notes. Sam was surprised how simple it was. It made perfect sense, and after a few squeaks, he ground out a simple tune. Tom picked up a violin from the counter, and played a catchy line. Sam struggled, but played the same thing, albeit with quite a few squeals. Tom played it again, and Sam did better. The fourth time it was perfect. Tom did something harder and Sam copied. The second time it was perfect. Tom fired off a complicated melody, and Sam botched it half way through. Tom repeated it, and Sam did it right the second time. People clapped. Tom's wife sold someone violin lessons.

By the end of the day, Sam was playing the violin fairly well. It wasn't that difficult. In Sam's mind all he was doing was copying what Tom did.

As they were playing a passage, Sam heard a familiar melody. It was the song he had played at Jimmy's funeral, a haunting, passionate piece by Bach. He couldn't get the tune from his head. It called to him so loudly that it started coming from the violin. He closed his eyes and heard the music. It welled up in him like an irresistible force and spilled out onto the strings. He was there, back at the funeral, Jimmy's still form before him. He threw his head back and played, his heart overflowed, and the strings cried out the precious feelings. Tears streamed down his cheeks, and he played as if nothing else in this world mattered.

When the music ceased he was startled to hear someone sniffle. He opened his eyes and realized that nearly fifty people were looking at him with faces filled with emotion, some with tears on their cheeks. He lowered the violin and they began to applaud. He suddenly felt foolish, exposed, embarrassed. It was too private a moment to have shared with so many people. He suppressed the urge to run away.

Sam's old feelings of never wanting to play in front of people dominated him for a minute, then washed away. Suddenly he knew something about himself that he had never been able to understand before. His soul was filled with music. He was so full of music that he heard it night and day. At times it nearly flooded out conscious thought.

Like a new revelation, Sam realized music was one of his gifts from God. He realized music was not something for which he had struggled and practiced a million hours to perfect, but it had come as a gift, It wasn't even something he had asked for. It was simply and entirely a gift.

Somehow Sam had know this before, but it had never occurred to him how magnificent this gift really was, and until this moment, how wrong it was to hide it. The spontaneous and sustained applause of his listeners had drilled this knowledge home to his soul, and in silent prayer he thanked Heavenly Father and gave Him all credit. He knew where the music came from, and it wasn't from himself. Like all things of pure beauty, it was from God.

Tom and Linda drove them home that evening as they often did. Tom often didn't want them to leave, and they usually missed the last bus. As they pulled onto the highway, Linda sighed. She didn't often say much to the Elders. They were Tom's friends, and everyone in the car was surprised when she spoke directly to Sam.

"Elder Mahoy, I feel as if a miracle has happened before my eyes today. I'm not sure what it was. I mean, watching you touch a violin for the first time, then play it so beautifully just a few hours later, that was a miracle. But that's not what I mean. As I listened to you play, and saw the tears coming down your cheeks, I felt as if God were in the store with you. When you stopped, your face was glowing, and my chest was burning like it was on fire. I've never felt that before. I felt as if I wanted to laugh, and shout for joy, and cry, all at the same time. It was such a complex mixture of joy and yearning as I have never before felt, or imagined possible to feel.

"I want to know why your face was glowing tonight, and why my bosom was burning." Linda turned to face Tom. "I know we kind of have an understanding. They just come and play, and don't talk about their religion, but I simply must know. Tom, I want them to come to our house soon and answer this question. If you aren't interested, you can go to another room or something. I'm sorry, Tom, but I have to know what it was." Then, turning back to the Elders she asked, "Will you come teach me about this thing that happened tonight?"

It was Elder Tilley who broke the silence that followed. "Elder, what were you doing at the end of the music, while you were just standing there?"

Sam cleared his throat, embarrassed. "I was praying," he said silently.

"Why?" Linda asked impetuously.

"Honey, maybe its too personal," Tom interjected, but it was obvious that he wanted to know too.

"Sorry, I..."

"No. It's all right Linda. Really." Sam said softly, and smiled at her. She relaxed. "I guess the easiest way to explain it is that I have always been musical, and always embarrassed about it. I'm a big guy, and playing music isn't a thing big guys are supposed to do. So I never did, except for my baby brother who loved my music. I used to spend hours playing my flute for him. He would sit on my knee and I would play, and he would sing, mostly nonsense words, or ones he just made up. It was our connection I think. After my baby brother died, I never did play the flute again.

"Actually, except for my harmonica, and some church music, I hadn't played much until I walked into your store. I mean played from the soul, like tonight."

Tom nodded understanding, and Linda turned around to kneel in her seat so that she faced the Elders.

"Tonight, for a few minutes, I was back there at the funeral, playing that same music as I looked down into the casket. Back then, I laid my flute next to him in the casket and vowed I'd never play again. Tonight, I vowed I would play all I could to express my love to Heavenly Father. I think that's the miracle. I think, tonight, a part of me came back to life. In a small way, the musical part of my soul was reborn tonight. I was praying to thank Heavenly Father for that miracle."

Nobody spoke for the remainder of the drive. They pulled up to the boarding house. Sam was halfway out of the car when he paused, then sat back down. His heart burned within him. He didn't want to offend them, yet he knew what the Lord wanted him to say. He waited until peace swept over him.

"Tom. Linda. Tonight was a very special and spiritual experience for me, and you were an important part of it. Would it offend you if I said a prayer and thanked Heavenly Father for this blessing, and to thank him for your part in it?" They both shook their heads silently.

Sam bowed his head, and after a moment said. "Heavenly Father, I'm so sorry, that I hid behind my sorrow all these years. I know now that it was wrong. And I know that thou has brought Tom and Linda into my life to teach me this. I just want thee to know how grateful I am. Please bless Tom and Linda, and let them feel thy Holy Spirit as they drive home, so they will know how pleased Thou art with them for helping me understand thy blessings to me, and thy will for me. In the name of Jesus Christ, Amen."

March 6, 1974

We have continued to go to Tom and Linda's store three times a week. It has turned out to be a wonderful experience. We keep busy teaching all the rest of the week from appointments we make in the store. Since we started this, we haven't needed to do much tracting. Can't say I miss it. It wasn't very productive.

Tonight, Tom handed me a violin. I've never ever played one, but somehow, I was able to play it. It was as if I had played one all my life. I wasn't thinking about how to put my fingers on the strings. I was hearing the music in my soul, and causing it to come out of the violin. I have had similar experiences, like when I got my harmonica a few Christmases ago.

Something happened while I was playing. The Holy Spirit came over Linda and Tom, and touched something in their souls. I hadn't really thought of them as investigators, just friends. We will begin teaching them next Tuesday, after playing. I know they are ready for the Gospel. It will be a joy to teach them.

The hardest part of this evening was asking them to pray as we sat in the car. I felt my soul burning, and knew what to do, but for some reason, I was afraid to offend them. But, that feeling of peace flowed over me, and I did it. It was a wonderful experience. The Spirit was strong, and they felt it. I am learning to trust the promptings of the Holy Spirit. I honestly believe that in order to be a good missionary, I have to become totally obedient to the Holy Spirit, then I will be able to do His work, His way.

I think I learned something about missionary work tonight. We have been trying to influence people to listen to our message, and the ones we simply loved, and weren't even trying to influence, are the ones who the Lord has prepared.

I love missionary work. I love the Lord, and feel the power of His love as I speak to the people.

Tom and Linda's home was large and hidden deep in a lovely subdivision. Sam and Elder Tilley were impressed. Tom was proud, but brushed off their compliments. Linda beamed as she showed them around their place. The building was horseshoe shaped, with towers at both ends. A swimming pool was nestled in a lush court-yard formed by the house. It truly was impressive.

They suggested sitting around the dining room table for the discussion. Elder Tilley set up the flannel board and began the first discussion. Before Elder Tilley had finished the first concept, Tom seemed to grow restless, and Linda began frowning. Elder Tilley made his voice more sincere, and tried hard to teach with the Spirit. By the time it was Sam's turn, there was a strained feeling in the room.

Sam didn't pick up immediately with the next part of the lesson, but sat quietly, looking at his new friends. Elder Tilley assumed he had forgotten his part, and began with the second concept, but Sam interrupted him politely. Elder Tilley smiled and leaned back in his chair.

"Linda. Tom. I want to tell you about something I was taught by my family. Something very important to me, and I hope to you." They both nodded, and turned toward him.

"Ever since I was a little boy, I have had a very active conscience. You know, the voice that stops you from doing everything you thought was going to be fun?" They both laughed, and made comments about how well they understood.

"I didn't realize until my parents taught me, that that voice is the Light of Christ, coming from the Holy Spirit. Every person born into this world has a conscience, and knows the difference between right and wrong."

"Everyone?" Tom asked doubtfully.

"The scriptures say that every person born into the world has the Light of Christ. The important point here is that the Light of Christ comes from Christ, and is actually His voice in our soul. It is revelation to us."

"Wow," Linda said. "Are you sure? I mean, wouldn't that make us prophets or something? If we are receiving revelations?"

"In some ways, it does, or at least it can lead to that point. What do you think the reason is for Christ giving us this revelation?"

Elder Tilley cleared his throat. "Elder, would you like me take it from here?" He gave Sam a meaningful look which was to remind him that they were not supposed to deviate from the memorized discussions.

"Thanks. In a minute," Sam replied, his mind hardly registering his companion's words. "You both indicated that you had heard your conscience guide you in the past. Did you follow that guidance?"

"Sometimes I don't," Tom admitted. "I have always looked at my conscience as a nuisance, not as a guide."

Linda leaned on the table with her elbows, and put her chin in her hands. "I try to, but miss a lot of them I think. I try not to do anything real contrary to my conscience though."

"Why is that?" Sam asked.

"Well, because I always feel miserable when I disobey," Linda answered slowly.

"Could you say that in a positive way?"

"What? Oh, because I always feel good when I obey. Actually, that's true, but I had never thought of it before."

Sam nodded and asked, "Would it be a fair conclusion then to say that the purpose of the Light of Christ, our conscience, is to make us feel good, to make us happy?"

Tom straightened a bit and thought about the question. "I think that would be a fair statement, but it strikes me as being too simplistic. I get the feeling there has to be a larger purpose to anything God does, than just making us happy."

Elder Tilley put a flannel cutout of Joseph Smith on the flannel board, and began to speak. "Brother and Sister Snodgrass, as we were saying earlier, since all the apostles and prophets of Christ's time were killed by evil men, it became necessary for God to restore the things that were lost at their death. For this reason, in the spring of 1820, God again called a living prophet and he was fourteen years out. His name was Joseph Smith. Why do you think he called Joseph Smith to be a prophet?"

Linda looked impatient, and Tom smiled at Elder Tilley, who smiled back. "Elder Tilley, would you mind if Elder Mahoy finishes his thought before we get to Joseph Smith. I know about Mr. Smith and the gold bible, and frankly, I'm doubtful of the whole story. I want to know what Elder Mahoy is getting at. When he was talking to me my whole soul seemed to be on fire. When you started with Joseph Smith, the fire went out. I don't mean to be rude, but could you postpone your comments until Elder Mahoy is done?"

Elder Tilley's mouth was hanging open. "Oh, sure. Excuse me," he said graciously, but Sam could tell he was stunned. Sam wasn't sure quite what to say, so he relaxed for a few seconds. The Spirit touched him and he again knew what to say.

"The scriptures indicate that man was created for the very purpose of bringing joy to himself. But the type of joy the scriptures are speaking of isn't necessarily the type we might get from winning the lottery or finding a buried treasure. It's the type of happiness that comes to a person's soul when they finally enter into the Kingdom of God."

"So, what has that to do with the conscience," Tom asked, as if Sam still hadn't returned to the prior subject.

"If the ultimate object and outcome of God's plan for us is to make us happy, how would you expect to feel if you were on the correct course and successfully traveling toward that goal."

"Happy," they both said simultaneously. Linda added, "but happy in the sense that I felt happy as my bosom was burning after you played the violin. Happy in a deep, wonderful way."

"Exactly."

"No wonder I feel miserable, frustrated, and unhappy most of the time," Tom said loudly, only half joking. Linda jabbed him with an elbow, which he pretended really hurt.

"Every time we hear and obey our conscience, it brings us greater genuine happiness. Every time we disobey, we become more miserable."

"That's me." Tom said.

"It often takes courage to accept what our conscience tells us, because it's often contrary to our own will, even contrary to common sense at times. But if we know it is the voice of Christ, then we can be confident that obeying it will ultimately bring us great blessings, even if at the time we can't see how that could possibly be."

Tom leaned forward. "When we first met, I told you two you could come to my store any time, but to not talk to me about your religion. And you honored that request right up to the other night when you actually asked us to pray with you in the car. How did you know that wouldn't offend us and drive us away? Never mind. I know the answer."

Sam turned to Linda. "What is the answer to Tom's question?"

"You felt guided by the Holy Spirit, and because of your faith, you knew it wouldn't offend us."

"Not exactly. I felt guided, but I didn't know what your response would be. I only knew what the Lord wanted me to do. We seldom know the outcome of our obedience, only that it is what is right."

"I see." Linda pushed her long hair out of her face. "I can see why obedience may be scary, except for the faith one would develop through obedience."

"Tom, a minute ago you asked a question, then said you knew the answer. What did it feel like when you suddenly knew that answer."

"It felt sudden, complete, comfortable, as if I had known it all my life. I just knew it, that's all."

"And has it brought you happiness, has it been a blessing in your life yet? In other words, did that knowledge come from God?"

"I am certain it did. What you have already told me tonight is going to change the course of my life. I know what you are saying is true, and I have decided to live my life according to obedience. I don't know where it will take me, but I'm going to do it."

Linda slipped her hand into Tom's. "Me too. I know where Elder Mahoy would say it's going to take us. Back to God. Right?"

Sam ignored her question. She already knew the answer. Instead he said, "I want you both to listen with your hearts for a moment, not with your rational mind. I want you to feel, to listen to that still small voice, and after a moment, I am going to ask you to tell me what you feel. Elder Tilley, would you repeat what you started to say earlier about Joseph Smith?"

Elder Tilley was following every word, and smoothly flowed into the account of the first vision. He told the events as if he himself had been there, with wonder in his voice, and a sense of great joy. He told it as he never had before, and his heart soared as he recounted that holy visitation. When he was done telling, he knew even stronger than he had known before that it was true. He concluded and bore a powerful witness of its truthfulness, barely able to restrain his emotions.

Sam turned back to Tom. "Tom, what did you feel. You are a prophet, able to receive revelation. What did the Holy Spirit whisper to your soul as you listened to Elder Tilley?"

Tom cleared his voice and fidgeted in his seat. Linda placed a hand on his arm as tears pooled in his eyes. He looked at her, then Elder Tilley, then back to Sam. His voice was barely audible as he said, "I know its true."

Linda clapped a hand to her mouth in wonder and tears formed in her eyes. She gave Tom a hug, laying her head on his shoulder.

"Linda, would you like to add your feelings to Tom's?"

"I felt it too. It was like after the violin music. My heart felt like it was on fire. When Tom said it was true, I just knew with all my heart he was right."

"We are going to have a baptismal service exactly one month from today. Would you be willing to make the necessary preparations to participate in that service. Are you willing to commit your lives totally to obedience to the Lord, and be baptized in His church?"

They both nodded without hesitation, then turned to one another and kissed. For the briefest time, eternity paused, and a moment of joy was indelibly recorded in heaven.

March 23, 1974

    Brother and Sister Snodgrass committed to baptism tonight. It was a wonderful discussion, but it got me in trouble with Elder Tilley. I didn't feel that they needed to hear the first discussion, and when it was my turn, I taught them about the Holy Spirit, and how to discern truth. When we did give them the first vision, they accepted it. They wouldn't have otherwise.

    Anyway, Elder Tilley gave me the lecture about not deviating from the lessons, and following his lead as long as he was senior companion. I felt like asking him who I should obey, him, or the Lord, but I didn't. The important part is that Tom and Linda are committed to baptism. I hope we can teach them every time with the spirit. I have a feeling that they will not respond to the missionary lessons exactly as they are written. They seem offended when we start rattling off memorized words. In this, and in all other things, I will do as the Lord commands. It is my only hope, and my only joy.

After scripture study the next morning, Sam finished a pencil sketch he had begun three weeks earlier. The image was clear in his mind, and the paper received the image. Sketching was another thing that came easily to him, though he had never developed the talent past rudimentary art. He had found a piece of stiff white paper which worked perfectly. When he was finished, he showed Elder Tilley the sketch.

"I've seen this little girl before!" he said in surprise.

"It's the little girl at the first house I did the door approach to, three weeks ago. Remember?"

"Now I do. This is really good. It looks just like her. Why'd you draw a picture of her?"

"On our way to the tracting area, I'll show you." It was the only explanation he felt inclined to give. Elder Tilley accepted that, and they hiked off. They arrived at #355 about thirty minutes later. It was nearly 10:00 in the morning.

"This is going to turn out badly," he said as Sam led the way up the walk. He rang the doorbell, and waited. After a long time, the mother opened the door. Her eyes were ok, as if she had been sleeping. She gave a small sign of recognition, and a big sign of annoyance. She was not pleased to see them again, but didn't say anything.

Sam held out the picture without explanation, which she took after a slight hesitation. She studied his drawing with a dull expression, a smile tugged at her lips, then she looked back at him. She was a pretty woman, not a whole lot older than Sam. She had short dark hair and high cheek bones which gave her an almost noble appearance. Her lips were full and gave the impression of being willing to smile. Her eyes were a most startling brown, almost black.

"It's her birthday," he said. "I drew her a picture." He was beginning to agree with Elder Tilley, that this was going to go badly. He started to back up to leave, but felt a hand in the middle of his back. He stopped, thinking he was about to trip over Elder Tilley, but realized with a start that his companion was standing beside him, and had both arms folded across his chest. Yet the feeling had been very real. A sweet peace settled over him and he knew he should not leave until the Lord had finished whatever it was they were there to do.

A tear trickled from the mother's eye, and she held the picture to her heart. Her lips said 'Thank you' but no sound came out.

Sam was not sure what to do, and was grateful when Elder Tilley said:

"Is there something we can do? Is everything all right?"

She shook her head, and Sam wasn't sure which question she was answering. Perhaps both of them.

Sam said, "Ma'am, is something wrong with your daughter? I'd like to help if I can." Instead of answering she stepped back, and motioned for them to enter. The living room was small and dark. It had a brightly polished hardwood floor, and worn, but functional furniture. They found a seat on the sofa. After closing the door, she took a seat in a big chair which groaned as she sat in it. A few more tears coursed down her face before she said.

"Juanita is ill. She has a blood disease. The doctors didn't expect it to advance as quickly as it has. There's nothing they can do for her…I'm afraid…" Just at that moment a young man walked into the room from the back of the house. He was tall and blond. Sam thought he looked like someone had peeled him off of a poster of California surfers. He walked into the room to stand beside his wife, a look of displeasure on his face. Sam could almost hear him thinking: 'What are these Mormons doing in my house?"

"Sean, these are Mormon missionaries. I'm sorry, I don't know your names."

Elder Tilley introduced himself and Sam. Their names were Connie and Sean Van Dangen.

"Look, Elder Mahoy drew a picture of Juanita," she held the picture up for Sean to see. The hard expression on his face softened. "It's a birthday present for her…" she added, but her voice trailed off. A look of concern and question crossed her face.

"She's sleeping. I gave her another pill," he said in answer to her unspoken concern. He turned to Sam. "It's a beautiful picture. Her birthday's actually two more days away, but I'll give it to her…" Sam heard the rest in his soul. 'If she lives that long."

His heart began to ache, and he remembered the pain of Jimmy's dying. He remembered those two long weeks when he was unconscious, and they all hoped against hope that he would live, and yet somehow knew he would not. His heart began to break, and without realizing it, he bowed his head. He understood their pain perfectly, and it was more than he could bear to see them going through it. Tears began to fall onto his hands. After a moment he realized he was weeping and wiped his eyes. He realized with a start that everyone was watching them.

"Excuse me," he mumbled. "My little brother died when he was two, and I remember the waiting and the wishing and the unbearable hopelessness at times. I guess I know a little bit of how you feel and it...breaks my heart, I guess. Forgive me."

There was a moment of silence, then Sean and Connie exchanged glances. He had seen his Mom and dad do the same thing, and knew they had silently arrived at a decision.

Connie stood, and asked. "Elders, would you like some Roi bush tea? I know you don't drink regular tea, but I heard you did drink Roi bush." They accepted and she disappeared into the kitchen.

Sean cleared his throat. "Please forgive me for being rude earlier. I didn't mean to be inhospitable, its just that this is a very hard time, and we weren't wanting to get tangled up in religious arguments right now. You see, I'm studying at the seminary to become an Anglican minister. My Father is an Anglican minister. So, you would kind of be wasting your breath. I probably know more about Mormonism than you do." He said all this in a subdued but haughty tone.

"Connie already said you weren't interested, and we respect that. I just wanted to give Juanita a birthday gift. I have a little sister, and she reminds me of her. When I saw Juanita the first time, I guess it made me homesick. We'll be going soon and won't bother you again."

At that moment Connie returned with a tray. "Please don't misinterpret our words. We do missionary work ourselves, and know how hard it can be. And I appreciate the beautiful picture you drew, and your remembering. Its just that we are very comfortable with our lives and happy with our involvement in our church. We were just not in the mood to have a religious debate at this time. Perhaps sometime later, after..." her voice caught, and she busied herself with the tea.

Sam sipped the tea. She had brewed it very lightly, and the delicate sent seemed to echo her fragile feelings.

Unexpectedly, it was Sean who broke the silence. His voice was searching, almost reverent. "You said your brother died when he was two years old. Did he have a disease too?"

"No. He drowned in an irrigation ditch. We didn't find him until he had been dead for over an hour."

"I'll bet your parents were devastated," Connie commented. "But you said you waited and felt hopeless at times. Why was that?"

Sam's mind tumbled about, groping for the right way to explain what had happened. He couldn't think of a way to explain it without interjecting his faith into the explanation.

"My mother pulled Jimmy from the irrigation ditch. She and my dad gave him artificial respiration for over an hour. After all that, he still was not breathing, and my mother asked a neighbor friend, a man who was an Elder in the church, to give Jimmy a blessing. Immediately after that, he took a breath."

"Oh!" Connie said. "Then he lived?"

"He lived for exactly two weeks. During that time he was in a coma, but his body seemed normal. One evening my mom and dad were holding his hands, and he opened his eyes, and told my mom he loved her. When he said that, my mom knew he would be leaving. Shortly thereafter, he passed away."

"Why do you suppose the blessing didn't work to keep him alive? It seems odd that it only worked for two weeks," Sean commented, a little harshly.

"We knew Heavenly Father wanted Jimmy to come home to Him, because he could have let him stay. There was nothing wrong with his body. He didn't die because of the drowning. He just went home to be with Heavenly Father. I think he let Jimmy live the extra two weeks to soften the blow to my family."

"Suppose it wasn't the blessing at all, suppose it was that the artificial respiration finally worked, and the blessing had nothing to do with it? I find it hard to believe that such miracles even happen in this day and age, and even harder to swallow that a Mormon Elder has any power to order the dead back to life. I don't mean to be heartless, but the whole thing is preposterous." Sean folded his arms across his chest and awaited Sam's reply.

Sam was amazed that Sean could doubt such a blessing from Heavenly Father. It had never occurred to him that Jimmy's coming back to life might be anything other than a miracle, wrought by the hand of God. His mind reeled at the suggestion that it was anything else.

When Sean saw that Sam did not have an answer he continued with a little more fervor. "Furthermore, I think it's cruel of any religion to teach their members that miracles can happen if their faith is strong enough. When the miracles don't occur, it makes them think God doesn't love them, or their faith is too weak. It cheats them out of true faith, which is to get them to believe in Christ."

Elder Tilley bridled a bit and leaned forward. "But Christ and his apostles worked miracles. If they occurred in the primitive church, is there any reason they shouldn't happen in today's church? If they had the power, shouldn't Christ's church today have that same power?"

"Miracles were given in olden times to proclaim Christ and to establish the truth of Christianity. It was not given to divert their minds from their faith in Christ, to faith in miracles. Today, we are only required to have faith in Christ. The miracles have already testified of Christ and have ceased. They would serve no purpose in our lives today."

"But..." Elder Tilley began, however Sam cut him off with a slight wave of his hand.

"Sean, I didn't come here to interfere with your faith, or to tell you about my little brother. I came because I felt impressed to draw a picture of your beautiful little daughter. My faith, my beliefs, my perspective on these things is different from yours. I wish you well, and with your permission, I will pray for Juanita." He set his teacup aside and stood. Elder Tilley followed.

They were standing on the front porch when the spirit moved within him. His face flushed and his heart pounded. But the peace came, and he knew what he must say. He turned to Sean. "I know there is a power which can heal your daughter. I hold that power, and my faith is strong enough to use it to that end. However, it isn't my faith which is the determining factor. It's yours." He shook both their hands, and left before another word was uttered. He heard their door slam as they walked down the sidewalk.

March 29, 1974

Today we met with Juanita's parents, Connie and Sean Van Dangen. They are fine people, but Sean is very rigid. I drew them a picture of their daughter who is dying. I felt very strongly that Heavenly Father would allow us to heal her with the priesthood, but not until her parents have more faith. I believe that Sean was right to some extent about miracles. Miracles are seldom given as a witness, they more often come as a confirmation of faith than a source of it.

That same evening I prayed with great strivings for Heavenly Father to allow us to use the holy Priesthood to heal their daughter. I was startled when the Spirit plainly said that I could not. It further said that such a blessing would work as a condemnation to their souls, because they would reject it. I was stunned, but felt immediately impressed to ask Heavenly Father to allow us to heal their daughter in such a way that it would not be a witness to the parents. I heard nothing but silence from the heavens after that.

Something else is happening, Elder Tilley is beginning to keep quiet around me. We don't laugh and chat about simple things any more. I can't tell if he resents me, or if he's angry, or what. I try so hard to do what is right and to be obedient to the voice of the Lord, I don't think he under-

stands that. I sometimes feel like he misinterprets my yearnings for obedience, as a form of arrogance, or phoniness.

Tonight I was reading in Mosiah 5, about how King Benjamin's people were born again following his great discourse. I have decided to seek the rebirth. It came to me very strongly that the key to the rebirth is obedience. They made a covenant to be obedient in all things in verse 5, and because of that covenant, they were changed. I want to have this mighty change in order to serve the Lord with greater power.

Three days before the Snodgrass's baptism, the zone leaders unexpectedly showed up at Sam and Elder Tilley's boarding house. The zone leader's went with them to their appointments. Sam and Elder Coleman, the senior zone leader, went together. That evening they taught Tom and Linda the sixth discussion. The lesson began well, and the spirit was there, but it was rigid and given word for word from the memorized discussions. He felt apologetic, and Tom and Linda wondered what had changed. They were used to a more free flowing, spiritual experience with he and Elder Tilley. About half way through the lesson, Sam could stand it no longer, and following a question by Tom, began explaining the plan of salvation. He was interrupted by the zone leader, who returned to the sixth discussion. Sam waited patiently, then returned to their discussion of the degrees of glory. Tom had a particular question about his parents, and where they would be going after this life. They were not members of the church, and he was troubled.

For a few moments Sam wondered if Elder Coleman would chastise him in front of his investigators or insist on returning to the memorized text, but he did not. When it became apparent that the discussion was permanently derailed, Elder Coleman relaxed, and in time made several moving comments about the plan of salvation and told of an experience he had had when his grandmother had died. She wasn't a member either, but he had felt strongly that she would accept the gospel in the Spirit World. The Spirit was strong and testified to all present. In the end, they reconfirmed their determination to be baptized this Friday, just three days away.

Once they had regrouped at their boarding house, the four of them knelt in prayer and thanked Heavenly Father for the blessings of the day. Without warning, Elder Colemen announced that Sam was being transferred to Germiston, a suburb of Johannesburg. He was to leave that evening, that very moment as a matter of fact.

A thousand thoughts assailed him simultaneously, not the least of these was that he would not attend Tom and Linda's baptism. Second among these was that he would not be able to speak to them before he left, to wish them goodbye, to bear his testimony one more time, to play music one more time with Tom. It was heartbreaking, and tears welled up in his eyes. They were just at Tom and Linda's a short time ago, and he had not been allowed to say goodbye. It didn't seem fair. He started to ask the very questions now beleaguering his soul, but was cut short.

As Elder Coleman answered he seemed twelve feet tall, and Sam felt like a child again. He simply said, "its not my decision, nor within my power to change."

Sam and Elder Coleman loaded his things into the VW bug, and drove the short distance to the main road. No sooner had they come to a complete stop, than Sam suddenly straightened in his seat. He looked around, as if lost, then a look of determination came over his face.

"Elder Coleman, we need to turn around."

"Did you forget something at the boarding?"

"No. We have to go visit an investigator."

"Elder Tilley can handle that. It's in his hands now. Relax. He's a good Elder," the Zone Leader replied, and started out onto the street.

Sam grabbed the emergency brake handle between the seats and slammed it on. The car skidded to a stop. The zone leader turned to him with anger on his face.

"Look, Elder Mahoy, I'm the zone leader, and I have instructions. What you did was dangerous, and rebellious. Now let go of the emergency brake, and let's get going. We have a good hour's drive ahead of us."

"Elder Coleman, as we were sitting at the stop sign, I felt the Spirit come over me and whisper that we needed to go give a little girl a blessing. It's someone we met tracting. We haven't even given them a lesson yet, and I don't understand why we have to do it now. But I'm afraid if we don't, the little girl will die. This is not something I thought up, it's what the Lord wants us to do. Please."

The zone leader pondered this for a moment, then closed his eyes. "OK. We're here to serve the people. The transfer can wait. Now release the brake?"

Sam smiled, and released the brake. They made a 'U' turn, and Sam directed them to their tracting area. As they turned the corner toward #355, Sam was startled to see flashing lights. An ambulance was parked in the street outside the house. A half dozen other cars lined the street. Several of them were big Mercedes, and other expensive cars. They quickly parked and hurried to the gate. A team of white coated men were carrying a stretcher into the house. They didn't seem to be in any hurry. Sam and Elder Coleman followed. A large, black woman sat on the front steps, rocking back and forth, mourning loudly, every once in a while breaking into mournful singing in her native tongue. Once inside, the small house was packed with weeping people. Sam noticed that two of them wore ministerial collars and were obviously consoling the people. One of those with the collar was Sean.

Sam quickly made his way toward Connie and Sean. As soon as Connie saw him coming, she broke away from her husband and made her way toward them through the press of people. Her face held a mixture of grief, and frustration. It was almost as if she were angry at Sam.

"Where have you been? You gave me hope, and I prayed and I knew that your words were true, but you didn't leave your name, your phone number, your address. For weeks I have hunted, watched every day for you to walk past, waited..." She buried her face in her hands, and sobbed. Sam was grief stricken. He had not considered the possibility that they might try to contact him. He was just waiting for the Holy Spirit to direct him back to them. He wanted to scream, to explain, to beg forgiveness, but she calmed herself.

"It isn't your fault, of course. I'm sorry. I'm not thinking clearly right now." She waved her hand weakly, as if brushing away the whole affair. At that moment, Sean came to her, and put his arm around her trembling shoulder. He nodded toward the Elders, but said nothing.

Sam introduced Elder Coleman who shook their hands. Sean introduced his father, a senior minister in the Anglican Church. They also shook hands.

"Please, tell me what has happened," Sam asked. By this time, the crowd had fallen silent, and everyone in the room had turned toward them.

Connie shrugged. "There's not much to tell. My baby just kept getting worse and worse. Tonight, about six o'clock, she...she...stopped breathing." She sobbed once then recovered enough to continue. "The doctor came, and pronounced her..." She couldn't bring herself to say it. Tears flowed down her cheeks, and she looked directly into Sam's eyes. Her lips formed the words, "If only you had come sooner," but no sound escaped her lips.

It was Sean who spoke next. "Elders, thanks for coming. But this isn't a good time, as you can see. I'll have to ask you to excuse us." Sam felt Elder Coleman put a hand on his shoulder, and he started to leave, but again, felt as if someone had put a hand in the middle of his back. This time, he did not try to figure out who it was.

"Can I see her, just for a moment? Then we'll go." Sean opened his mouth to object, but before he could, Connie was nodding and taking him by the arm. She led him a short distance to a small bedroom and opened the door. The room was painted pink, with ruffled curtains and bedspread. In the corner stood a pink crib, its side lowered. Inside, a small form laid perfectly still.

Sam stopped in the doorway and turned to Connie. "Would it be all right if just you and I went in? She nodded, and pushed the door closed in the faces of her husband and Elder Coleman, both of whom were voicing protests.

Once inside, Sam turned to Connie. She looked into his face, tears streaking down her own. "I believed," she said. "For a while, I believed what you said, about your little brother, about the power to heal. I believed it with all my heart. But my faith was weak, and I'm afraid its gone now, my baby's gone now."

A feeling of calm flowed over Sam, even still, he struggled to find consoling words to tell her. He opened his mouth to speak comfort to her, to tell her about how little children are saved by the atonement of Christ, to tell her of the better place her daughter had gone, but that was not what came out. "She isn't dead, Connie. Just sleeping. I have come to awaken her."

They both started at his words, Sam as much as she. Connie took a step back, and looked from him, to the crib. She put a hand to her mouth, as if she would cry out, and then lowered it. Slowly she nodded, and smiled. A feeling of peace came over him, and he walked to the crib. He looked down at the innocent little face and felt tears of gratitude forming in his eyes. Slowly, he reached out and brushed golden hair from her face.

"Juanita. In the name of Jesus Christ, and by virtue of the Holy Melchizedek Priesthood, and according to His divine mercy, I call you back. Juanita, come back to your mother. Amen." He lifted his hands from the small head, and when the tiny eyes remained closed, he felt the calm flow even stronger. He took a step back, and placed his hand on Connie's arm. Connie looked at him, a struggle of faith manifesting itself on her face. Yet she looked down at her baby, and smiled. Still, still as death, she laid there, not moving.

Sam turned her toward him, and spoke the words that formed in his heart. "Go tell them. Go tell the others she was only sleeping." Connie's face remained blank. Finally, she smiled weakly and nodded. She looked one more time at her baby, and left the room, pulling the door behind her. As soon as it closed, Sam fell to his knees, praying earnestly. Not for the still form before him, but for her mother. Tears cascaded down his face, and he waited, praying in mighty strivings such as his soul had never before called upon. It seemed as if a silence passed over the room beyond the door, and he heard, as if he stood inches away, Connie's voice explain. "She was…" then a long pause. "She was…only sleeping." A murmur of disbelief arose, and he heard footsteps coming toward the door.

He quickly stood, and on impulse, reached into the crib, and lifted the limp form into his arms. He was just turning as Sean burst into the room, a look of shock, anger, and disbelief on his face. His fists were balled, and he came toward Sam with violence written on his features. Connie made her way around him, and came to Sam.

He leaned forward and gave her his precious bundle. As he did so, a small arm looped around her neck, and a sleepy little voice said, "Mama, why did you wake me up? I was sleeping."

A cry of astonishment came from everyone except Sam and Connie. The word was quickly passed until all knew, she was only sleeping. As quickly as warmth follows sunshine, sweet relief and joy swept through the house. Connie and Sean were swept into the living room. Someone began singing, and a baby's voice laughed in the distance. Sam, again alone in the small room, fell to his knees, gratitude filling his soul to overflowing. After a moment, he felt a hand on his shoulder and looked up to see Connie, a look of solemnity on her face.

"Thank you," she said, her voice faltering, tears of joy coming to her eyes.

Sam stood, and said "To Heavenly Father, she was only sleeping." Connie nodded, a look of partial understanding in her red eyes. Sam joined Elder Coleman, who was waiting patiently in the hall. He smiled at Sam. Even he thought the child was only sleeping, and Sam felt no need to tell him otherwise. They departed without further comment. Everyone was too happy to notice them leave.

April 1, 1974

April fools day! I've been transferred. On the way out of town, we stopped and gave a little girl a blessing. The veil between life and death is very thin. Heavenly Father saw fit to honor her Mother's faith, and awaken her from that sleep which is unending. It was a precious experience, and one I would not have had, had I not been obedient to the still small voice. Everyone besides her mother and myself, believes the child was only sleeping. Miracles are not given to testify, only to bless those who believe.

It is interesting that Heavenly Father honored her faith, yet I doubt she associates this miracle with His true church. Perhaps in time she will come to an understanding of what truly happened tonight. What an interesting April Fools experience. Everyone in that house witnessed a miracle, and all were fooled so as to not recognize it.

Yet, this is what I requested, I realize now. I asked Heavenly Father to allow me to heal this child without it being a condemning witness to the child's parents. What a sweet, sweet blessing it is. I marvel at His mercy, His love and gentle kindness. With all my soul I thank Him for allowing me this precious blessing.

It is three days before Tom and Linda's baptism. I hate missing it. I didn't even get to say goodbye. I hope Elder Tilley can make them understand. I love them, and will miss them. I don't even have their mailing address. I never thought to ask them. Elder Tilley promised he would write me and tell me about their baptism, and give me their address. I will miss playing music with Tom, and Elder Tilley will have to go back to tracting. What a waste of time. Tom and Linda have had a marvelous effect on my life, and I hope, I on theirs.

I am going to Germiston, about an hour outside of Johannesburg. I will be junior companion to a South African Elder named Elder Beesler. I don't know too much about him, but hear he is a goof off. The one thing I could not bear, would be wasting this precious time. There is too much to do, too many miracles to work, too many wonderful souls who need the Gospel. My soul feels on fire, and my every thought is to bring glory, and honor, and souls unto the Lord. Blessed be His name!

eight

Bars and Stripes

Sam and Elder Coleman arrived at the mission home late that evening and spent the night there. The next morning he was asked into the office to speak with President Carlson.

"Elder Mahoy, my boy, how are you? How did you like Pretoria?"

"President, I was transferred three days before a baptism. I loved Pretoria, but feel devastated about missing their baptism. I could have spent the rest of my mission there and done a wonderful work."

President frowned, then noted, "I'm sorry, but this transfer was urgent. I have had to send a missionary home, and needed a strong Elder to put in his place. The Lord needed you in Germiston, more than your investigators needed you at their baptism."

Sam considered this, then nodded. He was willing to go anywhere, but it helped to understand why. "What should I know about where I'm going?"

"Your new companion, Elder Beesler, is a good missionary, but he's had bad examples. He and his last companion, the Elder I just sent home, got into some trouble. Bad trouble. Elder Beesler was only partly involved, but he is on a short leash. I need someone I can trust to not be sucked into his ways. I have to send him a junior companion because he's already a senior. So you can see why I needed you. I trust you to do what is right no matter what."

"It doesn't sound easy. President, I just want to do missionary work. I don't want to have to fight my companion to get it done. It shouldn't be that way."

"No, it shouldn't. But sometimes the reality of things isn't as perfect as our image of them. I know this will be difficult, but after much prayer and fasting, I am confident you are the right one for this assignment. If you can't influence Elder Beesler, then I'm afraid he will be sent home too. It would be a tragedy I hope to avoid. Will you accept the call?"

"Accept? Do I have a choice? Don't answer that. I don't want to know. I'll do as you say. I hope I don't let you down."

President smiled, and stood from behind the big ornate desk. "I appreciate your faithfulness. There is something else I wish to discuss with you. I have had many reports regarding you. It seems that you have a hard time sticking with the memorized discussions in spite of our instructions to do so."

Sam had no idea this was coming, and was dumbfounded for a moment. He started to reply, then decided there was no point in defending his position. Instead he simply said, "Its true. I do deviate sometimes when I feel like the people need to hear something different. I don't know what else to do."

"And how do your investigators feel about this? How do they respond?"

"Well, when I say the things the Holy Spirit wants me to say, it always works out well. Sometimes, what the Holy Spirit wants them to hear is the discussions, sometimes not."

"And how do you tell the difference?" President Carlson sat on the edge of the desk.

"I listen. When I'm in tune, I just listen, and once I know what to do, I try to have the courage to just do it."

"I see." President Carlson stood, and walked to the bookshelves which covered the walls on three sides. He opened a leaded glass door, and motioned to the books inside. "I love books. You may not know that I have a law degree and have read extensively on almost every subject you can name, and some you couldn't name, I imagine. When I first came to this office and saw all these books, I spent days reading titles and marveling at the value of what is sitting on these shelves. Almost every book in this room is priceless. I couldn't afford more than two or three of them if I sold everything I own. It's almost unbelievable to see such a marvelous collection in one room. Yet I imagine that few people who enter this room recognize their worth."

He pulled a book from the shelf. It was bound in rich leather and had gold lettering on the side. "This is a first edition copy of Charles Dickens' Oliver Twist." He opened the book, and tipped it so Sam could see the signature inside. "It's signed by Dickens. It's exceedingly rare and fantastically valuable." He slid the book back into place and closed the door. "Yet in an eternal sense, its worthless. It has almost no redeeming value."

He picked up a paperback copy of the Book of Mormon from his desk. "This book sells for about two dollars and is almost worthless by worldly standards. Yet it has been the instrument of bringing millions of souls to Christ. It's value is impossible to overstate. It's the most perfect of any book written, yet was not a part of this collection of valuable books. I have purchased a leather bound edition of the Book of Mormon, and when I leave, it will be a part of this collection.

If I could, I would get Mormon or Moroni to sign it. The difference between these priceless books and this perfect one, is this book was written under the influence of the Holy Ghost."

Again he sat on the corner of the desk. "Missionaries are like these books. They are all of great worth and precious to the Lord. Even that Elder I sent home today is precious. Yet some of them are not inspired, and to the extent that they are not, their value is not great in missionary work. By my earlier comments, you may have thought I was upset by your deviating from the memorized discussions." Sam nodded. "I just wanted to ascertain that your deviations were being inspired by the Holy Spirit. I am comfortable that they are."

"What I'm going to tell you now, you must keep to yourself, because others would not understand what I'm going to say. The memorized lesson plan is inspired, yet it's not a substitute for inspiration. We have them to guide us until the Holy Spirit chooses to take over. When that happens, we teach by the Spirit. Until it happens, we teach by the book. Unfortunately, some Elders never reach beyond the book. This is my instruction to you, just to you. Its not instruction to the whole mission, and I urge you to accept it as such. You have my full and complete approval to teach whatever the Spirit directs, as long as it is the Spirit. Just be certain that you are responding to the Spirit, and all will be well, and you will serve a great mission for the Lord."

"President," Sam said as soon as it became obvious President had finished. "I am relieved. I promise I will make every effort to ensure that all I say is under the direction of the Holy Spirit. You can't believe how relieved I am to know that what I knew was right, is acceptable to you, and to the Lord. It causes my heart to rejoice."

"It causes my soul to rejoice to have such a faithful young man serving with me in this great missionary work. God bless you Elder," he said as he stood. They shook hands, and then embraced.

Not many minutes later he met Elder Beesler, and they began the long drive to Germaston. While Sam was a large individual, Elder Beesler was even larger. He was the first missionary Sam had seen whom he knew could twist him into a pretzel. The part which caused him even greater wonder, was that he was sure Elder Beesler would enjoy doing it.

"Elder Mahoy," his new companion began shortly after they had gotten into the car. "I have to admit that today has been a shock. When President Carlson called me into the mission home, I thought he was going to make me a district leader out in Germiston. Now I find out that I'm in trouble because my companion got sent home. Well all I did was follow my senior companion, just like I was supposed to. When my companion was going to bed with that girl, I sat in the front room, and did nothing. I kept my nose clean, and I thought President was going to make me district leader. What good did it do me? Now I'm in disrepute, and I'll never be a DL. All I wanted was a chance to show everyone that I could be as good a DL as any one of you Americans. You guys come over here so smug and so self righteous, thinking you know everything. Well we South Africans should be the district leaders, and Zone Leaders, and now its not going to happen.

"How many people have you baptized Elder?" He didn't pause for Sam to answer, even had Sam been willing to answer such a preposterous question. "Well I've baptized twelve. Twelve people have come into the church because of me. And what do I get for it? I get accused of being lazy, and told I'll never make mission leadership.

"Now I don't even want to finish this miserable mission. And here you are to dog me, and make sure I don't do anything wrong." He paused for a moment, but Sam didn't interrupt the silence.

"I want you to know that I hate your guts, and nothing you do is going to change me. If President Carlson would not have lied to me, I would have felt differently. But nothing is going to stop me from enjoying the rest of my mission. I am going to be a missionary, and not do anything to get sent home, but you can bloody well bet I'm not going to be kissing President Carlson's ass, and certainly not yours. So keep your holier-than-thou bullshit to your flaming self."

Sam's head was swimming. Elder Beesler sneered at him, and jammed his foot onto the accelerator. They zipped past other cars and swerved dangerously into oncoming traffic. Elder Beesler made an obvious show of getting within inches of cars he was passing so the other motorists would jerk away from them. Each time, Beesler gave Sam a glaring, 'I dare you to say something,' look. Not very many minutes later flashing lights appeared behind them, and a police officer pulled them over.

Elder Beesler swore in Afrikaans as he pulled over, but spoke calmly and rapidly to the policeman in Afrikaans, mentioning his name, and Sam's several times. Sam had difficulty following the conversation.

The following morning, they went to court and waited and waited. The court room was a large theater-like room, with the judge, prosecutors, and attorneys on a low stage in front of stair-stepped seats. The judge sat behind a raised pulpit, where he could look down on everyone in his court. He wore an elaborate black robe. It reminded Sam of an old-time courtroom in England. The only thing that was missing was the white, powdered wig.

The prosecuting attorney just wore a simple black robe, but seemed to have great authority in court. He directed everything, telling people what they could say or do. He often became belligerent or insulting, and would occasionally turn to the judge and make sarcastic observations about the witness. The judge seemed to have almost no control over what occurred in the court room, except to render judgment after evidence had been laid out. At times, the prosecutor appeared to give legal advice to the person on trial, even making suggestions on what to do. It was all very different from the Perry Mason movies Sam remembered. What was more amazing was how swiftly they did things. Usually the judge formed his opinion quickly, often banging down the gavel and pronouncing judgment in the middle of someone's testimony.

Sam watched as dozens of people were brought before the judge. The trials were conducted in Afrikaans. Late in the day Elder Beesler was finally called to testify. He spoke in Afrikaans, periodically pointing back at Sam. Sam could barely tell what was happening. After a long time, they called him to the stand and began to question him in Afrikaans. He asked them to switch to English, which they did.

The prosecutor spoke very good English, though with a heavy accent. It made him sound British, but with a guttural overtone. He dropped r's on the end of words, and rolled r's amid word. Words which ended in 'uh' were pronounced 'er'. America would have come out Amerrricer, with the rrr being rolled like a child making a engine noise for his toy truck.

"You are accused of speeding, dangerous driving, and evading arrest. How do you plead?" the prosecutor in the long, black robe said with his heavy accent, obviously annoyed that Sam did not speak Afrikaans.

Sam was mystified. "I, I wasn't driving. I was the passenger. Elder Beesler was driving…"

The prosecutor laughed, and exchanged a knowing look with the judge. "So you were the passenger?"

"Yes, sir."

He produced the ticket and pointed to the signature. "Is this your name?"

Sam studied the signature, and was surprised to see his name on the ticket. "That's my name, but its not my signature."

The prosecutor smiled and took back the ticket. "Do you have another piece of identification with your signature on it?"

Sam thought for a moment. "No sir. I don't. Not on me."

"That's what you told the officer too. The citing officer asked for your license, and you said you were from America and didn't have any on you. Mister Beesler, who is a citizen of South Afrrrica..." He pronounced it 'Off-rrre-kuh' with heavy accent on 'Off'. "...has told us that you were, in fact, driving the car. Why are you lying about it?"

"I'm not lying. I wasn't driving. I haven't driven a car in South Africa yet. You drive on the wrong side of the road, and I..."

"Why would he lie about driving the car?" the prosecutor demanded.

"He was angry at me or just angry at the world, and was driving like an idiot to try to scare me."

The prosecutor spoke to the judge in Afrikaans, and the judge banged the gavel. "Guilty," he said in a very heavy accent. "I sentence you to the fine of two hundrrred rrrand."

Sam sputtered. "I'm not guilty! I don't have two hundred rand!"

"Then twenty lashes, and ten days in jail." He banged the gavel again, and an armed guard took Sam by the arm. He caught sight of Elder Beesler, who sneered at him, turned, and left the room.

They took him to a hall, down a flight of stairs, and to a small room with concrete walls. There, they took everything from him, including his shoes, socks, belt, shirt and tie. When they were done he only had his pants left. They took him down a flight of stairs to a small room. They quickly clamped his hands to the wall and his ankles to the floor. He was facing the wall, with his feet behind him so he had to lean against the wall awkwardly on his elbows. Someone fumbled with his snap, and pulled his pants and underwear to the floor. He was too terrified to protest. He had no idea what was going on. For a moment he thought they were going to rape him. A stiff canvas was unrolled from near the ceiling until it covered his entire backside. The canvas smelled of sweat, and blood.

Nothing happened for several moments. He could hear people moving around in the room. A man's voice whispered, then another laughed. Suddenly, he heard a whistling sound, and something exploded across his back. He had never felt such incredible pain. If felt as if someone had hit him with a sword and severed his body several inches deep. Someone said "twenty" in Afrikaans. Again the whistling sound, and the pain exploded a little lower. His legs buckled as he lost all feeling except the horrendous pain in his buttocks. He became aware of his wrists nearly breaking off in the manacles, and struggled to stand just as another blow struck near his shoulders. "eighteen," the voice said. Just as the feeling began to return from the first blow, another landed atop it. This time his scream drowned out the "seventeen," He felt his mind retreating further inside with each blow. Each blow seemed to land in a new spot between his knees and neck.

With a start, he heard the voice say "six," and he suddenly realized that he had passed out. He wished for oblivion to return as the lash whistled again. It seemed as if the moment lasted forever, the screaming of the whip, and the agony of knowing it was going to flail his flesh, and the terror of not knowing where it would hit. When it struck, it landed just above his waist and wrapped around his body, so that the greatest force of the blow landed on his side. The force of the blow caused his feet to slip, and he fell against the wall. He tried to stand, yet his feet slid again on something wet. He looked down and was surprised to see a puddle of water, and realized he had lost control of himself. The humiliation was almost greater than the pain, and he cried out even before the lash landed again. By the time the voice said "one" his body and soul were in agony. His legs refused to support him, and he hung helplessy by his wrists. What seemed like hours later, but was in fact just a few moments, they undid his shackles. Two guards held him, or he would have crumpled to the floor in his own urine.

They helped him stand, and pulled his pants back up. He heard someone scream, and was startled to realize he had done it. It had sounded as if it came from someone else. Each step caused his wounds to rub against his clothing, and his mind refused to move his legs, even when he ordered them to take a step. They half drug him to a cell, and laid him face down on the cot. They were surprisingly careful with him, considering they had just flogged him. A moment later a man in a white smock came in and rubbed an ointment on his back and legs. He explained something matter-of-factly in Afrikaans, which Sam could not understand. He wondered at the dichotomy; how they could be brutal, then passionless, even sympathetic seconds later. He sensed that it was just their job, and knew that they would have just as emotionlessly executed him had they been instructed to.

There were no windows, and the room smelled thickly of disinfectant. The cot was hard, and the only blanket was thin, but clean. He alternately felt feverish and freezing cold. He had felt this way before, and knew that he was slipping into shock. He focused his thoughts on prayer, and felt a gentle peace come over him for a while, but his mind could not ignore the pain for long. His back felt on fire, and he feared his clothing would stick to the wounds and become infected. Struggling to the toilet was further torture, and sitting was beyond agony. The toilet in his room had no seat on it, only the porcelain fixture, and only cold water in the sink. In spite of any prayer he could utter, he fell into despair, and finally into a tormented sleep.

The following day no one spoke to him, or brought him any food. It was nearly noon before someone appeared. It took him a second to recognize the prosecuting attorney without his robes. He spoke to him through the bars. Sam struggled, and finally managed to stand up. His back no longer felt aflame, but felt as if every muscle had been stripped from his skeleton, then carelessly replaced in all the wrong places.

He tried to understand, but finally said in his best Afrikaans.

"I am much sorry. I don't speak Afrikaans very much well enough, not. Could you please speak English, please."

"That's what I thought," the man said in English, and motioned to an armed guard whom Sam hadn't noticed. "You don't speak Afrikaans, do you?" he said, as the guard unlocked the bars.

"Well, I have been learning, but I'm afraid most people speak too fast for me to catch everything." Sam stumbled into the hallway and the jailer slammed the door shut.

The attorney gave him a sympathetic look, almost an apology, but not quite. "Last night," the attorney said, "as I was going to sleep, something was bothering me about your conviction. I woke up in the middle of the night and knew what it was. I know the officer who cited you, and he does not speak English. Not even a little bit. This morning I called him, and he said you spoke excellent Afrikaans, and described you. The description could have fit you, or the other man with you, but you don't speak Afrikaans, and he does."

"I wasn't driving the car," Sam said, hope rising in his heart.

"I believe you. Why didn't you say something when he was accusing you?"

Sam struggled to think that far back, it seemed a century ago. "He said it all in Afrikaans. I had no idea…"

"Yes. Of course. I should have seen that. Well, I can get the charges dropped. I have to apologize for the lashes," he said at last. "It's very unusual to sentence someone to lashes for a traffic violation, but perfectly legal. The judge was angry because you were, or at least at the time appeared to be lying, and refused to speak Afrikaans when the citing officer and the other man said you spoke perfect Afrikaans. And because you are a Mormon missionary. His brother and sister-in-law have joined that church, and it has divided the family. I'm afraid you were his first Mormon missionary in court since then, and he was, shall we say, somewhat severe.

"However, you will find that the scars are more psychological than physical. The canvas is to keep the whip from cutting. You will only see bruises when you look. You will heal quickly. Perhaps you can look on this as Peter did. Not many people get to take stripes for their faith, do they?"

Somehow, it made him feel better, but did not take the sensation of having been skinned alive from his back side. Each step sent a thrill of agony through his body. He could not believe a human body could be made to hurt so badly in such a short event. He was in greater pain than when he was beat up by all those guys at the lake. Far greater.

"Do you have someone you can call to come get you? And , do you know where that other man is? At the very least, he is guilty of perjury, probably the speeding citation also. He will undoubtedly be sentenced to lashes for letting you unjustly take his place."

Sam stopped amid stride. "I don't know where he is. If my opinion means anything, I beg you not to whip him. If there is ever a circumstance when whipping is justified, save it for rapists or something, not traffic violators." This he said passionately and the attorney nodded, as if he agreed.

"One more thing," the prosecutor said, turning to face Sam. "This is not America, and you have no rights here. Our laws are very specific toward non-citizens. If you complain to anyone about your treatment, or start any legal action, you will simply be expelled from the country. My suggestion to you, is that you tell no one. For your sake, and for your church's being able to continue to do missionary work in this country. I realize your treatment was unjust, but there are many who would like to lash all Mormons and send them back to America smarting. Do you understand?" He was dead serious, and Sam believed him.

They walked to the prosecutor's small office filled with books. It had no windows, and looked as much like a cell as the room they had imprisoned him in last night. The prosecutor showed him the phone on his desk and turned to leave.

Sam interrupted his departure. "Thank you for liberating me. I applaud your sense of justice. I realize you could have left me in there just as easily." The prosecutor bowed slightly.

"But you were wrong about my not having any rights in this country. No matter what your laws are, and no matter how insignificant my standing before your law is, there is a higher law. I am a servant of Jesus Christ, and before His law I stand innocent. All men will one day be judged by that higher law. I would rather be flogged to death unjustly according to the laws of men, than to stand before the bar of God having ordered that flogging."

The prosecutor's face slowly drained of color, and Sam felt his heart burning with the Holy Spirit. He suspected for a moment that he might be thrown back into the cell, but the prosecutor just nodded and said. "Let me know when you have finished your call, and I will bring you something to eat." He walked to the door and opened it, then turned back toward Sam. "It's high irony to me that you can barely walk, and with a word I could confine you to prison for a very long time. Yet you speak boldly to me, and for reasons which escape me, I feel no anger toward you. You stand to lose a great deal by your boldness, yet I am the one who trembles with fear."

President Carlson picked him up about three hours later. Sam had spent the intervening hours talking to Prosecutor Van der Kerk, who had canceled his court duties for the day. During that time, Sam taught him the Gospel, and bore testimony in a way he had never experienced before. They talked a great deal about justice, mercy, and judgment. The attorney listened intently, and occasionally made notes on a yellow pad.

Sam was not surprised to find him knowledgeable about the scriptures and highly intelligent. Mr. Van der Kerk would quote a scripture which seemed to contradict what Sam was saying, and immediately, Sam would quote the verse before it, or another verse, which brought the meaning into true perspective. The wonderful part was that these were scriptures which came to mind from a cursory reading of the New Testament in seminary before his mission. Yet he could visualize the verses, even quote them, as if he were looking at the page. It was a marvelous experience, and by the time President Carlson arrived, they had become, if not friends, at least respected opponents. Yet there was a feeling of discovery, and the glow of the Holy Spirit was upon them.

President Carlson had brought a member who was also an attorney. They arrived with flames shooting from their nostrils. Sam wouldn't have believed it possible for President Carlson to become this incensed. They would have launched into the prosecutor with a blue vengeance, except for the feeling of peace which existed in the room as they entered. It became obvious that there was no need for a defense, and the Holy Spirit overshadowed their indignation.

Sam introduced President Carlson, and briefly explained Van der Kerk's role in setting him free, without mentioning his role in getting him lashed. They shook hands, and as they were about to depart, Van der Kerk pressed a business card into Sam's hand.

"You have impressed me, young man. I wish I had your simple faith and your black and white perspective of the world. I would to

God that it was as simple as you say."

Sam transferred the card to his pocket, then took the prosecutor's hand in both of his own. "With all my heart, I know that it is true."

Looking deep into Sam's eyes he replied. "that is what's most troubling about you," he said. "I know you know its true. Your simple faith is more powerful that any sophisticated argument I have ever heard. And believe me I have heard many."

"God bless you," Sam said, and released his hand.

"I think he already has," was his sincere reply.

———

Sam stood outside the car, looking at the soft seat, immobilized. He could not bring himself to lower his bruised flesh onto it.

"Get in Elder and let's go," President urged him. Sam looked up at him, tears pooling in his eyes.

"President, would you give me a blessing so I can get into the car?" President came around to his side of the car and drew within whispering distance.

"What's troubling you Elder? How can I help?" So saying, he placed a hand in the middle of Sam's back which made him groan and turn away.

President's eyes grew big with disbelief. "What did they do to you?" he demanded, anger rising in his face. He glanced back toward the court house, and then at Sam. Sam could tell he was on the verge of marching back into the building.

"President. You may help me by giving me a blessing so I can bear to sit in the car. Please. Everything else is as it should be. Just my body needs help." Sam gave him a calm, but pleading look.

President surprised Sam by suddenly raising his arm to the square, and in a voice of authority saying, "In the name of Jesus Christ, and by the authority of the holy Melchizedek Priesthood, I rebuke the power of evil over you, and command your body to be at rest and to heal according to the timetable of the Lord. In the name of Jesus Christ, Amen." No sooner had he said these words than the pain changed in his flesh. It didn't go away, but it became different, tolerable, or perhaps even acceptable. Sitting was still agony, but it was an agony which made his heart soar in joy. He was swept over by a feeling of peace, and a sense of God's acceptance of his sacrifice.

As they drove home, Sam related all that had happened, including the prosecutor's warning. President wanted to drive him to a hospital, but Sam insisted he would be fine. They drove straight to the Mission Home, where he was given a proper meal and a soft bed. Sister Carlson wept when she saw his back. He fell asleep as she gently rubbed ointment onto his wounds. He awoke with a start when someone's alarm went off. He felt refreshed and considerably better. For the first time, he looked at his back in the mirror. He was surprised to see twenty distinct red welts surround by pools of black and blue. He expected to see open wounds and bleeding sores. Nowhere was his skin broken. The damage was deep and debilitating, but it would heal.

It was later that evening when the deep musical chimes of the front door announced the arrival of an unexpected visitor. All the Elders were out on teaching appointments, and only he and President were at home. President was startled to see Prosecutor Van der Kerk and an attractive woman at the door. In the circular drive was a limousine and two police cars. For a moment he was stunned into inaction.

"Excuse us for just dropping in. We have come to speak to Sam Mahoy. Is he available?" they asked.

President Carlson smiled, and invited them into the foyer. Sam was wearing the loosest clothing he could find and studying the scriptures when President popped into his room. It took him a few minutes to get himself looking like a missionary.

When he arrived in the big living room, President was explaining the history of the mission home. As soon as he arrived the Van der Kerks stood. For a moment they seemed awkward, almost intimidated. There was a moment of discomfort which threatened to stretch into eternity. Sam certainly didn't know what to say, and was grateful when Mrs. Van der Kerk stepped forward to shake his hand.

"I'm pleased to meet you. You have made quite an impression on my husband. He spoke so highly of you that it was I who insisted on meeting you. I didn't believe you were not angry for the rough treatment you received. I can see from the expression on your face however, that anger is not part of what you are feeling. What are you feeling, Sam?"

Mrs. Van der Kerk was a slender woman in her mid forties, her demeanor was regal, and her carriage proud. She had dark, almost black hair, and vibrant blue eyes, which sparkled with keen intelligence. Her face was friendly and most pleasant to look at. He found himself liking her. It was obvious they were wealthy, and she comfortable with status, position and power. However, he did not get the feeling she used her status to indulge a small, petty spirit. Instead, she seemed to use her position as a means to a larger end. He could not guess what that end might be, nor how he fit into it, but he was quite sure they would not be here if he didn't figure into it some way.

Sam cleared his throat, and still holding her hand, said: "I'm feeling like I should tell you why I'm in South Africa. Why don't you take a seat, and with your indulgence, I'll tell you." The Van der Kerks took a seat on the large velvet couch, and he stood near the piano. He began with his youth, and the faith his parents taught him. He told them about Jimmy, and the lessons his passing had taught him. He told them why he had come on a mission, and what joy it had already brought into his soul. He told him how much the gospel meant to him, and how he knew it was true.

He concluded by saying. "You asked me what I am feeling. I'm feeling overwhelmed with His love and with the breathtaking beauty of His eternal plan. And I'm feeling very grateful for this opportunity to explain my feelings to you, Brother and Sister Van der Kerk."

During the nearly forty minutes of his recitation, Mrs. Van der Kerk remained intent, occasionally nodding, sometimes laughing, sometimes frowning with deep thought. When he finished, she stood and walked to where he stood. When she was directly in front of him, she studied him intently until he began to feel foolish.

Finally she said: "We are members of the Dutch Reformed Church and hold responsible positions therein. We have fought the incursion of your church and several others into our country with all our energy. Our efforts are directly responsible for the limited number of representatives your church is allowed to have in our country at any one time.

"I have always seen your missionary efforts as an invasion of sorts. When my husband came home speaking highly of one of these, please forgive me, detestable Mormon missionaries, I decided that I would meet you and discredit you before his eyes. My husband is the City Prosecuting Attorney and in line to be elected Regional Prosecutor of the whole nation. I am a lawyer, and of no small consequence myself in powerful circles." She cocked her head to one side.

"I had planned to reopen his eyes to the threat that your religion poses to our way of life, and to belittle your gracious response to his rough treatment of you in jail as a ploy to win him over. It would have been quite a conquest, to win one of your greatest opponents over to your way of thinking, would it not?"

She turned toward her husband as if he were the judge in a criminal trial. "However, I would bet considerable money that Sam was unaware until this moment of who we are, or the threat we represent. He has said nothing of his ordeal, and has spoken quite plainly from his heart. He has rendered my cross examination impotent, and silenced the voice of opposition without even knowing I had come here to disembowel his arguments."

She turned back to Sam. "Either you are the most ingenious liar of all time, or you are speaking the truth. In either case, I beg your permission to hear you again on this matter to determine which of the two it might be."

Sam wasn't sure all that she had said made sense, and could only nod. Her husband stood, and as they were turning away, his mouth opened without his permission and said: "Until tomorrow evening then."

They paused as if considering, then nodded, and replied, "At seven." President Carlson ushered them into the night, and they were gone, but a sweet spirit rested upon those remaining in the cavernous expanse of the Mission Home.

April 5, 1974

Yesterday, I had the dubious privilege of being falsely accused and whipped. They gave me twenty lashes. I have never felt such incredible pain in my life. They placed a canvas over my back to keep the whip from cutting my skin, and still my back is a mess which will take weeks to heal. I can't imagine what Christ must have endured when they scourged him. He must have nearly died from that alone. Prior to that, he had suffered unknown horrors in the Garden, and would later be crucified. It causes my mind to balk and my soul to anguish. It makes my soul cry out in His behalf just to think of His pain.

The man who prosecuted me later released me. I felt no anger toward him, and he found that sufficiently novel, that he and his wife came to the Mission Home. I bore my testimony, and taught them a little. They asked if they could come again. I think they still hope to convince themselves that my faith is insincere. They don't realize that they are investigating the church, and already have a testimony. Missionary work is so amazing when done the Lord's way. I think this whole lashes thing was an elaborate door approach.

The following evening they came prepared to debate, and brought several pages of notes which they carefully referred to. As soon they were seated, they began with the first item on their list, and laid siege to Sam and President Carlson. Sam was aghast at the change in their demeanor, and had almost nothing to say. Accordingly, they shifted their assault to President Carlson, who entertained their questions, and tried to answer as plainly as he could. Even though the tone was friendly it was still a debate, and they plainly intended to win. President Carlson had been a lawyer, even a federal judge, and knew how to debate, but it was plain from his posture that he was not enjoying the evening. The Van der Kerks were, however, and with each question President could not answer to their satisfaction, their attitudes were more triumphant.

After nearly an hour, Mrs. Van der Kerk suddenly turned to Sam who had become a non-participant in the discussion. "Why have you stopped participating in the discussion, Elder Sam?" she asked. He had earlier asked them to call him Elder, and she had misinterpreted his words, so he became Elder Sam.

Without preamble, he said exactly what was on his mind. "I didn't come six thousand miles to debate doctrine. And you didn't come here this evening to learn. Given those incongruities, this evening was futile from the moment you walked through the door. Neither of us is being edified. If you wish to strengthen your own beliefs, then go talk to your minister. I'm not interested in wearing a bulls eye on my forehead so you can bolster your own opinions by lobbing arrows at me to see which ones stick."

Brother Van der Kerk smiled. "That's pretty direct. You seem to have a way of cutting to the chase on matters, Elder Sam. Since we have monopolized the evening with our debate, would you care to occupy the last remaining moments in whatever format you approve of? It was, after all, you who initiated this event through your unfortunate experiences in my jail, and we are guests in your home."

"Yes, Elder Sam. Please do. We are both lawyers, and are most comfortable with debate and cross examination. You choose the format that is most comfortable to you, and we will listen."

Sam was suddenly on stage without a script. He paused, waiting for the right thing to come to mind. The Van der Kerks waited patiently. When it came to him it was so bold that it startled him, yet peace washed over him, and once again he knew what the Lord desired of him. As before, he prayerfully sought the courage to 'say what you want me to say.'

"Brother Van der Kerk, when you released me from jail, you said that I was like Peter who was whipped unjustly for preaching Christ, and that I should see it as a blessing. I have endeavored to do that, and it was your words which initiated the peace I now feel concerning those events. In that same spirit, I would like to propose that you, both of you, are like Saul of Tarsus. You have gone about with great conviction attempting to destroy the work which God is bringing forth through the Church of Jesus Christ of Latter-day Saints.

"Like Saul, you have believed with all your hearts that you were doing good, and that the church is a threat to your way of life. As a result, you have persecuted the Saints and unjustly cast some into prison and caused some to suffer unjust punishment. And, like Saul because your heart was good but your actions misguided, the Lord has seen fit to interrupt you on your road to Damascus. He has sent you a witness of sufficient power to turn your hearts away from your misguided course and to cause you to look upon His latter-day work with a new perspective and to feel within your hearts the need for change.

"I now say to you in words to echo in your souls as they did to Saul: Brother Van der Kerk, Sister Van der Kerk, why persecute thou the church of God? It is hard for thee to kick against the pricks."

Sister Van der Kerk fell back into the couch as if struck in the face, and Brother Van der Kerk held his chin between thumb and forefinger, elbow upon his knee, as if deep in contemplation. A long silence fell upon them as they pondered his words.

It was Brother Van der Kerk who broke the silence. "Saul's vision was accompanied by a sign. He was struck blind and dumb as I recall. Your invocation of his vision is well chosen, but impotent without an accompanying sign. What sign shall we expect to accompany our conversion on the road to Damascus?" he asked. His voice was soft, but it held an edge of disbelief, of challenge.

"This is the sign I give you," Sam heard his lips say, and had time to wonder what the sign was to be before he heard himself say, "You are an adulterous man."

Four people gasped simultaneously, including himself. A stunned silence hung over them as the accusation seemed to bounce back and forth across the room. Sister Van der Kerk stared at Sam with contemptuous indignation, waiting for her husband to slam him into the ground with his denial. But when no denial came, her expression turned to disbelief, as her gaze reluctantly swung toward her mate.

"Deny it," she hissed in Afrikaans, barely loud enough for Sam to hear.

After a long pause, he looked up into his wife's face. There was pleading in his eyes. But his words were more startling than a denial. He spoke in Afrikaans, and unexpectedly, Sam understood every word as easily as if they had spoken English.

"I asked for a sign, and this is a true sign. Only God has known these many years, and it could only have come from Him. Would you have me add to my crimes perjury before God? Would you rather be married to a lying adulterer, or just an adulterer?"

Mrs. Van der Kerk bolted to her feet, grasping her handbag. "I think it's time to leave" she stated tersely, and turned toward her husband who remained immobile on the couch. "I will get a ride home in one of the escort cars." She took two hasty steps toward the door before Sam's voice brought her to an abrupt stop.

Without knowing why, or even how, he spoke in Afrikaans. His pronunciation was awful, and his sentence structure sloppy, but his message was perfect. "There is one more lesson Saul learned from his sign, which you both will learn when you come tomorrow night."

She turned toward him, her face red with anger. Her voice hissed with wrath as she stabbed the air with her finger, punctuating her words. "What lesson could possibly change the fact that my husband is an adulterer who has betrayed my trust and our marriage vows?"

Sam cocked his head to one side in a perfect imitation of her own expression of irony, and whispered in Afrikaans, "Forgiveness."

————

They did not come the next night at seven or even eight o'clock. It was nearly nine p.m. when a Mercedes pulled up in front without a police escort. It was nearly ten minutes later when the doorbell rang.

President and Sister Carlson met them at the door. This was the first time they had met Sister Carlson, and she greeted them warmly. Sister Van der Kerk seemed especially grateful to have Sister Carlson join the meeting. Brother Van der Kerk seemed oppressed and brooding. They were not in a pleasant mood, and whatever portion of the Spirit of the Lord had been there, seemed to evaporate with their arrival. When they were seated, Sister Carlson brought them Roi Bush tea. They sat on the couch several feet apart, an almost visible barrier of enmity separating them.

President Carlson suggested they begin with a prayer, a thing they had failed to do in earlier meetings. The Van der Kerk's immediately stood and bowed their heads. President Carlson offered a beautiful prayer. When everyone was seated, all eyes turned to Sam. He knew this would happen, yet didn't have a clue what to say. Still, even knowing this would occur, he had resisted the urge to prepare something, preferring to wait upon the Lord to fill his lips with words of truth. He suppressed the urge to ad-lib as the seconds pushed toward a minute. Still nothing came, and the second minute came and went in silence.

"Elder?" President asked quietly, but Sam just shook his head.

Silence stretched on for several minutes until everyone but Sam grew impatient. Finally, Sister Van der Kerk asked impatiently, "why haven't you said anything?"

It was Brother Van der Kerk who answered her question. "Because, like before, we didn't come here to learn. We came here to be angry, and nothing he could have said would have made a difference. Silence is the only thing that could penetrate the wall I came here with. In reality, it is I who needs to speak. I need to beg your forgiveness and God's forgiveness. Believe me when I say that my crime was many years ago, and was never repeated. I have anguished over it for years and wanted to tell you and to wash this taint from my soul, but I have never known how. I don't understand how. I only knew that telling you would break your heart. And I couldn't bring myself to do that."

At this exact moment, Sam's heart flooded with understanding, and he opened his mouth and taught them the truths which could heal their souls. He began with the garden of Eden, and told of Adam's long separation from the Lord because of his transgression. He told them of Adam's eventual understanding of the mission of Jesus Christ and the unspeakable joy of becoming a participant in that atonement. He told them of human nature, the natural man, and how all men sin. He taught them about the restoration of priesthood power in our dispensation, and of the cleansing power of baptism. He invited them to be washed clean and become whole through the power of that holy ordinance.

Brother Van der Kerk wept, and Sister Van der Kerk held his head against her bosom and comforted him. When he could speak, he asked them to arrange for his baptism and to help him prepare so the cleansing would be absolute. Of all the most beautiful things Sam had ever seen, the look of love on Sister Van der Kerk's face was the sweetest. He thought of how the Savior might look as he gazes down upon a humble, repentant soul, and considered the look in her face must be a reflection of that perfect love.

They came nearly every night for the next two weeks, and were baptized exactly sixteen days from the day Sam had been hauled before him in court. Their baptism was a solemn and joyful affair. Since he worked for the government, and the government was controlled by the Dutch Reformed Church, he fully expected to lose his job. Already, dozens of friends had abandoned them and heaped ridicule upon them. Family had disowned them, and their closest allies had rejected them. Yet they considered it a small price to pay, and walked away from it all with no apparent remorse. It was simply what they chose to do, and the great price they paid was of little consequence to them. Over 150 people attended their baptism, not a single one of them from their former circle of friends and family.

Days later, Brother Van der Kerk was fired from his job. Sister Van der Kerk was demoted at her law firm until she finally quit. They lost their home after a few months, and eventually moved into a small apartment. They sold their possessions to pay for their needs, and inwardly rejoiced. Their faith was fantastic, and their joy in finding the true church, utter and complete. They brought a sense of renewal and determination to the ward which revitalized and blessed everyone who became their new friends. The ward rallied around them, and formed an impenetrable circle of safety. Their humility and gracious acceptance of the cost of righteousness won them friends of everyone they met. In time, their story was told and retold, until those who did not know them thought it a fabrication. Yet by and large, every word of it was true. Except for life itself, it's not possible to give up more for one's conviction of truth.

In time, Brother Van der Kerk ran for election as Regional Prosecuting Attorney. The money he used was all donated by his new friends. His opponent ran on the whole argument that Van der Kerk was a Mormon. Every advertisement published bashed him for his membership in the "Mormon Cult." Brother Van der Kerk ran on the campaign slogan that he had the courage to do what was right, regardless of the cost. The campaign caught national attention, as his opponent became bitter and hateful. Brother Van der Kerk remained aloof, pressing his message of courageous honesty.

In congregations throughout the nation, sermons were taught, with no other message than to urge people to "defeat the Mormon threat." The government itself donated money to the other man's campaign, and armed guards had to be stationed outside Van der Kerk's apartment at night.

Because of the vigor of the opposition, his campaign cost very little. He had all the publicity he could have desired. In the end, he won a decisive victory. Everyone in the nation knew that a Mormon had been elected to high national office for the first time in written history, and missionary work surged ahead with unprecedented energy.

June 1, 1974

I have spent almost a month in the Mission Home. My back is healed enough so that I can get around without much pain. I still can't sleep on my back or right side. The skin is still black and blue, and has shrunken, or at least feels tight. I have been doing stretching exercises to try to regain full movement. Sister Carlson has been wonderful, and every evening rubs ointment on my back, and massages the muscles to keep them from balling up. Her ministrations have greatly lessened my suffering.

About the only missionary work I have done is teaching the Van der

Kerks. They were baptized on the 29th of May. It was a glorious experience. I baptized them both, and President confirmed them. Brother Van der Kerk bore his testimony after the service, and said that he had felt the burden lifted from his shoulders. He turned toward me and asked me to forgive him for the abuse he had heaped upon me. No one except President, Sister Carlson and myself knows about the lashes, and everyone wondered what he meant. Afterwards, I gave him a hug, and told him I loved him. He wept on my shoulder, and I on his.

President told me today that I was being transferred back to Germiston. At least I will be in the same ward with Brother and Sister Van der Kerk. It just occurred to me that I didn't know their first names until I asked their full names in the waters of baptism. His first name is Joseph. And hers is Emma. Somehow, their names became precious to me the moment I heard them. What a fantastic, almost poetic coincidence, that they should possess the names of the greatest prophet of all time, and his beloved wife. They didn't realize their names had significance in LDS history until I explained it to them. They both wept, and proclaimed themselves unworthy.

My new companion is Elder Snider, also from the Mission Home. He is not happy about the transfer. He was President's personal secretary, and wanted to become Assistant to the president. He sees this as a demotion. This last month I hated to be around him. He is arrogant, demanding, and self centered. I just hope he's a good missionary. I can put up with almost anything except not doing the work. We'll see I guess.

Sam and Elder Snider loaded the VW beetle, and drove away from the mission home in silence. At almost the exact spot where Elder Beesler told him that he hated him, Elder Snider cleared his throat. Sam winced and waited. Elder Snider gave him a surprised look and smiled.

"Elder Mahoy, I know you have been in the Mission Home recovering from an illness. I also know that you think I'm an insufferable brat. I guess I am, at that. But we have something in common. We both love the Lord. If you will be patient with me, I will be the best senior companion you have ever had. What do you say?"

Sam could hardly believe his ears, and felt himself relaxing. "Elder, I just want you to know that I recognize you as the senior companion, and that I will do whatever I can to serve the Lord and to be a good junior. Let's give it a try."

They drove to a different boarding house than the one he had spent that one night at with Elder Beesler. This one was a big old building apparently built as a boarding house. They were on the third floor, and there were no elevators. On their floor were perhaps twenty-five rooms. There was one big bathroom.

The first morning there, they went into the shower together. They were obligated by mission rules to remain within one another's sight, which included public rest rooms. The shower was a large room with shower heads on three walls. Each shower head had a stubby enclosure on two sides about armpit high, but which was open to the main room. At one time there had been shower curtains, which had long since vanished. Sam was just about finished when he heard a woman's voice mutter something about forgetting shampoo. He turned in time to see a completely naked woman stepping into the shower next to his. He was so stunned that he froze for a few seconds, and only began to breathe again when she asked to borrow his shampoo. He handed it to her without looking her direction.

At that very moment his eyes took on a will of their own and even as his mind was shouting NO! his eyes swept across her bare body as he turned. He hurriedly left without a second thought about his shampoo. As they were leaving, two younger women walked past them. One had a towel wrapped around her waist, naked above that, and the other was completely naked except for a towel tossed across one shoulder. Sam bumped into Elder Snider three times before either one of them found the door. All three girls were giggling as Sam and Elder Snider bolted from the shower. They ran to their rooms soaking wet, with only a towel around them.

They sat in their room, breathing heavily, shivering even in the heat of an African summer. Finally Elder Snider stood and suggested they both fast today. Sam thought it a wonderful idea. He could not get the image of those woman from flashing in his mind. Even when he read the scriptures, he periodically had to force the images from his minds. To make matters worse, they were attractive woman. He wondered if the images would be more or less haunting if they had been ugly. He derided himself for even having wondered that, but could not force the images to leave for any length of time.

The next morning they waited until the girls left. They took a quick shower in lukewarm water. It made them shower about an hour later than they would have otherwise, but at least they were alone. The water was heated by a big wood burning boiler which the landlord stoked up each morning except Sunday. They kept the water warm until about eight o'clock. After eight, they could have the shower to themselves because the water quickly went cold. If they timed it right, they could catch the last few minutes of warm water.

Their room was not much larger than a walk-in closet. There were two beds with about two feet separating them. At one end of the room was a wooden wardrobe large enough to hang their shirts. The next

Saturday a servant girl came by and collected laundry. They gave her their shirts. She returned them that evening all washed and pressed. She had done a good job, and they paid her several rand. However, there were little black spots all over their shirts. They questioned her about it next week, and she only shrugged. They were out tracting that afternoon and came upon the girl washing their shirts and garments. She was sitting on the curb in front of a house. The curb was running with water from the street. She had a lump of asphalt in her hand pounding a shirt on the curb. Their garments were spread out on the grass in a long row to dry, plainly visible to passing motorists. They were aghast, and scooped up their wet clothes, paid the girl, and left. The little black spots were from her lump of asphalt. Sister Van der Kerk heard about this and insisted on doing their laundry thereafter. They were grateful beyond words.

Elder Snider turned out to be an incredibly hard worker. They diligently tracted hours each day. They worked and worked and worked, all without success. Without exception, every door was closed in their face. The more discouraged they became, the harder Elder Snider pushed. They began tracting several hours more each day than required by the rules and still had zero investigators.

Sam suggested a special fast, which Elder Snider readily agreed to. They decided they needed special help, and planned a two-day fast. The weather was turning cooler, but was still hot, about ninety degrees and eighty percent humidity. They strained themselves to complete the fast. Still, they had no teaching opportunities.

The next Sunday at church, Bishop Fanstein handed them a referral. These people were friends of his, and even though he had not discussed it with them, he felt they might be receptive. He asked the missionaries not to use his name. They were disappointed about that, but agreed, grateful for the referral.

That evening Sam and his companion drove to the subdivision indicated on the referral card. There was a street name and house number on the referral. The subdivision was new and extremely large. The houses were nearly identical, hundreds of them in tidy rows. However, there was not a single street sign. They could not tell which house was the correct one. Several dozen houses had the same house number.

"Well Elder, the only way to work this is to knock on every house with that number, and introduce ourselves. Let's do it."

Sam sat in the passenger side of the vehicle, frustrated that Elder Snider did everything the hard way. He had once suggested that they could rely on the Spirit to guide them in their tracting, and by doing so they would not have to rely on their own labors to find investigators. Elder Snider had frankly told him that was foolishness. He insisted that they were to "find" the investigators, and not to expect the Spirit to dump them in their laps. He refused to entertain the thought of divine guidance in anything except at special times or in desperate circumstances.

"Elder Snider, if we were willing to rely on the Spirit, it would guide us to these people. The Lord knows where they live. Why don't we just try?"

Elder Snider gave him an indulgent look, as if he were a child who needed to be taught a lesson. Elder Snider brought the VW to a complete stop near the entrance to the subdivision and turned toward him.

"OK, here's what we'll do. As I pull up to each intersection, you listen to the Spirit and tell us which way to turn. OK?"

Almost immediately Sam felt his heart burn and said in response. "I have a better idea. You're the senior companion. As we pull up to each intersection, you tell me which way you would go. After that I'll tell you which way I feel inspired to choose, but we will go the direction I pick. Good enough?"

"Yeah, whatever you want. When we're done goofing around, we'll go tract them out like real missionaries." He drove to the first intersection, a 'T'.

"Right," Elder Snider said.

Sam did not know the way to the home they sought. What he did know was that had been prompted to chose the opposite of whatever Elder Snider said. "Left," he countered. They turned left.

Shortly they came to a four way intersection. Snider chose right, taking them into the heart of the subdivision. "Left," Sam countered.

At each intersection they went the opposite of every choice Elder Snider made. Finally, they ended up on a street still under construction. It was a dead end street, and none of the houses had yard lights on so they could not see the house numbers. There were no street lights yet, and it was impossible to tell which house was which without pulling into each driveway and shining the headlights onto the house.

"Well you lose. We're on a dead end," Elder Snider said triumphantly.

Sam chose the opposite, and said "this is the right street. You choose a house."

Elder Snider gave him a 'don't you ever give up,' look and drove slowly down the dirt road until he picked a house on the left which looked like someone was home.

Sam pointed to a dark house on the opposite side of the street. "That one," he said. They pulled into the driveway, and immediately saw that it had the correct house number.

"Well, we'll never know. No one's home. Let's leave."

Sam chose the opposite. "I say we knock." Snider shrugged, willing to put this foolishness to rest.

They walked up to the door, and knocked. It was dark inside, and they knocked again. Just as Elder Snider was turning to leave, footsteps sounded in the house. The porch light snapped on.

"Good evening," Elder Snider said to the woman who came to the door.

"Are you guys Mormons?" she asked suspiciously. Sam had heard that question a thousand times. It was usually followed by a door slamming in his face.

"We're from the Church of Jesus Christ of Latter-day Saints. People sometimes call us Mormons," Elder Snider answered with his best missionary smile.

"Really?" she replied. "For a minute I thought you were Jehovah's Witnesses. They have been around a lot lately. Let me get my husband. His best friend at work is a Mormon bishop. I think he has been wanting to learn more about the Mormon church. Could you come in for a minute?"

Sam gave Elder Snider a smile and led the way into their investigator's home.

Brother and Sister Solomon were golden beyond golden. Teaching them was like giving the discussions in the LTM. Their answers were almost word perfect with the mythical "Brother Brown" in the discussions. Elder Snider insisted on giving the first discussion word perfect, and the Solomon's enjoyed every word. The Spirit was strong and they rejoiced. Before the evening was over, the Solomons had committed to baptism three weeks away.

On the way home Elder Snider was quiet. He drove with both hands on the wheel, eyes straight ahead. Sam knew what was on his mind. He was disturbed about how they had found the Solomon's home.

"Elder?" he said finally, stealing a glance at Sam who didn't reply, but waited for him to continue. "I have been thinking about what you did in directing us to the Solomon's house. I have to admit that you were right. I still can't believe that every decision I made was wrong. That hurts."

When Elder Snider didn't continue, Sam said, "It wasn't I who directed us to their home. It was the Lord, through the whisperings of the Spirit. I had very little to do with it. I just think the Lord wanted you to have a graphic lesson in what the Spirit is able to do, if we use it."

"Tell me the truth," Elder Snider responded almost instantly, a note of disbelief in his voice. "Did the bishop draw you a map to their home? You must have known how to get there, and set me up. Huh? Tell the truth."

"The truth is, it happened exactly as you saw it. I had no map. You can ask the bishop if he gave me a map. You know that it was actually you who said which way to go at each intersection. All I knew was that I was to pick the opposite of whatever you said. I got that instruction from the Spirit, and I was willing to be obedient."

Snider gave him a sidelong glance with a knowing smile. "We'll see," he said. "I find this all hard to swallow. I know that the Spirit doesn't work like that. I'm as spiritual as any missionary, and it just isn't like that. You have to work things out for yourself, then ask for confirmation. The only way the Spirit could have led us to that house is if we stopped and fasted and prayed at every street corner. Even then, I doubt the Lord would have shown us. He expects us to do His work, not the other way around. We're here to serve Him, not He to serve us. See what I mean?"

Sam felt his heart sinking. If Elder Snider couldn't see the truth of such a powerful example of guidance by the Spirit, nothing Sam could say would penetrate his heart. Sam bowed his head and said, "I know where you're coming from." That seemed to satisfy his senior companion, and they drove home in silence.

June 22, 1974

We have been teaching the Solomons for nearly a month. Each of our discussions has been wonderful. Their baptism is scheduled for this coming Friday. They are excited, especially Sister Solomon.

The Solomons are our only investigators. We have tracted the soles off of our shoes, and there just doesn't seem to be anyone to teach. Elder Snider works harder than any missionary I have seen, but still refuses to listen to the Spirit. He told me that when he returns home, he wants to be able to say "he served a good mission." He doesn't want to report that "the Spirit served a good mission, and he was there to provide backup." I feel sorry for him. He has a good heart, but is inflicting unnecessary pain on himself. He ignores anything I tell him, and except for a few times when I was able to make suggestions which he agreed with, he has completely ignored me, and I think the Spirit as well.

I received another letter from home today. It was in the mail for over a month. The family has settled in the Matanuska valley, near Wasilla, Alaska. They just finished building a new chapel, and have divided the ward. Dad was made bishop of the new Wasilla ward. Because he was made Bishop, he has quit his job on the Trans-Alaska pipeline, and is looking for work in Wasilla or Anchorage. The pipeline job was two weeks on, two weeks off, and he knew he couldn't be the Bishop on that kind of schedule. They have been living in a camp trailer, and almost have enough saved up to start a house, but will wait until he finds other work before thinking about building a house. They have to do something before winter comes. He says winter in Alaska is fierce, and everyone tells him he doesn't want to go through it living in a camp trailer.

As soon as they pulled up to the Solomon's drive, Sam knew something was wrong. There was a bad feeling surrounding the house.

"Do you feel that, Elder?" Sam asked.

"What?"

"That negative feeling. I think the Solomon's are in trouble."

"The Solomon's are fine. I think you have an overactive imagination."

Sister Solomon let them in. Her eyes were puffy, and red. She didn't offer them a seat.

"Elders I'm sorry. My husband has decided that we're not going to be baptized. He doesn't want you to come around anymore." Sam was thunderstruck, but not surprised. The feeling inside the house was like a cold shower.

"Are you sure this is what you want?" Elder Snider asked. He was terribly disappointed. "If it's what you really want, then we won't come back. It's your decision, but I would like you to be very sure."

Sister Solomon glanced toward the back of the house as if unsure, then nodded bleakly. "I don't think he'll ever change his mind. I've seen him like this before, and he is adamant. I'm sorry. I know the church is true, but it wouldn't be right for me to be baptized against his will. It would probably cause a divorce. Please leave now, before he becomes even more agitated."

Elder Snider nodded sadly, and turned toward the door. He was halfway through it before he realized his companion had not followed. He placed a hand on Sam's arm, but Sam shrugged it off.

"Sister Solomon? May we speak to Brother Solomon? I feel like we need to talk to him directly."

Her eyes brightened a bit, then sank back into despair. "I don't think he'll come out. But if he does, it won't be pleasant. He'll probably scream at you, just like he…" She cut herself off. "Let me see." She disappeared into the back of the house.

She was gone for a long time before returning. After a few minutes, Brother Solomon stomped into the room., his hair standing on end, and his clothing crumpled. His face was white with fury, and his eyes wide and darting like a wild animal.

No sooner had he rounded the corner, than he snarled at them. "I told you to leave this house. You, and your evil religion are to never come back here! Do you understand? Now go. Go before I go get my shotgun!"

Elder Snider was pulling on Sam's arm, urging him to leave, but Sam's feet seemed riveted to the floor. A quiet urging brought his arm to the square, and he heard his voice begin to speak as if he were a spectator. "In the name of Jesus Christ, I command you to come out of him."

No sooner had these words escaped his lips, than Brother Solomon took two steps backward as if slugged in the chest. He fell to one knee, and took his head in his hands. Sister Solomon gasped, and rushed to his side. After a moment he stood and struggled to a chair. Sam backed up to open the way.

It took several minutes for him to recover. His eyes were tired, but normal as they fastened on Sam. "Elder. I don't know what to say. For the last three days, ever since your last visit, I have fought a terrible battle. Every evil thought, every temptation, every hour of every day has been hell. I haven't been able to sleep or eat for three days. I feel as if I have literally wrestled with the devil. And at this point, I'm not sure if I lost or won."

"Brother Solomon," Sam began, but was cut off by a wave of his hand.

"I don't want to hear it. I strongly suspect the church is true. My wife says it is, and for a while, I believed it was. But if I have to go through this to be a member of God's true church, then I'm just not willing to do it. It's just not worth it. The first time I felt peace was when I told my wife to tell you to never come back. As soon as you stepped inside this house the battle returned. It went away when you raised your arm, but I feel it beginning to return. Please go now. Let's end this like gentlemen, rather than with me threatening to shoot you. Believe me, ten minutes ago, I would have done it, just to stop the battle in my head. Now please go."

This time, Sam let Elder Snider tug him toward the door. But before he closed the door he said, "Brother Solomon?" He looked up at him with an expressionless face. "You lost," Sam said, and closed the door behind him.

Elder Snider chastised him all the way home, and lectured him on opening his mouth without permission, and not following his senior companion's instructions. Sam just shut off his ears, and ignored the whole tirade. He felt very tired inside.

August 3, 1974

Received a transfer notice today. I am going to be transferred to Rhodesia. It's another country north of here. Elder Snider has been a good companion as far as teaching me diligence and work. I feel badly that we never really got any missionary work done. I think he blames me for our lack of success. He has hinted at it, but not said why. In Rhodesia I will be co-senior with Elder Palmer. He came out in the group just behind mine. I am looking forward to finally being able to get some missionary work done the way I feel inspired to do it.

August 5, 1974

I am on the train to Rhodesia. This is day two of a five day trip. The train is a coal burning puffer belly, and never goes over 20 mph. I am in the third car from the engine, and the cabin spends about half the time filled with coal smoke. I have started coughing constantly.

The countryside is beautiful beyond description. It is rolling hills covered with low trees and brush. The colors are breathtaking. There is an unbelievable number of animals. We have gone past many herds of deer-like animals, and I have seen lions, elephants, a bazillion monkeys, and other animals I had no idea existed. I have taken lots of pictures.

The train stops at every black village it passes to let off packages and people. We usually spend about an hour at each village. We are not allowed off the train. While we are stopped, armed guards walk up and down the train to keep people from sneaking onto the train. The little kids of the village come up to the windows and sell things. Usually oranges and bananas. They also sell lots of hand carved animals and trinkets. I have bought a few because they are so cheap, but I don't have much money. The kids start out begging, then as the train starts to warm up, they start telling us we are selfish. Rich and selfish, and demanding we buy something. As the train pulls away, they start cursing at us for not buying enough of their stuff. Interesting sales tactics.

One cute little boy picked out a lady in the car ahead of mine, and was saying "Very beautiful rich lady, please buy an orange. I am so hungry." As the train began to move, he was saying. "Hey rich lady, why you so selfish. I think you very mean to me, rich lady. Please, my baby sister is so hungry." Then as we were pulling away, "Hey mean rich lady. Why you hate me? You are too ugly to be nice. I hate you, ugly, mean, rich lady!"

It was kind of funny. The kid was obviously not malnourished. He was as plump as the rich lady.

nine

Bulawayo, Rhodesia

By the time Sam arrived in Bulawayo, Rhodesia, he was sick from coal fumes. His new district leader met him at the train station, and drove him and his companion to their new area. He left them off on a street corner.

"Elders, this is a new area. Missionaries have never been here before, and there is no boarding. Your first tracting assignment will be to find yourselves boarding. I will come back to this street corner at six o'clock to deliver your bags. If you haven't found any, you will have no place to sleep." He hopped back into the car and drove away.

This was something unexpected, and neither he, nor Elder Palmer had a clue what to do. Finally, Elder Palmer suggested they have a prayer. So, standing there on the street corner they bowed their heads, and Elder Palmer offered a prayer. When he was done, they both started walking down the street as if they both knew where they were going. Without a word or signal, they turned into the fourth house and knocked on the door. An older woman answered the door. She seemed surprised and openly pleased to see them.

"Good afternoon, Ma'am," Elder Palmer said. "We're missionaries for the Church of Jesus Christ of Latter-day Saints, and we're looking for accommodations in this area. Do you know of anywhere we might inquire?"

She said she thought a Mrs. Whiting took in boarders, and gave them directions. They walked several blocks and found the house. Mrs. Whiting was indeed looking for boarders and welcomed them. They offered the amount the district leader had suggested, and Mrs. Whiting's eyes grew big. She declined that amount, but insisted on a lesser amount. Their room was a large bedroom with two beds, a large wardrobe, an attached bathroom, and a beautiful view. It was almost more than Sam or Elder Palmer could believe. They paid her the first months rent, and she gave them a key to the house.

Elder Palmer was nearly six feet tall, a full two inches taller than Sam. Where Sam's weight was compact and hard, Palmer's was loose and flabby. The skin on his face sagged and looked sallow. He wondered about Elder Palmer's health. In time, he learned that his companion was suffering from various health problems, and had had to get special permission from the First Presidency to go on the mission. Perhaps that was why he took missionary work so seriously, because it cost him dearly to do it. Each day he came home, he was exhausted.

They tracted for the rest of the afternoon before realizing they had gotten lost. They really had no idea which corner the district leader had left them at. It was approaching six o'clock when they rounded a corner, and quite by accident, ended up at the right corner. Minutes later the district leader pulled up and they climbed in. They drove to their new boarding and unloaded their bags.

Rhodesia was a small country of about 150,000 square miles. It sat on some of the most beautiful and mineralogically wealthy real-estate in the world. The soil was a dark red, some places a bluish-black, and in others, a deep green. The soil colors changed according to the type of minerals present. Red soils indicated iron deposits. Blue-black soils indicated gold or silver, and green indicated copper deposits. It was not uncommon to go into someone's home and see gold nuggets on their mantle piece as large as tennis balls.

Rhodesia was a country settled by whites from England, originally as an English common-wealth. Their neighboring country, Northern Rhodesia, was as well. In the late sixties, their English charter expired for both countries, and England began the process of turning the country to the indigenous peoples, the blacks of the Xota, and other tribes. Northern Rhodesia was a thriving colony because of their vast copper mines. At one time, they had the largest copper mine in the world, and exported more copper than any nation in Africa, and more chromium than any nation on earth.

Northern Rhodesia was renamed Zambia by the new government. Less than one year after their charter expired, a local black man made himself king and ordered the whites to work without compensation. In response, the white people flowed across the border into Rhodesia, leaving him without technical workers in the mines. He ordered his troops to kill any white person fleeing the country, and a blood bath began which ended up in a civil war. Before the king had been overthrown, over 30,000 whites had been slaughtered, and tens of thousands had been taken into slavery. In the meantime, the mines had flooded with water. When the white workers failed at the impossible task of evacuating the mines of the water, many of them and their families were slaughtered. Some escaped in daring rescues by friends and relatives from Rhodesia.

Rhodesia's charter expired in 1965, and England began the process of dismantling the local government. The settlers, led by then president, Ian Smith, rebelled. An election was held, and the people, black and white, overwhelmingly reelected Smith, and commissioned him to issue a declaration of independence.

England condemned Rhodesia before the United Nations, and the United Nations voted to sanction Rhodesia. Member nations were no longer allowed to trade anything except certain humanitarian supplies with Rhodesia. Trade with South Africa continued unaffected.

The economic shock was catastrophic. The huge gold, copper, and silver mines shut down over night. Without a buyer, even gold became valueless. Since South Africa produced huge quantities of these minerals, they had no need to buy Rhodesia's. Needed repair parts to keep vital utilities running became impossible to find, and utilities began failing. Electricity only ran at certain times of the day, water and fuels became scarce. Gasoline was rationed. Jobs were nonexistent, and money, currently the British pound, became scarce.

President Smith coined the phrase, "prosperity through independence," and asked people to report to their jobs without expectation of pay. He ordered the printing of the Rhodesian, "dollar," and asked the citizens to accept it without question. They did. In time, textile mills were built from smuggled parts. Machine shops made repair parts for automobiles. Utilities became more reliable as they learned to manufacture their own repair parts. People created cottage industries to create things normally purchased overseas, and the economy of the nation stabilized. In less than ten years, they became a struggling, though independent, nation.

The year Sam arrived, President Smith announced the completion of the nation's only auto manufacturing plant. It cranked out a small vehicle oddly similar to a Toyota Corolla. The church bought one of the first models to roll off the line. It was that vehicle which the district leader drove. To Sam's eyes, it was an incomplete mess. It had holes drilled in the body for chrome trim, but none was installed. The front and rear bumpers were painted iron, rather than chromed steel. There was no heater, radio, or horn, and air constantly blew through the heater vents. The clutch chattered, and the engine belched black smoke, but it ran, and it became a symbol of national pride to own one.

One thing Sam quickly learned was that everything was cheap in Rhodesia. Cheap in cost and construction. When he arrived in the country his first purchase was a new pair of shoes. They cost him less than four American dollars. They were handsome, lightweight shoes. They lasted until he stepped into the first puddle. In three steps they fell apart. He walked back home in his socks. The shoes were made of paper. The soles, sides, everything was paper. He simply bought another pair and avoided puddles. The shoes lasted about a month, after which he simply bought another. No wonder they were so cheap. The new shoe industry thrived on a marketing necessity impossible under any other circumstances.

Unlike South Africa, black people were welcome to participate in the economy any way they chose. As many black students attended college, as whites. There were black doctors, dentists, and lawyers, many of whom excelled at their trades and saw many white clients. The race barrier was still there, but it was much thinner than in their large neighbor to the south.

The people were divided into classes along economic lines. There was almost no middle class. Those who understood business, started one, and almost invariably found success. Mansions began to dot the hillside outside of town, and large cars were smuggled into the country. Those who understood only labor were paid paltry wages, and lived in small, nearly unfurnished homes. It amazed Sam that you could walk four blocks and go from mansions to shanties. What even amazed him further, was that they found their greatest missionary success among the near-slums of Bulawayo.

The only difference between these rows of tiny houses, and a true slum, was pride. The people loved their country, understood sacrifice, and willingly gave of themselves. There was no filth, no litter, no chronic malcontent, and little, if any, crime. Everyone who wanted a job had one. The opportunity to progress was wide open, and people felt no limitation on their future. They had seen the country go from bankruptcy and despair, to economic stability and hope. They believed in their future, and it showed.

Elder Palmer and Sam divided the days into even and odd. Sam would act as senior on odd days, and Elder Palmer on evens. It soon became obvious that Elder Palmer was a hard worker. And he understood, at least on an instinctual level, the workings of the Spirit. Sam soon found out that Elder Palmer had a grasp on the scriptures which made his head swim.

The mission published a list of four-hundred scriptures for missionaries to memorize. They were encouraged to memorize one each day, until they knew 365 of them. The remaining thirty-five were bonus scriptures. Elder Palmer knew nearly all of them, and Sam less than a third. On Elder Palmer's days, they played scripture chase while they tracted. The object was to quote a portion of a scripture, and then your companion had to finish the scripture and give the reference. If they failed, they lost a point. At lunch time, whoever was behind bought the other a soft drink. Soft drinks in Rhodesia contained no artificial flavors since they had no technology to create them. They were pure, carbonated, fruit juices. Sam found them delightful, and he decided to win as many of them as possible. Neither of them could afford to buy many soft drinks, so whoever lost, bought one, and watched while the other drank it, usually to appropriately exaggerated grunts and sighs of delight.

Elder Palmer also taught him how to "tip" rocks. This was done by placing the inside of your shoe beside a rock as you were walking, and just as you were about to lift your foot, to give the toe a flip. With practice, the rock became a projectile inflicting non-lethal damage to the other missionary's shins. Elder Palmer was a pro, and for weeks, Sam had bruised ankles. Elder Palmer would give a little skip whenever Sam tipped one at him, and the rock would invariably miss. At first, it seemed like a brutal, un-missionary-like sport, but there was a small satisfaction in it which allowed the release of pent-up frustrations which otherwise went unexpressed. They soon developed a set of defacto rules. No rocks bigger than a golf ball. Never in the tracting area or other public places. Only when walking to and from the tracting area and so on. It kept it friendly and relatively private.

In a short time, they had teaching appointments, and their missionary hearts soared. The first Sunday meeting was a shock for Sam. They walked nearly two miles to the chapel. It was on a major thoroughfare, and visible for miles. It was nearly the biggest building in that part of town, certainly the biggest church.

They were mobbed by happy members as soon as they stepped inside. They were escorted to seats on the stand, and were treated like visiting General Authorities. They were each invited to bear their testimonies, and tell where they were from. The branch President was Brother Braythwaite, formerly from England. He conducted the services with a humble heart, and the Spirit was present in abundance. The talks were simple, yet inspiring, and the music was sung without accompaniment.

The congregation consisted of about ten families, with a total membership of about sixty people. Their Sacrament meeting attendance was about sixty people. After the meeting, Sister Braythwaite invited them to lunch at their home. They gratefully accepted. While they were waiting for President Braythwaite to finish his branch president branch business, Sam investigated the organ in the chapel. It was locked, but he found a key in the bench. He was amazed to find it was a new Allan organ, made in America. It still had a manufacturer's sticker on the keys to keep them from vibrating during shipment. He removed the strip, and turned it on. The sound was rich, full, and inspiring. He played "I Am a Child of God," and before he began the second verse people had drifted back into the chapel and were singing. By the time the song finished, the whole congregation had returned.

Someone called out a page number. "The Spirit of God like a Fire is Burning," thundered through the small chapel. He had never heard it sung more enthusiastically, nor with such righteous feeling. Somehow he knew that angels were also singing with them. He played for nearly two hours before he finally could play no more. He had not played an organ since the ward in Idaho, yet it was a wonderful experience. The Braythwaites were ready to go, so he turned off the organ to loud, but loving protests.

Sister Braythwaite bundled them off to her home which was in a somewhat more affluent section of town. The entire ward came too, all sixty or so of them. Sam could not believe his eyes. Everyone who came also brought food. They ate, laughed, and eventually, held a testimony meeting. It was fantastically spiritual, and the fellowship was like unto nothing he had previously experienced. It felt to him as if he had entered a small portion of the Celestial Kingdom. The Braythwaites had no children, and Sister Braythwaite was not shy about telling everyone how desperately she wanted a baby.

Sister Braythwaite, Sharon as she preferred to be called, was thirty-five, blond, blue eyed, and unusually beautiful. She had a model's body and a dazzling smile to melt any man's heart. Her laughter was second only to her keen sense of humor. She loved her husband with deep passion. She was a fairly recent convert to the church, yet possessed a spiritual depth that bore testimony of premortal greatness. From her high energy enthusiasm, to her fast speech and zest for life, she almost seemed to be living life double time.

Yes, Sharon had everything, including leukemia, and was not expected to live much more than another two to three years. The doctors insisted she did not have the health to carry a child full, term. She had tried, and had suffered three miscarriages. They feared that another attempt would be fatal to her. Reluctantly, she had given up her immediate hope of bearing a child, yet steadfastly maintained her faith that she would have her precious child before she left this earth.

Her greatest hope in the whole world was to go to America, where she just knew she could be cured of her disease and have her baby. Sam and Elder Palmer looked at one another when she said this, but neither of them tried to disabuse her of her dream.

Missionary work in Bulawayo was a joy. They rarely had a door slammed in their faces, and at least among the poorer class of people, most everyone they met seemed pleased they were there. They were a curiosity, an anomaly in that land, and people hungered for news of the outside world. Their challenge became finding a way to determine who was interested in the gospel and who was just interested in them as visitors from another planet. They would often be walking down the street and have someone open their door and call them over to visit. It was so different from South African missionary work that Sam wondered if he were walking in a dream.

Still, the bulk of their investigators came from the poorer section of town. Elder Palmer was a joy to work with. He was sensitive to the Spirit, and as obedient as Sam. Together, they taught with power, and people began requesting baptism.

———

The day was over, and they were walking down a darkened street through an area they had previously tracted. It was nine o'clock and time for them to hurry home. They were both tired and footsore. As they came to the middle of the street, both of them came to a stop. It was Sam's day, so he said what they were both feeling.

"Elder, I think we need to knock on one more door." Elder Palmer nodded, and started up the walk directly in front of them. Sam grabbed his arm, and pointed across the street.

"Just testing you, Elder." Palmer laughed, and together they crossed the dark street. The house was unusually small, and had no porch light on. Only a dim light in one of the rooms gave any hint of occupation. Sam knocked, and waited as someone walked noisily through the small house. In a moment a woman opened the door. Her hair was stringy and disarrayed. She snapped on the porch light as she opened the door, but left the screen door closed between them. They could see very little of her features, except that she was tall and dressed in a loose fitting cotton smock which was torn at the neck. A small child clung to her left leg and made whimpering noises. Her expression was not unfriendly, but it definitely was not welcoming. A feeling of darkness and despair emanated from her which Sam found oppressive. He started to give a door approach, when something unusual came from his lips.

"Good evening, Ma'am. We are missionaries for the Church of Jesus Christ of Latter-day Saints. We have come to tell you about the family home evening program, which strengthens families, and helps them draw closer together. Would you have a few minutes for me to explain it?"

"Do I have to buy somethin'?" She asked suspiciously.

Sam chuckled. It was the first time he had been asked that one. "No. Nothing to buy." She nodded meekly, and pushed open the screen door.

The room they entered was smaller than Sam's bedroom at home had been. It had a rough wooden floor and a single couch against one side. She turned on a lamp without a shade which made a harsh glow in the room. She brought a chair from the kitchen and put it against the opposite wall of the room. When they had sat, their knees were less than three feet apart. She lifted the child to her lap. She was a pretty little girl in a thin cotton dress. Both mother and daughter were barefoot. Sam noticed that the little one's front teeth were missing, and the mother had the remains of a black eye. The mother introduced herself as Elaine Knight, and her daughter as Eleanor. Eleanor buried her face in her mother's chest and curled up into a ball. Sam guessed her age at about four years old.

"Mrs. Knight, the Church of Jesus Christ of Latter-day Saints is led by a living prophet, and one of the things he has given us is the family home evening program. It's where families meet together each Monday evening, and share Gospel stories and have fun together. It strengthens families and builds bonds between them."

Mrs. Knight stared at him as if she did not understand a word he was saying. He continued. "Would you be interested in having us come back and share a Family Home Evening with you, to show you how it may benefit your family?"

"Does it have to be a Monday?" she asked. Sam actually was surprised she had understood that much.

"No. Any night. We would like to do it when your husband is home though."

Her face soured, but she shrugged it off. "How about this Friday? I think that was the day Thomas was coming home."

Sam consulted his pocket diary, and they made an appointment. In minutes they were out in the street, and the porch light snapped off. They made their way back to their boarding in silence. Palmer didn't even tip a rock at him once.

Friday came, and they found themselves standing a half block away from the Knight's home. Elder Palmer was not sure he liked what Sam proposed.

"I've never done a family home evening with an investigator. What are we going to do?"

Sam shifted his weight to one foot. He wasn't sure himself, but felt sure they needed to carry through. "We are going to have a family home evening with them, just like they were our own family. We'll say the prayers, sing the songs, and teach the lesson. I have some cookies Sister Braythwaite baked for us, and we will share them. It may be a bust, but we have to try."

"Elder, I sing like a dying cow."

"Me too," Sam admitted, and they both laughed.

"We'll soon know if you were inspired, or just at wits end, won't we?" Elder Palmer said quietly as he rang the buzzer.

A tall, balding man answered the door. He looked too young to be going bald. The man scrutinized them for a second, then pushed open the screen. Sam introduced themselves just as Mrs. Knight came beside her husband.

"You should know that we are Jehovah's Witnesses and aren't interested in Mormonism," he said in reply. His voice was gruff. Mrs. Knight punched him in the side, and he laughed.

"Just kidding. Come on in. You going to show us how to have a happier family? If anyone in the world needs that, we do. Sit over there," he said indicating the only couch in the room.

They sat in exactly the same spot as before. Sam asked Elder Palmer to offer the opening prayer. Afterwards, he slowly recited the words to the first verse of 'I Am a Child of God.' The idea was for the investigators to join in. It didn't happen and he and Elder Palmer sang the verse alone. Neither of the Knights made any attempt to sing. Elder Palmer had told the truth, he did sing like a dying cow. During their song, Mr. Knight struggled to keep a smirk off his face, and Mrs. Knight punched him in the side again.

Sam gave a short lesson on trust. He told a story about a little girl who had the job of taking her daddy's lunch to him each day while he was digging a well. Each day the well was a little deeper, and eventually she had to drop his lunch down to him. Each day she would hear her Daddy catch the bag, and she would return home. Finally the well was so deep that she could not see her father, only hear his voice from far below. Even when she couldn't see him, he caught the lunch every time. One day, as she came to the well, she found that the forest was on fire. She was too small to climb down the rope, and her father did not have time to climb up to her. She was very afraid, and the heat of the fire was growing nearer. She called down to her father who called up to her with a single word. "Jump!"

Sam turned to Eleanor who was cuddled on her mother's lap. Her mother called her "Ellie." "Ellie," he said. "What do you think happened? Do you think her Daddy caught her in his arms?" Ellie looked at her father with large, frightened eyes. Then at her mother, then back at Sam. She stuck two fingers in her mouth which her mother pulled back out with a loud sucking noise. Finally, Ellie nodded.

"You're right. Her daddy did catch her, and they were safe from the fire. Sister Knight, why do you think the little girl was able to jump into that dark well?"

"Because she trusted her daddy, and knew he wouldn't drop her." Her voice was sure, and a little accusatory. She glanced at Thomas.

"Is it possible for us to help our children develop trust in our love for them, so that when the need arises, they will trust us like the little girl in the story?"

"I would like to know how," Brother Knight said in all seriousness. "I would never trust someone with my life like that. Nobody ever inspired that kind of trust in me."

"How we do it is by earning that trust. The little girl in the story came to trust her Daddy to catch the lunch sack a little bit at a time. As the well grew deeper, her trust grew stronger. We can earn our children's trust. That's what this lesson is about. In the absence of learning to trust, children fear and mistrust. But it can be earned if we are willing to take the effort to do it."

Through all this the Knights had sat with wooden faces, hardly involved in the meeting and obviously not enjoying it. An air of strained dicomfort hung in the room.

Sam felt foolish and wondered why he had gotten himself into this mess. They passed out the cookies, skipped the closing song, and had a closing prayer. With no desire to remain in that uncomfortable situation a moment longer they both stood as if on cue. As they were leaving, Elder Palmer handed Brother Knight a Joseph Smith pamphlet, and told them about living prophets in the church today. Brother Knight tossed it on the sofa without giving it a glance.

They both breathed a sigh of relief when they regained the street. It had been an uncomfortable, unpleasant experience, and they were both glad it was over.

As the days slipped by, the Knight family evaporated from their minds. It was nearly two weeks later when they were again walking past their home, that they both came to an abrupt stop.

"I think we..."

"Should visit the Knights," Elder Palmer finished for him.

They both wondered why as they crossed the street, but they were there to do the Lord's work and they both felt impressed to stop. Their previous meeting still rang a dull tone in their memories, and neither looked forward to another meeting.

Mrs. Knight opened the door. As soon as she saw who it was, her face brightened, and she called into the house. "The Mormons are back!" In moments, Thomas joined her, and pushed open the screen. They went inside. Thomas brought two chairs from the kitchen, and Elaine got the pamphlet. As soon as they sat down, she held it open for them to see. Many paragraphs were underlined in red.

"We read the pamphlet together about the new prophet. We had no idea there was another Prophet on earth. I read it three times before I realized the dates. I assume Joseph Smith is dead now? Who's the current one? Is there a current one? What's his name? Why isn't this in all the newspapers? This is important, you know!" Thomas told them with some urgency in his voice.

A brief, yet lively discussion followed about living prophets. A missionary's greatest happiness is teaching someone ready for truth. It follows then, that a missionary's greatest joy would be teaching someone of simple and pure faith literally starving for truth. For the second time on his mission Sam tasted the sweet, sweet fruits of missionary joy, and it thrilled him to the center of his soul. The Knights questioned them with eagerness and simply believed. There was no doubt, no cross examination, no dispute or debate. Their hungry souls simply received the truth with child-like faith.

Elaine poked Thomas in the ribs. "Told ya," she said. "Tom said that Joseph Smith died, and there wasn't another one. But I told him God wouldn't start something, and then let it die out again. Told ya." . Thomas chuckled at her.

Thomas leaned forward. "I have been trying to do the trust thing, and guess what," he leaned forward as if he were going to tell a secret. "It's working. A little. She doesn't trust me since I busted her teeth out. Don't blame her none. But I was drunk, and I didn't even remember doing it. I even gave Elaine a black eye too. Don't remember that either. I still feel terrible about it, but it was the drink, not me. The best thing is that Ellie is acting better toward me already." He leaned back. "I just need to figure out how to do it with Elaine now. She still won't let me sleep at home. Don't blame her though." Elaine punched him in the side, and gave him a meaningful look. He gave her a frown, but his eyes were smiling.

At that moment Ellie came from the back of the house. She was in pajamas, and clutching a threadbare teddy bear. She scanned the room, and walked to Sam. She held up her arms, and he lifted her onto his lap. She was as light as a feather. She curled up against him, and started sucking her fingers. With her other hand she began twisting his tie.

Thomas cleared his throat. "Elder Palmer, would you give us an opening prayer so we can get started with learning about this new prophet?" Palmer's mouth dropped open, but he quickly recovered and offered a simple, but lovely prayer.

As soon as they had said amen, the Knights began peppering them with more questions. It was all they could do to answer one before they came up with another. Every answer given was accepted. It was as if they had been starved for months and now were being allowed to eat a great feast. During the meeting, both of them smoked constantly. In a short time, the room was dense with smoke, making it unpleasant in the cramped and stuffy little home. Thomas noticed this and opened the front door. Several hours passed before they finally left. It was later than they should have stayed out. The Knights begged them to come again the next evening, which they did.

The following evening, the Knights looked restless, and fidgeted with their hands. After the opening prayer, they announced simultaneously that they had quit smoking.

"Well," Sister Knight said matter-of-factly, "my parents are Jehovah's Witnesses, and they told us that you Mormons don't smoke or drink. They are furious that we are talking to you chaps, because they have been trying to convert us for years."

"So," Thomas interjected, "we figure if we're going to join the true church, we had better start acting like it. So we gave up smoking. Well, actually, Elaine gave up smoking, and I'm about half there. She gave it up just like that." He snapped his fingers. "I'm struggling with it, but I'll make it."

"He will too," Elaine said. "He's bullheaded like an ox. When he sets his mind, its set. He said he wants to join the Mormon church, and that's that. So I had to scramble to make up my mind. I know its true, I just don't know anything much about it. Know what I mean? So you better teach me fast."

"And I want to know," Thomas added, "if it's true that we have to give up tea and coffee too?"

"Yes. Isn't it wonderful how much Heavenly Father cares about us?" Sam replied, a smile on his face.

"Damn!" Thomas said, and Elaine poked him in the ribs. "Oh, sorry. What I mean is, I'll get to that next. Smoking first. Drinking next. Then tea and coffee. Damn! I mean, darn." She poked him again.

"Ask them about tithing." Elaine urged Thomas. "Ask them."

"Tithing too?" he asked.

"A tenth," Sam said.

"Only a tenth? That's not much. I spend more than that on cigarettes. I'll get healthier, we'll pay tithing, and still have some left over. This will be great. When can we start? Do we have to be baptized first, or can we start tithing next Sunday? Do you Mormons pass a basket for donations, or how do we do the tithing?"

"You put it in an envelope and privately hand it to the Branch President."

"I like that way much better. There's so much pressure when they pass the basket, never thought that was right for God's church," Thomas said.

Elaine's voice was excited as she informed them; "we want to come to church next Sunday. Is that all right?"

"Oh, absolutely. Yes. It will be wonderful to have you," Sam responded, his head starting to spin. Elder Palmer gave him a bewildered look. Neither of them would have been surprised if they had both jumped up and shouted "April Fools!" Except they were both serious.

By this time, Ellie had twisted his tie until he was choking. He took the tie from her sticky little hands and untwisted it, then put it back into her hands. "Here, twist it the other way for a while." Ellie smiled, and said "OK," almost in a whisper.

Thomas bolted to his feet, and Elaine clapped a hand over her mouth. He turned to his wife, and exclaimed. "Did you hear that?" Elaine nodded, tears forming in her eyes.

"What?" Sam asked, completely baffled.

"Ellie has never spoken to a stranger. Not one word. Not ever. Nothing. This is the first word we have ever heard her say to anyone but us. She said 'OK.' It's a miracle. A miracle!" her mother cried.

"OK," Ellie said again, and twisted furiously at his tie.

"Well, she's still pretty young. Some kids are very shy for a long time. How old is she, about four?" Elder Palmer asked.

"She's almost eight," Thomas said.

Sam felt tears pooling in his eyes. Somehow, the twisted tie felt sweet against his neck.

"OK?" little Ellie asked, and Sam could only nod.

That first Sunday, Brother and Sister Knight acted frightened. Sister Knight wore excessive makeup, and Thomas had polished his shoes until he wore through to the paper. Ellie sat on Sam's lap and twisted his tie. Sam had tried to explain that they should wait until they were baptized to take the sacrament. When it was passed to them, they both partook. Elaine leaned over to him and whispered, "Sorry, but in our hearts, we are already members, you know." She poked him in the ribs. Sam just nodded. In his heart, he knew her words were true.

As the days progressed into weeks, the change which came over the Knights was miraculous. Each day they came, they felt a sweeter spirit in the home. Thomas surprised Elaine by buying her a refrigerator with money he had saved from not smoking. It was an old, American made model with the large coils on top. It was probably made fifty years ago, but it ran, and it made cold air, and to them it was a miracle. Their kitchen was so small that they had to put it in the living room, where they proudly showed them the carton of milk for Ellie.

Each day, Ellie spoke a little more until she practically became a jabber box. Sam had to bring trinkets for her to play with to keep her quiet. Without exception, if Sam was in the room, she was in his lap. He loved little Ellie, and his heart ached for her. She was so small, and her heart so hungry, that he wished he could give her something to feed her body and soul all the nourishment she had missed in her short life.

With the extra money they ate better, and Ellie began to grow. Elaine sewed her a new dress, and she began to laugh and play like a normal child. Every once in a while she lapsed into the tie twisting silence, but that became less frequent and eventually vanished.

The branch nearly swallowed the Knights whole. They lavished love upon them. In a short time the Knights were friends with everyone and would have continued to attend church even if they had been denied baptism. Sam watched all this with a sense of wonder, and thought how this little branch, lost thousands of miles from anywhere, was more like Zion than any place he had ever been.

The Knights were baptized exactly fout weeks from the night of the botched family home evening. Sam baptized Thomas, and Elder Palmer baptized Elaine. The whole branch was there. Every priesthood holder present stood to confirm them. It was a token of the absolute unity they felt one toward another.

Afterwards, they held a dinner party to celebrate. Ellie ate about half the food on the table. Her parents consumed as much love and fellowship as their souls could absorb.

The next Sunday, Thomas was ordained a deacon, and he helped pass the sacrament. Tears streamed down Sister Knight's face the whole service. Her eyes were glued to him as he moved reverently from row to row. It was as if she were shouting "I love you! I love you!" over and over. Everyone in the chapel sensed it, and few eyes were dry, including Sam's.

That following Monday, they met with the Knight's. They taught them how to study the scriptures and how to use the index and bible dictionary. It was a fun meeting. When they were about to leave, a feeling of concern came over Sam.

"Brother and Sister Knight, I have a concern I want to share with you."

"Sure Elder. What's on your mind?" Brother Knight replied.

"World wide, about half the people who are baptized later fall away."

"Oh, I'm surprised," Sister Knight said. "I can't imagine anyone falling away."

"I know what you mean," Sam agreed. "However, you can also imagine that your joining the Church is a great disappointment to Satan."

"I hadn't really thought of it that way. Well, let the old bugger be disappointed. I don't care," Brother Knight laughed.

"Still, I feel impressed to tell you, that I have observed a particular pattern that Satan seems to use in trying to get people to leave the church. Usually, it starts by someone giving them some anti-Mormon literature. So I want you to tell me when that happens. OK?"

"As a matter of fact, it has already happened," Sister Knight said as she stood and walked out of sight. In a few seconds she returned with a handful of pamphlets. "My mom and dad brought these over. We weren't going to read them, but I did anyway, and they are disturbing. I just figured they mostly are lies, but even still, it makes one wonder about things. Did I do wrong by reading them?"

"No. As a matter of fact, let's talk about your questions. It's like I said, it usually starts this way. You can just accept it as a witness that you have done the right thing. The gospel is true, and Satan has a plan that works, so he uses it over and over."

"We can talk about the anti-literature in a minute. I'm curious, what's the next thing that usually happens?" Sister Knight wanted to know. She picked up a pad and began making notes.

"Usually, the next thing is that the new member is offended by a member of the church. This is a big one, and usually works. The members of the church are wonderful, but they are just people, and Satan can usually get one of them to give an offense. Lots of new members leave because they feel offended, or perhaps embarrassed. When it happens, you have to overlook it, and forgive them, and go on."

"OK, we'll let you know when that one happens. What's next?"

"Next, people usually come across some doctrine they thought they understood, but which is actually different, and which challenges their testimonies. When that happens, you need to fast and pray, and perhaps get some council from church leaders. The church is true, and the doctrine is beautifully complete. You just have to be humble enough to always understand that our understanding of it is never complete."

"That's a good one. OK, what's next?"

"Well, at some point, a person in a position leadership will make an error, or even commit a sin against the new member. At least, it may appear to be the case. The key to overcoming this one is to forgive the leader, and to allow even leaders to make mistakes. Sometimes this one gets harder when they don't seem to be repenting. But even then, the principle is the same. We have to forgive. And we have to remember that the truthfulness of the church does not crumble because a leader makes an error."

"Well of course not," she asserted. OK, what's next?"

"From here, I don't know of any particular pattern. But by this time, you should be strong enough in the faith that you can handle most anything that comes along. Just always remember that your faith and testimony are more important than anything else, and never sacrifice them to justify your pride or to punish another for some offense."

It was barely two weeks later when both the Knights came up to the Elders outside the church. They seemed excited to get them where they could talk privately.

"Guess what, Elders," Sister Knight said excitedly, placing a hand on each of their arms. "It happened. Someone offended me and embarrassed me right in Relief Society. I gave the opening prayer, and then the lesson was on prayer, and the lesson was about not doing almost everything I had done. I was so embarrassed! It was awful, and for a few minutes I thought about just stomping out of the room and never coming back. Then, I felt really angry, but I remembered what you told me, and I walked right up to that Sister and asked her to forgive me for saying the prayer wrong.

She was surprised, because she didn't realize she had offended me. She got this look on her face of total embarrassment when she realized what she had done. She said she was thinking about her lesson during the prayer, and hadn't really heard it. She was so ashamed and asked me to forgive her. We hugged and are best friends. It was wonderful, and I am so grateful for the warning. We are going to watch real close for the other things and not let them throw us off. Just thought you'd like to know."

———

In the Southern hemisphere, winter comes in May and lasts for several months. Winter consists of two months of rain, sheet lightning, terrifying thunder storms, and wind. The temperature never drops below 50 degrees, nor the humidity below 80%. The first rainstorm of the season caught them out walking. The rain hit the pavement so hard it bounced back up. They ran nearly a mile home, arriving thoroughly soaked.

When they were almost there, a clap of thunder crushed against them, and a flash of lightning exploded from east to west, then rolled horizontally along the underside of the clouds until the entire sky was a huge, dazzling, blinding electrical discharge. In less than a heartbeat it had roared across the sky from north to south with a crackling scream that was terrifying. Seconds later, Sam was lying on his face, covering his head with his arms, and Elder Palmer was kneeling beside him, his face a sheet of white, his hair standing on end.

"What was that?!" Sam screamed.

"Satan!" Palmer screamed back, only half joking.

"Run!!!" They cried together, and ran the remaining several blocks home, half crouching as they went. Each time the sheet lightning exploded over them, they fought the urge to hit the ground. They found out later that sheet lightning is one of the most spectacular and least dangerous of all the lightning phenomenon.

They dried off in their room, and put on dry clothes, except clothing is never dry in 90% humidity. In a tropical country like Africa, homes are not heated. The inside of the house was the exact temperature as outside. They shivered in their damp clothing as they tried to study the scriptures. When they finally went to bed, the thin blankets did nothing to warm them. After a few hours, Sam got back up and pulled a rug off the floor onto his bed. After that he began to warm a bit, and finally slept. He was still cold when he awoke. His first thoughts were of a hot bath, and he hurried to draw the water. In Africa, trees and lumber are scarce, and homes are constructed of brick and concrete. The bathtub sat on a concrete floor, and by the time he climbed in, the water was already luke warm. Even filled with hot water, the tub was cold on the bottom. Before he climbed out, he felt colder than when he had gotten in. He hurriedly toweled off in the cold room, put on damp clothing, and shivered the whole day.

Sam had never been so cold in his life. The only time he got warm was when they walked briskly to their tracting area. As soon as they stopped however, the breeze would whip through their damp clothing and the cold would return. Being inside a house made no difference. Most homes were not made tight against the wind. The main rooms were open at the eves of the roof to let air circulate. To seal a house tightly was to condemn it to destruction by mildew and mold. Even the doors had no thresholds to keep out the breeze. Even in the snow storm and sub zero temperatures at home, he had not felt this cold, this long.

The next time the district leader appeared, he informed them he had challenged the city basketball team to a game. Sam couldn't believe his ears. The district leaders, Elder Tingley, was tall and wiry, and had played basketball in college. His companion was short and quick and was almost as good as Tingley. Sam had never played basket ball because of his poor vision. Elder Palmer only said that he could hit the basket if he tried hard enough. One other set of missionaries were coming from a neighboring town to join them.

The game was scheduled for the following Monday. They arrived at the field house, which contained a nice basketball court and bleachers. The stands were packed with towns-people. Almost all the members of the church were there, and several hundred others. Someone handed him the local newspaper. The front page held a story about the "Americans" challenging the local team. The article only mentioned in passing that they were all missionaries for the church.

Since there were six players, Sam took a position on the bench. He was grateful, because his basketball skills were badly underdeveloped. The referee blew the whistle, and Elder Tingley out jumped the other center and grabbed the ball. In less than thirty seconds he flew to the other end of the court and made a basket.

The other team put two players on him, and it was the last free basket he got. The other team was good, and in less time than Sam believed possible they scored three baskets, and the score was 6-2. Tingley was all over the court, running constantly, shooting every time he got the ball. But he was double teamed, and few of his efforts were fruitful. The other four missionaries on the court did almost nothing. When the score his 12-4, Elder Palmer called a time out.

Elder Palmer quietly scolded Elder Tingley for trying to win the game by himself. Elder Tingley nodded, sweat running down his face. Elder Palmer suggested they pass the ball around, and see what the other members of the team could do. He mentioned that if he was outside the key, to toss him the ball. He wouldn't let them down.

The ball went to Tingley, who dribbled it to the key, quickly became surrounded, and bounced the ball to Palmer who was standing at the top of the key. Elder Palmer tossed the ball toward the hoop as if it were a wad of paper. The ball swished through the hoop.

The other team missed their shot, and the ball came back to their end. Palmer had stayed about half court. Tingley's companion rebounded, and tossed the ball to Palmer. He turned, took two steps, and swished the ball.

As the game progressed, the strategy became one of getting the ball to Palmer, who generally stayed between half-court and the key. He hit the vast majority of every shot he attempted, many of them from nearly half-court. When the other team ganged up on Palmer, he passed the ball to Tingley who easily made the open shots in the key. The other Elders dribbled and passed and had opportunities to make a few baskets themselves. The crowd roared with approval. They cheered every time a basket was made by either team. They had come to watch basketball, and who won was secondary to the fact that this was real entertainment, real people, real basketball.

By half time, Tingley insisted Sam go in for him. Sweat was pouring down his face, and he was approaching exhaustion. Sam huddled with the guys, and only made one request. "Throw the ball to me slowly, or bounce it, or I won't even catch it." In the first few seconds of his entering the game, Palmer bounced the ball to him. He turned and made a basket. The ball rolled around the rim sloppily and went it, but it was worth as many points as Palmer's swishes. It was the first basket Sam had made in his life. It was the only game he had been in in his life. It felt electric to hear the crowd roar approval. He was flattered when two of the other team started to guard him. They soon figured out that he was no threat, and went back to Palmer. As soon as he was not guarded, they tossed him the ball, and he made another sloppy basket.

Sam stayed in nearly the whole quarter, during which time the other team got ahead. He wasn't much help, and the other team easily stole from him. He learned by sad experience what double dribble was, what traveling was, and a host of other violations, but no one became impatient, or ordered him off the floor. As he became familiar with the ball and his own ability to actually catch the darn thing, he began playing in earnest, and ran until his legs felt quivery. In the finaly wash, he made six baskets. A lifetime high for him.

When Elder Tingley replaced him, the score was 35-47, the other team's favor. It was the fourth quarter, and everyone was exhausted. Sam wiped sweat from his face and cheered the guys on. Tingley passed the ball more than he shot it, and Palmer continued to swish nearly every shot he threw. The other team began surrounding Palmer, and the others took advantage of the open court. When the game ended they lost 62-65. The crowd roared and ran out onto the floor. They were slapped on the back until it hurt, but the crowd was delighted. Each person who shook their hands also got a Joseph Smith tract. It was unusual missionary work, but in that setting the people thanked them like they had received a precious, American-made souvenir of the game, for free.

When the crowd started to thin out, the other team came over and enthusiastically shook their hands. They said repeatedly that they were amazed they had beaten a team from America. They were so impressed with themselves, that no one had the heart to tell them they were just a few missionaries, and not the Harlem Globe-trotters.

Sam and Elder Palmer baptized three more families before Sam was transferred. One of them was Sister Knight's Jehovah's Witness parents. In all, they spent eight months together, and both of them wept when the letter came announcing Sam's transfer. The branch quickly organized a going away picnic at the chapel. After the meal, they herded Sam to the organ and he played for three hours, while the saints of God sang with great zeal.

Finally, Sam began to play "God Be With You Till We Meet Again." He could barely see the music for the tears in his eyes. He played the last verse almost without anyone singing, for their hearts were too tearful to make more than a whisper. He closed the organ lid and slid from the bench. He quickly shook every hand, hugged those closest to his soul, kissed Ellie on the cheek, and slipped out into the night. His heart was soaring with both rejoicing and anguish. He loved these people and knew he had righteously served the Lord among them. He also knew he would never again visit this part of Zion. Leaving them was bitter-sweet.

ten

A Distant Melody

The train left Bulawayo April 28, 1975, and headed south. During his train ride to Rhodesia, Sam had gotten sick from coal smoke. It was approaching winter again, and Sam was dreading the ride and breathing coal smoke and fumes for five days. However, the weather was cool, and the windows were kept closed. His cabin had a heater in it, which actually blew warm air. He huddled by the register and let the warm air blow up his pant legs. It felt sweeter than any feeling he could remember. Every few seconds his body shivered with delight.

On the second day, late in the afternoon, the train suddenly lurched. Sam felt the wheels beneath his car lock up, and scream in protest. He grabbed onto the seat for support. A series of sharp jolts was followed by his car pitching to the left. For a moment it felt like the car might roll onto its side, then it settled back. A series of minor jolts followed in rapid succession as the cars behind slammed into the couplings. A large escape of steam roared from the engine a few cars ahead, and the heater quit blowing hot air. It made Sam feel like crying. Simultaneously, the lights in the train went out.

Sam watched out the window as armed guards ran to positions beside the train, and began patroling back and forth. Sam pushed open the sliding door to his cabin and took a single step into the hallway beyond. Other people were emerging into the hall, some pressing bandages to their heads, or other injuries. He stooped to look out the windows and could clearly see the engine lying nearly on its side a short distance from his car. The train had derailed. The car immediately following the engine was nearly on its side. His car was the first one still upright.

It was nearly an hour later when the conductor came through his car, explaining what had happened. The rails had been sabotaged, and the engine was hopelessly derailed. They had radioed for assistance and expected another train by morning. The conductor said people from the forward cars had to be evacuated and asked if some could join Sam. He had a private berth, but his room had four seats and four beds. Sam agreed without hesitation. The church bought the three extra tickets to his cabin to give him privacy. The thinking was, rather than send another missionary along to be his companion, keeping him isolated on the train would serve the same purpose.

161

Consequently, he had three empty seats in a nearly full train.

In just a few minutes, the conductor introduced him to two young women. Marcia and Melody MacUlvaney. The girls were sisters, traveling to boarding school in Cape Town. Both were frightened, and refused to share his cabin. Marcia was eighteen and Melody sixteen, and they insisted that they would have nothing less than a private cabin.

"I understand your concerns," the conductor said with thinly veiled impatience. However, there are only three sleeper cars on this train, and yours is lying on its side, as you recall. The third one is full, and this one has two rooms with space. The other one has two young men your age, also traveling away to school. And this one."

"This gentleman is an American missionary, a Mormon. They have the highest moral decency, and I trust you would be best served here, than in with the other two gentlemen, who are in the process of getting drunk even as we speak. There simply are no other options I'm afraid." So saying, the conductor threw up his hands without waiting for a reply, and stomped away.

The girls stood just outside his cabin, still uncertain what to do. Sam correctly interpreted the look on their faces as terror and stood on impulse.

"Forgive me. I'm not thinking clearly," Sam said. "I'll go spend the night with the college students, and you two take my cabin. That will be better, I think. Then you won't be afraid to have me here with you."

Marcia nodded, and Melody shook her head. They both wore long brown riding coats which covered them from neck to ankle. Both wore huge wool caps and gloves. They were dressed warm enough for Alaska, let alone Africa. The few soft curls of hair which hung from their hats were light brown. He could see very little of their faces because of their large caps.

It was Melody, the younger, who finally spoke. Her voice quivered as she spoke, but the words were calm. "No. I should be ashamed to put you out of your own cabin to accommodate us. No, I think not. You are kind to offer, and your kindness settles my fears somewhat. I think perhaps we can trust the American missionary. Ne?" she asked, turning toward her sister. She spoke with that musical, lilting accent some British people acquired after living in Rhodesia. Her accent almost sounded Australian.

Her sister merely walked past him, sat down primly, and turned her face toward the window. Sam couldn't tell if she was disappointed, angry, or terrified. Melody sat beside her, and pulled off her large wool cap. A tidal wave of hair spilled over her shoulders and flowed nearly to her waist. Sam was amazed so much hair could have been inside. She pushed the flows of hair away to reveal an unusually beautiful face. Her eyes were dark brown, her nose small and turned upward. Her lips were full and seemed as if they might be comfortable with laughter and smiles.

Under different circumstances he would have found himself smitten by her beauty but he was a missionary, and the thought didn't occur to him that her beauty was anything other than beauty and meaningless to himself as a member of the opposite sex. Before sitting, he pulled the door to their cabin closed and latched it. He took the seat opposite the girls. The cabin was sufficiently small that their knees were nearly touching.

Sam felt the chill starting to seep into the cabin, and pulled his jacket from his bag. Without heat in the train, it was going to be a cold night. It was only a few hours before dark, and without the engine running, there would be no electric lights in the train. The guards were building large fires on both sides of the train to keep the night from overtaking them entirely.

Before there was time for an awkward silence to develop, the lock on the door spun open, and the conductor shoved the girls bags into the cabin, banging them against their legs. Sam helped Melody stack the bags in the luggage rack overhead. Amid the luggage were two violin cases. He picked up the first and held it for a few moments before carefully placing it on top of their other luggage.

Melody cocked her head inquisitively. "Do you play?" she asked.

"Not really. A close friend showed me a few things, and I tinkered around. But I've never had any lessons or anything."

"I see," she replied, disappointment in her voice. There was a meaningful pause before she continued. "We are going away to continue our studies on the violin. Papa wants us to play professionally. Mama played beautifully before…Anyway, we are going to school at Jan Smutts conservatory of music. So, you might say, we love and hate the bloody things."

This earned a snort from Marcia. Sam let his eyes widen in response. In this culture, bloody was a curse worthy of a hardened criminal, not a proper young woman on her way to boarding school. Yet she seemed unrepentant, and Sam smiled in response.

"Good," she responded resolutely. "You're not a prude. I just wanted to see if you were going to lecture me on cursing."

"Did I pass the test or fail it?" Sam asked suspiciously.

"Fail," Marcia muttered simultaneously with Melody's "Passed."

Sam chuckled. At that instant a rifle fired, then another. With each report Marcia slumped lower and lower in her seat, and Melody flinched as if she herself had been shot. Sam wasn't sure whether to be scared, or curious. After a moment, another detonation sounded from the other side of the train. Sam could hear someone in the car behind him begin to cry. It sounded like a small child. Someone cursed in the distance, and something banged inside the train. It sounded more like someone threw some baggage around than anything more dangerous, but it had an electric effect on the passengers. Panic seemed to become palpable, and people began running in the hall outside their door. Voices shouted, demanding explanations.

Melody looked up at him anxiously. Twin tears slipped down her cheeks. At that moment the door to their cabin was wrenched open. Two young men teetered in the opening. One had a bottle clutched tightly in his hand. They were both drunk.

"Came to see if you ladies," he slurred the word sarcastically, "needed some comforting?" the one closest said loudly.

"Go away Kirt," Marcia said sternly. "We don't want anything to do with you."

"Why not?" He demanded. "Oh, I see, you got some other dandy to twattle with then?" he said, motioning toward Sam.

"Don't be rude, Kirt." Melody demanded. "This gentleman is a Mormon missionary, and much more pleasant company than you and your liquor." The latter she said with a poisonous tone to her voice.

"Yes, well. I promised your father I'd take care of you two, so you're coming back to my cabin. We can keep each other safe and warm, and whatever else comes to mind." The man behind Kirt laughed drunkenly.

In a single motion Kirt stepped into the room, and grabbed Melody's arm. She struggled to free herself, but could not. He drug her to her feet.

At exactly that moment Sam came to his feet, his heart pounding, his fists doubled. He was furious, and every muscle was tensed for battle. He took a step forward, but was brought short by a blow to the chest, not from any visible source. It felt as if he had run into a wall of solid air. It brought no pain, but had the effect of stopping him absolutely. A feeling of calm swept over him, and he raised his arm to the square.

Kirt was shouting and Melody screaming protests, so that neither of them heard him say, "in the name of Jesus Christ, and by virtue of the Melchizedek Priesthood, I command you to come out of him, and trouble us no further."

Whether Kirt heard it or not, it had an immediate effect. He suddenly released his hold on Melody and staggered back, shaking his head as if dazed.

He turned his eyes toward them, and Sam saw confusion and apology in them. "Melody...what?" Kirt stammered as Sam turned him toward the door, and helped him out. In seconds it was over, and the door was shut. He fiddled with the locks until he found the one that could not be opened from the outside. He slammed it home with finality. He was getting tired of that door bursting open. Besides, there was near pandemonium in the hall. People were running in both directions, knocking one another down in the narrow passage.

When he sat again, Melody had a look of confusion on her face, but Marcia was staring at him with piercing brown eyes. He realized that she had heard every word. Without preamble, she said. "You cast an evil spirit out of him, didn't you." It was not a question.

Sam didn't know what to say. He wanted to explain, to tell them about the priesthood, but didn't know where to start. Just then, another rifle fired, and someone started fighting in the hall. The train jolted as bodies grappled not far from their door. Men cursed, and the sound of blows echoed in the train.

On impulse Sam stood and retrieved one of the violin cases. He opened it to find an expensive instrument neatly packed in velvet. He picked it up and strummed the strings. The instrument was in perfect tune. The small instrument smelled of wax as he tucked it under his chin. He pulled the bow across the strings and made a long, solemn tone. Then he slowly began to play the only tune which came to mind. "Abide With Me, tis Eventide." He played slowly, carefully, his fingers unsure what to do next. He was grateful to find that even though his fingers may be unsure, his soul was not, and the music swelled within him flowing out of the little violin. He played with feeling, and peace settled over him.

Somewhere in the middle of the piece, the brawl in the hallway stopped abruptly. He switched to another hymn and played with deep feeling. After two or three hymns, he stopped. The silence in the train was almost as if everything outside their door had ceased to exist. The crying in the adjacent cabin had stopped.

From far away, a small, frightened voice called, "Amazing Grace." Sam loved that song. He played it with a sense of joy, and was vaguely aware of voices singing in the distance. Marcia stood and retrieved the other case as he played. She lovingly lifted the instrument and tuned it quietly. Afterward, she handed it to Melody who tucked it under her chin. Sam began the second verse, as Melody played a quiet harmony.

It was the most beautiful thing he had ever heard. He watched her eyes close, and felt the power of her love for the instrument she held. She played with great skill, her touch sure and masterful. She allowed the harmony to flow unrestrained. It made his own music seem amateurish with its complexity and unabashed beauty. Yet as powerfully as she played, her music was like a full orchestration and made Sam's simple melody sound like a beautiful violin solo.

Another request came from outside the train. The name of the song was French, and unfamiliar to Sam. Melody smiled and pulled the bow across the strings in quick, sure strokes. A joyful melody danced through the train, lifting hearts and causing toes to tap everywhere. After the tune capered to its conclusion, someone requested "I Am A Child Of God." Sam knew the person must be a Latter-day Saint, and it warmed his heart. He lifted the bow and played with a joyful heart. Melody listened carefully and joined him on the second verse, again quietly playing harmony. Again, it was breathtakingly beautiful. The person who had made the request began to sing in a powerful tenor voice. The words of the precious hymn rolled through the train like a summer breeze. Peace settled upon them. Few even noticed the next few rifle shots. Sam and Melody certainly did not. All they heard was the music in their souls as it spilled from the strings.

They played for over an hour, mostly answering requests shouted from their unseen audience. They played until someone rapped on their door. It was the steward, who handed them a tray of bread, cheese and mineral water. In the middle of the tray burned a single candle. Darkness had descended completely during their playing, and the candle brought a cheery glow to the room.

As they unfolded the table from the wall, the steward explained that the rifle shots were intended to keep lions and hyenas at bay. If they did not fire periodically, they would sneak up on the train. He told them to ignore the intermittent shots. Sam accepted the explanation, yet wondered what threat wild animals could be as long as they remained inside the train. He wondered if there weren't another explanation.

They were hungry, and the food was unexpected. They ate in silence. By now it was dark outside, and people were settling down. He could hear others pulling the bunks down in adjoining cabins. The steward came and showed them how to pull down the beds. There was a moment of awkwardness after he left. Sam excused himself and walked the length of the train. Candles had been left burning at intervals along the train. With darkness on every side being haltingly held back by the flickering candle glow, Sam felt as if he were inside a medieval castle.

Everywhere he went, people were humming to themselves and

speaking in hushed voices. The effect of the music upon the people had been magical. They, of course, had no idea it had been he who had played the music. It was somewhat mystical to walk the halls, nearly invisible in the darkness and enjoy the peaceful effect of the music. What the people could not guess, was that the peace they felt did not come from the music, it came from God. The music had only opened their hearts to the divine. Praising the music for calming their souls would have been like applauding the velvet curtain at a performance. All the curtain did was open the performers to their view.

When he returned, Marcia and Melody were both in bed, their coats and dresses hung on hooks on the wall. He pulled off his shoes and tie, and climbed into bed fully clothed. There were extra blankets, and in a few minutes he was warm and comfortable. He could hear the girls breathing slowing and deepening. He blew out the candle.

From the darkness a small voice asked him. "What did you do to Kirt?" He could not be sure which of them asked the question, but was fairly sure it was Marcia.

"I relieved him of his motivation to hurt."

"You mean you cast an evil spirit out from him, ne?" she asked, using a colloquial expression of polite inquiry, which one word roughly meant: Is this not true?

"That's one way to put it, I guess." Sam replied. He knew evil spirits afflicted people, yet was aware of his imperfect knowledge concerning them. This was only the second time he had used the Priesthood to cast one out, and was not totally sure of what he had done. He only knew that he had done what he felt prompted to do.

"Why? Why do that, as opposed to fighting him. You are bigger than him and look capable. Why do what you did, hey?"

Sam thought about this. It was actually a good question, and he didn't have an immediate answer. When the answer did come, it was as informative to him, as it was to Marcia and Melody.

"To be a disciple, is to do the bidding of the master. I did as I was directed, by the authority of he who directed me. Nothing more."

There was a long pause before Melody's voice asked. "I didn't know anyone could command evil spirits to depart in these times. I thought that all ended with the bible times."

Sam waited until the right answer formed in his heart. It felt important to him to give exactly the right explanation. "It did," he replied. "It was lost shortly after that, and was not on the earth again until a new prophet was called in 1820. As a missionary and Elder of that restored Church, I hold the authority of the Priesthood which has been passed down from that new prophet unto this day. It's a wonderful thing. If you like I will tell you about it in the morning."

"Sam?"

"Yes, Melody?"

"Can such an explanation wait until the morning. I think I should not be able to sleep for wondering what this all means. Would it be too much of an imposition to ask you to explain tonight? Please?"

Sam was still quietly explaining the restoration of the Gospel as the sky began to lighten outside. He realized with a start that he had taught and testified to them the whole night. He began to apologize, but they both urged him to continue. He continued by bearing his testimony, and promising them he would continue after a few hours sleep.

It was the most peaceful sleep he had ever had. The Holy Spirit blessed that little cabin with its sweet presence, and they slept the sleep of angels.

———

Sam awoke with a start to a sudden volley of gunfire. He rolled from his bunk and hopped to the floor. He was surprised to see his breath in the morning air. He raised a blind just as another volley of gunfire exploded from the small circle of men guarding the train. At that moment he heard something thud against the train, and a split second later, the distant report of a gun. The guards answered with a volley. Silence followed for a few seconds before a spatter of bullets again thudded into the train. He heard people shouting in adjoining cars, and several people screamed.

Marcia and Melody tumbled from their bunks, and pulled their dresses over their heads. He kept his back turned, intent on watching the day dawn on the drama outside his window.

He noticed for the first time that they were in a large valley surrounded by low, rolling hills. The train track cut through the lush desert on a raised bed of red gravel about three feet high. A short distance beyond the gravel pad the bush began abruptly. What everyone called bushes were actually small trees, each somewhat taller than a man. The larger bushes were a milky, olive green, with darker green plants growing in clumps closer to the ground. The ground was covered with a patchwork of grasses and wildflowers. The guards were kneeling on the gravel pad to give them the advantage of height. They had brought some wooden crates from the train to act as a barrier to protect them. The closest guard was only about six feet from his window.

While he was observing this, he spotted a figure darting between the bushes in the distance. The guards responded by firing toward the figure. Seconds later, the sound of breaking glass was followed by a distant report.

Without warning, about ten men suddenly appeared in the bush and fired at the train, then quickly disappeared. Bullets ricocheted through the air, and glass shattered on the train. A guard near Sam's window lurched backwards, spun in the air, and landed on his face, a red stain quickly forming on his side. He thrashed on the ground for a moment before rolling over onto his back. A similar stain was forming on his shoulder, near his neck. Sam could clearly see his face pinched in pain. The man pulled a white cloth from his pocket and pressed it against his shoulder. It quickly turned red. Another volley from the bush smashed against the train, and the guards began backing from their wooden crates. They grabbed their wounded comrade, and retreated to beneath the train. At least there they would have the big steel wheels to give them some safety.

"Sam?"

Sam had momentarily forgotten about the two girls, and turned toward them. They were huddled on the floor, against the door, as far from the windows as possible. As he watched, Melody pulled Marcia's head onto her chest and held her, stroking her hair. With each gunshot Marcia flinched as if she, herself, had been shot. Marcia was immobilized by fear, while her younger sister seemed grimly determined. Melody's face was a study in conflict between terror and icy, cold determination. It created an expression on her face something like a young mother might have while confronting a charging lion to protect her child.

"Sam, aren't you afraid?" Melody asked incredulously, her voice small and strangled.

It suddenly occurred to him that he was being foolish to stand in the window, and knelt down. He wondered for a moment if he was too foolish to be afraid, or too American to comprehend that people actually did attack passenger trains. He briefly wondered if he thought he was watching TV, and the violence could not get past the glass of his window. Her question was a good one, and he pondered his feelings. When he knew the answer, he spoke it.

"No," he said honestly. "I'm not afraid."

At that moment he heard a whistling sound which grew louder and higher in pitch until it ended in a deafening explosion near the train engine. The whole train shuddered, and jolted from the impact.

It was the loudest thing Sam had ever heard, and he wondered if he were deafened. They were only two cars from the engine, and the explosion sounded as if it actually hit the derailed engine. Seconds later, another whistling sound arched toward the rear of the train. It landed further away, but still the train bounced on the tracks. It seemed their attackers had bigger weapons than rifles. The obvious occurred to Sam and to everyone who was not too terrified to think. Their attackers had no particular interest in capturing them alive.

"Why?" Melody asked simply, ignoring the explosions.

He wondered how to answer her question and waited for the right answer to form in his heart. When it came, it answered his own question as well as hers.

"When I made the decision to be a missionary for the Lord, my father gave me a blessing in the name of Jesus Christ. My dad is a High Priest in the church, and a former bishop and a man I know to be close to God. Among other things, he blessed me that if I was obedient to the commandments and to the promptings of the Holy Spirit, that I would serve a wonderful mission, bless many lives, and return home safely. As he spoke those words, I felt the Holy Spirit confirm their truth. I'm not afraid because I have implicit faith in the promises made to me in His name."

Melody pondered this as another bomb whistled directly over-head and exploded on the far side of the train not far from their car. The glass on the opposite side of the train shattered with a roar, and the train rocked against the explosion. Finally, she said, "I envy you your faith, Elder Mahoy. I have always believed in Jesus, yet my faith is not sufficient to bring me your sense of safety. I guess my faith just isn't strong enough to know He will keep us safe."

"Many people believe in Christ," Sam replied. "Not many are able to believe Christ."

"I don't understand the difference," Marcia said, turning fright-ened eyes toward him. Sam was glad to see that she was listening.

"Many people believe IN Christ, that He is the Savior. What they don't believe is that He will keep His promises. He promises us great blessings if we obey Him and keep His commandments. Lots of people don't keep His commandments because they don't think He will bless them as promised. They doubt He will give them something as wonderful as whatever they are getting from their sins. So they keep sinning. If we really believed Christ, we would trust Him to keep His promises. I have the added comfort of having my father give me a blessing in Christ's name, in which I also have great faith. I believe Christ, I guess you might say."

"OK, I guess I understand that. If we truly believe IN Christ, then we should believe He will keep His promises. That feels true. I guess I just wish I had a blessing from your father too, and your faith to believe in it," Melody replied, her eyes lowered.

At that exact moment, a blaze of machine gun fire erupted like the roar of a demon. Bullets impacted the train from one end to the other, and glass exploded into their cabin. Fortunately, it was safety glass, and did not cut them, but they were suddenly buried in a avalanche of broken glass. Sam could see a half dozen bullet holes in the walls not far above their heads. Marcia buried her head in Melody's bosom and trembled there. She was too frightened to scream.

Melody cocked her head to one side and studied Sam through squinted eyes, as if trying to see through him. "You really aren't afraid, are you?" She observed.

Sam did not answer that question, he was thinking of her earlier statement. "Melody, I hold the same Priesthood power that my father does. If you want, I could give you a blessing too. I don't know what its content will be. That's up to the Lord. But I know it will come true, and I know it will help you."

Marcia's raised her head, and turned tear, filled eyes toward him. "Oh, please. Please, could you give us your father's blessing?" she implored. Melody merely nodded, and smiled weakly.

Sam crawled the short distance which separated them until their knees were touching. He reached out and placed a single hand on Marcia's head. She trembled beneath his hand as she lowered her head onto Melody's chest.

"Marcia, in the name of Jesus Christ and by the power of the Holy Priesthood which I hold, I give you a blessing of comfort and peace. Fear not the battle of men, nor the harm that men can do. You will live many years beyond this day and will see your dreams fulfilled. You will become a noted musician and teacher of music. In time, you will reflect upon this day as a happy memory, and tell it with wonder to your children, about the day God saved you from sure destruction by the power of His arm and simple faith in His love. In the name of Jesus Christ, Amen."

Marcia looked up, an expression of wonder in her eyes.

Since Melody was closer, Sam placed both hands on her head. As he did so he was suddenly filled with a glowing warmth and a powerful sense of her spirit. The impressions which crowded into his mind were so sudden and powerful, that he gasped involuntarily. It was as if he knew Melody, perhaps had always known her, and this sudden realization took his breath away. It took him a moment to speak.

"Melody, in the name of Jesus Christ and by the power of the holy Priesthood which I hold, I also give you a blessing of peace and comfort. You are a noble daughter of Heavenly Father, and a precious spirit in his sight. In order for you to fulfill the measure of your creation, you will be called upon to endure many trials, the present difficulties being a mere shadow of what will follow. You are the first and the last. You are the last to inherit the curse of your fathers, and the first to triumph over it. Your quest will take you to many nations and bring you full circle. When you finally find what you seek, you will have returned to this moment, and it will bring you joy. In the name of Jesus Christ, Amen."

She looked into his eyes as he took his hands from her head. They were pooled with tears, and when she blinked, they coursed down her cheeks. A deep feeling unexpectedly stirred within him which he suppressed almost without noticing it. He could not help but feel the sweetness and purity of her spirit, and it thrilled him in a way he had never before experienced.

"Sam, your blessing both comforts, and frightens me. Do you understand the words?" Sam merely shook his head no. "I thought not. But I felt the warmth and the peace. I believe what you say will be, and it will bring me joy," she said.

"I think you gave part of Melody's blessing to me," Marcia said. "She's the great musician, and I'm the one who's always getting into trouble." Her voice was brighter, almost peaceful.

Sam smiled, but did not answer her. He had given them the blessings the Lord intended. He reached for his scriptures on the seat behind him, opened it to a blank page in the back, and wrote down the two blessings as nearly as he could remember them. When he finished, he signed it, wrote the mission home's address beneath his name, carefully tore it from his scriptures, and handed it to Melody. She and Marcia read it together.

At that moment, an amplified voice boomed across the desert. The voice spoke in heavily accented English. Oddly, Sam thought the accent sounded Spanish.

"You will be now throwing your guns away, now! We have much bombs, and will kill you all very much, badly! Immediately surrender! Now!" The guards beneath the train responded by firing. The detonation seemed to come from directly beneath their train car. They fired again, and again a hail of machine gun bullets riddled the train. Some of them hit below the windows, but did not penetrate the thick steel of the old train cars. At that moment another bomb whistled toward them, and exploded outside their window, showering them with dirt through the open windows. Sam's ears were ringing, and he found himself huddling with the girls. They pressed themselves against him and tried to make themselves small. Another bomb exploded a distance away, then another. Sam did not hear the guards from beneath the train return fire.

Sam could hear men shouting in a foreign language outside the train while sporadic gunfire came from beneath them. At that moment, a machine gun of much larger caliber belched with a deafening roar. It was so obviously a larger gun, that it made the former machine gun sound like a toy. This gun spat bullets in a slower, more booming roar of heavy weaponry. The gun belched in short, authoritative bursts. Sam knew such a gun would easily penetrate the steel of the old train, yet no bullets hit the train. All he could hear were the shouted commands and curses of men outside.

Suddenly, an engine roared a short distance away, and the big machine gun belched. This new vehicle sped past their car as the big gun bellowed its rage. No bullets hit the train for a full minute, and the shooting from under the train ceased. Sam heard men cheering outside. He crawled toward the window on shattered glass. What he saw outside was the most beautiful sight in the world.

An old World War II vintage, armored, personnel carrier spun around on it's huge rubber tires, spraying the bush with bullets from twin machine guns mounted on the top. The big gun blazed and threw a flame six feet from the end of the barrel. Off in the bush, he could see figures scurrying away from the train. Cheering began up and down the train as more and more people recognized their salvation.

Sam heard the tell-tale whistle of incoming artillery, and an explosion nearly flipped the old vehicle on its side. It slammed back to the ground, its wheels on that side falling into the bomb crater. It tipped into the crater, and sat there immobile as if stunned. There was the whistle of another shell just as all six wheels on the faithful old machine churned the ground. It lurched up out of the hole in a roar of smoke, dust, and bravado. Seconds later, another shell landed in the exact spot where it had been. Sam could see that the left side of the armor was dented in nearly a foot. But the old machine roared ahead, blazing from the twin machine guns overhead. It zigzagged through he bush, firing almost steadily. It was gone nearly a half hour. When it returned, it was nearly destroyed. It limped back to the train, its wheels on the side of the explosion bent and wobbling severely. One of the big guns was drooping, as if it had gotten too hot. Its side was pocked with bullet holes, some appearing to almost have penetrated its armor.

The big machine came to a stop, spun slowly to face outward, and the motor clanged to a stop. A steel hatch slammed open on top, followed by a blue cloud of smoke. A head appeared in the smoke and looked all around. A large man climbed out onto the top of the tank. He looked much too large to have been inside the tank. He was dressed in a khaki colored uniform, and had a huge handlebar mustache. He was broad of shoulder and slim of hip. His whole demeanor was confident, yet shaken. His smile displayed a wide gap between his front teeth.

"Daddy!" Melody and Marcia screamed simultaneously, and bolted from the cabin. "Daddy, Daddy!" they cried as they pushed past people in the narrow hallway and jumped from the train to the ground. Sam was just jumping to the ground as their father caught them both, and in an effortless move lifted them both, one in each arm, and swung them around. "Daddy! Daddy!" they cried, holding onto him with all their passion, and love.

"I made it!" he bellowed repeatedly in a voice much too loud. "I found my babies in time! I came for you! I did it!" His voice was huge, booming. He made no effort to suppress the tears running down his cheeks.

"Daddy! You came for us! Thank you!" Marcia nearly screamed at him.

"You lost a shoe?" He shouted at her.

"No, Daddy. I'm delighted you came."

"What's the same?" he shouted.

"Daddy, what's wrong?"

"This is no time for a song," he shouted, and roared with laughter.

Sam tapped Melody on the shoulder. She merely glanced at him. "He's deafened by the gunfire, and explosion," he said to her back. She nodded. She had already figured that out.

Melody made hand signs to him, and he nodded. "Yes," he shouted. "The bloody explosion and bloody machine gun bloody deafened me. It will pass. Just give me a few minutes. It will bloody well pass."

Marcia said something about cursing, which he misinterpreted. She ignored his nonsensical response.

Two other men climbed from the old war machine and were surrounded by cheering people. They were equally deaf, yet had no difficulty understanding the joy and adulation the people lavished upon them. When everyone on the train had come to thank their rescuers, there were about a hundred and fifty people.

In a few minutes his hearing improved, and he demanded to speak to the engineer. A man in a conductor's uniform informed him that the engineer had been killed in the wreck. It took a few minutes to get the people back onto the train, and to assemble the remaining railroad people. Marcia, Melody, and Sam were invited to stay.

Melody introduced Sam while they were waiting for the passengers to return to the train.

"Daddy, this is Elder Sam Mahoy. He took good care of us while you were coming. He is our friend, our very good friend," she added.

"Donavon MacUlvaney," he said, taking Sam's hand in a powerful grip. "So, you're the Mormon missionary on the train. I thank you for taking care of my babies. You will find that my gratitude means something young man. Thank you."

"Pleasure, sir," was all Sam could think to say. A part of him wondered how he knew he was "the" Mormon missionary on the train. He dismissed the thought as the train people had finally gathered.

Donavon started speaking without preamble or introduction. "I have just drove over 200 kilometers. Four vehicles started out, the rest broke down part way here. They have weapons and food, and are expecting reinforcements. My vehicle is out of petrol and out of ammunition," he said, as he looked at the old armored vehicle. "I'm afraid the old girl has fought her last battle," he added wistfully. His demeanor quickly turned business-like.

"We are in the bushlands of Botswana, as you know. Shortly after the train left Bulawayo, a rebel faction declared civil war and threatened to disrupt transportation. As soon as I heard that, I organized a private force and launched out after this train and my girls. I was afraid I wouldn't get here fast enough. Thank God..." his voice trailed off.

"The point is, we can't expect help from Rhodesia, since they are trying to negotiate a treaty with Botswana as we speak. We can't expect help from South Africa, since this is a Rhodesian Express train, they have no legal right to interfere. In short, we're on our own. We can't stay here. The rebels will go for reinforcements, and as soon as they realize I am by myself, they will attack with everything they have. As some of you may have correctly surmised earlier, they are not after hostages. They intend to kill us after they have..." Donavon didn't finish the sentence. It required little imagination to understand what he didn't say.

"We have to get started immediately. My chums are about a day's march away. If we march all night, we can make them by late tomorrow. If we stay here, we are surely doomed." A chorus of agreement arose from the railroad people.

Sam was about to agree also, but felt a reluctance flow through him. He pondered this for a moment, trying to determine its origin. He bowed his head, and supplicated with all his soul. The stakes were very high, and he did not want to misunderstand. He closed his eyes, and sought guidance, searching the inner reaches of his soul. A feeling of peace flowed over him and he rejoiced.

"Sam? Sam?" He started when he realized Melody was speaking to him. He opened his eyes, and was startled to realize everyone was looking at him, waiting.

"Sorry," he mumbled.

"Sam, what is it? You look troubled," she asked, placing a hand on his arm solicitously.

"I..." he wondered what he should say. He didn't know what they should do, he only knew what they shouldn't do. They should not start walking back toward Rhodesia. "I don't think we should start walking toward Rhodesia," he said quietly.

"Why not, man!" Donavon demanded in a booming voice. "We're less than fifty kilometers from the Rhodesian border. We can't stay here, and we're over three-hundred kilometers from South Africa."

"I'm not sure. I only know that we shouldn't go toward Rhodesia."

"Look, lad," Donavon said, his voice lowered in a patronizing way. "I know you're scared. I am too, but I have been fighting these bloody rebels for over twenty years. I know how they think. They'll be back about daylight tomorrow morning. There is food, ammunition, and friends less than fifty clicks from here. Logic dictates that we go that direction."

"I'm not speaking of logic. I'm saying I feel that we should not head north. If we must leave, it should be to the south."

"What you're saying doesn't make sense, lad."

"I'm not claiming it does. I'm just saying its the right thing to do."

"Well, OK. Let's put it to a vote." He raised his voice. "All who want to head north immediately, raise your hand." Everyone except Sam raised their hands.

"All who want to go south, raise your hands." Sam raised his hand timidly. He was the only one. However, just as Donavon was about to speak again, Melody raised her hand.

"Melody, what are you doing, baby? You're coming with me, back home," Donavon thundered, his voice sure and demanding.

Melody cleared her throat, all the time looking steadfastly on

Sam. Without lowering her hand, she said, "I'm going with Sam, Daddy. You take the others, and go north."

"But why?" he thundered. "The Mormon doesn't know this country. I do. I came to take you home, and that's what I'm going to do," he concluded with finality.

Without looking away from Sam, she said. "Are you prepared to hog tie me, and carry me screaming and kicking for fifty kilometers? No? Then I'll be going with Sam."

"Tell me why. At least give me the satisfaction of explaining your foolishness. Give me something to write on your grave marker, at least," he concluded with frustration.

"Daddy, forgive me. I trust you, and I'm so grateful you came for us. But, you see, before you saved us, there were bombs bursting, and machine guns firing, and people screaming, and I was terrified. But Sam wasn't. I asked him why, and he said because we were going to be safe. Daddy, he knew something that seemed illogical at the time. He believed something that seemed foolish and impossible."

Donavon grunted, as if to say that what Sam was going to do was still foolish.

Melody ignored her father. "When Sam told us those things he had a particular look on his face, a look of calmness and peace. He has that same look now. Look at him and you'll see it."

"I don't see a bloody thing. I see a bleedin' Yank, Mormon, fool. That's what I see." Donavon leered at Sam, as if pretending to see beyond the obvious.

Sam was surprised at Melody's words, yet they were true. He didn't want to be their leader or to be contrary to Donavon. He just knew as surely as he knew anything, that he should not be going north with them. If necessary, he would remain here alone. While these thoughts were going through his mind, Donavon's expression changed, softened somehow.

Unexpectedly, Marcia turned toward her dad. "I'm staying with Elder Sam too. I can see that expression same as before. Daddy, please don't make us go north. I'm afraid we will all be killed. Do what Sam says. Please," she pleaded.

"Bloody!" Donavon exploded. He scrubbed his face with both hands, as if dry washing it. "You two stubborn women will be the death of me. You're just like your mother, God rest her sweet soul. And you, Sam the Mormon, are going to be the death of us all. If you are wrong, we are all dead. You know I won't leave my babies. But you better know this, if you're wrong, I'm going to save my last bullet and put it between your eyes. Do you understand me?"

Sam swallowed hard. It was a deadly serious threat. He considered apologizing, or offering a compromise, or waffling somehow. But knew he should not. Instead, he excused himself and walked out into the bush. When he had gone a short distance and was beyond hearing, he knelt upon the sandy, red, soil and prayed with all the energy of his soul. It seemed as if a long time elapsed before he felt comfortable with what he must do. He returned to the train, and found Donavon, who was still grumbling.

"Donavon? I wish to travel south. Since Melody and Marcia are planning to come with me, and I know nothing about the bush or survival in the bush, I would be very grateful for your company and leadership. I don't mean to cause you problems, and I am humbly asking for your help and protection."

Donavon stood and faced him. A multitude of expressions crossed his face before he merely nodded. He turned toward the train employees. "Tell the passengers I am leaving to travel south. I will conduct anyone who wishes to go with. Tell them no guarantees. It will be hard and dangerous, but less dangerous than staying here. Tell them if they wish to travel north they should just follow my old tracks. Divide whatever food is left equally among the passengers. We leave in thirty minutes."

The group scattered to pass the word. Melody and Marcia returned to the train to get spare clothes and their violins. Sam tied some things into a small bundle around his scriptures. He picked up his coat, camera, and an extra roll of film. Everything else would have to catch up with him later, if ever.

It was nearly noon by the time they struck out. Less than half the passengers on the train joined them. About fifty people remained aboard the train, and about twenty people started north, toward Rhodesia. Most of the railroad employees remained with the train.

Of the nearly 75 people in their group, well over half were black, who picked up the bundles of food, balanced their baggage on their heads, and strode off with an easy gate. They hummed or sang as they walked, and seemed perfectly at ease. Sam picked up a box filled with loaves of bread and carried it under one arm. Under the other he held his bundle of clothes. In just a few minutes his arms were aching, and he was struggling to hold onto the box. A young African girl caught up with him and through hand signals, made him understand she wished to carry the box. Though awkward, it wasn't heavy, and he felt silly surrendering it to a young woman. She persisted and he handed it to her. She wrapped a sweater around the top of her head and deftly balanced the box on her head. She smiled at him, took her own small bundle of clothes, and tossed it onto the top of the box. It landed neatly in the middle of the box. With one hand on a corner to steady it as she turned, she began walking briskly away. He smiled, and caught up with Melody.

They walked along the train tracks, stepping from tie to tie. The black folks seemed to prefer walking among the bushes, weaving in and out to make their way. He could see parcels bouncing just above the tops of the bushes on both sides of the tracks. Donavon led the way, walking at a moderate pace. His eyes constantly scanned the country-side, but they heard and saw nothing but an endless reach of train track and desert. As it began to grow dark, they stopped and built small fires. Donavon insisted they only build very small, smokeless fires. He had to show them how. The blacks already knew how, and deftly built small cook fires. They passed out their meager rations. Sam got two slices of bread and a tin of sardines. He hated sardines, but he was so hungry they actually tasted good. He sat by Melody as they ate.

During the whole hour they ate and rested, neither of them spoke. But they communicated just the same. It was spiritual and deeply personal. When it was time to leave, Donavon carefully extinguished their camp fires and strode off into the twilight. At first, Sam found it impossible to walk on the ties in the darkness, but soon got the rhythm of it and found that he could do pretty well. Eventually, he ended up holding Marcia's right hand and Melody's left. Between them, they could keep lined up on the tracks and stop each other from falling and hurting themselves.

When daylight finally began to peek above the horizon, they were bone weary, their ankles, shins and knees scraped and raw from numerous falls. Donavon called a halt, and again they built small fires. Sam nibbled on bread while Melody slept against his shoulder. Marcia found her father, and curled up beside him. He let them sleep for several hours. Sam awoke to the feel of warmth on his face. He opened his eyes to broad daylight and the welcome warmth of the sun. Melody had slumped to the ground, her head resting lightly in his lap. He resisted the urge to stroke her hair. Instead, he took off his jacket and laid it over her. She stirred and seemed to sleep more peacefully.

They were just beginning to stand and stretch their limbs when Sam heard the distant thrum of a helicopter. Donavon shouted for everyone to get into the bush. They ran into the trees and tried to hide. In several minutes a big helicopter passed over them, moving fast and low to the ground. It suddenly looped around and came back to their camp-site. Sam could see men through the cockpit glass. A man stood at a machine gun in the open side door. There were no markings on the helicopter, it being painted a sand-colored camouflage.

A speaker squawked, then a man's voice boomed across the desert. "Greetings from the South African Air Force. Glad to see you are all right." The voice bore a heavy, South African accent and sounded cheerful. "We will radio in your location and proceed on to the train wreck. Please remain at this location. A train is on its way and should arrive at your position in several hours. You are safe here. Good luck. Goodbye." The big chopper turned and powered away. It was obvious they were in a hurry.

Everyone cheered, and began hugging one another. Melody hugged him, then ran to find her father. They built a roaring fire and consumed all the rest of their food and water. There was a lot of laughing and back slapping. Donavon sought out Sam. He arrived with a daughter on each arm.

They sat down by him, and after a few minutes Donavon handed him another tin of sardines with a smile. It was as much of an apology as the big man had ever made, and it was sufficient.

The train arrived as promised, and they were helped onboard by concerned men in uniform. There were no sleeper cars, only military style coaches. Sam sat by himself, and Donavon and his daughters squeezed onto a bench meant for two. The train was heavily armed, with soldiers in every car. One of the cars ahead of them was a train version of an army tank, with a heavy cannon, and many machine guns protruding from slots in its sloping sides. Sam felt perfectly safe and was soon asleep.

He awoke later as the brakes squealed. They ground to a stop. Sam followed Donavon out onto the ground. They had arrived back at the train wreck. The train had been heavily bombed. Only a few people had survived. They told a tearful story of trying to fight against hopeless odds. It was the helicopter that had finally delivered them from certain destruction.

The survivors were helped aboard the train. The big helicopter settled onto a flatcar on the train and refueled. A short time later it headed north. It was gone just a little over an hour when it returned. It landed back on the flat car, and they began the long journey south. Except for meals, Sam slept the entire trip.

They arrived in Pretoria twenty three hours later. President and Sister Carlson met Sam and hustled him away. As they were leaving the train station, they unexpectedly ran into Donavon, Marcia and Melody climbing into a cab. Donavon waved vigorously and trotted up to Sam, the girls close on his heels.

Sam introduced the Carlsons, and they shook hands. Without preamble Donavon said, "Did you hear about the group who walked north toward Rhodesia?" Sam shook his head. He was not anxious for more bad news. "They were ambushed. No survivors."

Sam dropped his head, his heart heavy. It seemed such a short time ago. "When we were about to head south," Donavon said, interrupting his thoughts, "I threatened you. I meant what I said. What I didn't say, was that if you were right, I would be profoundly grateful. I owe you a great deal, young man. If there is ever anything I can do for you. Anything at all…"

"It just so happens there is something," Sam said, and pulled his leather bound Book of Mormon from his small bundle of possessions. He held it out. "I will consider the debt settled if you will read this book and sincerely pray about it." Donavon took the book, looked at the title, and smiled.

"You Mormons don't give up easily do you?" He chuckled. "I'll gladly do as you ask. God bless you Elder Sam Mahoy," he said, as he squeezed Sam's hand without shaking it. The grip was so fierce it brought tears to Sam's eyes, tears of joy. Donovan shoved a hand into one of the many pockets in his vest and pulled out a tiny parcel tied in a white cloth. He nodded to Sam and handed him the little bundle, then spun on a heel and walked briskly away, hands clasped behind his back.

Marcia gave him a warm hug, and turned away. Melody paused momentarily, unsure of what to say, then impulsively held him for a long moment. It was much more than a hug. She kissed him on both cheeks, and blinking tears from her eyes, turned and ran away without a word. No words could have been adequate to express the feelings of deep sadness mingled with joy which coursed through her heart.

Sam and the Carlsons had driven many miles in heavy silence before Sam remembered the little bundle. He carefully unwrapped it, and to his astonishment, found a perfectly cut diamond the size of his thumbnail.

May 12, 1975

I only have one more thought to add to what I have already written about Rhodesia. I find myself thinking about Melody. Not in a romantic or worldly way, but in a way that makes me feel as if our lives will intersect again. I wish I had kept a copy of the blessing I gave her on the train. I remember something about her going full circle, and coming back to that moment. I don't know what it means, but feel myself involved in her life again, perhaps far into the future.

I take that back, I do feel romantic. Strike that too. I love her. I suddenly realize that I have never loved someone before. Not like this. It is exquisitely sweet, and sharply painful. I'm quite sure I don't like the feeling of discovering love, and losing it at the same moment.

President Carlson has kept me at the mission home for nearly a week. He doesn't let me go out tracting, or teaching, or anything. I have been filing papers in the mission office. He says I need a rest. He spends a lot of time on the phone. I know he is trying to find out exactly what happened on the train.

I told him the entire event, and showed him the diamond. He took it without promising to return it. He didn't seem angry, but also didn't seem pleased. I think I get into too many unusual problems for his perception of a good missionary.

Well, at least I can add one more thing to my list of things I don't want to be when I grow up. I don't want to be a clerk or typist.

"Elder Mahoy my boy, come. Sit down," President said cheerfully, waving him to an overstuffed leather chair. Sam sat, a feeling of weariness settling over him. He really was tired and didn't feel ready for this interview.

President pulled his chair from behind the ornate desk around to where they were nearly touching knees. He smiled and sat, one elbow propped on the corner of his desk.

"Elder, I apologize for keeping you cooped up in the mission home this last week or so. I know you have been anxious to get on with your mission. In all candor, I have spent the last ten days on the phone with nearly every government agency in South Africa and Rhodesia. Almost without exception, they have been glowing in their reports of your conduct on the train. The glaring exception to this, is the Rhodesian embassy, who feel that your involvement in urging the people to go southward was an affront to the rebels they were negotiating with, and doing so inadvertently led to the attack on the remainder on the train…"

"President, I…" Sam began, but was cut off by an upraised hand, and friendly smile of dismissal.

"No need to defend your actions, son. I'm satisfied that your actions were what saved those people. I'm also certain that if you had stayed, you would have been killed along with the rest. The difficult part of all this has been keeping you away from reporters and out of the newspapers. They have been clambering for your story. I hope you don't mind that I have shielded you from that." It was not a question, and Sam shook his head slightly and stared at his hands in his lap. All this was news to him, and he honestly did not want publicity. It would make the rest of his mission impossible.

President Carlson leaned back in his chair, and looked thoughtful. "What I don't understand is how you manage to get yourself into so many difficult circumstances. Mind you, I know you don't plan them, but you do seem to attract them. You're the only missionary, the only one, for whom I have had to twice intercede with the government. Once to bail you out of jail after being flogged, and once to keep you from becoming a national hero. You are a most unusual young man, Elder Sam Mahoy."

Sam didn't know what to say, so he kept quiet. This only seemed to make President Carlson uncomfortable. Sam sensed what his question was, but waited until President asked it.

"Elder, why do you have these astonishing experiences?"

"President, my grandfather used to say, if you aren't making waves, you don't have your oars in the water."

President Carlson chuckled at that, yet waited politely for him to continue. He wasn't going to be put off by a clever answer. In reality, Sam was aching to understand all this himself.

"President, I'm not sure I understand myself why these things happen to me. I certainly don't want them. I would be very grateful if you would explain it to me. I'm afraid I am not good for the mission. I seem to get into a lot of trouble without asking for it. If you want to send me home, I wouldn't blame you," he said meekly.

"Nothing could be further from my intent or from the truth," President Carlson replied, his voice filled with surprise. "My reason for asking you these questions was to see if you understood what is going on in your life?"

"I sure don't," Sam responded dejectedly.

"Have you studied the life of Joseph Smith, Elder Mahoy?"

"A little, but not as much as I'd like to."

"You are of course aware that he lived a life that basically moved from one difficulty to another. His life was a continual course of tragedies and set backs."

"He certainly paid a high price for his righteousness," Sam observed.

"And that is the key." President added quickly. "Opposition is always meted out in direct proportion to righteousness. The greater our efforts and ability to serve God, the greater the opposition. It is my opinion that you experience what seems to be more than your share of trials because you try harder than most to be obedient and effective in your calling."

"It doesn't seem fair," Sam observed quietly.

"Oh, but it is! Its perfectly fair, and just, and according to divine law. Through all the ages of time, those who have set the course of their lives in service of God have, by that same course, brought into their lives great trials. Yet, consider this my boy, that every single one of them rejoiced in their blessings. I am convinced that if we were able to question any one of them, they would bear powerful testimony that the reward is gloriously worth any price.

"I am concerned about you, it is true. But, you must understand that my concern is not that you have these trials, but that you aren't defeated by them. You must never interpret the fact that opposition arises as an indication that God has abandoned you, or that you are failing in your calling. Do you understand?"

"Yes, and no," Sam admitted. "I do feel like a failure at times, and I do feel as if can't bear up under my trials sometimes. I feel like I need to apologize to you, and to the Lord. Yet in my heart I feel Heavenly Father's love, and I do rejoice in my blessings. It is all quite confusing to feel both ways."

"I think it's important to observe here that we can bring trials into our lives through unrighteousness and disobedience. It would be foolishness to assert that all trials are a result of opposition arising from righteousness."

"I understand that, President."

"I'm sure you do. However, I think it equally important to point out that these trials on your mission are a result of your righteous efforts to serve the Lord. That being the case, I want you to fast and pray until you no longer feel like a failure because of your trials. All such feelings do not come from the Holy Ghost."

"I hadn't considered that," Sam admitted, his mood lifting.

"Think about it until you understand and believe it with all your hear, my boy. At the same time pray for courage and strength equal to your faithfulness. It would be tragic if one was not able to endure the very trials his strivings to righteousness ordained. Along with the spiritual fortitude to press forward into righteousness, we must have the moral courage to endure the outcome, which includes fantastic blessings and great trials."

"I'm not sure I have the courage you speak of. I have felt utterly defeated so many times on my mission that I could write a book about them."

President Carlson chuckled and made a dismissive motion with his hand. "You say that, but here you are, ready to move forward. I think you have plenty of courage. Perhaps you just need to rely upon the Lord more, and upon your own courage less. You will have to work that out with the Lord. But never let your heart faint or become discouraged in these matters."

"I will try, President. I really will."

"Very good!" he said enthusiastically, bringing that subject to an abrupt close. "Now, I have one more item to discuss with you."

"Yes, sir?" Sam replied, unsure again.

"I am calling you to serve as the district leader in the Natal District. You will have a new missionary directly from the States, and will be leaving this afternoon for your new assignment."

May 20, 1975

Transferred once again. This time to Durban, in Natal, near the Cape. I will have a new companion straight from the LTM, and will be the District Leader in the Natal District. President Carlson is wonderful. He expressed the utmost confidence in me when he called me to this position. After talking to him I feel a new hope and lifting of my spirits.

Who's counting, but I only have seven months left on my mission. I feel like I haven't gotten anything done yet.

eleven

The Atheist

Elder Kim Hall was directly from the LTM and as green as grass. Sam picked him up at the bus station. Elder Hall was dark haired, black eyed, half a head shorter than Sam, and half his size. He was smiling when Sam picked him up, and still smiling when they arrived at their digs. Sam found himself liking Elder Hall. He was so eager to please and willing to serve, that Sam found himself rejoicing inwardly.

"Where you from, Elder Hall?" he asked once they entered their small room.

"It's hard to say," he replied blandly.

"Why is that? Most people know where they're from," Sam replied with a chuckle.

"Well, its like this. My mother's current domicile is in San Jose, California with my father. Well, that is my step father, who is actually like a real father to me. My biological father, who is less of a father figure than my step father, currently lives in San Francisco with his wife, who is more like the sister I never had than a step-mom. I have spent every other six months of the past twelve years in one of those two places, so that I really don't know to which one I owe the prestigious honor of calling my home. So you see, it is difficult to say."

"Geepers, Elder. I see what you mean." Sam said. "How old are you?"

"Why do you ask such an inconsequential question?" Elder Hall asked.

"Just curious. You talk like a college professor," he replied as he unloaded pamphlets from his pockets.

"Would it cause a substantial shift in your opinion of me if I told you I was just nineteen?"

"Uh, no," Sam answered, not sure if Elder Hall and he were even from the same planet.

"I'm nineteen."

"Finally, a sentence with just two words in it," Sam muttered to himself.

"Sorry, Elder Mahoy. I'm used to communicating on a substantially higher level than is usually considered conversant in non-academic circles."

"Are you speaking English?"

"Actually, no. I'm speaking Stanford. It's quintessentially Californian and somewhat more expressive, though a little more verbose and snooty than village English. Some call it High English as a joke. It's required of anyone in graduate school. And a bad habit, I see now."

"You're a graduate student at Stanford?" Sam asked, amazed.

"I had hoped to avoid this subject," he replied dejectedly.

"You brought it up. And why would you want to avoid it?"

"Because few people find me socially tolerant when they find out I speak High English, am a graduate student at Stanford University, and only nineteen years old. I guess I've grown defensive over the years."

"You've also grown vocabularily abusive."

"There's no such word, Elder."

"I know," Sam admitted. "But it was the only big word I could come up with on the fly."

Elder Hall laughed so heartily that Sam decided once and for all that he liked him. For Elder Hall's part, he found Sam a welcome relief and a gentle introduction to missionary work. He made himself a promise to drop the 'High English' and speak like everyone else.

Sam was thinking along the same lines when he said: "Tell you what. I know a perfect way to slow your English down to mere village English, as you put it. Let's go through the discussions in Afrikaans. I've been in Rhodesia for seven months, and they only spoke English there. It would be a good refresher for me."

"I don't know them in Afrikaans. They cut our stay in the LTM short because our visas came through early. I only learned through the second in Afrikaans."

"In that case, why don't you study the third in Afrikaans while I fill out these district reports. OK?"

"Sure," Elder Hall replied. He grabbed his book, and curled up on his bed in what appeared to Sam to be a very uncomfortable position.

Sam filled out reports until his head spun. When he looked at the clock he was startled to observe that three hours had passed, and it was time for bed. He noticed that Elder Hall was reading the scriptures.

"I thought you were going to work on the discussions," he said with mild rebuke in his voice.

"Did it. Got it here," he replied, tapping his temple.

"You memorized the third?" Sam asked in amazement. It was a

long discussion on the Word of Wisdom, and had taken him days to memorize.

"Not actually."

"What do you mean, not actually?"

"I didn't just memorize the third. I memorized all of them."

"You what!?" Sam demanded, disbelief in his voice. Elder Hall just nodded and went back to reading.

Sam flipped open the book and thumbed to a random place in the fourth discussion. "Give me the third concept of the fourth."

Elder Hall rattled it off word-perfect. Sam corrected his pronunciation in several places. Sam turned to various places in the discussions, and was startled to find that Elder Hall had spoken the truth. He knew them verbatim.

"How did you do that?" Sam demanded, amazed nearly speechless.

"I have a small gift. I memorize easily. Actually, I just read it once, and I've basically got it. I'll read it again tomorrow, and it will stick forever. It's nothing, I have always been able to do it."

"Do you understand what you've memorized?"

Elder Hall looked up with a quizzical expression on his face. "Ah, now, that's the rub. I don't have a clue what it means. They are all just sounds to me. I would appreciate your going through them and giving me the translation. That would help immeasurably."

Sam was even more flabbergasted. He had memorized the whole set of discussions in three hours, in a foreign language, without having a clue what the words meant.

As the weeks progressed, Elder Hall became more and more of an astonishment. He was studying medicine at Stanford, was in his second year of graduate school, had a 4.0 GPA, and was president of a fraternity. The fraternity he created and was president of, was called the "Anti Protest Fraternity." They opposed anyone who opposed anything.

He said it started as a joke, but actually became popular because it gave kids a chance to be have a voice against the radical groups so prevalent on campus. If someone held a sit-in to protest a rule not allowing men and women to live in the same dorm, Elder Hall's group staged a protest to support the rule.

In time, his group had more members than any radical group on campus, and their protests drowned out the real protesters. He grew long hair, a scruffy beard, and wore beads and torn Levis. Because they looked their part, the real protesters were not offended by their anti-protesting, and Stanford University was delighted by their effect.

They offered to fund Kim's Anti Protest fraternity. He published the letter in the school paper and held a protest.

Equally as astonishing was, that Elder Hall had been a member of the Church just a little more than a year. One of the protests staged during the spring of '71 was against the building of a Mormon Institute of Religion building on campus. His group protested in favor of the 'Mormons.' Consequently, he met a few Mormons. One of them was a red-headed coed from San Diego. He described her as a 'glow in the dark' kind of Mormon. Sam supposed he meant that she radiated the Spirit. Kim said she radiated everything; happiness, virtue, beauty, spirituality. He made Sam want to meet her just to see if she were actually mortal.

Her name was Olivia, and he wanted to know what made her glow in the dark. She told him, and he believed her. He investigated the church, read all (Sam wondered if he memorized) the standard works, was baptized and proposed marriage to Olivia, all within three months time. Olivia told him she had her heart set on marrying a returned missionary. In reality, she was already engaged to a returned missionary.

However great this disappointment, the seed was planted, and he patiently waited the year required between baptism and going on a mission.

Sam had had no concept of what it meant to be a district leader. Like everyone else, he assumed it was wonderful, filled with spiritual experiences, and opportunities to do powerful missionary work. The district leaders he had known were spiritual giants in his estimation, and he desired to be like them.

The reality of the situation was that being a district leader was a lot of work that had nothing to do with teaching. There were lots of meetings, interviews, traveling between cities, solving problems, finding boarding houses, transferring Elders, taking Elders to doctor's appointments, and the paperwork. He hated the paperwork. It seemed futile and demanded time he would have preferred to spend teaching the people.

As the weeks turned into months, he slowly accepted the fact that he was no longer able to proselyte full time. He did his job with as much energy as he could. Yet he grew more and more disillusioned with his new position. He desperately missed teaching the people, and yearned for the opportunity to bear testimony to humble souls. Yet without time to tract, they did not meet the people, and consequently, the only investigators Sam met were when they worked with the other Elders.

Sam saw the remaining precious months of his mission slipping through his hands like fine sand. He mourned and wept inwardly. This wasn't the way he wanted to finish his mission, locked in some administrative position, unable to meet the people or teach them. He felt useless and depressed. It seemed that the more depressed he grew, the hotter the fire burned inside him until it seemed as if he might burst from the unresolved conflict.

It was late at night, and Elder Kim had long since slipped into deep sleep. Sam knelt on the concrete floor beside his bed, tears of frustration sliding down his cheeks.

"Oh, Father. How could I have come to this dark hour. How could I have accepted this job where I have no power to bless the people. Father, my soul is on fire. I desire every minute of every day to be teaching the people. Yet I cannot. I know the job of District Leader is important. The other Elders depend on me, and look to me for encouragement. I know I did before I became the DL.

"Father, I promised I would do anything thou asked me to do. I have done that, and will continue to do so, with all my heart and with all my soul. I most humbly apologize that I will not be baptizing any more..." He had to stop as tears flowed down his cheeks. Even his silent voice could not continue for the lump in his heart.

"Dear Heavenly Father, I beg thee to forgive me, that I cannot do the missionary work my heart yearns for. Forgive me. Forgive me. Still Father, with what little I have left to give, I give it all. Freely. Completely. Father, I beg thee to use me for what little I am worth, and allow me to complete my mission in righteousness."

A heightening of the Spirit flowed into him, and he felt his heart and mind quicken. "Father, I know thou lovest me. I feel it in the very fabric of my soul. And even though I have little to offer, I covenant with thee that I will be obedient to every command. From now until the end of my life, and verily, through out eternity, I will obey thee, and do thy will, and walk in the paths of righteous, as thou will reveal them to me. I confess my profound love for thee and do it in the name of Jesus Christ, Amen."

A feeling of warmth flooded over him like a flow of warm water. He felt the tiredness of his heart lift and suddenly felt like singing. He lifted his head toward heaven and silently spoke the words which vibrated through his soul. They were more than words, more beautiful than poetry, and more lovely than angelic singing. They flowed from his soul in an unending symphony of love. Such worship, such honor, praise and glory came from his heart that he wept as he worshipped, and felt the earthly world roll back to reveal a powerful outpouring of love from the eternal realm. He lost track of time as his soul became immersed in praise such as he had never considered possible.

Hours later he climbed into bed, his body cold and stiff, his soul burning with joy. He drifted off to sleep in the embrace of love, and dreamed dreams of great services performed in Father's service.

When the alarm went off he awoke with a warm burning in his bosom, and even though he had slept less than three hours, felt completely rested. His heart was buoyant with joy, almost giddy. Everything was sweetly perfect, and he rejoiced.

Elder Hall took one look at him, and covered his eyes with his forearm as if shielding his eyes from the sun. "Glow!" he said in mock surprise. "Glow in the dark Elder!" he exclaimed in a loud voice.

Sam ignored his companion, and ignored the pile of reports waiting for him. They hurried from their apartment and drove to their tracting area. They did have one, even though this was the first time they had gone to it in weeks. They picked a block of small homes and knocked on the first door. His heart thrilled as he waited for the door to open. Though not interested, the man behind the door hesitated, and looked quizzically at them.

"What you see is our testimony," Sam told him. The man gave them a puzzled look and slowly closed the door. Sam slid a Joseph Smith tract under the door. Each door was an exciting experience. Even those who slammed them did so after feeling something. Before they broke off for lunch, they had three appointments to teach. By the end of the day, they had taught a first discussion and had five appointments, two for that evening.

As they were walking back to the car, Elder Hall turned to Sam. "What happened last night? I saw that you stayed on your knees after I went to bed. I awoke hours later, and you were still there. What happened?"

"Elder, I'm not sure. I did pray long into the night. I've done that before, but this time it was different. Something happened to me. I feel different. There's something different and wonderful inside me now. I feel so much joy I feel like I'm going to burst. My bosom is burning so hotly it would be painful if it didn't feel so wonderful. I don't understand it. It just is."

"Elder, when I first laid eyes on you this morning, I knew something had happened. You remember my calling you a 'glow in the dark Elder?' Well, you were, I mean, you are. You have to tell me what you said, what you did last night. I want to do it too."

"I'm sorry, Elder. I really don't understand it myself."

"I've never seen such a transformation in a person. You speak differently, you bear testimony more powerfully, you make suggestions instead of command decisions. You are more friendly, you laugh more, your prayers are sweet and loving, you talk to everyone with patience and respect. Elder, if you don't tell me what you did, or at least, how you did it, I'm going to have to be very disappointed in you."

"Well, we don't want to disappoint you," Sam laughed. "I'll try, but it's not a simple story."

"I have two years," Kim answered. They both laughed.

Sam began with Jimmy's death, with the lessons which had been impressed into his mind. He taught Kim how to distinguish the voice of the Holy Spirit, and how to obey. He said again and again, "obedience is the key to righteousness." He told him about his experiences in Rhodesia, about learning to obey each and every prompting. He told him about the train wreck, about saving those people's lives by listening, and having the courage to obey.

He told him, as nearly as he could, about his mighty prayer of the night before. He told him of his feelings of worthlessness, of feeling as if he had nothing more to offer, yet of covenanting to obey and serve with all his soul. It was immediately after that that he had felt the powerful influence of the Holy Ghost flow over him.

Kim listened intently, asking only question which brought out rich, inspiring answers. By the time he had concluded, it was late at night, and they were in bed.

"Elder," Kim said quietly after a long silence. "There is a scripture which describes your experience exactly. It's in Mosiah, chapter 5."

He sat up and pulled on a pair of pants. It was July, the middle of winter, and even though the days were often in the 80's, it still dropped to the 40's at night, far too cool to run around without clothing.

"Let me read verse one. It describes the change you have experienced."

> And they all cried with one voice, saying: Yea, we believe all the words which Thou hast spoken unto us; and also, we know of their surety and truth, because of the Spirit of the Lord Omnipotent, which has wrought a mighty change in us, or in our hearts, that we have no more disposition to do evil, but to do good continually.

"Does that fit with your feelings, I mean, having no more disposition to do evil, but to do good continually?" Elder Hall asked.

"It does. I've read that verse many times, and it never occurred to me that I might be able to do the same thing as King Benjamin's people. I guess I have always considered it a unique experience of those ancient people, not an indication of what might happen to me."

"There's more. This is verse five."

And we are willing to enter into a covenant with our God to do his will, and to be obedient to his commandments in all things that he shall command us, all the remainder of our days...

"See, they made a covenant of obedience, similar to what you described."

Sam thought about this. "Although it seems that they are making this covenant after they experienced this mighty change. In my case, it seems to have preceeded it."

"Not necessarily," Kim replied after some thought. "The next verse says this is a covenant they had already made. The gospel only works one way, Elder. If it worked this way for you, it is going to be the same for all people."

"I believe that's true as long as we are all dealing with the fullness of the gospel."

"Sure. Let me read verses six and seven."

And now, these are the words which king Benjamin desired of them; and therefore he said unto them: Ye have spoken the words that I desired; and the covenant which ye have made is a righteous covenant.

And now, because of the covenant which ye have made ye shall be called the children of Christ, his sons, and his daughters; for behold, this day he hath spiritually begotten you; for ye say that your hearts are changed through faith on his name; therefore, ye are born of him and have become his sons and his daughters.

"Oh my gosh," Sam exclaimed.

"Elder Sam Mahoy, I believe you have been born again."

"Oh my gosh," Sam said again. There was a protracted silence while he tried to understand.

Finally, he said. "I just find it hard to believe that could actually happen to me. I'm nobody special. I just try to do what's right. I make mistakes, lots of mistakes. I'm not perfect, far from it. I find it hard to accept. Perhaps this is something else."

"I know I'm your junior companion, and you are my teacher in these things. But let me give you some spiritual counsel. Don't doubt the gifts of God. Don't let your humility interfere with your blessings. Accept it. Rejoice in it. It's true. You said you are nobody special? I tell you, you are a son of God in the purest respect, and that is very special."

Sam took his companion's counsel and rejoiced with all his soul. He recognized that doubt is not a gift of the Spirit, and when it came, he rejected it without exception. Each time he did, his soul rejoiced until he felt as if his blessings were too great for him to possess them all.

June 2, 1975

It is with the greatest joy in my heart I have ever felt, that I record tonight, that I have recently experienced the rebirth. It was quite unexpected, and far from my thoughts. I was completely depressed, and felt as if I had failed the Lord. I thought I was going to go home having been a failure as a missionary. It pained my heart to the point of death, and I fell down, and begged the Lord to forgive me.

While I was feeling so devastated, I still had this powerful desire to dedicate what was left of my soul to the Lord. I spent many hours in prayer, and covenanted myself to absolute obedience. It was more than a promise, it was pure, profound, and absolute. Even though I was mostly worthless as a servant, I still wanted the Lord to have whatever I had left.

A marvelous feeling swept over me, and my depression evaporated as quickly as fog before the bright sun. The Holy Spirit enveloped me, and I felt unbridled joy, so intense that it confused me. I had never before experienced joy so profound. It was joy in the Lord, His joy in me, all rolled together. Some part of me changed in that moment. I came away from that experience a different man.

Since that time, I can not even think of sin without feeling repulsed. I look upon the world with different eyes. The things which previously excited me and to which I looked forward with great hope, no longer even interest me. Everything about the world seems almost meaningless to me. Money, a problem through out my mission, suddenly became meaningless. The only thing that matters is people, and my relationship with God.

My heart is continually filled with prayer. Every waking moment is prayer, and my heart rejoices continually.. As soon as my heart turns to prayer, the Holy Ghost overflows me, and I am directed in powerful prayer. The words flow like a mighty river, and come fourth in more beauty than the most beautiful music. At times, it seems as if the words rhyme, and have meter. When I am fully caught up in prayer, it becomes pure, absolute praise, and my soul rejoices in it. When I thus pray under the influence of the Spirit, I get everything I ask for.

I feel absolute humility. Having had a small portion of the perfections of God opened to my understanding, I am struck with the fact that He, the most perfect, and powerful being in all existence loves me. He LOVES ME. Such unspeakably beautiful words. HE LOVES ME. Tears come to my eyes to think it. I AM HIS SON. Think about it. He who is most perfect, powerful, loving, kind, and holy, is my Heavenly Father.

For the first time in my life I understand how the Gospel can bring us to a measure of the stature of the fullness of Christ. In a way too beautiful for mortal man to understand, through obedience, we qualify for this mighty change, this rebirth, this remaking of the soul, which makes us like unto Him. Not perfect yet, just more like He who is perfect.

I have long believed that we had to become perfect largely through our own labors. We had to develop faith, humility, love, kindness, hope, charity, and all other Christ-like attributes. And after we had done all that, He would apply the atonement, wash away our sins, and we would finally be like Him. It all seems so distant, so incredibly hard, so remote, that even the brave hearted faint by the way.

What I understand from this experience, is that the primary thing Heavenly Father wants us to develop in this life is obedience. Obedience, absolute obedience, is the key which unlocks the doors of righteousness. Obedience to the commandments, obedience to church leaders, and obedience to the will of God as made known to you through the Spirit.

Having at last developed that faith which leads to obedience, the door has opened, and I understand at last that the attributes of godliness are to a large extent, gifts. They are gifts of the Spirit. What a wonder it is to finally see clearly. It opens a thousand doors, and brings the Gospel into sharp focus. It makes it all do-able, unscrambles the scriptures, casts bright light upon the straight and narrow way, and illuminates the darkness of the world.

In a tiny way, I now perceive the perfectness of the plan of Salvation. Every person born lives their lives surrounded by the voice of revelation, and all have an equal chance to hear and obey. To hear and obey is to be led along the path of righteousness, until we experience this might change which makes a new creature in Christ. (As Paul expressed it.) Suddenly, Paul's words make sense, whereas before, they were nonsensical. Paul understood the rebirth profoundly, because his experience therewith had been profound. With every letter he penned, he taught them about the power of the change which had saved his soul from destruction.

Oh, how I rejoice in these things, and worship He whose plan this is.

Their first appointment was with a Mr. And Mrs. Van der Kerk. It was a common name, and they were no relation of the state attorney he had baptized. Their home was small, yet very tidy and clean.

Mrs. Van der Kerk opened the door and smiled. She was a lovely, dark-haired woman in her late thirties. Immediately inside the door was a huge drafting table which took up most of the foyer and part of the living room. On the table were immaculately drawn electrical drawings. Sam studied the drawings. He had taken drafting in high school, and these were very professionally done. He was bending over the drawings when Mr. Van der Kerk came from the back of the house.

Sam extended his hand. "Good Evening, I'm Elder Mahoy, and this is Elder Hall."

"Anchenama Kennis," (Pleasuree to know you) he replied, switching to Afrikaans and shaking both their hands. He noticed Mrs. Van der Kerk giving her husband a quizzical look. He just smiled at her, and turned his attention to the missionaries.

It was considered rude to change the language being spoken. If someone started speaking English, it was socially correct to continue in that language. Their prior conversations with Mrs. Van der Kerk had been in English. He knew they both spoke English as well as he did. He felt a momentary pang of panic. He hadn't had a conversation in Afrikaans in eight months. Yet he knew the language, and felt confident the Holy Spirit would aid them.

After polite conversation, Sam told them briefly about the apostasy and restoration. He asked them if they would be interested in hearing more about the man who had been called to be a prophet in this dispensation.

They both expressed interest. Sam began the first discussion, and they went through the apostasy in greater detail. The Van der Kerks understood and agreed. He told them about Joseph Smith, and the first vision. As soon as he mentioned the appearance of God to the boy prophet, Mr. Van der Kerk objected. He said no one had seen God, and stood to retrieve his bible.

Sam could see that the bible was well worn and marked in many places. Mr. Van der Kerk turned to one of them and read a verse which said that no man had seen God. Sam had not read the scriptures in Afrikaans, and it took him extra mental effort to translate the words into English. He recognized the verse, and was about to reply when Mr. Van der Kerk launched off into another verse.

From there, the conversation deteriorated into an argument, except that no one was participating in it except Mr. Van der Kerk. Sam felt himself growing more and more restless as Mr. Van der Kerk pounded them with scriptures, not waiting for a reply, or in fact, being interested in one.

"Wait!" Sam shouted just as Van der Kerk was about to thumb to another verse. The sheer volume of his voice brought the conversation up short. Sam filled the silence by saying. "I have sat here and listened to you attack my faith without allowing me to answer a single accusation. This is not the way Christ would have us do it. You just read a scripture in First Corinthians."

Mr. Van der Kerk nodded, glancing back at his book. He had not given the reference, and was impressed that Sam knew it. In reality, he could not remember reading that verse in English or Afrikaans, but, nevertheless, Sam knew the reference with great certainty.

"Read the two verses prior to the one you read." Mr. Van der Kerk did so. Sam had difficulty following the words, yet knew what they said. "As you see, those two verses show us that it actually is possible to see God."

"You are misinterpreting the scripture," Mr. Van der Kerk replied. "One must use each verse separately. Each is inspired, and each bears a message. To apply the meaning of prior verses to warp the meaning of the next, is to twist the scriptures. Each verse stands alone." This he said haughtily and with indignation.

"You say God has called another prophet. I say that none are needed. We have the holy book of God, the Bible. It is all we need." He thumbed quickly to a verse and read.

Search the scriptures; for in them ye think ye have eternal life: and they are they which testify of me.

This he read with great emphasis, punctuating the words by stabbing his finger in the air. He had switched into High Afrikaans, which was only used for preaching sermons and powerful prayers. It was never used when speaking to another person, and was a great insult.

"So you see, you poor misguided Mormons, that salvation is in the scriptures. You don't need a prophet. Your whole argument is void. You have come to deliver a message which has no meaning. Go back to America, and quit wasting your time and ours."

Sam remained unperterbed. "When Christ spoke these words, he was speaking to highly educated men, who refused to accept him as the Christ. They used exactly the same argument you just did. They said they had the scriptures, the law and the prophets, and had no need of a living prophet."

"That is not true." He insisted

"Read the verse just prior to the one you quoted," Sam requested. He had no idea what that verse said, but the fire was burning in his bosom, and he knew the words he spoke were true.

And ye have not his word abiding in you: for whom he hath sent, him ye believe not.

Silence filled the small room after the reading. Sam let it linger for a few moments. "He was being sarcastic. He was saying 'Search the scriptures all you want if you think they will save you, but they are they which testify of me. And if you don't accept me, and those I send to you, then you cannot find eternal life. How can you come unto Christ if you reject His prophets. Read the next verse, please."

Mr. Van der Kerk slowly looked back at his scriptures, and after a pause read.

And ye will not come to me, that ye might have life.

Sam waited until the Spirit moved him. "Mr. and Mrs. Van der Kerk, I want you to know that a prophet has been called anew in this era. His name was Joseph Smith. He was a prophet in the same respect that Moses, or Peter, or Isaiah were prophets. I want to bear you my testimony that the true, and living church of God has been restored to the earth, and all the blessings which were found in the ancient church, are found today. I know you feel the burning in your soul, testifying this is true. In the name of Jesus Christ, amen."

Mr. Van der Kerk sat silent for almost a full minute. Finally, he closed his bible, and set it on a table beside his chair. His eyes studied each of the missionaries in turn before fixing upon Sam. For a moment, his face was aglow with wonder, but darkness seeped across his face, and his brow furled into a frown.

"You two are dangerous," he finally said. "You almost deceived me. Very clever. I will inform the pastor about you two, and we will see that you have no success teaching in this town. I will see to it that you two are miserable in every possible way. You take my words as true, and consider my words prophetic, for they shall surely come to pass. You are evil!"

Sam stood suddenly. Elder Hall followed, gathering up their things.

"Mr. Van der Kerk," he began, "you have been given the true witness, and you felt the power of it. In all fairness, I want you to understand that you will be held accountable…"

"Hold on there!" Mr. Van der Kerk bellowed. "Be very careful what you say. Your words are being recorded in heaven, and will echo in the halls of justice. Don't condemn me to hell, unless you wish to go there yourself." This he nearly shouted.

Sam lowered his voice, and held his gaze steadily. "You, sir, will be called to account on the day of judgment for the testimony I have born to you this day. Good night." So saying, he walked solemnly to the door, opened it, and stepped out into the night. He was vaguely aware of Mr. Van der Kerk storming into the back of the house. His wife quietly closed the door behind them without a word.

Sam stood on their porch for a long moment. Elder Hall stopped half-way down the walk, and turned just in time to see Sam lift each foot, and brush the dust from each sole.

They climbed into their VW beetle. "Elder," Kim said as soon as the engine chugged to life. "I thought you didn't speak Afrikaans that well."

Sam looked at him and shrugged. It hadn't occurred to him that he had spoken far beyond his abilities.

"Don't shrug this off. I just heard you speak for two hours, bearing testimony, quoting dozens of scriptures, answering difficult questions, and all of it in flawless Afrikaans. I know you don't speak it that well, and I know you haven't read the bible in Afrikaans. Yet you quoted those scriptures verbatim. You used words I doubt you had ever heard before and quoted scriptures you probably never read before. Have you read the Old Testament?"

"I've read at it, but I haven't gotten clear through it yet."

"Then how were you able to quote those scriptures in Isaiah?"

"I did that?" Sam asked, having difficulty remembering. Now that the power of the Spirit was subsiding, his memory of what he had said was fading as well. It felt to him as if someone else had conducted that interview, and he had merely watched the whole event. He had vague memories of quoting those scriptures and of answering those questions, but his memories included statements he had made in Afrikaans which even now he had difficulty under-standing their meaning.

"You did. And how about those scriptures in Jude, and in first John. Had you memorized those? They're not on the memorization list."

"No, I guess not."

"What about that scriptures in John? Had you ever before consid-ered what he meant when he said 'Search the scriptures for in them ye think ye have eternal life?"

"No, I had never really considered the meaning of that scripture."

"That's what I thought. I can hardly wait to get my hands on my journal tonight."

They drove in reverent silence all the way home. Sam turned off the car and put a hand on his companion's arm.

"Elder Hall, thanks."

"For what?" he asked with a puzzled expression.

"For helping me finally begin to see the blessings of the Lord. I think I have taken many things for granted without rejoicing over them. Tonight was very special, and I probably would have overlooked the sweetness of it without your comments. Thanks."

Elder Hall closed his eyes in thought. When he opened them, they were moist.

"No. Don't thank me. I was just a witness of tonight's miracle. I'm astounded that I actually followed the conversation. I heard hundreds of new words I have never heard in my life and understood them perfectly. This is literally my first experience in actually hearing a complete conversation in Afrikaans. When he was railing at us prior to your inspired remarks, I didn't understand a word he was saying. But as soon as you started speaking, I felt the Holy Ghost come over me, and I instantly understood every word.

"I tried several times to make comments, but even though I could understand perfectly, the words would not come to my tongue. I could say nothing. It seems obvious that you had the gift of tongues tonight. I guess I had the gift of ears." They both chuckled.

"Elder Mahoy, we have much to be grateful for."

"We certainly do, Elder."

———

At church that next Sunday, Bishop Van Halen stopped them in the foyer.

"Elders, have you tracted out a family named Whitehall in the Sunny Side subdivision?

"Yes, Bishop, we've already given them a first discussion." Kim replied while Sam's mind was still rummaging through his memories for a match to the name.

"Good. Very good. The wife is a friend and coworker of my wife. They have been good friends for years. She has been anxious for the missionaries to meet them, but didn't want to directly refer them. When you see my wife, she has something to tell you about them."

They had no trouble finding the bishop's wife. She was a very happy, active woman, who seemed to be the heart and soul of the ward. They found her putting up pictures in the Relief Society room.

"Her name is Judy," she told them as she motioned them to a seat.

She sat on the edge of the table before them. I have known her and been working with her for years. She has always resisted my attempts to share the Gospel with her."

Elder Hall cleared his throat. "We taught her a first discussion, and both she and her husband seemed interested, or at least polite. They did invite us back."

Sister Van Halen clapped her hands together in joy. "Oh, wonderful!" she exclaimed. "Just wonderful. She told me at work that some missionaries had knocked on her door, and she thought they were from my church. She also told me something else. I'm not sure I should tell you."

"Why is that?" Sam asked, his curiosity piqued.

"Well, I don't want it to influence your teaching, or make you go too quickly."

"We will teach them only as quickly as the Holy Spirit directs, Sister Van Halen, regardless of what you tell us."

"Yes, of course, certainly. I'm sorry, its just that I've been working with her for so many years, you know."

"We do understand. Don't worry, we'll teach her as carefully as we can. What she chooses to do with it will depend on whether she gets a testimony, as you know."

"Well, that's what I wanted to tell you. She already has a testimony."

"Oh?" both Elders asked in unison.

"She told me at work and actually swore me to secrecy. She said one evening about a week before you tracted them out, both she and her husband had the same dream. She said she saw a sea of faces, as if it were the whole world. They were wandering back and forth in her dream, without paying any attention to her. She felt lost and afraid.

"She could tell that some of the people were bad, because they had blackness surrounding them. Some people were good, because their faces were surrounded by light.

"She told me that there was one face in the crowd which glowed brighter than all the others and was coming toward her. She watched, anxious to know who it was. Finally, it got close enough that she could distinguish the features, and it was a young man she had never seen before.

"At that moment an authoritative voice told her, 'This is my true messenger.'

"She knew it was the voice of God, and it frightened her. She was afraid she wouldn't find the person, or wouldn't recognize him.

"About a week later, you two knocked on the door, and she opened it with the determination to send you two packing. Imagine her surprise when one of your faces was the face in her dream!"

Sam glanced at Elder Hall, who looked back with raised eyebrows. They both wanted to ask which of them it was she had seen, but neither did.

"She said she was so amazed that she didn't even say hello, but ran to get her husband."

"I remember that now," Sam interjected. "I thought she was going after a gun or something. Instead, she brought her husband who immediately invited us in. I thought it was strange at the time, but was so glad to be able to teach them that I had forgotten about that."

"My point in telling you this is so you will understand how precious they are. Heavenly Father really must want them to accept the Gospel. Aren't you curious which of you she saw?"

"I'd rather not know," Kim replied, and Sam agreed. He would feel much more comfortable not knowing.

They had an appointment with the Whitehall's on Wednesday evening. They fasted, and made spiritual preparations. As they walked up the path to their front door, Sam had a bad feeling.

"Elder, do you feel that?" Sam asked in a hushed voice.

"I sure do. Something's blacked out inside." It was his way of saying there was a negative spiritual feeling from the house. Sam had felt it before, and it invariably ended up with them being asked not to return.

Sister Whitehall opened the door before they knocked and pushed open the screen door. She was very solemn and barely greeted them. It did not look good to Sam. She left to get Brother Whitehall. He came into the room with a young man about Sam's age.

"This is our son, Sean. We invited him to come hear your message tonight. We hope that's all right."

"Certainly," Sam said cheerfully as he shook Sean's hand. It was like shaking the hand of a spiritual corpse. Darkness emanated from his eyes. This young man was one of the most completely evil men he had ever met. It caused his skin to crawl.

"Brother Whitehall, would you ask someone to pray?" Sam asked.

Sean coughed, and half under his breath said : "To what?" then chuckled derisively.

Elder Hall gave a nice, though brief prayer, during which Sean snorted at every mention of God.

"Thank you for having us by this evening," Sam began, not quite sure how to approach this situation. He wanted to teach the Whitehalls, but knew Sean would not allow it. He prayed silently for the Holy Spirit to inspire his words. "It's a pleasure to meet with you again."

"That's precious. Begin your teaching with a lie," Sean snorted.

"What do you mean?" Sam asked.

"You lied. It's not a pleasure for you to have me here. You feel alienated from me because I represent the exact opposite of what you represent. You feel uncomfortable around me, and its not a pleasure. Let's at least be honest. You claim to represent God. At least you can do it without lying." His voice was insulting and charged with hate. Sam was almost bowled over by his assault. He considered arguing that he was pleased to be with the Whitehalls tonight, and that was the truth, but knew it would only derail their discussion.

"Truth," Sam began, "is what we are here to discuss. Truth in its purest form, as God has revealed it ..."

"Another lie!" he bellowed. "God reveals nothing! There is no God." He turned to his father. "Do you really expect me to sit here and listen to this tripe. He can't say one sentence without lying. They're like all the rest, they have this mindless fixation on a being that does not exist and presume to be His spokesman. They aren't even entertaining. Some of the others, at least I got to laugh in their stupid faces. These are just congenital liars." Sean proclaimed.

His father blanched and raised a hand as if to restrain his son, but Sean ignored him.

"Prove to me there's a God." He demanded, turning back to Sam.

"Prove to me there's not a God," Elder Hall interjected hotly. Sam knew the discussion had just gotten out of hand. There was really nothing else to lose, and he let Elder Hall trade logic with him for a while. Elder Hall had apparently had this argument with some intellectual atheists before, and handled himself well. Still, the Spirit departed, and nothing of worth was being taught. Sean certainly wasn't going to change his mind, no matter how sound the logic Elder Hall might bombard him with.

Sean leaned forward and lowered his voice. "Just this morning in the paper, it told a story of a little girl who was abducted, raped and murdered. An innocent little girl. Tell me where God was while she was crying and screaming, begging for her life. Where was God while she was stabbed over and over. Tell me. I'm really curious."

Kim sputtered, and Sean jumped down his throat with both feet. "You can't explain it, because there is no God. If there was a God, that kind of insanity wouldn't happen. God would stop them. Or, if He chose not to stop it due to some all mighty," he said sarcastically, "plan of His, then God would punish them on the spot. Make them hurt as much as that little girl."

"We have free agency," Kim insisted, "and sometimes people use it unwisely. God doesn't stop people from exercising their free will."

"God doesn't stop them because he can't. God doesn't stop them because he doesn't exist. You call God Heavenly Father, right?"

"Yes," Kim replied.

"Father? What kind of a father, an all powerful, all mighty, all knowing, all loving, father would allow His little girl to be brutalized before His eyes, and not intervene. Would you? I know you think I'm a wolf, and I am, but I wouldn't allow someone to do that to my daughter. I'm better than God, and I'm a scum bag."

"I..."

"Excuse me," Sam said politely, interrupting Elder Hall's reply.

"There is no excuse," Sean bellowed. "Either you produce God, or you shut up. If God exists, give me a sign. Prove to me that God exists, and I'll prove to you that He's a hateful God. Make God come stand right here, and I'll scream in His face, and tell Him He's a failure as a God. A God who can't save His little girl, and thousands like her! Who would even want to believe in such a being, let alone worship Him!?"

"I will give you no such sign," Sam replied calmly.

"Why not? Because you can't, that's why. If there truly was a God, and you truly were his representative, you would be able to give me a sign. None of the others could. You can't. There is no God."

"You're right. I can't. But if you insist on a sign, then let God give you a sign."

"Well, isn't that a convenient, coward's way out. God doesn't exist, so here we are back to the original lie." He threw his hands in the air in exasperation, a smile of triumph on his face.

"I said, I personally can't give you a sign, but, as God's mouthpiece, I can give you a sign." Sam heard his own words with curiosity, and wondered what the sign would be. It would be whatever the Lord directed, and he waited with anticipation to hear it.

"This ought to be precious," Sean said sarcastically, crossing his legs, and lounging back into the sofa. "What are you going to do, strike me blind?"

"Here is your sign. Your best friend raped and murdered that little girl."

"What!?" he screamed, bolting to his feet. His parents leapt to their feet at the same instant. For several minutes pandemonium reigned, while his parents shouted, not at the Elders, but at their son. Demands, accusations, and denials punctuated the air. While they fought, Sam sat in silence, barely hearing their words. He pondered why he had said such a thing. It had just come out. His heart had been aflame with the Holy Spirit, and he had been speaking the words which came to his heart. These had come out without his editing them.

At the instant he said them, the thought occurred to him that Sean's best friend was Satan, and that the evil one had inspired the deed in someone unknown to Sean. However, the more he contemplated the words, the more he realized how they were literally true. Sean's hot denials proved their truth. If he had perceived it as a lie, he would have calmly called it such, as he had all evening.

Without a word from Sam, the argument came to a sudden stop. Sean took his seat.

"Let me tell you all something," Sean began calmly, but his voice was like a knife, and he hoped to wound with it. "I'm sure you read the papers just like I did. My parents undoubtedly told you that the little girl's father is my best friend. What you said was an incredibly cheap shot. He is more devastated by his daughter's death than you can imagine, and your accusing him is just another indication of how hollow your claims to truth are."

What Sean did not know, was that missionaries were not allowed to read the papers, and until Sean mentioned it, Sam did not even know there had been a little girl murdered.

"Besides, that's not a sign," he continued vigorously. "A sign has to be irrefutable, undeniable. All you did was start an argument, not give me a sign. You'll have to do better than that." He pushed long black hair from his face with his hand, and flipped his head to keep it there. His eyes were filled with hatred and defiance.

Once again, Sam felt the flow of words begin and steeled himself to speak them. It took courage to allow his voice to speak words he chose not to edit.

"If you want another sign, you choose it. By your own words, you will know the truth."

"Oh, this ought to be fun," he said mockingly. "OK, let's see. Blindness? No, too obvious. Disease? No, too common. Shot by a jealous husband? No, too likely to happen anyway. I think I'll go for a body part, something small, but important. Nothing crippling, but big enough to be obvious. What do you think, Mister Mormon Missionary? You call it."

"As you wish," Sam heard himself say. "That part of your person which you value most will be denied to you until you repent of your sins. As a further witness, it will begin the next time you curse God."

"Well, God damn it, let's get the show on the road! Consider your phony God cursed," he shouted, and stood up. "I've had all of this foolishness I can stand. Besides, I have a doctor's appointment." So saying, he nodded to his parents, strode to the door, and slammed it behind him.

They spent the next short while speaking with Sean's parents, who were mortified by what had happened, and apologized profusely. They had hoped their son would be touched as they had been. Sam stayed just until the Spirit returned to the home. They made another appointment, and left them with a prayer.

Late that very night, they were awakened by an insistent knocking at their door. It was about three in the morning.

"Who is it?" Sam called through the door.

"Bishop Van Halen, and Sister Van Halen," the voice came through the door.

They scrambled to get their clothes on, and let them into their small room.

It was Sister Van Halen who explained. "A short while ago I got a call from my friend, Virginia Whitehall. Something has happened to their son Sean, and they want you to come to the hospital. She didn't know how to get in contact with you, so she called me. Can you come with us? Its a long drive."

They threw on their clothes, shaved quickly, and climbed into the bishop's Mercedes. They drove for almost exactly an hour and a half before coming to a large hospital on the outskirts of the city. It loomed before them like a lost city in the dim light of dawn.

Sean's room was on the twelfth floor and down a long hall. The hospital was surprisingly busy for so early in the morning. Of greater interest was that no one made an attempt to stop them, or ask where they were going.

"Thank you for coming," Mrs. Whitehall said as she pressed Sam's hand. She led him to the side of the bed. Sean's black hair looked stark against the sea of white sheets and pillows. His face, however, was nearly the color of the sheets. He was looking away, toward the opposite wall as if ignoring them. After a few moments, however, he slowly turned his face toward them. He had been weeping. Even more startling than that, was the fact that most of the darkness was gone from his eyes. In its place was a total absence of light. It was still unnerving.

"How did you know?" he asked Sam, his voice barely audible. Only Sam heard him clearly, since he was closest to the bed. The others whispered his question behind Sam's back, until all understood.

"Know what, Sean?" Sam asked, his voice soft, but not patronizing. He felt the presence of the Holy Ghost, and knew that he had a further task to accomplish for the Lord. He also knew that Sean would not like what he had to say, even though he had no idea what it was.

"That my friend Charles was the murderer?" he said, his voice almost tiny.

"I personally didn't know. I told you what the Lord wanted you to hear. Until this minute, only my faith told me that it was true."

"I was certain you'd say something like that," he said, and turned his eyes toward the far wall. His voice was still filled with doubt, but it was no longer dripping with vitriol.

Sean spoke without looking back toward him. "Charles and I have been ..."

"Lovers," Sam interjected, surprised at the words himself.

There was a long pause, then: "lovers," Sean admitted. His parents gasped, his mother began to cry.

"We have been...lovers for many years. His daughter lives with her mama, and is the cutest thing. She was ten years old, and I loved her, and Charles loved her. I just don't understand..." There was a long pause.

"When she...when she died, Charles was devastated, and so was I. He wept, and mourned, and howled, and thrashed on himself so badly that I was afraid for him. I could not believe he could, or would even do such a thing.

"Just a few minutes after the doctors gave me their bad news, Charles called me, and told me the whole story. He's in jail now, awaiting sentencing. He'll probably be executed before the week is out."

Bishop Van Halen explained softly when he saw Sam's puzzled look. "In our country, a confession coupled with evidence to support it, cancels the need for a trial. There is a sentencing hearing, and the criminal is put away. In this case, he will, almost certainly, be executed." Sam nodded understanding. He had heard that justice, or injustice, as the case may be, was swift in this country. He had experienced some of that himself.

When Sean turned his head back toward Sam his eyes were pooled with tears. At first Sam thought it was for the loss of his lover, but when he spoke, it was something else which was torturing his soul.

"I have cancer," he said, and both he and his parents wept. When he regained control of his emotions, he continued. "You'll recall that I had a doctor's appointment after our meeting yesterday. I came here, for what I thought was a urinary tract infection. I have had several. Its one of the hazards of being, how shall I say it delicately...attracted to men." The term 'gay' had not as yet been coined. At that time, in that country, there was no polite term for homosexuals.

"The doctor did some tests, then some more, then some more, and finally informed me that I have an advanced stage of prostate cancer. He says it is probably the result of my deviant lifestyle." He laughed ruefully and paused to reflect. When he began again, his voice was filled with irony.

"If they don't operate, I will die within a few weeks. If they do, I may live, but I'll lose the use of my...my sexuality," he said, obviously struggling for words.

"Do you want to know the hardest part of all this?" he asked, looking into Sam's eyes. Sam did not respond.

"It's knowing that you were right. You have given me a sign I cannot deny."

"God has given you a sign," Sam corrected him in a sterile voice.

Sean pondered this for a long time before saying. "God has given me a sign."

Behind him, Sam heard Sean's mother gasp, and begin weeping. She mumbled something about being too late, too late. Sister Van Halen held her in her arms.

"You know?" Sean continued. "If it had just been Charles being guilty, I would have discounted that, and rationalized a way you might have known, or guessed his guilt. But with that, and this cancer taking away the part of my body I value most, it's beyond dispute. Checkmate," he said with finality.

"I'm sorry you have to have this experience," Sam said, not sure what to say. "In the long run, I believe you can use it to your advantage. At least you know there is a God now."

"Oh yes, I'm convinced of that. The problem is, I'm also convinced He hates me. A few hours ago, I would have argued that I don't want to believe in a hateful God. Now...now, I believe, and I still think He hates me. Its an awful feeling."

"Why do you consider His treatment of you hateful?" Sam asked. "Since there is a God, there is also salvation, and conversely, damnation. I think we would all agree that you were on the fast track to damnation just a few hours ago. At least now, you have the choice. Your eyes have been opened by this experience. Now, when you choose, you can choose salvation. I know this experience is difficult for you, but this sounds like the work of a loving God to me, not a hateful one."

"I hope you're right, Elder Sam," he said quietly. "I do hope you're right. I know God loves you, because you keep the commandments, and you're on a mission for Him. Its easy to see why God would love you. But me? Believe me when I tell you I've done everything wrong a person can do. I've broken every commandment except murder, and I'm not so sure I didn't contribute to that one too. I've been in and out of jail a dozen times. If I were put in jail for every criminal act I've done, I'd still be in jail.

"I hated God, and worshipped, what you would call, evil. I reveled in it, rejoiced in it, and bathed my whole soul in it. I don't see how I can be forgiven. I can't imagine a God willing to forgive such a long list of sins. I am not just bad…I'm evil." He said with deep conviction.

"Your words are the beginnings of repentance. Whether you understand it or not, you just confessed your sins. It is a beginning. Its up to God, but I believe you can be forgiven. What do you have to lose by trying?"

"That's certainly true. I have nothing at all to lose. Nothing." His voice trailed off into silence.

Sam patted him on the shoulder and turned to leave.

"Elder?"

"Yes, Sean."

"Before you go, can you remove the sign. I see the evilness of my life. Isn't that enough? Can you undo what you did? Can you release me from the sign?" His voice was child-like, desperate, and pleading.

"I cannot," Sam said without hesitation. "It didn't originate with me. It's up to God to release you from it, not me. I simply can't do it."

Sean began to weep uncontrollably as Sam backed away. It was as if his last hope for life had been yanked away from him. His mother rushed to his arms to comfort him. Even in the hall, Sean's voice wafted through the heavy door, the long, forlorn, wail of an anguished soul. Sam heard it for what it was, the beginnings of a long, hard, repentance. He didn't know if he would make it, but at least the process was begun.

As he climbed into the car, Sam suddenly realized that he was exhausted. He leaned back in the soft leather seats and slept.

June 22, 1975

After leaving Sean's hospital room, I was so exhausted that I slept all the way home. I had a vivid dream about Alma the Younger. It was almost as if I were there, watching him fight against the church, angry and vengeful. I watched, in my dream, as he was struck down, and went through an accelerated repentance process. I couldn't help but wonder if the dream was meant to parallel Sean's experience.

I no longer view Sean as an evil, unredeemable soul. And I can see that there is real power and the potential for goodness in him. He could be a great asset to the church if he put as much effort into serving God as he did in hating Him.

Elder Hall is a great blessing to me. He is the first companion whom I have truly loved. All the others I have appreciated, or valued, or been friends with. Kim is like a brother, and I will be most sad to leave him.

———

The Whitehalls delivered a message through the bishop's wife, that they would appreciate not being visited by the missionaries until after Sean's operation and recovery. They promised to contact them when they were ready to resume their discussions. Sam took the note, and carefully folded and dated it. He put it in the envelope along with many other such notes and sighed.

twelve

Dawn Brought the Sun

The subdivision was surrounded by a high, concrete wall, with armed guards by the gate. Sam came to a stop outside, by the guard's window. The man leaned out the window and waited for Sam to speak.

"We have been requested to pay a visit to Mr. Oliver Pauley," Sam told him, not sure what else to say. He passed the referral slip to the guard. It was a two inch strip of paper, cut from the visitor's book at Temple Square in Utah. Mr. Pauley had signed it, and said he would be glad to have a visit from a representative of the church.

The guard disappeared back inside the room for several minutes. When he leaned back out the window, the big iron gate was beginning to swing open. Sam felt like Alice in Wonderland. The guard handed him the slip, and said: "Number 224."

They drove past buildings more like palaces than normal homes. It took them a while to find number 224, yet they did not mind slowly driving past all the beautiful homes. Every one of these homes was newer and more beautiful than the mission home.

Deep within the subdivision, they found another large fence and gate. On one of the massive gate towers was '224'. The gate was open, so they drove in. They followed the narrow road, lined with flowering bushes and immaculately sculpted shrubs, until the road forked. A small sign directed all deliveries to the left. Sam took the right fork. Almost immediately the road grew wider, with a low stone wall on each side. The wall was of gray stone, designed to look like a castle wall with regularly spaced turrets. Flowers grew from the turrets. When they spotted the house a second later, it was like driving into another world. It was, in fact, a castle, complete with drawbridge and moat. They stared open mouthed as they rounded a bubbling fountain before the huge front door. Everywhere they looked, the gardens and trees were immaculate. They could see a huge swimming pool far to the right, also decorated castle-like. A single figure, obviously female, lounged on a chaise beside the pool.

The only difference between this castle and a real castle, was that everything here was smaller. Yet it was proportionately correct, giving the appearance of being much larger than it actually was. It was a carefully crafted optical illusion. The two story walls appeared to be four stories tall, with small windows cut in the walls to complete the illusion.

They walked across the drawbridge, over a moat filled with goldfish and flowers, and knocked on the massive door. They were just about to give up and leave when they heard a bolt click back. The heavy door opened with an appropriate groan to reveal a young woman standing in the shadows. She had apparently been the girl by the pool, for she wore nothing but a very small swim suit, a large towel draped over one shoulder. She stared at them with a curious expression.

"Hello?" she said, more as a question, than a welcome.

It was Elder Hall who recovered first. "Good afternoon. I'm Elder Hall, and this is Elder Mahoy. We were asked to visit Mr. Oliver Pauley. He visited Temple Square in Salt Lake City, Utah, and requested we visit him."

"Oh, yes!" she responded happily, pulling the door open wider, and motioning them to come in. "I was there too. We had a wonderful time and loved the Temple." She motioned them to a large couch before a fireplace taller than Sam's head and twice as wide. "Would you excuse me, I need to put on something more. I was by the pool. I'll be right back." So saying, she smiled apologetically, and disappeared up the circular stair in the foyer.

Both Elders walked slowly around the room, looking at the unusual decor. The room, while very large, felt like it was too small. The illusion of the building gave the feeling of a huge castle. Now they were in a room which should have been vast to complete the illusion, yet was not much more than a very large living room. It was still impressive. The room was two stories high, with tall slotted windows. The wall to their left held a huge tapestry which covered the entire wall from side to side, and nearly to the ceiling. All around the room near the ceiling were rows of animal trophies. There were lions, bears, water buffalo, rhinoceros, zebra, and a host of others. In all four corners stood medieval suits of armor holding swords and spears. The opposite wall held a collection of portraits. The figures all wore the ornate clothing of medieval times, but the dates on the portraits were more recent.

They had barely begun discovering all the strange trappings in the room when the girl returned. She had pulled on a silken robe over her swimming suit. In reality, the robe did little to cover her, and only added to her attraction. Sam had to admit, she looked stunning coming down those large stairs. Yet, by the way she hopped down the stairs two at a time, he doubted she was trying to impress them.

"My name is Dawn Pauley," she said offering Sam a slender hand.

"Don?" Sam asked, taking her hand. It felt warm, and delicate, almost as if it might break if handled roughly.

"Dawn," she repeated, "as in the rising of the sun." She pronounced her name by prolonging the vowel sound. It came out 'Daauwn.' It sounded exotic and magical when she spoke it.

"Oh, excuse me, Dawn. Pleasure to meet you."

She smiled at him, and shook Elder Hall's hand. She motioned for them to sit, and took a large chair by the fireplace. She crossed her legs, and the robe slid open, leaving very little to the imagination.

"Look at the floor," Sam whispered to his companion, whose eyes were having a hard time staying in his head. Kim nodded, and obediently looked at the floor with an obvious effort.

Sam felt as if he was being swallowed by the huge couch. He had never sat in a chair with such massive cushions. Since it was Elder Hall's day, he resumed, still looking at the floor.

"Dawn, as we said earlier, we are from the Church of Jesus Christ of Latter-day Saints. We're glad you enjoyed your visit to Temple Square. Your father indicated that he would enjoy a visit from us, so here we are."

"Do you chaps realize that we visited the Temple Square over two years ago?"

"I'm sorry," Elder Hall replied, glancing at her face, then back to the floor. "They don't date our paperwork. This far from Utah, it sometimes takes a long time to follow through."

"That's fine. It's actually sweet that you remembered after all this time. Daddy will like that. But he isn't home. He usually gets home about six o'clock." She glanced at a huge grandfather clock to her left. It read a little before three. "I wouldn't want him to miss meeting you. He was very impressed and has been anxious to have someone call from the church. If you like, you can join me in the pool. We have lots of bathing suits. That would be a fun way to spend the next few hours. Daddy usually comes home and takes a dip anyway. It would be perfect."

"Actually," Kim explained. "As missionaries, swimming with attractive, young women is one of the things we aren't supposed to do. Appealing as your invitation is, I hope you will forgive us if we decline." He handled that so smoothly, that Sam was proud of him.

She let her lip slip forward in a pout, then smiled at them. "I should have guessed as much. Of course you can't. I meant no disrespect. Well, then the best I can do is invite you back at seven. He will be pleased to receive you then." She stood gracefully, and adjusted the gossamer robe around her. It covered very little. Sam had to look away to keep his eyes off her body. He felt ashamed that he had no more self control than that.

Once back in the car, they both wiped sweat from their brow, and not from the heat. "That was as close as I want to come to being tempted by a beautiful woman, Elder." Kim said with a sigh. "And she wasn't even trying to tempt us. Man, I need a three-day fast!"

Sam laughed, and nodded agreement. He liked Dawn, but hoped she had more in her wardrobe than the bikini and silk robe.

Seven o'clock found them again knocking on the huge door. This time, a butler answered the door. He was dressed in a butler's uniform, and invited them in with a sweeping bow. He led them past the big living room and into a study.

"The master will join you shortly," he said matter-of-factly, and closed the double sliding doors. The study walls were lined on three sides with book shelves. It reminded him of the study in the mission home. Many of the volumes were ancient, and probably very valuable. This room was also tall, with the bookshelves extending far higher than any person could reach. Above the shelves, a silent zoo of smaller trophies stared at them with glassy eyes. One shelf held birds, some with their wings fully extended. Sam noted that they were all birds of prey. Another wall held a fine collection of small cats. He saw several which reminded him of the American bobcat. While the collection was impressive, it made him feel slightly uncomfortable. A lot of animals had died to decorate his walls.

They were so intent on the trophies, that neither of them heard the study doors open. "It is an impressive collection, isn't it?" a voice said behind them. They both turned to see a middle-aged man dressed in a red smoking jacket and silk pants. He held a pipe in his teeth. He was slender and obviously athletic, with sandy hair, and a slim mustache. His eyes were a very light blue. He smiled and shook their hands.

When he spoke, his accent was heavily British. It completed the impression of the great white hunter. "Damn decent of you to finally look me up after all this time. Please, take a seat." They pulled plush chairs toward the desk, and sat. He took a seat behind the desk. "Dawn told me you're from the Mormons?"

"Yes sir, the Church of Jesus Christ of Latter-day Saints," Kim replied.

He nodded, and puffed a cloud of blue smoke which rose slowly toward the ceiling. The pipe had a sweet, fruity smell which Sam did not find at all objectionable. It smelled more like fruit and roses than tobacco.

"As you know, Dawn and I visited there several years prior. Very impressive. Most enjoyable. We went to every little performance and attended every tour. Had a splendid time. Had you come the day I returned to Africa, I probably would have joined your church without much of a to-do. As it is, I've kind of lost interest. Don't want to put you two lads off your feed, but I'm really not interested in discussing religion. I hope that doesn't offend you. I know you've traveled a damn long ways to visit me. Terribly sorry and all."

Kim straightened in his chair. "Mr. Pauley, we live in South Africa. We didn't travel from America for the soul purpose of visiting you. So you owe us no apology. We are on a mission for the church, and will be here in your country for two years."

"Quite right. Of course. Much the better then. I haven't put you out as much as I had originally thought. I'm much relieved then. Still, I have to say, I did anxiously await your coming for several years. Perhaps I'll go back some day, and that will rekindle the spark."

At that moment, Dawn entered the study. She was carrying a tray with four teacups. This time, she was wearing a soft, blue dress which extended from under her chin, to her ankles, and left everything to the imagination. In many ways it made her more beautiful. For the first time, Sam noted how finely chiseled her face was. She had her hair done up in soft ringlets. She could have walked from the room and attended any formal ball.

"Ah, there you are, Dawn. Thank you dear, very thoughtful of you. Elders? Would you care for Red Bush tea?" he asked, using the English name for Roi Bush tea. "Dawn says you can drink it. Not real tea, or coffee though, I understand, hey?"

Then nodded, and accepted the teacups she handed them. After offering them cream and sugar, she took a seat near Sam and sipped her own tea.

"Dawn," Mr. Pauley continued. "I was just telling these lads that I'm no longer keen to become a Mormon. What about you dear? Do you still want to listen to these chaps?" He said it all so calmly, that it sounded as if they were discussing whether to have one lump of sugar, or two.

"Daddy, you were the one who was so enthusiastic back then. I'm surprised you've lost it. You have often talked about it. As a matter of fact, I have anticipated the missionaries coming, only because of your interest. But now that you're no longer interested..." she paused.

Sam could feel the rejection hovering in the air, unspoken. He silently braced himself. He had been sent away so many times, that another would just be another. He had long ago overcome the sense of personal failure at each rejection. Still, his heart ached as each of Father's children turned away their opportunity to know Him better. He looked into Dawn's eyes and saw more than a lovely woman. He saw a precious, spiritually significant, daughter of Heavenly Father, and he prayed her heart would feel the need as keenly as his did.

"...I think I still want to know more. Would that be OK Daddy?"

"Sure, my dear. You check it out. If its really good, let me know, and maybe I'll come listen in," he said, blowing a blue cloud of smoke, and leaning way back in his big chair.

"In that case, I'm going to go for a dip in the pool. You three carry on without me. Cheery-O," he said, and left the room.

They taught Dawn a first discussion, which she enjoyed. It was a delight to teach her, she was sweet, unassuming, and believing. Her questions, while deep, were for the purpose of exploring the truth, not to challenge or dispute.

As they came to know her, they learned more about the Pauley family and their amazing house.

The castle had been built by her grandfather, and passed on to his son, her father. The grandfather had made a great deal of money by publishing a newspaper. He loved castles, and could afford to make his dream home look like one. The castle was, in fact, much larger than it appeared. There were over one hundred rooms, twenty-five of which were bedrooms. There was a six-car garage, two pools, two tennis courts, an indoor squash court, four formal living rooms, two libraries, two kitchens, four dining rooms, several game rooms, and a host of other rooms. Since her mother's death, they had closed off most of the huge building, and occupied only a small portion of the whole.

On impulse she stood and walked to the book shelves. "Daddy doesn't like me showing these things to people. I only found this one a few weeks ago while cleaning." She pulled down on piece of trim near the third row of books. A latch clicked, and the book shelf swung inward silently. She motioned for them to follow.

Dawn flipped a light switch and they found themselves in a narrow, carpeted hall. The walls were expensive paneling, and the carpeting, a lush green, though coated with dust. A few feet away the hall came to a tee. She led them to the right, and they came to a stair. "This stair rises in a cavity below the stairs in the foyer. It goes up, and has a secret opening in most of the bedrooms upstairs."

She walked past the stairs to a blank wall. She placed the palm of her hand on the panel, and slid it to the left. Beyond, was a dark piece of glass. Sam stepped forward and moved close to the glass. He could see a darkened room beyond, and immediately recognized it as the main living room. They were looking through the large mirror on the wall. Dawn slid the panel closed and led them back to the tee. She walked straight past the hall they had entered by and on for a fairly long distance.

"Many of these panels open to allow you to see into other rooms. Some of them open into secret doors. I have spent most of my childhood exploring these passageways. I know more about them than Daddy. He doesn't seem to be too interested. I can get from one end of the castle to the other, without stepping out of these secret hallways. I have found several rooms that have no other entrance than by these halls. One of them has a whole lot of guns and things. Several of the doors are very thick and locked. I think Grandpa was afraid someone would discover these secret passages, and locked even some of the secret doors. I don't know who has the key, if anyone does."

She turned left, then right, and stopped by a panel. She pushed left, and it slid open. A gust of frigid air rushed through the opening. She chuckled when the Elders seemed startled. She stepped through, and flipped on a light. She was standing in a cooler. Stainless steel shelves filled with food stuffs surrounded her. They followed her through. The secret door slid closed of its own. She pushed open the heavy door to the cooler, and they stepped out into a huge kitchen.

"I sometimes go this way to get a midnight snack," she confessed sheepishly, and led them to a counter which held a plate under a domed crystal cover. She lifted the cover to reveal three huge cinnamon rolls. "The prize at the end of the maze," she said happily, and carefully lifted one onto a china plate. She handed it to Sam, then the next to Elder Hall. She led them to a small, sunny dining area, where they laughed as they ate the sticky sweet rolls.

Sam found Dawn's father intriguing. Oliver Pauley was forty-seven years old, a diamond cutter by profession. One evening, instead of teaching Dawn immediately, they listened to him describe his line of work.

"I'm a cutter," he explained. "And without being presumptuous, I'm one of the best. I have a type of spiritual connection with the stones and can feel their inner beauty and instinctively know how to cut them. However, I haven't cut a stone for years. I presently manage a cutting house for Goldstein, Goldstein, and Meyers. I direct the other cutters on how to find the magic in each stone."

"Wow," Kim exclaimed, "it must pay really well."

"In fact," he replied, drawing deeply on his pipe. "I work for nothing."

"How can that be?" Sam asked.

"Come on, Daddy. Tell them the whole thing," Dawn urged, her voice childlike.

He laughed. "When they offered me the position they gave me two options. One was a fairly handsome salary. The other, was the pick of any stone that went through their shop, at their cost. The only limitation is that I cannot sell any stones in this country. I chose the latter. It has proven to be a wise decision."

"But if you can't sell any diamonds in this country, how could you make a living?" Elder Hall wondered.

"Twice a year I take two or three of my favorites, mount them in jewelry, and Dawn and I go on a vacation. First we go to England, where we sell the stones for a handsome profit. Since they are mounted in jewelry, there is no import duty. We deposit the proceeds from the sale in a Swiss bank, and head off to some new exotic destination for a couple weeks."

"Wow, that's amazing," Sam admitted. It makes me wonder why more people don't do it.

"Few people can buy stones at the cutter's cost. The only reason they let me do it is because I make them millions of rand each year. They know I could get a similar, or better deal anywhere I go. Few people have my affinity for the stones, you see."

"Amazing," Sam said again.

"As a matter of fact," he continued, leaning forward as if this were especially important. "I'm looking for people to do the traveling for me. Anyone with an American passport would be perfect. If I trusted them, we could do some amazing business. I have a South African passport, and if I go more than twice a year, the customs laws allow them to tax my stones whether they are mounted in jewelry or not. They wouldn't pay any attention to a person with an American passport."

"What are you getting at?" Kim asked, a suspicious tone to his voice.

"I'm a business man, and this is a business proposal. It has nothing to do with your teaching Dawn, or your mission. Here's the deal. After your mission, you go home and raise 10,000 dollars. Come back to me, and I will sell you 50,000 dollars worth of diamonds, already mounted in jewelry. I'll introduce you to my buyers in England, where they will help you sent up a Swiss account, and transfer the money for you. You return home with 40,000 dollars in your hands. I make 5,000 on each transaction. I have enough buyers that you could make the trip once a month, and never go to the same place twice. I have several people doing it already. They make their entire living doing it, and they live very well. It works to everyone's advantage. You could make nearly half a million a year, and travel all over the globe."

"I don't mean this to be an insulting question," Kim said. "But, is it legal?"

"Certainly. It's very common practice. I've had several international lawyers check the various customs and import laws, and they all concluded that it is perfectly legal. You are welcome to read their letters so stating, if you wish."

———

Kim could not sleep that night thinking about diamonds. Mr. Pauley's proposal seemed to echo in his mind. It was still on his mind when they returned three days later to teach Dawn. However, she was home alone.

"I'm so sorry," she said as soon as she opened the door. "But I have an unexpected matter I need to attend to. A neighbor has lost their youngest son in a tragic accident. He was killed while playing soccer at school, of all things. Broke his neck." She sighed and stepped out onto the front porch. "They are having a gathering of friends at their home, and I really need to go. They have been friends for years. I hope you understand."

They did understand, and assured her it was just fine. They made another appointment for the following day, and were just climbing into their car when she walked toward them, a smile on her face.

"I just thought of something. Why don't you come with me. They know I'm studying with the Mormon Elders, and they were quite supportive of the idea. It may be nice to have you come. What do you think? Afterward, if you still have time, we could do our discussion."

They exchanged glances, and then said in exact unison, "sounds good." She smiled and turned away. She trotted several steps toward the garage, then stopped suddenly.

"Do you chaps want to ride with me? Daddy said I could take the Jaguar. I'm a good driver, and I don't speed." She pronounced it 'jag-your.'

They watched as the third garage door opened smoothly, and the roar of an engine filled the yard. A sleek, red, Jaguar convertible backed out into the lane. Sam noticed it was a model XKE. It had a V12 engine, and looked as if it were faster than a bat out of the hot place.

Sam climbed into the passenger seat, and Elder Hall squeezed into the tiny space behind which passed for a back seat. Sam gripped the door as she shoved it into gear. She touched the gas and the car lept forward, belching smoke in a roar of burning rubber.

"Oops," she said, and gave him an apologetic look. "I always forget how powerful this thing is. She started again, this time rolling smoothly down the lane. When she reached the road, she carefully powered onto the road. Even driven conservatively, the mighty roadster was a thrill. Sam felt his heart pounding as she touched the gas, and it leapt down the road. She took them on a fairly short, but dizzying journey deeper into the subdivision. Every home they passed was a palace. Finally, they pulled up to a huge English Tudor style home. She stopped on the curb, and killed the car. There were nearly a dozen other vehicles parked nearby. Sam counted four Rolls Royce, and two Cadillacs. A butler met them at the door and ushered them into the living room. It was palatial in size, with two, huge, gold and crystal chandeliers at opposite ends of the high ceiling.

At the far end of the room, a man and woman stood side by side, their faces gripped with grief. They tried to entertain their guests, but every few minutes, one of them would have to turn away. He watched as the mother turned her back, and her shoulders shook with silent sobs.

He was momentarily transported back to the tragic days following Jimmy's accident, and it was as if he were watching his own parents grieve, and his heart felt as if it would break. Without waiting for an invitation, he walked directly toward them. He was only vaguely aware of Kim following in his wake through the crowded room.

Dawn arrived at his side, and following a hug to both of them, turned and introduced Sam and Elder Hall. To their left, a picture of a young boy stood on a grand piano. It was surrounded by cut flowers.

"Mr. and Mrs. Feinstein, this is a friend of mine, Elder Mahoy," she introduced as they shook hands. He was a short, balding man in his late forties with sandy blond hair and a Roman style beard. He shook Sam's hand without enthusiasm and almost immediately looked back at the photo on the piano.

Mrs. Feinstein held his hand, and looked into his eyes. She was somewhat younger than her husband, and possessed the most penetrating ice-blue eyes he had ever seen. A twin course of tears spilled down her cheeks, and he suppressed an urge to take her in his arms. Somehow, she sensed his emotion, and smiled wanly.

A powerful urge to give them something swept over him, and he pondered what he possessed that might ease their pain. He had no flowers, no sympathetic cards, no poetry, no inspiring thought. He glanced at the piano, and realized there was something he did possess. The music which endlessly played in his mind was there, sweet, flowing, comforting. He stepped back, and Mrs. Feinstein released her grip.

He nodded toward the piano. "May I?" He asked.

Her eyes brightened, and she nodded, taking a step toward the big, black piano.

Sam sat and raised the lid. It was a Knab piano, considered by many to be the finest piano in the world. Made in America, they routinely sold for sums exceeding 50,000 dollars. He played a short scale and found it perfectly tuned. The music was there, waiting in his heart, but something was missing. He wanted to give them something, not just entertain them. Give meant something more permanent than music which evaporates into memory with the last note played.

"Do you have a tape recorder?" he asked. Mr. Feinstein nodded toward the door, and took several steps toward the piano. A moment later, the crowd parted as a servant rolled a cart containing a large reel to reel recorder into the room. The servant placed a microphone on top of the piano, and another aimed at Sam, as if he were going to sing.

Instead, he picked up the mike, and handed it to Mrs. Feinstein. She took it hesitantly. The servant clicked on the big recorder, and the reels moved ahead slowly.

"Mrs. Feinstein, what was your son's name?

"Lawson," she said hesitantly, "Lawson Levi Feinstein Junior," she said with pride in her voice, which wilted as soon as the words had escaped her lips.

"Tell me about Lawson. Start with his age, and tell me the special things about him, what he liked, the things he loved doing. His favorite things. The things that made you love him most. When I start playing, I'd like you to keep talking. Speak up so I can hear you. Whatever comes to your mind, just say it. OK?"

She looked frightened, then slowly began to speak. "Lawson was twelve. I guess his favorite thing in the whole world was camping. We all love to camp. We have this favorite place, where there's a small waterfall, and a brook with clear, cold water."

Sam could almost see the waterfall, and the music it made as it happily tumbled over the rocks. He began to play, light and happy, spilling, rolling. His fingers caressed the keys, and the music became a warm summer day, and a giggling water fall.

Mrs. Feinstein stopped, momentarily mesmerized by the music. Sam nodded at her to go on.

"I believe it was by that stream that his father first showed him how to kick a soccer ball. He was eight years old and took to it immediately. We played all afternoon. We ran, and ran, laughed and kicked that ball until we were so weary and so happy that we could hardly walk."

Sam closed his eyes, and the ball flew through the music in long, intricate runs and bounced happily from person to person.

"It was almost dark, and my husband kicked the ball one last time. Lawson missed it, and the ball rolled into the stream. We tried to catch it, but it was quickly gone in the dark." She paused, remembering, as if she were there once again. "Lawson cried."

The music tumbled, turned minor, and rumbled like thunder. Then, just as suddenly, became happy again.

"Besides camping and soccer, I think he loved Mickey Mouse the most. I'll never forget the first Mickey Mouse cartoon we took him to. We had to stay and watch it three times!" She laughed as the music played M-I-C K-E-Y M-O-U-S-E. Everyone in the room chuckled and clapped their hands.

"His favorite movie was "Doctor Zhivago," which surprised me at the time, because it is such an adult movie. But he loved it, especially the part where they meet again after so many years in that mansion filled with ice and snow. I remember watching him cry, as he thought of their sadness and joy. He was an unusually mature child, I think."

The music became those dark days of the Russian revolution, and the bitter sweet love story of Doctor Zhivago rolled majestically from the piano.

"I think the thing I will miss most," his father said, now standing very close, facing his wife, both their hands on the microphone which was now forgotten. "Is his laughter. He was so alive, so, so happy," he said, searching for words. "He was a bright star, a flash of sunlight in my life. Every time I saw him, he smiled at me, even when he was angry at me for punishing him or missing a soccer game. I can't remember one time when he didn't smile..."

"Yes," she agreed, "that was my son. I wish I knew where he is, if he's happy, if he still loves soccer..." her voice trailed off into silence, and her hands fell by her side. The music continued for almost a full minute, aching, wondering, weeping, seeking answers.

"Let me share something with you," Sam said, and they started, and looked at him as if seeing him for the first time. She nodded, and as an afterthought, set the microphone back on the piano.

"I want to tell you what my heart tells me; what my faith tells me." As he spoke the music quietly turned to "I Am a Child of God." The music flowed magically from his soul, as if inseparably connected to his words.

"I believe we are children of a loving Father in Heaven. All of us. Since we are children of an eternal being, we also possess the seeds of eternity within us. As tragic as dying seems, it is not an end, but a beginning. We leave this life and enter the next still the same person, but freed from the limitations of mortality. It is my firm conviction that Lawson still lives, as a spirit person, in the presence of God. And it is my great joy to have complete faith in the truth that you will one day hold your son in your arms again. Until then, we endure this brief separation we call death, with faith in God."

He turned back to the piano and finished the song with a reverent and beautiful flourish. He lifted his hands, and quite unexpectedly, a voice carried across the room. It was a man's voice, high and melodious. The voice carried across the room, as if from another world, sweet and pure. It was as if an angel had come to add his testimony to Sam's. The crowd parted once again, and a man walked forward, singing "I Am a Child of God." He sang with reverent passion, pressing both fists to his chest, raising his chin, as if singing directly to God. His eyes glistened as he stopped beside the piano. Sam began once again, playing, not the melody, but an intricate harmony. His fingers did a ballet on the keys, as the stranger's voice penetrated every soul.

The singer knew all three verses, and he sang them as if they were the final act of his life. Sam felt his heart soaring and tears ran down his cheeks. For him, nothing existed but the music and the words he had known since childhood.

I am a child of God
And He has sent me here.
Has given me an earthly home
With parents kind and dear.

I am a child of God
And so my needs are great.
Teach me to understand His will
Before it grows to late.

I am a child of God
Rich blessings are in store.
If I but learn to do His will
I'll live with Him once more.

Lead me, Guide me, Walk beside me.
Help me find the way.
Teach me all that I must do
To live with Him some day.

The music ceased, and he slowly closed the lid on the piano and stood. Lawson's mother embraced him and held him as she both laughed and wept on his shoulder.

"Thank you," she said quietly in his ear. "I will long treasure this moment, and the memories you have created for us. Until you said those words, I did not realize that I also know that Lawson is still alive, somewhere, somehow. We are Jewish, and I don't think we believe these things, yet I know them to be true. Would you come back and teach us what the words of that song mean? Come back and teach me why, against logic, against hope, I still believe Lawson lives?"

His single nod was all she needed, and she released him, tears of joy and relief falling from her cheeks. She stepped back, and was swept into an embrace by Dawn.

Mr. Feinstein took his hand in both of his.

"Thank you," he mouthed, no sound coming from his lips.

His purpose done, Sam walked quickly to the door and out into the hot afternoon.

He was sitting in the passenger seat of the Jaguar waiting for Dawn when the stranger with the beautiful voice appeared at the door. He caught sight of Sam and walked directly toward him.

"Elder," the man said, taking Sam's hand in a hand unaccustomed to work. "I am Sir Philip Domigo. I doubt you know me, but I sing opera with the South African Operatic Company. I have to say, that I have heard many renditions of that charming little hymn you Mormons sing, yet I was so deeply touched by the one today that the words literally burst from me. I hope you will forgive me if I upstaged you. I didn't mean to."

Sam shook his head, but said nothing. "I thought not," the man continued, a smile softening his face. "What touched me so deeply was the beauty of the message of the words. I had never seen them as a testimony of the eternal nature of the soul, yet as I sang them, I almost felt as if I could see into heaven and glimpse the endless joy God ordains for those who return to him with unstained hands."

He paused for a heartbeat, which in reality seemed longer. Something was heavy on his mind, and he was searching for words which seemed hidden to him. He continued in a voice soft with emotion. "I am intimately familiar with the performing arts and with persons of vast talent. Yet I must say, my young friend, that your music is superior to all those others. Not because you possess a greater talent. Indeed, almost all my acquaintances could perform circles around you. No, not because of your obvious talent, but because of the purity of your soul. You believe the message of your music with all your soul, and the power behind your music is nearly divine. Thank you, my friend, for showing me the music the angels sing. I have long hoped to one day hear angels sing, and today, I sang with them and my soul rejoiced. Thank you."

So saying, he released Sam's hand, and quickly departed. Sam shook his head as if to clear it, and then bowed his head in rich joy.

––––

That evening, as they studied the scriptures before going to bed, they were surprised by a knock on their door. Sam straightened his tie, and answered the knock. Two uniformed officers stood before him. A moment of panic swept over him as the grim faced officers handed him an envelope. His panic vanished as he read "Elder Sam" in flowing script. The envelope bore the return address of the Regional Prosecutor. The letter inside was in Sister Van der Kerk's flowing script.

My dearest Elder Sam Mahoy,

It has come to our very pleasant attention that you are now stationed in Durban, Natal. Since Brother Van der Kerk won the Prosecutorship, we have purchased a new home in Pretoria, to be near the seat of government. However, we spend three months each year in Durban.

We are presently here, and anxious to meet you once again. Some very good friends want missionary discussions, and we hoped you would teach them.

Actually, we know they are out of your teaching area, and all the above is just a ploy to see you again.

We formally invite you, and your companion, and all other fellow missionaries in your area, to join us for dinner this Friday evening. Be sure to bring everyone, and a hearty appetite.

If you are able, please send word with the gentlemen who delivered this

*letter. They will pick you up at six p.m. that evening if you agree.
Until then, we leave our love,*

Brother and Sister Van der Kerk

Six o'clock Friday evening found his small room crammed with eight Elders. When their car arrived, it was a stretch limousine, into which they comfortably fit. The Van der Kerk's home was spread out over a hill near the coast. As they drove up the cobble stone drive to their home, his heart pounded in his chest.

Sister Van der Kerk flung open the door, and ran to the car as it pulled up. As soon as he emerged, she swept him into her arms, and kissed both cheeks, releasing him only after the other missionaries cleared their throats.

"Well," Elder Hall said under his breath, his voice alive with humor, "I'll bet that greeting was against mission rules." She heard, and turned toward him.

"I have vast experience getting rules changed. If need be, young man, we'll change this one. It must be a stupid rule anyway." She laughed at her own humor, and laced an arm through his. She led him into the large foyer of her new home. She explained that it was a home owned by the government, set aside for the use of government officials. It seemed as if no expense had been spared. She led them from room to room, letting them ooh, and aah at the lavish furnishings and grand design of the home.

"Our home in Pretoria is much smaller. You would be proud, Elder Sam," she said happily. "Since joining the church, our desire for opulence has diminished to zero. Our home is just adequate. It is kind of embarrassing to live in this great home, but we suffer along as best we can." That brought a laugh from everyone including her. However, she was serious.

She led them to a huge dining room which held a table adequate for seating as many as forty guests. The ceiling was arched, with open woodwork of great skill and beauty. Along one side, near the ceiling, were flags of the various cities. Along the opposite, were flags of the nations. The table was spread with a single white cloth and set with golden table ware. She showed them to their places and indicated a place for Sam near the end. She sat on the end, leaving a vacant seat beside her for her husband.

At that exact moment, a door closed in the distance, and Brother Van der Kerk scurried into the room. Sam stood and embraced him. He had been detained, but was finally here. A servant took his briefcase and coat and they sat. Brother Van der Kerk asked Sam to pray.

The meal began with half an avocado stuffed with chilled shrimp. The avocado was the size of an ostrich egg, sweet, and smooth. The shrimp was in a light cocktail sauce and was the finest Sam had tasted. Sister Van der Kerk urged them to only sample each dish. The combination of avocado and shrimp was unique and difficult to just sample. Sam allowed himself to slowly savor the exotic flavors. Next came a soup made of water buffalo and black beans. The taste of the soup was so complete, that it awakened taste buds never before used. Again she urged them to lightly sample each dish.

Next came a fruit salad in half a pineapple shell. It was made entirely of kiwi, grapes, pineapple bits, and narchi. The narchi was a large, grape-like fruit with its single pip removed. The meat immediately around the narchi seed was so bitter that no human could eat it. Once the bitter fruit was removed, there was no sweeter fruit than a narchi. The whole effect was so exotic, and sweet, that it should have been a desert.

Following the salad came a plate with a single Larenzo Marx Prawn upon it. The large prawn was the size of a lobster. The mission-aries had never seen a shrimp so large, or so ugly. Some of them just stared, their eyes growing large at the idea of eating such a grotesque monstrosity. Sister Carlson lifted hers, and demonstrated how to open the shell and get the sweet meat within. After some encouragement, the missionaries gamely pried, twisted, and poked, until they succeeded. The meat was rich beyond belief. One taste was all it took to make them believers. Sam's mouth almost refused to believe that something this succulent existed in the whole world. Each bite was a tiny bit of heaven. He found himself wishing there had been ten of them on his plate, rather than one. Yet, by the time the shrimp had deteriorated to a pile of loose shells, he was feeling quite full.

Next, the servants brought a frosty parfait glass filled with a bubbling liquid. Deep inside the liquid were three, tiny scoops of ice cream. They sipped the almost-bitter liquid, and ate the ice cream with long handled spoons.

As they ate, Sister Van der Kerk explained: "In a traditional feast, what you have just eaten would be the appetizers. This drink is unsweetened mineral water, with a tiny bit of ice cream for sweetness and flavor. It settles the stomach and freshens the palate. In a moment you will begin to feel hungry again, which is a good thing, because we have prepared what we hope is a very American treat."

At her words, servants began laying large bowls of food before them. All around them swirled familiar smells. As each plate was set down, Sister Van der Kerk described the dish. There were mashed potatoes from Idaho, candied yams from New York, corn on the cob from California, honeyed ham from Kentucky, corn fritters from Kansas, crayfish from Lousiana, and a host of other dishes, all from the States.

As each dish was introduced, some missionary in turn sighed with delight. The Van der Kerks had done their homework, and there was a treasure for each Elder, carefully chosen to remind him of home. The last dish to appear was a gigantic turkey. No one was disappointed.

Sam later found out they had telephoned the parents of each of the Elders weeks ago and asked what his favorite dish might be. Sister Van der Kerk's love of the Elders, and her desire to please them was reflected in the great cost of an international phone call to the States, which was nearly a hundred dollars apiece.

By the time dessert was due, not a single soul could eat a bite more. Sister Van der Kerk stood and disappeared for a few minutes. She returned with a New York cheesecake, complete with blueberry topping. Sam loved blueberry cheesecake above all other foods. Atop the cake were twenty one candles burning brightly. Behind her, a stream of servants brought in deserts for each Elder, each different, each burning cheerily with birthday candles. Elder Hall's dessert was a huge cantaloupe half, filled with orange sherbet ice cream, his favorite dessert. She set the cheesecake before Sam, and began to sing; Happy Birthday...Though a little confused, everyone joined in. Birthdays are the hardest days for missionaries. They often go unnoticed, uncelebrated, and unsung.

"I know it is none of your birthdays today," she said as soon as the singing ceased. I also know, you often don't celebrate them much because your families are so far away. This is my way of giving you my love, and saying thank you, and telling each of you that I am so grateful you came to our land. Please, make a wish, and blow out your candles before you have to eat wax." They all laughed and blew. An amazing cloud of smoke wafted up from the table. Servants appeared with plates and deftly cut huge pieces for them, while another scooped ice cream of exotic flavors.

Not a single fork moved as they stared at the enormous plates of dessert, yet the sweetness was not on their table, it was in their hearts, and they treasured the joy of the moment. The only one who finished his dessert was Elder Hall, who also ate the other half of the cantaloupe.

An hour later, Elders were sprawled all over the huge living room, groaning in various states of blissful consciousness. With the exception of Elder Hall, they had all dismantled the word of wisdom with their forks.

Sister Van der Kerk found Sam lying on an oriental rug, and indicated with a nod that she wished him to follow. With some difficulty, he rolled to a kneeling position, then pushed himself to his feet using the sofa. She chuckled at him from the doorway. Elder Hall stood to follow him. She led them through several rooms and halls until they came to a game room. Brother Van der Kerk sat on the edge of a large billiards table, which was illuminated by an elaborate stained glass lamp hanging low over the table. He was holding a cue.

He handed them both a cue, and Sister Van der Kerk picked up one from the rack.

"Elders, have you ever played billiards?" he asked, motioning to the oversized table. It was larger than a pool table. Neither of them had. He explained the rules. They played one game, then Brother Van der Kerk grew serious.

"Elder Sam, I have looked forward to this day for nearly a year now. We haven't spoken since our baptism, and I have longed for this day."

Sam turned to face him. Sister Van der Kerk walked to her husband's side, and slipped her arm through his. It was clear that what he was about to say was important to them both.

"I have some unfinished business," he said, his voice breaking. He lowered his head. There was a long moment of silence. Elder Hall made a loud shot, and mumbled something about the seven ball. It was his way of not being involved in the conversation, and it was appreciated.

"Elder..." He paused. "Sam, my soul has been tormented almost without respite. I wake up in the middle of the night in a sweat, and can't sleep. It is the one part of my life which my baptism did not wash away, and I need your help."

Sam was mystified and a little frightened by his words. "What is it, how can I help?" he asked, his voice echoing his deep concern. These were people he loved and cared about deeply.

"How you can help, is by hearing my confession," he said.

Sam felt an electric bolt of fear stab through him. But before he could say a word, Brother and Sister Van der Kerk exchanged a quick glance, and he continued.

"Well, that isn't what I mean, exactly. I guess what I need is to beg your forgiveness."

"Whatever for?" Sam demanded, his voice curious.

"For having you whipped that day in court," he said, his head lowered. His hands trembled, and tears dripped onto the deep green carpeting.

Sam felt himself begin to brush it all aside with a dismissal, but was stopped by a gentle urging from the Spirit. Instead, he said nothing.

"You see, I was so arrogant, so, so official. I felt no remorse at the time. I thought you would learn a lesson, that we didn't want you in South Africa, that we were willing to cause you physical torment to deliver that message. I thought you deserved it for bringing a false religion into my beloved country." He fumbled with the cue, his wife still holding onto his arm.

"Yet, you know well the effect that event has had upon me, upon us. We have found the truth. Heavenly Father, through you, gave us truth and love and hopefully eternal life in response to my evil treatment of you."

Sam took a step forward and laid a hand on his arm. He didn't know what to say, and felt no words flowing from the Holy Spirit, so he said nothing. Brother Van der Kerk was not finished. After a moment, he continued.

"I was the one who made the observation that you were like Paul who had been whipped for teaching Christ." He paused here and sobbed twice. "What I was blind to at the time, was that I was like the wicked men who ordered Paul scourged. Since this thought entered my heart, I have lain awake nights terrified that I have jeopardized my exaltation. I allowed a representative of Jesus Christ to be scourged. It is the same as if I had stood by, and allowed Christ himself to be whipped, when it was within my power to stop it. My soul mourns more than words can express that I had so little valor, that I stooped, willingly, to such evil. I can scarcely pray, my guilt is so heavy on my soul. If God were to walk into this room, I would beg the house to fall on me, to hide me from His presence." It seemed to Sam as if the only reason he did not fall to his knees was because Sister Van der Kerk still held his arm. It was as if the weight of damnation were on his soul.

Sam stood quietly, tears trickling onto his cheeks, until his heart flowed with the right words. "There are two observations I want to make, if you'll allow me."

They both nodded solemnly, Brother Van der Kerk without lifting his head.

"Firstly, as you already know, I do forgive you. In fact, I look back on those events with rejoicing. I consider it a small price to pay to be able to find you, and teach you. I love you, and you need never think otherwise."

"We know this is true," Sister Van der Kerk said softly.

"Secondly, I believe your answer lies in a statement you made." Brother Van der Kerk looked up, an expression of confusion and doubt on his face.

"You said, 'I can hardly pray, my guilt is so heavy.' Do you remember?" They both nodded.

"There's a scripture in Mosiah, which says in part, that it is the evil spirit which teaches a man not to pray. The whole effect of this long, painful, process of dwelling on the past and being harrowed up with awful feelings has taught you not to pray. Brother Van der Kerk, you are laboring under the effects of a false spirit. You have been listening to the wrong voice."

Brother Van der Kerk looked up, his eyes suddenly hopeful, yet confused. "I don't understand," he said. "I thought this was the effect of the Holy Spirit working on me, bringing me to godly sorrow, to repentance, to recognition of my woeful state."

Sam allowed a doubtful look to cross his features. "The process of repentance is often painful, and does bring a person to recognize their need for repentance, and often to feel very badly for their sins. But it never teaches a person they are worthless, or lost, or beyond redemption. It certainly never teaches then to stop praying.

"When the Holy Spirit works with a person, the end effect is peaceful, joyful, and brings a person closer to Christ, not further away. The Holy Spirit leaves one with an intense desire to pray, not to hide under the rubble of their own tortured soul.

"There's a scripture in Galatians which I memorized a while ago. It goes like this:

"But the fruit of the Spirit is love, joy, peace, longsuffering, gentleness, goodness, faith, meekness, temperance... (Galatians 5:23)

"Nowhere in that scripture does it list shame, fear, hopelessness, alienation, shrinking from the presence of God, or any of the negative emotions you described as coming from this experience. I think you need to reevaluate this experience. You have needlessly allowed yourself to be tormented by events long past and long forgiven."

"So, all this time I have been feeling worthless and like God no longer loves me, I have been deceived by Satan." It was not a question. He straightened, laying his cue across the table. The pain which formerly twisted his features, was gone. He took a deep breath, and smiled.

"I feel so much better. I was to the point of not wanting to go to church because I felt unworthy. Now that I understand, it seems so plain, so simple. I will remember from now on. If the effect of a thought process makes me feel worthless, or like not praying, or hiding from God, then those thoughts are not inspired."

"Or, they were inspired by an evil source," Elder Hall said. He had been so quiet, his presence in the room had been forgotten, and everyone turned to look at him.

"I couldn't help but hear what has been said," he explained in apology.

"Quite all right, Elder," Brother Van der Kerk said with an airy wave of his hand. "I realize mission rules require you two to stay together."

"I'm grateful to have been here," Elder Hall replied earnestly. His face lit up with a smile. "I have been learning the same lessons, mostly from Elder Mahoy. One of the great things he has taught me is that spirits may be discerned in the same way people are."

"Come again?" Sister Van der Kerk asked.

"I didn't say it well. We can judge if a person is inspired in what they do, and how they live, by their fruits. If their fruits are good, and they bring people to Christ, and teach them to pray, and to love and serve God; if their lives are Christ-like in content, then we may know they are inspired of God. Most people come to know Joseph Smith was a prophet by reading the Book of Mormon, one of his fruits of divine origin.

"The same is true of books, movies, talks in Sacrament meeting, and most other things. If their fruits are good, they came from God.

"In the same context, if a spiritual experience leaves us feeling uplifted, and like praying and worshiping, then it came from God."

Brother Van der Kerk was nodding vigorously. "I see. Yes, of course. Since all good comes from God, and all bad from Satan or one of his tempters, then they may be discerned by their fruits as well.

"What a fascinating tool. If I had understood that, I would have rejected messages of self loathing and feelings of wanting to hide from God as being evil in origin, and saved myself months of sorrow. Well," he concluded, rubbing his hands together briskly as if trying to warm them. "I'll be better armed next time."

"I wonder how all-encompassing that principle is?" Sister Van der Kerk asked aloud. "I sometimes will just be standing there thinking, and of a sudden, have an angry thought, or feel grumpy. Those kinds of feelings don't come from the Holy Spirit, I'm sure. Does that mean they came from an evil spirit? It makes me wonder how much the evil ones affect our lives. Its kind of spooky to think about." She shuddered, and wrapped her arms around herself.

Sam thought about this for a moment. Her question was one he had pondered himself. In reality, he was unsure, and was unaware of any prophet speaking on this subject.

"I really don't know the answer to that question," he replied. "I'm unsure what impact they have on our daily feelings, but I am sure that blatantly negative reactions are often evil in origin. Especially, I believe, if they lead us away from righteousness, or make us feel like not praying. I prefer to stay on the safe side and not attribute overly much to evil spirits. On the other hand, it really helps to understand what's going on when we have an experience which leaves us feeling alienated from the Gospel, or from Christ.

"There's a scripture in Moroni, Chapter 7 which says the evil one entices, and urges to sin continually. I'm not sure we can interpret continually to mean every thought we have, but I'm sure they do everything in their power to drag us down."

Sister Van der Kerk nodded. "I've noticed that the big things start small. What I mean is, when Satan does succeed in getting me to feel disobedient, or to feel alienated from the Gospel, that it started as a small thing. It may have been some small thing someone said to which I took mild offense, which he worked on until it grew into something grotesque.

"I agree that every small negative feeling we have may not be directly inspired by Satan, but he apparently is able to pick up on them and to try to use them against us. For my part, I prefer to avoid them all if I can," she said thoughtfully.

Sam took a step and sat on the corner of the billiards table. "There are two great forces at work in our lives. On the one side, there is Christ and the Holy Spirit, which enlightens and entices for good, and strives to bring us unto righteousness. On the other side, and in direct opposition to Christ, are the forces of Satan and the unholy spirits. These continually entice us to depart from righteousness, and to choose anything which interferes with our eternal progression, whether it is blatant sin, or just something mindless which saps our strength and keeps the Holy Spirit away.

"Somewhere in the middle is the mind of man. We are continually exposed to these two great sources of revelation. I know it sounds odd to call temptations revelation, but in a very real sense they are. We are continually given the opportunity to choose between these two. The scriptures indicate that we will be exalted, or damned, according to which voice we choose to obey."

Brother Van der Kerk pulled up an ornate chair with a green leather cushion. He sat and held his chin in his thumb and forefinger, elbow on knee. He didn't realize it, but it was his trademark posture. It made Sam smile. "I'm always hearing complex conversations in my mind. This is especially true since my baptism. They almost sound like arguments and are quite confusing. I have been having a hard time determining which is the voice of the Holy Spirit and which is not. Like this last episode, I have sometimes listened to the wrong voices, even while trying very hard to do what is right."

It was Elder Hall who responded. "I have had vast experience following the wrong voice. Before my baptism, I became quite familiar with sin and grew accustomed to that voice. Since my baptism, I have been able to avoid those enticements to sin simply because I recognize the flavor of the evil voice. But even more important, since deciding to be obedient to all revelation from the Holy Ghost, I have begun to be as familiar with the voice of truth, and can recognize the voice of the Holy Spirit much better now. It may be a matter of experience."

Sam nodded. "That, and testing the messages against the words of the prophets and scriptures. If I were to receive a prompting to steal something, I would immediately know it was of an evil origin because it conflicts with known truths. Conversely, a prompting to say my prayers is easily identified as a true prompting because it harmonizes with known truth.

"Something else which helps me identify the source of various promptings, is to notice their order. When I receive an impression that I should bear my testimony, as an example, immediately after that, I hear a barrage of reasons why I should not."

Sister Van der Kerk laughed. It had a musical, almost chime-like quality. "That's what I hear all the time! I'm beginning to understand, its like a cross examination in court. The defense makes a statement which supports their case, immediately thereafter, the prosecution offers a series of rebuttals, often many more than necessary to prove the point. I do it myself in court. Fascinating." Her voice was animated, filled with excitement and discovery.

"In fact," Sam continued, "it is one of the evil one's weaknesses, that they often tirade against what the Holy Spirit says."

"Of course," Brother Van der Kerk mumbled, "of course."

"The Lord expects us to search diligently in the Light of Christ, or the conscience, to determine the difference between the two," Sam added.

"As a matter of fact," Elder Hall said. "There's a scripture in Moroni, chapter 7 which speaks of the very things we have been discussing. He closed his eyes as if viewing something seen only by himself. "It goes like this…"

> "But whatsoever thing persuadeth men to do evil, and believe not in Christ, and deny him, and serve not God, then ye may know with a perfect knowledge it is of the devil; for after this manner doth the devil work, for he persuadeth no man to do good, no, not one; neither do his angels; neither do they who subject themselves unto him.
>
> "And now, my brethren, seeing that ye know the light by which ye may judge, which light is the light of Christ, see that ye do not judge wrongfully; for with that same judgment which ye judge ye shall also be judged.
>
> "Wherefore, I beseech of you, brethren, that ye should search diligently in the light of Christ that ye may know good from evil; and if ye will lay hold upon every good thing, and condemn it not, ye certainly will be a child of Christ." (Moroni 7:17-19)

Brother Van der Kerk stood, picked up his cue, and said; "Elder, every time I talk to you I feel as if I'm a newborn babe spiritually, and I'm growing frightened about what I will do after you leave Africa. I seem to get easily diverted from the straight course. When I talk to you it seems straight forward again. You don't suppose I could offer you a great job and entice you to stay on, do you?" Brother Van der Kerk was very serious. This conversation had come up several times before.

"We have time for one more game before we have to get back," he said.

Sister Van der Kerk sighed and said, "I didn't think so."

———

The following evening they met with Dawn. It was to be her third discussion. She met them on the porch, her face was tear-streaked, and her eyes red and puffy.

"Daddy has forbidden me to continue with our discussions," she said without introduction. She sniffled and wiped her eyes with a silk handkerchief. "He says his boss is upset that I am studying to become a Mormon, and has commented that he would not feel comfortable doing business with someone who let his daughter be abducted into a cult."

"Dawn," Sam said softly, suppressing an urge to place a hand on her arm. "I'm so sorry. Of course, we'll respect your wishes. I'm really sorry this has brought you so much sorrow."

Dawn's face turned from sorrow to anger in a flash. The transformation was so sudden that it startled both of them. "How dare you assume what my wishes are, and how dare you assume that I am so spineless that his objections would deter me from finding and serving God!"

Sam opened his mouth to apologize, but she cut him off with a small shake of her head. "I'm sorry, Elders. I didn't mean to snap at you. It's just that I have been fighting this battle in my heart for two days, and I thought you, of all people, would understand how important this is. I'm sure you do. My emotions are rattled. Of course you do."

"What do you plan to do, and how can we help?"

"I plan to continue taking the missionary discussions. I plan to join the true church," she replied quite simply.

"I have to ask you several questions. How you answer them will determine whether we will be able to continue teaching you. OK?"

"Yes, I understand."

"OK. Are you legally emancipated?" In that country, a teenager could become an adult any time after sixteen, if they filled out the paperwork and filed it with the court. Until they were legally an adult, the mission rules forbid them teaching a person without parental consent.

"Daddy had me file for emancipation last year. That way I could have my own passport, and we could export more gems. So, I am."

"Good. Next question. Will your father react violently, or throw you out of the house, or disown you?"

"I think he will. I know he loves me, but he is a worldly man, and I don't think he will sacrifice his business to let me become a Mormon."

"Last question. Are you willing to pay that high a price to join Christ's true church?"

"I am." She said without hesitation. "In fact, I want to accelerate the discussions and be baptized as soon as possible. Is that possible? I want to do it while the power of my decision is still strong, and before I can be persuaded against it."

Sam considered this for a moment. "It's possible," he said, "but I don't advise it. I suggest you allow enough time to elapse so that the fire of your decision does cool. When you go into the waters of baptism, I want your decision to be as hard and as cold as steel. I want it to be sufficient to carry you through the rest of your life. I don't want you to look back on that day, and wonder if you acted hastily, or if you should have done it differently. I want you to rejoice every time you think of your baptism."

Dawn let her lip slip into a pout, then just as quickly, recovered, and smiled. "I agree. I would still like to accelerate the lessons though, but out of a desire to learn. If we finish too soon, we can go through them again, or pursue some other teachings, but I want to learn as quickly as I can. I will stick with the baptismal date we originally set. I think its wise, and I think Daddy will eventually see that it was wise."

When Dawn told her father of her decision, he tried to persuade her otherwise, and failing that, asked her to move out. Both she and her father wept as she walked down their long drive. He wouldn't even let her borrow the car to move away. He didn't close the door until she was out of sight down the long drive.

Dawn walked to the Feinstein's home, where she stayed for a few days. Eventually, she moved in with Bishop and Sister Van Halen. They wrapped their arms and their love around her.

Sam and Elder Hall were teaching Dawn the sixth discussion in the Van Halen's home when the phone rang. Having been isolated from the sound of telephones for almost two years, it startled him. It sounded like a fire alarm. Sister Van Halen answered the call, and handed him a note. He waited until Elder Hall was giving the next concept before glancing at it. What he read more than surprised him.

Elder Mahoy, Sean Whitehall called to request that you come to the hospital and talk to him. His tele # 23-5225 room 1128.

They had been expecting a call from the Whitehalls, but their son Sean was the last person they were anxious to meet again. He was one of the most completely evil men Sam had ever met. Nevertheless, they used the bishop's phone to call as soon as the discussion was over. Sean was abrupt, and merely made an appointment for the following Thursday. Considering everything, it was not an appointment Sam was looking forward to.

The hospital looked smaller in the daylight. As little as Sam knew about hospitals, this one seemed quite modern, yet had an air of backwardness he found a little frightening. On the main floor was a large room filled with dentist chairs. He had never seen such a thing. The room was roughly the size of a basketball court, yet had a dentist chair every ten feet in every direction. About a third of the chairs had someone in them. The chairs each had the old cable operated drills. The sound and smell of drilling teeth drifted from the room. Sam was old enough to have had a couple teeth drilled using the old cable drills, and it made his teeth hurt to remember.

They found the elevator and made their way to the eleventh floor. Sean's room was windowless and felt cheerless. They found Sean lying in bed, his skin pallid and pasty looking.

"Hello, Sean," Sam said, much more cheerfully than he felt. Sean rolled his head toward them, and without changing expression motioned for them to enter. The bed was high enough that sitting would have made them invisible to Sean, so they stood.

When Sean spoke, his voice was raspy. Without any attempt at pleasantries, he got directly to his point. "I have been lying here for almost three weeks now, with nothing else to do than think about how I got here. I have gone over and over it in my mind, trying to figure out how you two fit into it all.

"Logic tells me that I had this disease long before I met you in my parents home, and your telling me I would have a disease which takes away my most valued body part could have been wishful thinking on your part.

"Logic tells me that you probably heard my parents mention that my best friend's daughter had been murdered, even though they say the did not. And logic tells me that you may have guessed, or suspected that he, himself, was the criminal." He paused here, as if struggling to find his next words.

"Logic...what a fickle thing," he mused aloud. "It is beyond logic, however, that you could have gotten all three of those things right. I have tried every avenue of logic, and there are none which come close to explaining your correctly guessing three incredibly obscure things about a total stranger.

"Logic, my faithful companion, my guide in hating God, my sword excaliber in battling religious stupidity, has betrayed me, and now suggests that the only way you could have known these things, is if you are either clairvoyant, or were inspired of God. I personally prefer the former explanation, yet logic is equally agnostic toward things paranormal, as it is toward the whole idea of God."

He fixed his eyes on Sam with such intensity that Sam felt like turning away, but something in his gaze pulled at Sam's heart. His intensity was as much a cry for help as it was a tirade against all things spiritual.

"So, you see, I have asked you to come, and if you would be so kind, to explain yourself. You know how I hate falseness, flattery, false religion, false spirituality, false emotions, and everything false. I beg of you, tell me only the truth, and I will do my best to believe your words. I'm floundering here, and for the first time in my life, I am reaching out to a fellow mortal to help me. Help me, Elder Mahoy. Please."

Sam was actually surprised when he felt the familiar warmth of truth in his bosom. He, for himself, had judged Sean unsalvageable, and had personally written him off. The truth which touched him was a chastisement, a rebuke from the Lord, and it stung him to silence. He wanted the truth to be a lesson for Sean, but it was a lesson for himself, and no words came to his lips. But the rebuke continued, and lashed against his soul in firm, yet loving admonition. Here was a son of God, a precious soul needing help, and God had prepared him, conditioned his soul for teaching, and Sam had failed to see anything but the facade Sean had erected around himself.

Tears formed in his eyes, as he struggled to repent, to readjust his soul, and to see Sean in a purer light. Sean saw his struggle, and without understanding the source of it, was touched.

"The truth," Sam said, "Is that I owe you an apology." Both Sean and Elder Hall were stunned. It was not what either had expected.

"I don't understand. If any apologies are due, they should be from me. What..."

Sam cut him off with a small shake of his head. "When you asked me for the truth, I felt overwhelmed by the Spirit. It's a familiar feeling, and often comes when its time to teach. Yet the truth which came to me was a rebuke. I stand rebuked by God for judging you, and for not seeing your worth in God's eyes. I completely overlooked the very thing I preach, and that is His great and abiding love for you as his son."

"I don't understand..."

"At this point, it is only important that I understand, and that you forgive me for pre-judging you."

"Elder, I'm not sure I understand. Your words shatter my thinking to splinters. I wanted to debate the existence of God with you, and you beg my — MY forgiveness? What kind of a person are you?"

"I'm a person who has wronged you, and who is asking for your forgiveness. That's all," he said, his voice small. He was, in reality, thinking of his failure as a disciple of the Lord, and not about Sean's confusion, nor how this might affect him. He only knew what he must do, not what its outcome might be.

"Elder Mahoy, I can see that you are in dead earnest here, and to whatever extent you have offended me, I do forgive you. However, I have to say that I can't think of a single way in which you have. You have been perfectly civil with me in every way. So, perhaps you could explain in what way you feel you have offended me. It wasn't at all what I wanted to hear from you, but has certainly gotten my attention." He pushed himself up higher in his bed, and rearranged his pillows behind his back.

"I am a disciple of Jesus Christ, and one who loves Him with all my soul. Nothing is more important to me than to represent Him well, and to lead others to understand and love Him as well. As near as I understand Him, His greatest attribute is love. He loved us so much that he was willing to die for us, all of us, whether we loved Him back or not, whether we even knew about Him, or believed in Him.

"When I first met you, I disliked you, and decided that you were beyond redemption. I concluded that you were one of the most evil men I had ever met. I thought of you as one beyond the love of God, or, perhaps, undeserving of God's love. In this way, I offended you. In reality, I offended God even more, to believe that He would not love you in spite of your anger against Him.

"It wasn't until I was overcome by the Spirit, and felt His love for you, that this became apparent to me, and has been a great lesson to me."

"So, God used me to teach you that He loves me." It was not a question, but a summation of Sam's words.

"It has been a stunning revelation to me," Sam said, then realized almost immediately that Sean may take offense at his words. But before he could say anything further, Sean merely added.

"Me too." After saying this, he seemed amused, and rolled back his head in a hearty laugh which echoed richly in the room. It was the most amazingly rich laugh Sam had ever heard, and almost immediately felt his heart lifting. Soon, he was laughing too.

"Now, I want to get something straight," Sean said, wiping tears from his eyes. "This Spirit you mentioned which you said told you God loved me, and which you said was a familiar feeling? What does it feel like?"

Sam was about to explain, when Sean interrupted him. "No, let me explain it, and you tell me if I'm right. Its a feeling in the center of the chest, almost a warmth or comfortable feeling. Am I right?" Both Sam and Elder Hall nodded.

"And the general effect it has upon the mind is one of peace and joy." He added.

"You've obviously felt this before," Elder Hall observed.

"Just now, a few seconds ago, just before I laughed. As a matter of fact, I believe that was why I laughed. I have lain here for three weeks in utmost turmoil, confusion, and bitterness, and when that feeling of peace hit me, it was absolute. What I mean is, not only did it bring me peace concerning what you were saying, but also concerning my illness, my future, my eternal welfare, and everything else. For just a moment, I felt complete, total peace. I don't believe I have ever felt joy before. It was just joy, unexplainable, unreasonable, unlogical, joy. It felt so good, I immediately felt like laughing."

"You have described it perfectly," Sam said happily."

"Do you want to know what is most odd? I felt it so strongly there for a moment, that I will never doubt for the rest of my life that it was there. But I can hardly feel it now. I seem to have returned to my former feelings of depression. Explain that to me."

"I don't understand why the Lord does a lot of things He does. But one possible explanation is that He wanted you to have tiny taste of His love for you. We are messengers for Christ, and His church, and if the people are ready when we speak, the Holy Spirit bears witness that our words are true. I suppose that since we were talking of His love for you, His way of bearing witness of that fact was to let you feel it for a moment."

"Fascinating. I would like to try that again. You don't suppose you could tell me about His love for me again, do you?"

"Let's try another subject. You already have that one down, I believe. I'm going to ask Elder Hall to tell you about a young man who learned about the existence of God, in a way not entirely dissimilar from your own. He was a young man who was also confused about God, and which church he should join. His name was Joseph Smith."

Elder Hall did most of the rest of the teaching that evening. Sam was grateful, because his soul felt wearied, and burdened by the recent chastisement from the Spirit. He had never felt such a thing before, and even though he felt cleansed and much blessed by all that had happened, he still felt as if the experience had inexplicably drained his spiritual batteries quite low. Elder Hall was filled with the Spirit, and his words were both inspired and inspiring. Sean was a demanding student, and asked pointed and detailed questions, but his questions were now to discover the truth, not to bury it.

Sean continued with his chemo therapy during all their visits. Each time they came, he was weaker, and seemed sicker. Yet as his body weakened, his spirit strengthened, until it seemed as if his body was an unfit habitation for his mighty spirit. Like Paul of Tarsus who had persecuted the church and been turned away from his sin in a single moment, Sean changed in a mighty leap toward righteousness. His face glowed with the Spirit, and his words rang with conviction. He read the Book of Mormon almost in a single sitting and rejoiced in it. He devoured every book they brought him and begged for more. He coerced them into coming every day for a while to complete his spiritual education.

It was just a little short of three weeks later that they returned to visit, only to find him too weak to sit up in bed. He greeted them weakly, but with a big smile. His face was aglow with the Spirit, and he radiated hope and love. This marvelous change in him was as miraculous to Sean as the raising of Lazerus from the dead.

"Elders, come closer so I don't have to shout." He chuckled. His voice was very small and seemed to wheeze from his emaciated body. "The doctors tell me I am too weak to undergo the operation. It seems I have wasted much quicker than they suspected. Without the operation, I will die. If they operate I will die. So you see, I am going to die. They have told me to get things in order."

Sam felt tears forming in his eyes, yet knew Sean's words to be true. He fervently wished the Lord had let them heal him, to lift the curse which he had pronounced upon his head by his own words. In all their many hours of teaching Sean, he had never once asked them to bless him to remove the curse. He had, however, many times expressed the thought that his curse was actually a blessing because it had brought him to the depths of humility necessary for him to finally find the Lord.

"I have one thing which remains undone, which I know with absolute certainty I must do before I can face God without shrinking from His presence."

"What is that," Sam asked, his voice breaking.

"I want to be baptized, by authority, for the remission of sins. Without this I fear death with all my being. When my sins are washen I can die in peace."

"Sean, I rejoice in your desire to be baptized," Sam told him. Elder Hall expressed similar feelings. "Is it even possible? There is so very little of you left, that I'm not sure the doctors will let you travel to the chapel, or even let you be baptized. Have you thought about this?"

"I have, and you are right. I wouldn't survive a trip from the hospital. However, one of the nurses said there is a small indoor pool they use for therapy right here at the hospital. The doctors have reluctantly given their permission to allow me to be baptized. What do you think? Will you do it?"

"Well, yes! Absolutely. When?" Was all Sam could think to say.

"Now. Tonight. As soon as we can get my parents and Bishop and Sister Van Halen here. Do you think we can pull it off? I feel a powerful urgency to do it tonight, as if I won't be able to tomorrow.

Please. Help me do this?"

Sam walked to the pay phone in the hall near Sean's room. He dialed Sean's parents. They were just on their way to come visit Sean, and when Sam explained Sean's desires, they were excited, and said they would be there in a little more than an hour. He finally found the Bishop in the Bishop's office. He was in the middle of an interview, but said he would immediately get Sister Van Halen, and they would come. He would make the appropriate phone calls, and bring the necessary paperwork. He also would arrive in little more than an hour.

Several nurses and an intern rolled Sean's bed through the big double doors of the pool room. Dawn came with the Bishop and Sister Van Halen. Sean's parents brought his older sister whom they had not yet met. Word had spread through the hospital, and one doctor and two nurses, all of whom were LDS joined them. Sam asked the doctor to offer the opening prayer. The nurse standing nearby asked if she might sing a special musical number. He asked Elder Hall to give a talk on baptism. Bishop Van Halen handed him a bundle of white clothing. He had completely overlooked the idea that white clothing was needed. He was grateful for the Bishop's thoughtfulness. Sean was no problem, since everything he wore was hospital white.

Sean had asked Sam to baptize him, so he quickly changed. Bishop Van Halen conducted the meeting. The prayers were sweet and brought the Holy Spirit in rich abundance. The nurse sang like an angel, her voice rich and vibrant in the small room. Elder Hall's talk was brief, yet inspired. Finally, it was time.

Sam stood, and approached Sean's bed. All his tubes had been disconnected and needles removed. He stopped by the bed, unsure how to help Sean into the water. Before he could utter a word, Sean's father stepped between them. He was not much larger than Sean himself, yet without effort, reached into the bed, and lovingly lifted his son. Their eyes locked, as if truly connecting for the first time in their lives. Sam turned and walked down into the pool. The water was very comfortable. Sean's father slipped off his shoes, and carried his son into the water until he was waist deep. He carefully transferred his son to Sam.

Sean's emaciated body was wasted to nothingness, and startled Sam with its lightness. He carefully lowered his legs into the water. Sean looped his arm around Sam's neck. Even with Sam's help, he had barely enough strength to support his own weight even in the weightlessness of the water. Sean's body trembled, as if from fear or anticipation or joy; perhaps from all of these.

Sam whispered in his ear. "Sean, I'll support you all the way. Trust me and keep your arm around my neck." Sean smiled and nodded. He raised his right hand to the square, and in a voice of quiet authority, said.

"Sean Eugene Whitehall, having been commissioned of Jesus Christ, I baptize you in the name of the Father, and of the Son, and of the Holy Ghost, Amen."

Sam slowly knelt down. Sean closed his eyes with a look of ecstasy. Sam only closed his at the last moment. He continued on down until his whole body went beneath the waters, so that Sean's arm around his neck was completely submerged. Just as carefully, he swiftly lifted him from the water. Sean's face cleared the waters beaming with joy.

"It's done!" he cried in a hoarse voice. I can finally meet God with a peaceful heart. I'm finally ready." A single reverberating laugh of exquisite richness flowed from his throat, and he fell silent, his strength completely spent. Sam heard Sean's mother gasp and begin to weep.

His father rushed back into the pool, and carried his son to the bed. The nurses efficiently removed his wet clothes, and dried him. In mere minutes he was dry and back in his own room.

Sean insisted that he be confirmed immediately. So, despite his weakness, all priesthood holders laid their hands gently on his head, and Elder Hall bestowed the unspeakable gift of the Holy Ghost. Among the words which he spoke, were these: "Sean, you have fulfilled the words which were spoken to you, the curse is lifted, and you are made whole through your faith."

The doctors, nurses and others left quietly, until only Sean's parents, the Bishop, and Elders remained. It was time to go, but it was hard to say farewell. Everyone suspected this parting might be the last. Sean was listless upon his pillows, yet his face glowed with joy. It was as if death were only waiting for them to leave, so that it might bear him away.

Sam held Sean's hand for many minutes, then tearfully, quietly, said goodbye.

They were a dozen steps down the hall when Elder Hall suddenly skidded to a stop. An idea had suddenly impressed itself upon him. It was so sudden, and so incredibly pure, that he instantly recognized it's source. He spun on a foot, leaving Sam walking by himself for two more steps. He ran back into the room. Every eye turned toward him as he slid to a stop on the slick floor. Sam plowed into his back, his mind whirling with wonder.

"Sean," Elder Hall said, straining to control his voice. "I have some bad news."

"The first time I met you I told you not to lie to me, Elder." Sean said sternly, then laughed weakly.

"You're not going to die!" he exclaimed as if the burden of his message was too big for his heart to keep inside.

"What!" Everyone exclaimed simultaneously. He was barraged by questions, none of which he answered until it again grew quiet.

"Sean, I don't think I ever mentioned it, but dropped out of medical school to come on a mission. I was a junior in my masters program. But that isn't my point really."

"No, I didn't know that," Sean replied with dullness tinted with hope.

"Well, you know how your cancer has not responded to any of the treatments?"

"Well, yes..." he said tentatively.

"And has actually grown worse?"

"Yes."

"Well, I know why. It came to me just as I was leaving."

"Tell me." Sean urged, his eyes brightening with hope.

"Its because you don't have cancer!"

"What!? What do you mean? All the doctors said I have it. All the tests, everything indicates cancer. But I don't?" he finally asked, his voice filled with wonder.

Sam stood there listening to this exchange a bit skeptically until the Spirit swept across him like a soft breeze. Peace entered his soul, and he also knew the truth. He stepped forward and laid a hand on Sean's knee. "Listen to him, Sean. Listen to your heart. Listen to the Holy Ghost."

Elder Hall glanced at Sam and smiled. But he wasn't through. "I'm not saying this because I studied medicine. I'm saying this because the Spirit wrought on me a few moments ago, and gave me this thought. I know its true because of learning to listen and implicitly trust the promptings of the Holy Spirit, and because of my training.

"It hasn't responded to cancer treatment because it isn't cancer. It's an infection, or something else. Have the doctors do another test. Have them look for something simple. Force them to give you antibiotics no matter what they find and take you off the cancer drugs."

"But they said stopping the drugs would immediately let the cancer kill me," he replied, his voice worried.

"Stop thinking with your logic and use the gift you just received. Let the Holy Ghost guide you. Feel instead of think. Let the Holy Ghost take you beyond your mind's ability to understand. Think bac on the original words of the sign you asked for. 'That part of your person which you value most …'"

"…will be denied to you until you repent of your sins." Sean finished quietly, as if intimately familiar with that fateful sentence. There was a long moment of silence before he said. "Until implies there will be something after, that the effect is not permanent," he said with determination.

Sean pondered this for a fraction of a minute longer, then reached up and pulled the tape from his arm where the nurses had already reattached his tubes. He pulled a needle from each arm, and with his father's help, one from his ankle.

"Elders, my soul has finally triumphed over my brain. I have repented of my sins, and the words are fulfilled. Whether I live or die now is irrelevant. I have finally triumphed." He asked his father to find the doctor and bring him to his bed. With these words he fell back into his bed and closed his eyes.

———

It was several days later, during the sixth discussion with Dawn, that the Bishop's phone rang once more. Again, Sister Van Halen handed him a note. This time, he did not wait, but interrupted himself to open it.

———

Sean Whitehall called to tell you his tests still indicate cancer, but he has refused further cancer treatment. He says to tell you he has succeeded in convincing the doctors to give him antibiotics, and feels stronger each day. He sends his love.

———

It took two weeks for all traces of the cancer to evaporate. The doctors were mystified, and to the end maintained that his cancer had spontaneously cured itself. Several were insistent that Sean's baptism had cleansed him, which was interesting because they were not LDS. However, they gave zero credence to the idea that the antibiotics had anything to do with his healing. It was interesting to Sam that they were far more protective of their medical beliefs than their spiritual ones.

Sean was released from the hospital, and after a brief convalescence at his parents home, began his life anew, completely cured of both cancers previously robbing him of life; cancer of the body and soul.

———

Dawn's eyes were bright with happiness as Sam read the note

aloud. She had said many times how she had enjoyed Sean's baptism and how it made her look forward to her own. Her own baptismal date was still several weeks away.

"I just know he will recover," she said, her accent even more British than usual. "I just know he will. I can feel it here." She pressed a palm to her heart.

"Elder Mahoy, how much longer until you return to America?"

Sam had to think for a moment. "Six weeks," he said, a little startled. "Just six weeks." It still seemed to him as if he had not accomplished a lot, and the short time remaining pressed upon him.

"I want to ask you something. I hope you won't get mad, but I have thought about this a lot, and ..." she paused as if unsure.

Sam was surprised at her timidity. Dawn was a lot of things, all of them wonderful, and timidity was not one of them.

"What is it, Dawn? What do you want to ask me?"

"Well, I want to go to America," she said in a rush.

"Well, I'm sure some day you will..." he began, but she cut him off.

"No, you don't understand. I want to go to American with you, six weeks from now." Her eyes sparkled with hope and fear. She blinked rapidly, as if trying to keep tears from filling them. He could tell she was very serious, and greatly feared his rejection.

He took a breath, and then blew it out. He could almost hear President Carlson's lecture. Yet President Carlson's fear would be that he was taking Dawn to America because he had fallen in love with her. It was true that he loved her, but he was not *in* love with her. He hoped the distinction would be sufficient for President.

On the other hand, Dawn was without home, without family, without support, and without work. She was too young to provide for herself entirely, yet old enough to make her own decisions. He knew his mother would wrap her arms around Dawn and love her as much as her own children. He could imagine his father's reaction, and the inevitable conversation, probably late that first night, about Sam's relationship with Dawn. In the end, he would be satisfied. No, the obstacle was President Carlson, and it was no minor roadblock. Mission rules were explicit about taking people home from the mission.

The obstacles were vast, and everywhere his mind turned, he saw another, and another. It seemed impossible, yet it felt right to him. Somehow, it felt right. He glanced at Dawn, who was fighting an unsuccessful battle to keep tears out of her eyes. She had lowered her head, tears falling silently onto her fists bunched in her lap. She had interpreted his silence as rejection, and her hope was quickly evaporating.

Again he drew a breath. "I think its a marvelous idea."

"You do!?" Dawn burst out, her head snapping up so quickly he wondered she didn't get whiplash. She jumped up, as if to rush to him, then thought better of it, and sat back down. She clapped her hands silently, and bounced her feet in excitement like a small girl. Elder Hall whistled that sinking tone which usually indicates a falling bomb, or sinking ship. Both metaphors were apropo.

"Dawn," he said as he closed his scriptures and set them aside. "I really do. I know my parents will welcome you with open arms."

"They will?" she asked, marvel in her voice. "I was thinking of getting a room, and finding a job, maybe going to college. But your parents would do that for me, a total stranger?"

"They love everyone, and would treat you like their own daughter," he answered with absolute surety. He had seen them do this very thing many times.

She clapped her hands together, and held them to her lips as if in prayer. Again, her eyes misted with tears of happiness.

"You need to begin immediately to get your papers in order, and to say goodbye to your father. I need to talk to President Carlson. I'm not looking forward to that at all. Do you have money for plane fare?"

"Elder Mahoy, I have more money than you can imagine. My father has been salting away a fortune in Swiss bank accounts in my name since I was a baby. I'm not sure, but I could probably by the airplane as easily as a seat on it."

"Won't your father transfer the money to another account now that you've moved out?" Elder Hall asked impulsively.

"In the first place, I don't think he would do that to me. Secondly, he can't. Since the day I became a legal adult, I have meticulously moved all the funds into accounts he has no knowledge of."

"Oh." Sam and Elder Hall said simultaneously. Dawn seemed so naive, trusting and unassuming, that seeing this side of her was surprising. There was a part of her personality which was very capable, and not a little shrewd.

————

Sam had tried to imagine what it might be like to kneel at an altar, across from a beautiful woman all dressed in white. He had replayed the scene many times in his mind, each time altering the face, or the room, or the dress she wore. Yet he had never imagined a woman more beautiful than Dawn, dressed in a simple white gown as she slowly walked down the steps and toward him in the baptismal font. Her face was radiant with happiness, and aglow with the Holy Spirit. His breath caught in his throat, and tears came to his eyes. Still a step away, she extended a hand toward him, a momentary look of wonder in her eyes. He reached out, and felt her slender hand slide into his. She smiled, partly at him, mostly at the joy of this moment.

The road from her front door, to this cleansing moment, had not been uneventful. Her father had kicked her out of her home, and thus far, refused to talk to her. She had repeatedly called, wrote letters, and even gone to visit him. The butler had tearfully refused to allow her to even enter the foyer. Sister Van Halen had told him that she often cried herself to sleep, or called out her father's name in her sleep.

The day after she had asked to go to America with him, she had gone to the bank to check on her accounts. She had been told that none of the accounts existed. Her father had been more shrewd than she. One moment she thought she could afford to buy an airplane, the next, she was destitute. Yet here she was, standing before him, radiating joy and anxiously awaiting the first of many ordinances on her road to exaltation.

These thoughts flowed across his mind like a gentle breeze on a summer's day, and warmed his soul. Here stood a beautiful, gloriously precious daughter of Heavenly Father, and it was his privilege to baptize her. His heart thrilled.

He directed her to stand to his left. He gazed into her eyes for just a moment, and then swept them across the Saints standing above them. He was ready. He raised his right arm to the square. A long moment of deep silence followed before he spoke the sacred words.

"Dawn Olivia Pauley, having been commissioned of Jesus Christ..." At that moment, a door opened and closed, and a man's voice boomed across the crowd.

"Wait!" the voice said urgently.

People parted, and a man came forward and knelt before the font.

"Daddy?" Dawn asked with wonder in her voice. Mr. Pauley reached out, and Dawn took a step toward him. Both of his hands closed over hers. What he said was so soft that only Sam and Dawn heard it in the hush that had fallen over the room.

"I love you," he said. So saying he released her, and nodded at her, then at Sam. She returned to his side. He raised his arm to the square, and in a voice of quiet authority spoke the words of salvation.

"Dawn Olivia Pauley, having been commissioned of Jesus Christ

I baptize you in the name of the Father, and of the Son, and of the Holy Ghost, Amen."

He opened his eyes, and found hers fastened upon his. It was as if their souls touched, and something electric passed between them. He lowered her towards the water, her eyes still upon his. As the waters rose, she slowly closed her eyes, and the waters flowed across her. Beneath the waters, her face was angelic. He lifted carefully and she arose. He could see her smile before she emerged, and when she opened her eyes, they were still upon him. Immediately she flung her arms around him, and held him tightly for a long moment.

"Thank you," she said quietly in his ear. Suddenly she broke free.

"Daddy!" she cried, and rushed toward the stairs in a swirl of water. Her father ran to meet her, and they fell into one another's arms with a watery sound. Dawn laughed, and wept loudly, and rocked back and fourth in his arms. He merely said, over and over...

"I love you. I'm sorry."

———

It was church policy that every missionary be interviewed by President Carlson prior to their being sent home. Sam had dreaded this interview for the several weeks between Dawn's baptism and this day. He entered the now familiar office and took a seat on the richly uphol-stered chair. It occurred to him that this was the same chair he had used every time he had entered this room. Not every experience here had been sweet, and he fully expected this one to trend toward the bitter.

Yet, the interview was rich with warmth and praise, both for him, and for the others who had entered the mission field with him. The requisite worthiness questions were asked and answered, and President was satisfied.

"My dear boy, what an asset you have been to this mission, to me personally, and the people of this continent. You can rest assured that you have made a lasting impact upon all who have known you. I have never known a missionary more willing to serve, more willing to do the Lord's work, nor more prone to cause problems." He laughed aloud, and Sam could tell that President's opinion of his problems did not include blame or wrong doing . His mission had been difficult in many ways, yet he had fought a good fight, and he felt his heart soar.

"Do you have any questions, my boy?" President asked unexpectedly.

"Well, yes, there is something I'm curious about. What ever happened to Elder Beesler?"

President frowned and turned his chair until he was profile to Sam. He seemed to be considering his answer. "Generally," he said, "we do not make public mention of what happens to other missionaries. However, I feel that you deserve an explanation, especially considering the circumstances.

"Elder Beesler did not return to his mission duties after leaving you at the courthouse. He just disappeared with the mission's vehicle. He was found several weeks later in the Cape and arrested. He was accused and convicted of perjury, several traffic violations, and car theft. The latter was dropped because the Church declined to press charges. He received a one year jail sentence, and is presently serving that sentence. However, I received a phone call just yesterday asking if he had been here. At first I thought it was a member calling, but the more I think on it, I wonder if it wasn't the police. I fear he may have escaped and means mischief toward the church." President interlaced his hands over his chest and lowered his chin in deep thought for several moments. Then he straightened and resumed his narative.

"As a result of leaving the mission field without permission, he was excommunicated from the church. It is all a very sad affair. You may be interested to know that he expressed considerable remorse for leaving you to be whipped. He said it didn't register to him what your sentence had been until after he had left the building. By then, he realized it was probably already in progress, and didn't have the courage to go back in and put a stop to it. The reason he ran away was because he was ashamed of himself beyond his understanding. When the Lord's will was made manifest to me that he was to lose his membership, I was shocked, because I considered his remorse genuine. However, when the verdict was announced, he grew extremely angry. He cursed and raged, and had to be taken from the room. I am certain the Lord's verdict included past acts much worse than those of the present.

"Since going to jail, he has called this office many times asking for your address so he could write you a letter and ask your forgiveness. I did not give it to him, because I felt you had enough to deal with without being exposed to his emotions. Besides, I had a hard time believing him sincere after his outburst, and suspected he had darker motives for wanting your address. I hope I did the right thing."

"I'm grateful," Sam said, not sure himself if he meant for not giving him the address, or for allowing him to know what happened to Elder Beesler, or simply for the fact that he had been caught and punished. He was grateful that Elder Beesler had not been whipped as Brother Van der Kerk had initially suggested.

"Before I officially give you my blessing to leave the mission field, I feel as if there is something you would like to bring up. What is it Elder?"

Sam was momentarily taken aback by his perceptiveness, yet knew he was a spiritual man upon whom the mantle of his office rested fully. Sam cleared his throat and struggled to find the right words. There were no right words to find. Finally, he just blurted it out.

"The young woman we just baptized…"

"Sister Pauley," president interjected, a look of understanding crossing his features.

"Yes, well, she was disowned by her father."

"I'm familiar with her story. Her father came to the baptism at the last moment, and they were reconciled. Its a touching account."

"That's mostly accurate. He has forgiven her and asked her to come back home. But she knows if she does, he will lose his business. For some reason, his employers hate Mormons.

"So now they are at odds again, but from the opposite positions. He wants her to come home and she refuses. She is determined to go to America with me. I honestly don't know what to do."

"There's nothing you can do," President said as he slipped a sheet of paper back into the file folder on his desk. "Its a free country, and though young, she's a legal adult. If she wants to go to American on the same plane you're on, I don't see a problem with that. Nor do I see why her doing so impacts you or your mission."

"But I know there are strict guidelines about missionaries doing this sort of thing."

"Elder, you taught me a valuable lesson, actually several of them. I know what the mission rules say, and in the strictest sense, this violates them. However, I feel at peace about the situation and choose to ignore the whole thing. You have served an honorable mission, that's all I need to know.

"My challenge to you is that you never allow yourself to forget what you have learned here. You have great potential for good, and consequently, great potential for failure. Everything has its opposite, which opposite is usually equal in power. You taught me this. Your spiritual greatness will bring you a lifetime of joy and a life filled with trials of great intensity.

"You are one of the few who has the power to achieve the promise of exaltation in this life, and one of the few who also has the power to become a son of perdition. These two are your possibilities. You will not achieve something in between.

"Beware, my boy. For God's sake...for your sake, beware all your life." There were tears in his eyes as he spoke barely above a whisper. Sam received the warning with an open heart.

———

Sam and Elder Hall arrived at Jan Smuts airport three hours early. He was met at the door by Bishop and Sister Van Halen who relieved him of his only suitcase. As they walked toward the ticket counters, others joined them, until nearly fifty people pressed around him.

Everyone he loved was there; the Van der Kerks were there with an armed escort, Tom and Linda Snodgrass came with their new baby, Sean, still looking very thin, and his parents came. The only people missing were Melody, whom he presumed was still in Rhodesia, the Knights, still in Rhodesia, and President and Sister Carlson. Sam realized with a start that Dawn was nowhere to be seen as well. He knew she had tickets on this flight, and wondered if all was right with her.

The crowd of well-wishers migrated to an unused boarding area. Soon everyone was laughing and telling stories of Sam's deeds and misdeeds. He felt embarrassed by the attention, yet his soul rejoiced in his friends and simultaneously ached at their impending separation. This was going to be much harder than leaving his family back in Salt Lake City. At least there, he knew he would return.

There was still an hour to go when Dawn arrived. Her face was aglow with happiness as she directed the servants carrying her many bags. Her father attended her like another servant, anxious to do anything to help. The entire time, she kept one arm laced tightly through his.

When she spotted Sam, she hurried over, and kissed him on the cheek. Elder Hall gave a meaningful cough.

"He's almost not a missionary anymore, so I can almost give him a kiss. When we get to America, I'm going to lay a proper one on him." Everyone laughed, and Elder Hall threw up his hands in mock resignation.

As the hour grew closer, the group grew more sober, until eyes were misty and words no longer seemed adequate. Sam found himself in a daze, looking at faces he loved, suddenly aware that he would probably never see them again. Bishop Van Halen looked at his watch, and pointed toward the gate.

"It's time," he said. A murmur of disappointment simultaneously escaped many lips. Sam stood and found himself facing Tom Snodgrass.

"Sam, I want to give you something. I know its small, and you said you no longer want one, but I felt impressed that this would be the most important thing I could give you." He held out a narrow box wrapped in colored paper. As soon as Sam touched it, he knew what it was. The feel, the weight, the very essence of the package was familiar to him. His eyes filled with tears. He didn't want it, yet his soul cried out in relief that he now owned one once again.

He tore open the paper, and flipped the shiny latches. A beautiful silver flute lay nestled in blue velvet. He snapped the lid closed and hugged Tom and Linda.

Sean stepped up next and handed him a long envelope. Sam pulled a bound manuscript from the envelope. The title read:

Atheists Never Die

Atheists

by Sean E. Whitehall

"I already have a publisher," he said as Sam studied the cover. "I was so heavily involved in the Atheistic movement, that my conversion to Christianity has created quite a stir. Thank you for all you've done for me." They shook hands, then embraced.

Brother and Sister Van der Kerk approached next, and held out a small package. Sam had no idea that this was going to turn into a birthday party. He took the small package with wonder in his eyes. He opened it to find a piece of knotted leather about six inches long, mounted inside a small viewing box which could not be opened. A small brass plaque held the following:

Acts 5:41

And they departed...rejoicing

that they were counted worthy

to suffer shame for his name.

"Is this..."

"It is," they replied simultaneously.

"In reality," Brother Van der Kerk told him, "it is your gift to us. I had two made, and keep the other on my desk. By your stripes I came to know Christ. I hope someday I can repay the great debt of your gift to me. God bless you..." His voice faltered. They embraced. He held Sister Van der Kerk, until she kissed him on both cheeks, and turned away.

Each of those present came forward until his hands and pockets were full. Dawn proceeded him through the gate, and just as he was turning to go, President and Sister Carlson ran toward them.

"Elder Mahoy!" They called from a short distance. They hurried toward him as the speaker announced the final boarding for his flight. As he hugged Sister Carlson he couldn't help noticing she smelled of smoke.

"Elder," President said as he grasped his hand. "We almost missed you. You would not believe what has happened. We awoke this morning to a smoke-filled house. We barely got everyone out. The mission home has burned to the ground!"

"*No!*" Sam cried. His mind reeled at the thought of all those beautiful paintings, marble statues, and other treasures being destroyed in the fire.

"The terrible part is that the police suspect arson. Not suspect, it was arson. Who ever set the fire also blocked the outside doors to trap us inside. We climbed through a window. It was a blatant attempt at murder, I'm afraid.

"Following my suggestion, they checked on Elder Beesler, and he has been released from prison. His parents had arranged for him to be deported to his home town, and he was taken to the airport, but apparently didn't get on the plane. They are looking for him now. I'm afraid if they find he had anything to do with this fire, they won't let him be deported, but will put him in prison for a long time."

"Do you really think it was Elder Beesler?" Sam asked, his hands trembling. It was standard procedure for missionaries about to go home to spend their last couple days in the mission home. By special permission, he had not. He had a bad feeling about the fire.

"Perhaps it's unjust of me to suspect him without greater evidence..." His voice trailed off into thoughtful silence.

"So much destruction," Sam replied, his mind walking through the plush interior of the old mansion. "So much destruction..."

"Yes. Its a tragedy. Yet no one was injured, and we were able to save most of the mission records. Only a few pieces of art were saved though. I did have the presence of mind to grab something very important, though." He pressed a small package into Sam's hand.

Sam opened the box to find a gold tie clasp holding a perfect diamond the size of his thumbnail. He inhaled sharply when he recognized the stone Melody's father had given him in gratitude for his part in saving his daughters. Others leaned over the box and gasped. Even in South Africa, where large diamonds were commonplace, this was an exceptional stone.

"May I?" Mr. Pauley asked, and took the box from Sam's hands. He produced a loop from his pocket, and held the stone to the light. His face frowned, then frowned further, until he lowered the stone.

"I know this stone!" He said in an excited voice. "It was cut in my factory. It's a full twenty-two carrots, D in color, ice blue, flawless under a X10 loop. It is almost priceless. I tried to purchase it and couldn't. It was sold to a wealthy land baron in Rhodesia. How did you come by it?"

"I don't have time to explain," Sam said, taking the stone back. "It was a gift. President Carlson can explain." He shoved the box in his pants pocket. He gave both the Carlsons a hug, and turned toward the gate.

"Elder," Mr. Pauley persisted. "I want to buy the stone. It is one of the few which escaped me then. I will give you its wholesale value here and now."

Sam stopped walking. Dawn came back and slid her arm into his. She whispered, "leave the stone with Daddy. Let him buy it, or send it to you later. It really is too valuable to carry around."

"How much is its wholesale value?" Sam asked.

Mr. Pauley leaned forward to whisper in his ear, "millions of dollars," he said. Sam's eyes grew wide, and he seriously considered it. But there was only confusion, not peace, and he rejected the idea. He shook his head slightly.

"Elder, I strongly suggest you leave the stone with me. I'll ship it to you if you don't want to sell it."

"That's OK, I'll just take it with me." Mr. Pauley was about to say something else, but Sam turned away. He did not see the worried look which crossed Mr. Pauley's face.

Dawn tippie-toed to kiss her father on the cheek. She whispered something quickly, then hurried away with Sam. Their plane was about to leave without them.

At the door to the concourse he turned once to wave, and then proceeded onto the plane.

He, Dawn and Elder Palmer had adjacent seats. She took her seat, and slid her hand into his. He wondered if it was against mission rules, but concluded that it didn't matter. Elder Palmer was too anxious to care what they did. Almost immediately the engines began to turn, and the steward came to check their seat belts.

"That diamond?" Dawn whispered in his ear. Sam nodded. "Is

too valuable to transport this way. Too many people now know you have it. There are those who will kill us both to get it. Believe me, I have done this many times, and I know. You should have sold it to Daddy, or given it to him to send to America for you. We have ways of safely transporting diamonds. This way is very risky."

"I wasn't sure what to do, and there wasn't time to think."

"I know. There wasn't time to convince you Father would deal honorably with you. You should have trusted me."

Sam thought about this. He was relatively certain it would have taken weeks to convince him to surrender the stone to Dawn's father, especially when he blamed Sam for her joining the church. Even though he had forgiven Dawn, he would barely talk to Sam. She was right, though. He should have trusted her. In fact, he did. At the time, leaving the diamond with Mr. Pauley hadn't seemed like an issue of trusting Dawn or not.

"What should I do, do you think."

"For now, give it to me. I know exactly what to do. We'll be making a twelve hour layover in England. When I kissed Daddy goodbye, I told him to have our contact in England meet us at the airport. He will come. Believe me when I say, you will not make it back to America with that stone in your possession. Diamond smuggling and diamond theft is a highly developed art in this country. They watch the airport 24 hours a day to spot this exact thing. I can guarantee that someone is on the phone this instant planning how to relieve you of it before you reach America. I don't expect them to try anything until we get to England. We'll be safe until then. Our problem will be to get it to our contact before the thieves get to us. We can do it...if we're lucky," she added. Sam didn't like the sound of this at all.

"I had no idea..." Sam said as he slid the small box into her hand, and she transferred it to her purse.

"I'm sure you didn't. We will be all right until we reach England," she said in a whisper. With a start, he realized she was right. Many people had seen the stone, including stewardesses and other people passing by. Naively, they had made no attempt to conceal the fact that he had it. Thinking back, he could remember several strangers being particularly impressed with the stone. He had that sinking feeling in the pit of his stomach, and wished he were still just doing missionary work. He missed it, and was already dreading the transition back to "normal" life.

"Why is my life always so complicated?" he mumbled under his breath, and laid his head back as the big plane roared into the sky.

———

Look for Book II of the Millenial Quest Series
At your LDS book retailer.